Loves' Conqueror

Renée Hand

Gypsy
Publications

Published in 2015, by Gypsy Publications
Troy, OH 45373, U.S.A.
GypsyPublications.com

First Edition

All names, characters, and incidents appearing
in this work are fictitious.

Hand, Renee
Loves' Conqueror / by Renee Hand

ISBN 978-1-938768-56-9 (paperback)

Library of Congress Control Number
2015933760

Edited by Gina Sudzina Smith

PRINTED IN THE UNITED STATES OF AMERICA

To my family and fans who have supported me throughout the years. Thank you so much. You are what made this happen.

PRELUDE

The wind whipped wildly, tearing at the sails, as the waves beat against the sides of the *Fighting Spur*, rocking the ship violently. Great waves rose up over the prow of the ship and crashed down, sending tides of white foam across the deck, causing the crew to slip and fall repeatedly as they fought to keep the ship under control. The squall had lasted an hour already, and the men were getting tired. Heavy squalls could blow up fast at sea, could last what seemed hours, and then end as abruptly as they came. When this vicious squall finally blew itself out, leaving an open night sky, the sailors were relieved. The sea slowly calmed, allowing the ship to sail smoothly and safely into port. As soon as the *Fighting Spur* anchored, the captain released the crew, allowing them to go ashore and enjoy the pleasures of the sinful Island of Tortuga. The lights of the town enticed them, energized them, and they eagerly filled the longboats. Tortuga never slept. The men would find food, drink, and women aplenty.

But the captain did not join his crew in their licentiousness. He had other concerns and another destination drawing him as surely as the needle of his compass sought north.

The sky sparkled with millions of stars, like jewels in a pirate's chest, as the captain and his first mate lowered the last longboat. As Davy, the first mate, started pulling on the oars, the quarter moon began to rise, its two horns punctuating the calm seas. But the sight of the moon gave little comfort to the man staring at its glowing horns hoping—no, praying—for considerable fortune.

Captain Stratton Mayne was a man built for adventure. He was tall, thick, and muscular. His sun-bronzed skin was framed by long blond hair that fell in waves to his shoulders. His blue eyes were as bright as the ocean on a sunny day and were always expressive, always cunning.

Davy pulled on the oars heading away from Tortuga for a quiet part of the island far from the recklessness of the port town. Davy was a man in his late twenties. Younger than Stratton by only a few years, his hair was as black as night and cut short to his ears. He was tall, about six feet, and his shoulders were enormous and wide, making the pull on the oars seem almost effortless. His size alone intimidated most men.

As the oars dipped again and again into the dark sea, Stratton's mind filled with thoughts of his wife, Miranda, and her beauty. She had bronze skin like his that often glowed against her soft brown eyes. Her chestnut hair looked like spun gold with its sun-struck highlights. Miranda was a pirate, just like him, and had stood at his side on many adventures. When Miranda married Stratton, he promised a life of adventure and freedom. That's what she wanted, and that's exactly what she got. For months on end, she sailed with her husband, traveling to various islands for exotic birds and valuables to sell to civilized ports. She loved the sea. Captain Mayne treasured memories of her standing at the rail, the wind in her luscious hair, her eyes reaching far out to sea. Together they had taken merchant ships and stripped them of the valuables aboard. Silks and spices they stole for markets in the New World. Exotic birds taken from ships leaving the New World were sold on the black markets of Europe and England. Heavily armed military vessels were plundered for their gun powder and weapons, making the pirates formidable opponents on sea or land, and food stores were taken to keep themselves at sea longer. Rum and sugar from the Caribbean found ready markets in any port, and cloth, combs, buttons, and other metal goods had easy sales in any New World city. Rarely would they come upon a ship with chests of gold or jewels, but even when they did, the wealth would never satisfy them or their crew for long. Lust of every sort was part of pirate life, and none in that profession were known for their frugality.

Miranda was a well-kept secret in that there were few women who chose the pirate life. On the rare occasion when an enemy would board the *Fighting Spur*, she would play the part of the innocent captive. Standing at the rail had saved their ship from being destroyed more than once. She would be handed over to the enemy and protected by them, but a true pirate she was. She would infiltrate the crew from the inside and turn the tables on the would-be conqueror. Miranda was a skilled swordswoman. On her own she could take on several men. Her beauty and sex would give her the advantage against disbelieving men; her abilities would give her the win. She was revered by the crew and, though sailors usually felt a female aboard was bad luck, she had proven herself and was accepted. She always wore breeches and linen shirts, like they did. She kept her long, brown hair braided down her back or tucked under a cap. She fit in perfectly and always treated each one of them with respect. She was as good at swearing as they were, was not loathe to climb the rigging, and could hold the wheel in storm if need be, being lashed by wind and waves. The crew loved her.

Then Miranda found that she was with child, and everything changed. Stratton forced her to stay at Eleuthera Island. They had built a house there, long ago, on a hill surrounded by jungle. With no settlement on the island or anywhere nearby and only one protected bay to hide the ship, no one knew of this hideaway, except for Stratton's trusted crew, and not a one of them would divulge the location. They respected and feared Stratton too much. Stratton also made sure that he always arrived at the island at night. His men only saw the rugged cliffs where the surf pounced mercilessly and not the protected bay or the caves that were underneath his home. No outsider had ever set foot on the island; no one had ever thought to land on the island. The caves' rocky passageways served their purpose as deterrents to all, and only Stratton and Miranda knew its secret winding way in.

Stratton knew that his wife and unborn child would be well protected there. However, a few months into the pregnancy, Miranda's pirate restlessness showed, and she begged to be aboard the *Fighting Spur* again. She missed Stratton and her life at sea. So deeply in love was he that he could deny her nothing, Stratton allowed her one more sail. He planned only a short voyage because he feared their rugged life might be too hard on her in her condition, and yet he wanted to satisfy her love of the sea. At the time, she did not seem troubled by her pregnancy and walked and acted the same as she did before. Thinking that it would cause her no harm, they sailed to Tortuga. While his men partook of the pleasures of the town, Stratton and Miranda traveled inland to see the wildlife on the other side of the island. That was what Miranda had wanted to do, and so they did it, but something happened that they did not expect.

Miranda started getting pains. These got so severe so quickly that both she and Stratton agreed she could not return to Eleuthera to have the baby as she would have liked. She was forced to stay on Tortuga until the birth of their child. Instead of begging for Stratton to stay by her side, she insisted he leave and return in a few months' time. Though she loved her husband dearly, she knew that he could do nothing for her. His time was better spent elsewhere while she dealt with the birth and its complications. Stratton left her in the capable care of a priest who was in their debt for the funding and building of his church that saw to the needs of the natives of the island.

Miranda was a believer of God, and Stratton gave to the priest when she asked. Miranda felt it was good for them to help others. She had a good and generous heart and soul, but she was also very clever. She knew that sharing some of their fortune with the priest and the natives would allow them safe access to the island of Tortuga, at least the wild parts outside the town. Their generosity gave them a place to hide, should they need it, and, on occasion, they had. Now it provided Miranda safety during her time of confinement.

Stratton and Davy beached on a quiet beach up the coast, and they pulled the longboat as high up on the sand as they could. As Stratton's eyes filled at the sight of the priest's house, located on the side of a hill facing them, he cursed himself for leaving Miranda. He cursed her a little as well, for being stubborn and keeping him at a distance when all he wanted to do was be at her side. Without a word, he began to run along the jungle path that led to the priest's house. Instead of knocking on the door, Stratton ran at it full bore and broke it down. As he and Davy entered into the room, they saw Miranda upon a cot. The priest was between her thighs, and his hands were bloody.

An instant protective anger filled Stratton as he stepped forward aggressively, but before he reached the cot, he saw the birth of his child. The priest was speaking encouragingly to Miranda as she gave one more push. He pulled the baby the rest of the way out and held it in his arms. He then began to clean the fluid from its lungs. Soon, the baby gave its first healthy cry, causing tears to spring from Stratton's eyes. He ran to his wife's side in excitement. Upon seeing him, Miranda gave her husband a weak smile.

Up close, Miranda's appearance shocked Stratton. Her face was covered in sweat, and her glorious hair had become a dull, dark mat.

Her hand clutched at her stomach periodically and her features wrinkled in pain. The warm glow of her skin seemed to have disappeared, and gone was any evidence of her energetic spirit and lust for life. She was pulling away from him, he could tell, and what angered him most was that there was nothing he could do about it, except watch. As he stared at her, he wished that they were back again on his ship. Often, he would stand by the helm and watch as Miranda stood by the prow breathing in the fresh sea air and letting her arms spread outward as if she could fly. She had been free and filled with life. It had been her spirit that he had fell in love with, her beauty that entranced him. Her strength could outlast any man's and yet here she was, her strength and sassiness gone, her features weak and pale. It scared him and filled him with sadness.

He glanced at the priest, who smiled briefly, his attention focused more on the baby he was bathing with a damp cloth. "It is a girl, Captain Mayne," the priest said quietly as he finished the task. Once done he wrapped the baby in a clean blanket.

Stratton finally tore his eyes from his wife's face to gaze at his new daughter. He fell in love immediately. He thought his daughter to be the most beautiful baby he had ever seen.

"Can I hold her?" asked Stratton uncertainly.

"Of course. Just be gentle."

Stratton could wield a sword with dexterous skill. He was a formidable fighter, and a deadly aim with rifle, pistol, and cannon. And, should he be bereft of all these weapons, he could fling a dagger with such accuracy that none stood against him. But he didn't know how to hold a baby. After standing awkwardly a long moment trying to figure it out, he looked to the gentle priest, who smiled and pressed the infant gently into his unsure arms. The baby's face was smooth and angelic, innocent and pure. Her eyes seemed to study him, and her little arms and legs twitched and pushed at the blanket. Stratton stared transfixed at his daughter, afraid to hold her tighter for fear of crushing her for she was so small and delicate. His eyes then returned to his wife, who also gazed upon their daughter.

"Miranda?" spoke Stratton, his voice cracking as he tried to gently pass his daughter to his wife. Miranda wouldn't take her, Stratton became concerned and returned his gaze to the priest. The man slowly shook his head. Once Miranda was cleaned, the priest lowered her legs into a relaxed position and covered her lower body with a blanket. Miranda winced from the pain the movement caused her. Davy glanced at Stratton and saw him open his mouth to speak. When no words came out, Davy decided to ask the question he knew his captain could not.

"What's wrong with her?" he asked, his tone filled with concern. Davy then glanced over at Stratton and saw him close his eyes and breathe deeply. He was preparing himself for the dreadful news that he knew was coming. The priest turned to face them.

"She's dying. She's lost much blood in the delivery. But that's not what's killing her, I think. She's weakening, and the pain she feels in her abdomen will not cease, which means that she is bleeding from the inside . . . or worse. There's nothing to be done. I'm sorry."

"No!" Davy said quietly, moving for the first time into the room from his station at the door. He knew how much Stratton and Miranda loved one another, knew this forced parting would not be easy for Stratton. The priest moved to a basin and washed his blood-covered hands. After taking a deep breath, he dried his hands on a scrap of cloth and watched Stratton. The captain's large hand caressed his wife's damp hair as he kissed her cheek tenderly. Stratton's eyes filled with sadness, and he had a hard time accepting the fact that his wife was going to die.

"Are you sure there's nothing that can be done?" pleaded Stratton, but the priest only shook his head again. The poor priest was filled with helplessness for not being able to help Miranda more, but he did not know what else to do. As his eyes fell upon her, he could not help but shed a few tears. For months she had kept him company and helped him and the natives he served with tasks around the island. She had loved walks on the beach and would often swim in the shallows near the shore. Further along in the pregnancy, she spent much time gazing out at the sea. When he would watch her, the priest had noticed the far away look in her eyes and knew that she was thinking of her husband and their past adventures. Her features would always fill with sadness and something else. At times he thought she felt regret.

"Unfortunately, there is nothing that I can do. If I could change places with her, Captain Mayne, I would, for that's how much my heart aches for her." The priest paused as he tried to compose himself. "The damage has already been done to her body. By the time I find someone who might be able to save her, she'll be gone. We are miles from someone competent in medicine." The priest's gaze moved hastily to the baby in his arms. Miranda then turned her head slowly to her husband as if wanting to say one last thing before her strength gave out. Stratton let a tear fall as he held his wife's hand and gazed lovingly upon her. "Keep our daughter safe, my husband. Don't let her live the life we have led. It is not right for her, the life of a pirate. We are rich enough for her to live a life of luxury.

See that she does. Let her know that I love her and never let her forget me." Miranda then reached for an object around her neck and placed it in the palm of her husband's hand. "This belongs to her now. It is no longer mine. One day, if she desires it, she should be given the chance to find the treasure that we could not. If she is anything like me, I know that she will want to, though deep down I hope she doesn't." Miranda's face contorted in pain and then she relaxed slightly. "I have many regrets, and the biggest one was not allowing you to stay with me. I have missed you so, and now I'll never see you again." Tears flowed down Miranda's cheeks as her sadness choked her.

Stratton could not help but to cry as well. "I know, Miranda. I should have stayed by your side. I shouldn't have let you push me away. I regret leaving you and have missed you so much. I don't want to lose you."

"Nor I you, but it will happen. It's meant to be. Stay strong for our daughter, Stratton. She'll need you. Be a good father to her. Don't let pride come between you. I love you, my darling." With those words Miranda Mayne cast her last breath, her hand still held tightly in her husband's.

"Miranda? No!" Stratton shouted. "No!" he leaned forward and held his wife in his arms, his body wracked with sobs. After several minutes, he let her go. As he was about to stand, he glanced at his palm to see what his wife had taken from her neck and pressed into his hand. Lying there gently was a cylindrical crystal. The clearness of the crystal shined and sparkled in the candlelight. It had a hole bored through one end where the necklace could go through. He wore a similar crystal around his own neck.

They were identical pieces except for an angled notch set into his. During his wife's first voyage aboard his ship, they'd came upon a Spanish vessel carrying goods to the Americas. The vessel didn't give up its stores easily, and they fought. The *Fighting Spur*, a fast sloop with fourteen guns, captured the ship and finally sank it, but not before they removed all of its precious cargo. Miranda, when snooping around the captain's quarters, found a small treasure box of jewels hidden underneath the berth. She snatched it up before even surveying its contents.

When she finally opened it aboard the *Fighting Spur*, she found diamonds, emeralds, and rubies of various sizes and shapes that shined brightly for all to see.

There also were the two uniquely shaped crystals, that when put together, formed a key. Lining the bottom of the box, she came upon a piece of parchment. Upon reading it, she learned that the crystals opened a safe or vault of some sort. However, half of the parchment was torn away, and the beginning of what looked like a map was gone. No location or any other pertinent information gave away its where abouts. Miranda immediately disclosed the information to her husband. They had searched for the treasure, but never found it. In the meantime, each wore a piece of the crystal to show they had an equal share. Now Miranda's share would go to their daughter.

Stratton held the pieces tightly in his hand recalling their promise to each other. He then turned to his daughter, fast asleep in the priest's arms, and stood. He reached for her, but was unsure how to take her without waking her. She was so small and fragile, and Stratton's hands were large and callused from life at sea. The priest, upon seeing the dilemma, again placed the baby in Stratton's open arms. Stratton held the baby tightly to his chest, tears of joy running down his cheeks.

"She's a precious child, Stratton. Do you have a name for her?" asked the priest. Stratton stroked his daughter's cheek as he thought of a strong name to give her. He then glanced at his wife, remembering what she had requested of him.

"Her name will be Miranda, after her mother. Isn't that right my little angel?" Stratton stared at his daughter. The child was still sleeping, but her lips moved slightly in response.

"What are we going to do now, Captain?" asked Davy.

"We're going to return to the ship and set a course for Eleuthera, Davy."

"Eleuthera? But, Captain," replied Davy. His words stopped when he saw the hard, determined look upon Stratton's features.

"My wife needs a proper burial. I won't leave her here. I won't toss her body into the sea. She deserves better, Davy. She deserves to be home where she should have been. I promised the men more booty, but there's something I have to do before we can sail again. I'm all that my daughter has now. I cannot continue this reckless life and bring danger upon her. The *Fighting Spur* will be dry-docked until my daughter's old enough to sail. Then, when we are ready to sail again, our destination will be for England."

"England, Captain?" asked Davy in disbelief.

"Yes, England," replied Stratton. "Will the men stick with me?" The thought of not having a crew alarmed him at first, but then he laughed. He could always find willing men to serve under him. His reputation was good enough for any man to want to join his ranks.

"Of course, they will, Captain. You've brought the men much wealth these past years. I'm sure that some of them would welcome time to enjoy their plunder before they die. All we need is about a half dozen faithful and trustworthy men to stay with us. The rest can be let go until we need their services again. I'll make sure they get paid in full. We do not wish to have any grievances."

"That sounds good, Davy. Thank you. Now, as my first mate and most devoted friend, it'll be your job to look after my daughter's welfare when I'm not able to be with her. If she's anything like her mother, she'll need us both to guide and love her. Can I trust you to keep my daughter safe?" Stratton turned toward Davy and placed his daughter gently into his arms. Davy looked down at the sleeping baby and felt honored for being given the task. His heart melted as she turned her head and moved her arms farther into the blanket. His blue eyes admired the beautiful child he was holding to his chest. He had always wanted a child of his own but did not see one in his future, especially not with his love of the sea getting in the way of settling down. He didn't want to change his ways for a woman and yet his heart started to melt at the sight of the infant in his arms.

"Yes, Captain, I'll take the responsibility of protecting your daughter when you cannot. From this day forward she will be my daughter as well, and I promise that no harm will ever come to her whilst I'm watching over her. You can have my life upon that oath." Satisfied, Stratton moved away from Davy's side, already thinking of the sad trip ahead of them. Miranda's last voyage.

"Good, then we'll raise her together, and she'll have the love and protection of two fathers. At this point I don't think I'll ever love another woman as much as I loved my wife, but a daughter is different. She'll always have my love. My heart aches, though, because I'll never be in love again. How could I? There's no woman out there who would accept me for who I am the way Miranda did. Love is a joke for fools like me who believe they're deserving of it. Oh, how I loved Miranda, Davy." Davy placed his hand on Stratton's back and patted it as tears came to his own eyes.

"You are young, Stratton. Miranda was a great woman, a great pirate who was as slippery as an eel when it came to stealing booty." The comment made Stratton laugh as memories of his wife's past exploits filled him. "She'll always be in your heart," Davy continued softly, "but don't scoff at the idea of finding love again. It is possible. Look at me. I once thought I'd never have a child to love and raise—now I do."

Stratton patted Davy on the arm and then shook his head and stared once more at his wife's lifeless body. He couldn't help but to go to her, caress her cheek and kiss her lips one last time before he stepped away from her and covered her with the blanket laid upon her.

"Some of my people can help you carry Miranda's body back to your longboat. She'll be sorely missed," spoke the priest. "Her laughter illuminated this place and brought music from the trees. I'm so sorry for your loss." The priest then left as a few tears escaped his eyes and ran down his cheeks.

Stratton nodded as he thought of his daughter's future. He wanted a new life for her. A life he knew would be hard for him to bear. He then thought of Davy's promise and smiled. He was thankful for his friend's help. His thoughts then fell upon his beloved wife as he watched a few of the natives walk through the door of the priest's house toward him. As they saw Miranda's body, their heads immediately bowed in sadness and respect. Stratton's hand moved swiftly to his lips as he closed his eyes, his heart aching. Tears began to flow like a river down his tanned skin, his chest filling with loss. He would miss Miranda dearly.

CHAPTER 1

Twenty years later

"Are you ready, Miry?" asked the deep voice behind the door. Miranda Mayne checked her appearance one more time before moving to the closed door. Her golden skirts flowed side to side as she adjusted the crystal necklace around her neck, tucking the crystal between her breasts and out of sight.

"Yes, Davy, I'm finally ready." Miranda opened the door with a smile, knowing that her faithful friend had asked her at least twenty times if she were ready.

"I don't know what takes you so long in your appearance. I take less than an hour," remarked Davy. Davy was the same man that he had been twenty years ago, except now his pitch black hair had various shades of gray mixed in. He had become much wiser with his age, as well as a tad bit softer. Raising Miranda had taken its toll, and he had changed into a different man. He had not only become like a second father to Miranda, but a mother as well, constantly nagging at her to behave. He was devoted to her and rarely left her side. Because of his guidance, Miranda had turned into the woman her father wanted her to be, and yet she had a wild side to her, too. Just like her mother, she loved the sea, cursed often, and was too free with her words, but she was also courageous.

"I have more to put on, I assure you. I am more than willing to make a trade and wear your breeches while you wear my dress." Miranda placed her hand on her stomach, adjusting her shoulders slightly. The dress had a low neckline and a tight waist, so tight in fact, that Miranda had a hard time breathing. "If father buys me one more corset I will scream." Davy grabbed Miranda's hand and placed it on his arm as he glanced over at her. He escorted her from the room, closing the door behind her, and walked down the hallway quietly. They were descending the stairs when he responded.

"Child, be thankful of your father's generosity. He only wants what is best for you." Miranda's brown eyes expressed her frustration with the dress.

"I am thankful, Davy. Forgive my outburst, but I can hardly breathe in this damn thing. Whoever makes these corsets should be shot, because apparently they have never worn one. A man probably created it. No offense to you, my faithful friend." Davy only smiled at the beautiful girl beside him as he placed his hand over hers. Miranda had grown into a beautiful and enchanting woman. She was almost the spitting image of her mother and had her spirit. Her hair was the color of a pale yellow satin, while her eyes shown their light brown splendor. Her skin was pale but had a hint of a tan from her time in the sun without a parasol aboard her father's ship. He let her sail with him every time he visited her in England, but never took her for very long trips. Stratton didn't want his daughter to love the sea as much as he did, so he limited the amount of time she spent on board, and yet for all of his efforts, she still loved to sail.

The pair left their townhouse and stepped into a carriage waiting for them on the street. After Miranda sat down she straightened the folds of her skirts. She then gazed out the window into the calming afternoon light.

"I long to be on Father's ship, Davy. I desire to feel carefree and alive again. When will he be coming to port?"

"To be honest, I'm not sure. I haven't received a letter from your father in several weeks, which is quite unusual." Miranda's brown eyes met Davy's blue ones.

"Should I be concerned?" Stratton Mayne wrote to his daughter at least once a week, if not more, telling her of his adventures. Often, he would come to port in the harbor and stay for weeks to spend time with her, bringing her various gifts like fabrics and linens, a parrot from the Caribbean, which she couldn't accept because of the cold weather. He brought her many things from his travels and yet all she wanted from him was his love and affection, but most importantly she wanted his time. If she was just able to spend quality time with him, no gifts, no broken promises, then she would be the happiest girl in the world.

The last trip that her father made was two months ago when he brought her jewelry and silk fabric from the Orient, which her seamstress made into several fine dresses for her, as well as some breeches and shirts for Davy. The idea of not hearing from her father in several weeks concerned her, and a frown marred her unblemished brow.

"There is no reason for us to be concerned yet, Miry, but if we do not hear from him soon we will go searching for him." Davy was also concerned for his good friend. Not receiving a letter from him meant he was caught, hurt, or worse—hung. Davy gave up his pirating ways to devote his time to Miranda like he had promised long ago, but Stratton refused to give up his freedom as a pirate. It was not the wealth he wanted or needed, but the adventure and freedom. He found life boring and spiritless, needing the sea to keep him feeling alive and young.

"You're right, Davy, and I respect your judgment on the matter. If we do not hear from Father soon, we will go looking for him. Now, let's talk of a different matter. Who am I eating supper with again? Is it Lord Covington or Lord Brussels? They all look the same to me with their long dark wigs and pale faces. Few men wear their hair short nowadays. What do you say to that?" Miranda adjusted her bodice, her gaze not leaving the man who was sitting across from her smiling.

"Lord Covington is getting married. You remember the invitation he sent. It was the one you threw into the fire." Miranda did not reply, her features unchanging. "And Lord Brussels stopped his pursuit after Lord Hammil stepped in. It is he who we will be eating supper with tonight. Over the past few months you have selected to forget Lord Hammil, and you know that is how long you have been seeing each other—a few months. He has asked me for your hand in marriage. Do you not remember this or do you simply choose to forget? And by the way, wigs are in style and do serve some importance. Some men choose to wear them because of their station. However, there are many men who do not."

"You don't!" Miranda blurted sharply.

"No, for I care little about style and what other men think important. Besides, wearing a wig itches my head and is unbearable to me. I can't stand wearing them. I have always liked the shorter and cleaner look with my hair; that, and I do not wish to spend very much time on it. " Davy rested his hands upon his stomach as he gazed at Miranda contently.

"Sometimes I think of our meeting as a bad dream. A dream I want to forget." Davy raised an eyebrow, not liking her answer.

Miranda exhaled a frustrated breath. "Yes, sometimes I choose to forget the man. Don't get me wrong, he is handsome and pleasing but I just don't enjoy the time we have been spending together like I used to. He is quite eccentric in his ways and mannerisms, and I just can't see us as being husband and wife. I guess that I can't see myself being happy with a man who makes me feel ashamed for being me. Whenever we are together, I feel like someone else. I feel like I have to be a different person to please him. I am slowly becoming a person I hate. Maybe that is the price of growing up, I don't know, but what I do know is that I am not happy." Miranda paused, taking a deep breath before continuing.

"But then I think about the good side of our relationship. Lord Hammil is quite devoted with his affection for me, so at least I know that he will love me. He is also well respected and rich, let's not forget that, so he will also be able to take care of me, to provide for all my needs. I would have a good life with him—a safe life. Father will be pleased with that and he will probably adore Lord Hammil and agree to the match. When I think about Father's happiness, I feel that I can sacrifice my own to please him. People do that for the ones they love, right? Sacrifice some things in their lives to please another?" Davy nodded his head and yet his heart filled with sadness.

"You are too young to have to make such sacrifices, Miry. If you are that unhappy with the man, I can make Lord Hammil quickly go away." Miranda's eyes grew wide as she shook her head.

"No, Davy! Let's wait 'till we hear from Father. If he is pleased with the match, I must obey his will. Has he said anything about Lord Hammil's proposal in his letters?"

"He has said nothing, but you already know that. There is not one day that goes by that you have not read those letters at least twice. I have seen you when you think I'm not looking." Miranda turned her face toward the carriage window and gazed out into the street.

"I miss him, Davy. I want to be by his side at sea, not here. This is not the life I was meant to live. Why won't he accept it and let me be with him?" Miranda turned her face back toward Davy, awaiting his answer.

"You know why, Miry. It was your mother's last request. She didn't want you to become a pirate like her, or your father."

"But why? They lived a life of excitement. A life filled with strange pleasures. They were happy, Davy," replied Miranda. "I want that same happiness."

"They lived a life with the fear of getting caught, Miranda. Pirates, when caught, are hung or worse. It is not a pretty sight. Believe me when I say that I have seen much in my day—too much. Now is especially not safe when most of their sanctuaries are being governed. The life of a pirate may seem glamorous to you, for one so naïve, but it is a dangerous lifestyle with many risks. Your father risks his life each and every time he destroys or loots a ship. I pray daily that he is never caught, and it is wise for you to never speak of him to anyone besides me. He is infamous, and the fact that he has never been caught is appealing to many. The bounty on his head is handsome. Men would gladly turn you in to catch him. Remember what I say, young one, for though I would never betray you, there are men out there who gladly would." Davy glanced one more time at Miranda before he turned to face the window.

After some time passed, Davy spoke again and turned to face Miranda. "Do you remember when you were twelve and your father asked what you wanted for your birthday?" Miranda nodded her head and smiled briefly.

"I told him that I wanted to sail with him for a year."

"Yes, and with much deliberation he agreed to the request," said Davy.

"He did, but afterward he brought us back here, and after staying only long enough to allow the men time to restock the ship, he left. I did not hear from him, or see him, for the next six months," spoke Miranda.

"But you know why he kept his distance, don't you, Miry?" Miranda shook her head quickly, still angry for the way her father had acted. "As you know, sailors do not like women aboard their ships. Even a child is unacceptable in their eyes, for as far as they are concerned, all women are bad luck. But during the time that you were aboard the *Flying Wasp*, you changed the men's opinion of you, and you could do no wrong. You cared for each man, respecting them as an equal instead of the filthy scum of the earth that everyone thought them to be. You were slowly turning into your mother. Even at such a young age your father could see it, and it scared him. He could not let that happen. You were wise to the ways of sailing, for your father and I taught you everything that there was to know, and yet you far exceeded our expectations.

"Your mother was a pirate—a good woman. You have to

understand that your mother didn't want that life for you, which is why you are here with me and not by your father's side. You are destined for something better, Miry. If you would stop being stubborn for one minute you would see that this course chosen for you is the better one."

"That may be so, Davy, but what frustrates me the most is that he could be with us right now if he wanted to. For his own selfish reasons he chooses to be alone instead of with me. He abandoned my mother when she needed him, and now he does the same to me. You gave up being a pirate for me, Davy, and as far as I am concerned you are more of a father to me than he is."

"Miry!" Davy shouted, chastising her for her behavior.

"You did, Davy! You sacrificed everything for me when you truly didn't have to," spouted Miranda. "Why couldn't he?" Before Davy could respond, Miranda turned her head away from him and focused her attention out the carriage window.

The rest of the ride was in silence until they reached the large estate of Lord Hammil's. As soon as the carriage stopped, a servant opened the door and held his hand out for Miranda to take. She took it freely and stepped out of the carriage assessing her surroundings. The estate was vast with trees and a stable. The house was large from the outside and looked to have at least fifteen rooms. Miranda looked beside her where Davy now stood and shook her head, imagining what it would be like to be responsible for the house and all the events that would take place there as Lord Hammil's wife. It all seemed overwhelming to her. Davy grabbed her elbow and walked to the door where a servant was waiting for them.

As they entered the house, the inside shined as brightly as the outside. The walls held portraits and pictures in every room. Wood tables and chairs littered the rooms with unlit candlesticks on top of them. A chandelier could be seen from the entranceway, and was radiant against the pale walls. The servant showed them into a parlor where there was a cushioned sofa and chairs for them to sit. A fire illuminated the room with warmth as well as light. Davy stood by the chair while Miranda surveyed the room more closely. Carpets lay upon the dark wood floor and furniture of different shapes and sizes filled the room. She walked past a table and dragged her fingertips across the top. She then glanced at her fingertips. Upon seeing no dirt, she knew the servants were doing their jobs.

"I wish to remind you to behave yourself. Men adore women who are obedient and humble. Act both with such an important man. Do not choose to embarrass me or your father."

"Yes, Davy," replied Miranda obediently as she rolled her eyes, careful not to let him see her. She knew what qualities men wanted in a wife, she also knew that she had very little of those qualities. Miranda was about to sit when the door to the room burst open and in entered Lord Hammil. Lord Hammil was a tall and slender man. He had short brown hair cut to his neck and a curling brown mustache. His blue eyes sparkled as they gazed upon her.

"Miranda, I am so glad to see you." Lord Hammil walked over to where Miranda stood and grabbed her hand, kissing it in welcome. "Supper is served and is waiting for us. Shall we?" Lord Hammil offered his arm for Miranda to take, which she did with reluctance. As they moved from the room, Davy followed quietly behind.

The meal was exceptional as usual. They started with soup and then ate lamb with potatoes and bread. For dessert there was a plate of fresh fruit. As supper ended, Lord Hammil started a conversation about his work, hoping to get Miranda to talk to him. She had been quiet throughout the meal and wasn't sure what to talk about other than the food on the table. To Lord Hammil's dismay, Davy filled in the gap. When their plates were being taken away they were all given a glass filled with a burgundy wine. Miranda didn't like the taste of it much, but still drank the contents to calm her nerves. She kept her eyes averted away from her host and stared frequently around the room with false curiosity. Now, as she placed her glass onto the table she could feel Lord Hammil's eyes upon her. It was then she knew that she couldn't escape conversation any longer.

"So, Lord Hammil, what is it, exactly, that you do again?" She knew he had explained it to her at least a dozen times, but was embarrassed to tell him that she wasn't paying any attention when he had.

"Miranda, please call me Leonard. We don't have to be formal when we are with each other." Miranda quickly glanced at Davy who was standing behind Lord Hammil and nodded his head. "If your father gives me permission to marry you, I would like you to feel comfortable calling me by my name, as I will be calling you by yours."

"Of course, Leonard," replied Miranda dryly.

"I am in charge of handing out the letters of marque for the queen to privateers. I also have many other important duties that I am responsible for."

"So, you are familiar with captains and their ships?" asked Miranda cautiously.

"Yes, I am familiar with many captains and their ships, though I can't tell you which ones, my dear," replied Leonard as he gave Miranda a charming smile.

"Why not?" Miranda's voice held her disappointment but as her eyes narrowed onto Lord Hammil, she noticed the slight shake of Davy's head to her right as he had taken a chair slightly behind him.

"Because, no one is to know what ships have that privilege. Now," said Lord Hammil as he changed the topic. "Does my house please you? You will have run of it, of course, when we wed. Will you be able to handle the responsibility?" Miranda noticed the way Leonard smoothly switched topics, but decided not to pursue her interest in his knowledge of ships.

"Your house pleases me very much. Would we be staying here all year round or do you have estates elsewhere?"

"We will be staying here, mostly, but I do have other estates that we will be visiting periodically." Leonard finished his sentence in a way that made Miranda feel uncomfortable about asking him the question. She then pursed her lips tightly, the corners of her mouth turning slightly into a frown.

"And where, pray, are these other estates?" Lord Hammil ignored the question as he smiled adoringly at Miranda.

"I must say, Miranda, you do please me. You are not only beautiful, but obedient. I like those qualities in a wife." Miranda smiled at Leonard as he casually glanced down the length of her. The ogling made her want to shout in protest. "Yes, you please me very much." Leonard quickly stood and approached Miranda, his eyes focusing on her lips. Miranda quickly glanced at Davy, who already rose from his chair to intervene. Her hands were clenching together, nervous about Leonard's intentions. Other than the occasional peck on the cheek, he had never kissed her passionately before. In fact, she had never kissed any man before.

"Would you honor me with a kiss, Miranda? I have often thought of your lips upon mine. If you were to be my wife, then I would wish to kiss you often. It would please me greatly to taste your lips, if only just once to see if there is any magic between us." Leonard reached out his hand for Miranda to take. She accepted his hand reluctantly and stood in front of him, her eyes glancing over at Davy pleadingly. He was now standing behind Leonard waiting for the moment to intercede. As Leonard slowly leaned forward, his lips moving closer to hers, Davy interrupted.

"Forgive the interruption, but I feel it would be better if you were to wait until you were wed to pursue such romantic intentions. I think only of her virtue." Miranda exhaled the breath she was holding. Leonard exhaled a breath of his own, but it wasn't with relief.

"Her virtue is safe with me, Davy, rest assured. Maybe there is somewhere else you need to be? When in my care, you can trust that I can protect her." Davy folded his arms in front of his chest and narrowed his eyes threateningly. His arms were still muscular and though his youth was gone, one would never know it by how good of shape he kept himself in. Davy was a man who took great pride in his appearance and did not want to fall prey to age.

"Forgive me, milord, but Miranda has only one protector, and it's me." Lord Hammil stood tall and threatening, and though his whole demeanor spoke of his power, his gangly physique spoke of his lack of strength. He slowly let go of Miranda's hand.

"I will take this time to inform you that once we are wed, your services will no longer be needed." Lord Hammil turned abruptly around to face Davy. The men faced each other, determination in their eyes.

"If he stays with me or if he goes, Leonard, the decision will never be up to you. It is up to me, and I say he stays." Lord Hammil glanced back at Miranda quickly, not taking his eyes away from Davy.

"When I am your husband, I will have the say over you, and he will go. I will not have him towering over me every time I wish to be alone with you." Miranda's eyes narrowed as she moved in-between Davy and Lord Hammil.

"He is my protector, designated to me by my father, and he will remain by my side for as long as he wishes to be. Forgive me, but becoming your wife isn't official as of yet until I speak with my father about the matter. So please, do not try to change what you do not have any control over. Now, if you will excuse us, we have somewhere else we need to be." Miranda moved toward Davy and pushed him to the door.

"Where is your father? I wish to get my answer from him soon."

Miranda faced Lord Hammil, trying to think up a good lie to tell him.

"He's currently away on business, but when he arrives home I will make sure that you speak with him. We are all eager to hear what he has to say upon the matter of our engagement."

"Yes, well, until his return I request that you join me for a ball I am throwing a week from today. I wish for my family and close friends to meet you. Will you attend?" Miranda thought of her future as well as the honor it would give her father if she were to marry such an established gentlemen.

"If that is what you wish of me, then of course I will attend as you request." Miranda bowed her head slightly to the ground. Lord Hammil moved forward until he stood just inches from her. He then bent down and lightly kissed her upon the cheek, his eyes daring Davy to stop him.

"I will see you in a week's time then?" She bowed in front of him again and turned for Davy to escort her out the door and into their awaiting carriage. Lord Hammil ran his fingers through his hair as he stared out the window watching the carriage move farther and farther away until it was only a speck on the road.

The week had passed by quickly for Lord Hammil. He was in his office mulling over paperwork when he was summoned to speak with the queen. He often did this when she was handing out or reissuing letters of marque to privateers to help her deal with her enemies, but today was different. When he arrived at the palace, it was not to speak with the queen, but with one of her closest advisors, Lord Havenor. When Lord Hammil stepped into a richly furnished room, Lord Havenor was waiting for him. He was a medium built man who wore a long gray waistcoat with white breeches. His face was solemn, his eyes a dark blue, missing nothing. He wore a long white periwig upon his head, which denoted the importance of his station. He did not appear to be a kind man, but a man who took his job very seriously. He was a man not to mess with.

Surprise filled Lord Hammil's features, not sure of what the advisor wanted with him. They seldom talked with each other but when they did, the information was always useful. Lord Havenor motioned for Lord Hammil to sit in a chair opposite him. Once Lord Hammil took his seat, the advisor started to speak.

"I am aware that you were supposed to see Her Majesty, but I am here to speak on her behalf. Here are the letters of marque for the following ships and their captains. As always, these men can't be punished for their crimes if they are captured. The queen looks highly upon these men and their crews to help keep her enemies at bay, as well as to fill her coffers." Lord Havenor handed papers to Lord Hammil, who perused them quickly.

"I see that she has given Captain Riveri a letter of marque. I thought she said that she was never going to provide him with one?" Lord Havenor rose from his chair and walked slowly around the room.

"Yes, I know she said that at one time or another, but the daring man came to see her and well, let's say that she was quite satisfied with what he had to say." Lord Hammil raised his eyebrows, understanding what the advisor had meant. "He has also been doing special favors for our dear queen for the past year, which has convinced her of his loyalty and devotion. The captain is an intelligent man and has been using his talents and ship wisely. Regardless of my opinion of the man—which the queen will not listen to—he will serve her well and has earned his position of freedom—or so I am told." Lord Havenor took a deep breath before continuing, trying to remove the disdain for Captain Riveri in his tone.

"I feel that Captain Riveri is going to be very useful to our cause, which is why I am appointing him to you. The queen needs you to sail to Port Royal and search for a particular item for her. Riveri knows the man who has this particular trinket. You see, it is a long crystal about the size of my pinkie finger and it has a mate. When these two pieces are united it becomes a key. This key opens a vault that was built by the Spanish many years ago. The vault holds unspeakable fortunes, which would explain our desire to have it. Many have tried to open this vault, but without the key, there are many traps and dangers that surround it. What that means, I have no idea. Your guess would be as good as mine at this point."

"Who is the man that has the crystal?" asked Lord Hammil, who was listening carefully to every word the advisor was saying.

"Captain Ditarius has the crystal in his possession, but only one of the pieces. We feel that he knows who keeps the other. I have received word that one of his men has been captured by the Governor of Port Royal and is to be hanged. However, the governor has agreed to turn the man over to us until we have no more use for him. Then we will have the honor of killing him ourselves. He knows where the captain is hiding, but will not confess. Even torturing has not loosened his tongue. You will be sailing there in a few days. I am sorry that you will have to leave the day after announcing your engagement at your ball, but duty calls." Lord Hammil nodded his head at the advisor understanding what he needed to do.

"Whatever Your Majesty wishes for me to do, I will do gladly. I have an estate on the island of New Providence and will arrange to stay there until we find Captain Ditarius and the other crystal. Where is the vault located?"

"Our sources say the vault is located in, or somewhere near, Nombre de Dios, which is near Panama. The vault is said to be buried into the side of one of the mountain ranges. Years ago the Spanish sailed to Nombre de Dios and picked up shipments of gold and silver. Twice a year they picked up the shipments that were dropped off in Panama and taken by mules to the little town. Here is a map to help you and more information about the crystal. What we do not have or know anything about, is how to open the door of the vault. There is a special way, but no one knows how, so you will need to find that out as well. Here is a pouch of coins to pay for your journey, and the queen would like you to bring back whatever you find. She will reward you handsomely for your patriotism." Lord Hammil accepted the pouch and the map thankfully.

"Captain Riveri is down at the harbor waiting for your instruction. He only knows that he is to take you to Port Royal and help you with whatever needs you desire. He is not to know the entire purpose of your journey. He needs to be kept ignorant of some facts."

"He is the captain of the ship, he will need to be informed," urged Lord Hammil.

"Let me briefly explain to you why you must keep some things from him. If Captain Riveri discovers the identity of the person you are after, or any of the information that I have just told you, he will prevent you from reaching your goal. He will feel honor bound because of his close relationship with Captain Ditarius. Personally, I hope he does, for it would give me an excuse to take away the letter of marque he has worked so hard to attain. He feels he's invincible, and I wish to crush him like rocks beneath my feet, just to show him how human he is." Lord Havenor had a crazed expression upon his face, then it vanished as quickly as it was revealed. Lord Hammil knew the reason for the man's distaste for the captain, for it mirrored his own.

"Unfortunately, he is aware that if he does betray us in anyway, we will revoke his letter of marque, and that we will hunt him down like the pirate he is. Knowing this, I am also sure that he will do as he is told and will walk a straight line. The man will not make a mistake, I guarantee it. He has too much to lose and he knows it. However, if you can think of a way to break him, by all means—" Lord Havenor let the rest of his words go unspoken, but Lord Hammil understood the implication. "Now, he has many men and a large ship. He will be able to handle any attacks that may come upon you. Good luck on your journey." Lord Havenor bowed his head to Lord Hammil in farewell. Lord Hammil stood, grabbed all the papers he acquired during his meeting and held them underneath his arm.

"There is one more thing before you go. Who is the woman you chose for your bride? The queen wishes to bless you with many gifts upon your vows." Lord Hammil smiled at the advisor and replied, "Her name is Miranda Smyth. She is a charming and beautiful woman. Her father is a traveler. I believe you have met her before, at Somerby's affair a couple of weeks ago?" The advisor only smiled and nodded his head.

"I remember it quite well. She's an enchanting creature indeed, a real beauty. Well, here is my wedding gift to you ahead of time. I believe you will find it most useful." Lord Hammil grabbed the parchment wrapped with a pretty red ribbon from the advisor and thanked him profusely for his kindness. He then turned away from the advisor to face the door, and after making sure that he had all of his papers, left the room. Lord Havenor was smiling evilly upon Lord Hammil's exit as if he were a cat eagerly awaiting his prey.

CHAPTER 2

Sounds of steel could be heard from the living room as Davy trained Miranda in the ways of swordplay. Daily, the furniture was removed from the room and the pair would practice for a few hours at a time. The servants would occasionally watch this tradition, and today was no different. Some of the men and women were gathered in the doorways watching with smiles on their faces as Davy and Miranda moved from one side of the room to the other. The fight between the two was getting heated, and Miranda was being aggressive. They would determine the winner by seeing which one could slash at the others clothing first. The skill between both was exceptional, though it wasn't always so. When Miranda was a child, Davy would end up with scars on his arms and legs. Even though he took special precautions by wearing protective covering, it never seemed to save him from her blade. Now though, the protective shields remained on his chest but nowhere else.

Miranda had her hair back into a braid while she moved around the room stealthily. Davy never took his eyes away from her for fear she would beat him again. Over the years, she had moved faster with a blade than any man had, including her father. Miranda was told to strike with her fists when she felt confident enough, and today she had her confidence. Davy swung at her head, but Miranda smoothly ducked from the blow. Instead, she punched him in the stomach. When she saw Davy hunch over in pain, she hastily went to him. She lowered her sword to her side and placed her hand on his back.

"Are you all right, Davy?" As she bent over to check on him, Davy moved his foot and brought it by her ankles, tripping her in one fluid motion. With his hand he pushed her to the floor and straddled her hips, his sword at her throat. Miranda cursed loudly as she felt Davy's cold blade. Davy's eyebrows rose arrogantly as he touched her nose with his finger.

"How many times have I told you never to let your guard down? If I was another man fighting you, I would have killed you."

"If you were another man, I never would have checked to see if you were hurt." Miranda punched Davy's thigh as he removed his sword and rose off of her. "You are getting up there in age you know." Miranda crawled away quickly, but not before Davy smacked her on the backside with his hand.

"If I am so old, than how come I can beat you?" Davy gave Miranda a crooked smile as he put their swords away along with his chest pad. Miranda rubbed her backside as she stood from the floor.

"You have to admit that I'm improving," returned Miranda arrogantly.

"The only way I will admit that is if you admit that I beat you fair and square." Miranda rolled her eyes as she placed her hands upon her hips.

"Oh, all right, you beat me fair and square. Unlike the last time, and the time before that when I beat you soundly." Miranda gave Davy a sassy smile as he started to chase her around the room. Her screams could be heard throughout the house, the servants only shook their heads in response. One servant, in particular, walked into the room and interrupted the pair.

"Excuse me, Miss Mayne, but Lord Hammil's ball is in a few hours and you need to be getting ready if you want to make it there on time. His note requested for you to arrive earlier than his guests so he could speak with you privately." The servant was a small, thin girl with curly brown hair and a round face. Her name was Melissa. "Also, I am to remind you that Madam Fairaday will be arriving shortly to assist you in your preparations. She will also be attending."

"I forgot about that. Thank you for reminding me, Melissa." Melissa bowed her head and smiled at her flush-faced mistress before turning away. "I better hurry before she arrives and sees me like this. The wonderful woman would faint if she saw me wearing men's breeches." Miranda placed her hand to her chest, her heart racing from her exertions. Her cheeks were flushed, and a smile was evident upon her face. "I don't see why you don't ask her over for supper some evening? She is a kind woman who could probably make you happy." Davy rolled his eyes dramatically.

"She is out of my league, love. Don't worry about my happiness. When I find a woman that I'm interested in, I will let you know."

Miranda slowly walked up to Davy, whose heart was also racing, and embraced him. They held each other for several seconds, then as Miranda pulled away she kissed him upon the cheek.

"Do you know how much I love you my faithful friend? I couldn't imagine my life without you by my side." Davy caressed her cheek as he smiled from her comment.

"Yes, my child, you love me as much as I love you. You are like a daughter to me. Now, go and get ready, and you might want to consider a bath with some of those scented oils your father brought you from France."

"Why? You won't let Lord Hammil close enough to me to notice." Miranda glanced back at Davy as she walked from the room to the stairs and winked. Davy moved to stand in the doorway the servants once occupied, who were now returning the furniture to its rightful place.

"If you desire for him to touch you or more, all you have to do is say the word and I will leave your side and let him." Miranda looked down at Davy from the stairs, her eyes narrowing.

"No!" Miranda spoke sharply.

"I thought as much. The look you gave me the last time Lord Hammil attempted to kiss you, begged for me to stop him." Davy folded his arms in front of his chest. His weight pressed up against the doorframe. Miranda played with the red sash at her waist. Whenever her and Davy practiced with the sword, she would wear breeches with a white shirt and sash pretending she were a pirate.

"I have never been kissed by a man, Davy. I am unsure of what I am supposed to do." Miranda looked down at the steps, averting her eyes from meeting Davy's.

"There is no shame in that, Miry. Your father and I are grateful for it. However, if you become Lord Hammil's wife, he will want you to show him affection. You cannot avoid it forever." Miranda glanced back at Davy, then proceeded up the stairs.

"I will think about it," and with that said Miranda walked the rest of the way up the stairs, Davy watching her go. He began to walk down the hallway toward the kitchen when he heard a knock on the door. He saw a servant walk toward the door and answer it. It was Madam Fairaday.

Madam Fairaday was an extremely wealthy woman with a full bodice and thinning figure. Her features were pleasing to the eye. She was at least in her early fifties, but one would never know it for her appearance never revealed her age. She had slightly graying black hair with beautiful hazel green eyes. Her skin was pale with a slight hint of red upon her cheeks. Her hair was wrapped delicately upon her head and her gown was of a dark green that flattered her figure. It had a low neckline and thinning waist but the skirt billowed out around her almost preventing her from walking through the door without help. Davy instantly hastened to her side and kissed her hand in greeting.

"Madam Fairaday, how nice it is to see you again."

"It is always nice to be seen, Davy."

"Miranda is upstairs getting ready if you would like to join her. I need to change as well so I will not be able to escort you." Madam Fairaday waved her hand in front of her carelessly.

"There is no need to escort me, Davy. I'm familiar with the way."

"Very good, then I will see you shortly." Davy was about to turn around when he felt Madam Fairaday's hand upon his arm.

"Can I speak with you alone for a moment?" Davy looked quickly around him, then escorted her into the library. When they walked into the room, he quickly closed the door behind them, neither wanting to sit.

"Yes?"

"I wanted to ask you something before I attend to Miranda. I know that you don't want to talk about this, but I have to ask you. Have you heard from Stratton lately?" Davy shook his head as he folded his arms in front of his chest.

"No! We have not heard from him in a while."

"Neither have I. I am concerned." Madam Fairaday bowed her head toward the ground, her stare focusing on Davy's feet.

"As are we, but there is no reason to worry yet." Madam Fairaday returned her eyes to meet Davy's and gave him a weak smile.

"There is one more thing. Does Miranda know about—?"

"No!" Davy quickly answered cutting her off. "And I don't think she should, at least not yet."

"But Davy, you are her guardian, how can you keep this from her?"

"And you, my dear woman, are Stratton's new wife. It is not my responsibility to explain what happened between you or why."

"But—"

"There are no exceptions!" shouted Davy angrily. "We all discussed this, remember?" Madam Fairaday gazed at Davy wide-eyed. "She should not know yet. Now is not the time to explain to her the relationship that you two have. She will not understand and will only feel hurt. Trust me on this. Stratton has to explain to her what is going on between you. I will not intervene on either of your behalves. It will only make the situation worse because I know of the deception. What you two did was spontaneously romantic, yet disgustingly deceptive. Both of you did not think of the consequences of your hastened marriage." There was a long pause before he continued, "What of your son, has he found out? Is that why you are bringing this up?"

"Yes, I have told him."

"And how did he take it?"

"Not well," responded Madam Fairaday sadly. "He didn't take it well at all, but we have talked and he now understands that my happiness is more important than his anger or surprise, though he's still vexed with me. Actually, he has not gone out of his way to speak to me about it, and every time I bring it up, he avoids the topic. He says it does not bother him, but I know he's lying. I know my son and when he first found out about my relationship with Stratton's months ago, he was—well—crushed. Now that he knows that we are married, his anger knows no bounds." Madam Fairaday paused before saying, "I cannot spend all this time with Miranda and not tell her the truth, too. I do not want to see that same expression on her face, that look of betrayal. No, I could not bear to see it from her. Seeing it from my son was painful enough." Davy placed his large hands on Madam Fairaday's shoulders and squeezed reassuringly.

"She will understand the feelings that you two have for each other but she will not understand anything else for her vision will only be filled with hurt. Her reaction will mirror your sons, I will guarantee it. No matter when you tell her, her reaction will still be the same."

"Yes, all the more reason to tell her now and get it over with before the lie spitballs into something bigger and more unforgivable."

"No, you are doing the right thing by keeping the truth from her, don't doubt yourself. What you need to focus on is still befriending her. Then, once she knows the truth, her anger won't be so terrible." Madam Fairaday shook her head at such nonsense, wanting to change the topic. Before she did, she raised her eyebrows and clucked her tongue loudly.

"There is one more thing. I have friends who are wives of some of the queen's most trusted advisors and chiefs of staff, and I have learned something very disturbing. You see, they said—" Before she could say anymore Miranda opened the library door and peaked inside. Davy instantly removed his hands from Madam Fairaday's shoulders.

"Madam Fairaday, I thought I heard your voice." Miranda gazed at Davy and then at Madam Fairaday curiously. "What are you doing in here?" Davy was about to speak but Madam Fairaday quickly interrupted.

"I was speaking with Davy about this evening's event. Are you in need of my assistance, for if so, then I shall move with haste?" Miranda glanced one more time at Davy before she answered.

"Please, my gown is complicated to get into. Your help would be greatly appreciated." Miranda smiled mischievously and winked at Davy as she turned around and left the room. Madam Fairaday stared at Davy as he shook his head slightly, again pleading with her to say nothing to Miranda. She didn't respond, but only lifted her skirts as she exited the library, following Miranda up the stairs.

An hour had passed and Miranda and Madam Fairaday were in her bedchamber still working on her appearance. Miranda was glancing into a mirror at her hair when she saw Madam Fairaday sitting behind her deep in thought. She hastily turned around and smiled politely.

"What's wrong? You are quiet today." Madam Fairaday smiled briefly as she stood from her chair.

"I will get Davy to finish tying the lacings in the back. No matter how hard I pull them, they are still not tight enough." Miranda stood from her chair. "You do look beautiful tonight."

"As do you. In fact, I think that you already have an admirer." Madam Fairaday stared at Miranda in confusion.

"What do you mean?"

"Davy! I think I know why you were alone with him." Fear crept into Madam Fairaday's chest.

"You do?"

"Yes, I think he has feelings for you, or you for him?" Madam Fairaday laughed loudly as she exhaled a breath of relief.

"No, dear child, that's not the case." She then walked up to

Miranda and embraced her. "You know that I care for you as if you were my own daughter, don't you?" Miranda nodded her head as she smiled brightly. "I have no daughter of my own so I'm blessed to be able to dote on you. It's meant so much to me." After squeezing Miranda again gently, Madam Fairaday pulled away. "If there's nothing more, my dear, I will see you later at Lord Hammil's?"

"Of course, if he will free me from his grasp long enough to talk with you."

"Don't worry. I will make sure he allows us time to talk. If he doesn't I will make a scene. I know how much he would love that." Both women laughed at the very thought of seeing Lord Hammil's embarrassed cherry red face. Madam Fairaday then kissed Miranda's cheek, walked to the door, opened it and left. Davy entered shortly afterward. He moved right toward Miranda's unfinished laces and pulled on them.

"Davy, may I remind you that today you need to watch what you say instead of me when we are at Lord Hammil's?" Miranda winked at her friend through the mirror. She then admired her appearance. She chose a brownish gold gown with gold underskirts. White lace wrapped around the bodice and sleeves. The color matched her eyes exactly and flattered her figure. The skirts flowed smoothly when she walked around the room. Miranda was thin with curvaceous hips and supple thighs, but neither assets could be seen by any man. Her breasts were full and round, her shoulders soft and narrow. When Davy pulled the last lace too tightly, she glared quickly back at him, knowing that he did it on purpose, though he apologized.

"Did you have a nice visit with Madam Fairaday?" asked Davy changing the topic.

"Yes! I always enjoy our visits. I almost wish we didn't have to go to Lord Hammil's so I could spend more time with her instead," poured Miranda as she admired herself in the mirror again. "I know what I can do, I will invite her over for tea tomorrow. Then we can gossip properly when we are not so distracted."

"You look beautiful, Miry, but we are running out of time and need to get going. Stop stalling." Miranda admired herself one last time in the mirror, then left with Davy by her side. Davy wore a dark brown waistcoat and black breeches with a white shirt shining underneath. His hair was slicked back and his face clean shaven. Davy escorted Miranda to a carriage waiting for them by the street and helped her inside. When he stepped in and closed the door, the carriage started moving. Silence filled the carriage until Miranda could see the torches shining outside of Lord Hammil's estate.

"I don't mean to be selfish, Davy, but what if Lord Hammil refuses to let you stay by my side?" Miranda focused on Davy's features, her concern for him bothering her ever since Lord Hammil had said the words.

"Have you been thinking about that the entire ride?" Miranda didn't smile or smirk, but remained still and serious. Davy placed his hand upon Miranda's and squeezed.

"You know I promised your father that I would take care of you when he was away. Even if you marry Lord Hammil, he cannot make me break my oath. I may not be by your side as often, but I will always be here for you if you need me." Miranda placed her other hand on top of Davy's and smiled, feeling reassured.

When the carriage stopped, Davy removed his hand from Miranda's grasp and opened the door. He quickly helped her step out and then walked slowly to the door. When Miranda entered into the hall, Lord Hammil hurried over to greet her. He lifted her hand and grazed it with his lips. He then nodded his head in Davy's direction.

"My dear, we have much to discuss. Shall we go into my study and talk before my guests arrive?" Miranda had no time to refuse as he placed her hand on his arm and walked her to the study. Lord Hammil casually walked her into the room and helped her sit into a chair in front of his desk. He then turned to Davy and asked if he would be so kind as to wait in the hallway. Davy glanced at Miranda who nodded her head, letting him know that she would be fine with it. Davy then turned and left the room, but not before saying, "I will not be far if you need me." Miranda nodded her head and noticed the glance that Davy had given Lord Hammil. She saw the irritated look on Lord Hammil's features and had to stop herself from smiling. Davy closed the door behind him.

Lord Hammil moved to his seat behind the desk and folded his hands to lay upon his flat stomach. His eyes glanced periodically up at Miranda who sat in her seat patiently, her hands lying in her lap, fingers clenched tightly together.

"You look beautiful tonight, Miranda. I appreciate you coming. I'm not ashamed to say how much pleasure it will give me in having you meet my friends. I will immensely enjoy seeing the envious looks upon their faces." Miranda smiled politely at Lord Hammil's comment, but didn't respond. The nervousness she felt prevented her from speaking. Lord Hammil traced a long slim finger along the edge of the desk as he said, "Any news yet from your father?" Miranda refused to tell Lord Hammil anything about her family, especially the truth. However, she knew that by stalling him again, he may be put off, and she knew that her father would no doubt bless the union between them. Her father often spoke of her living a normal life with a wealthy gentleman instead of being a pirate renegade sailing the seas. Though the sea was all that she craved for, Miranda wanted to make her father happy, so she told a lie.

"I received a letter from him this morning and he has given his approval for us to wed. He's sorry that he will not be able to say this to you in person." Lord Hammil rose abruptly from his chair, almost knocking it over, and hurried to stand in front of Miranda, his features expressing his joy.

"Does this news please you, Miranda? I must know." Miranda rose from her chair with confidence, arms hanging by her sides and her chin lifting firmly.

"Yes, Leonard, you are a fine man. It would please any woman to become your wife." Miranda told Lord Hammil what he wanted to hear, knowing that her words would please him. She then relaxed slightly and smiled, but her joy didn't reach her eyes. Lord Hammil failed to notice. He placed his hands upon Miranda's shoulders and pulled her to him awkwardly. Surprised by the action, Miranda placed her hands between them to rest on Lord Hammil's chest.

"I have wanted to do this for some time, Miranda," and without warning he leaned forward and pressed his lips against hers. The kiss was not passionate or exciting, but pleasant. Having nothing to compare it with, Miranda thought the kiss to be very satisfying. Feeling that Lord Hammil was taking enough liberties with her, she backed away removing herself from his arms and taking several steps away from him. She wanted to put plenty of space between them.

"You have made me a very happy man, Miranda. I will see that you are taken care of properly. Everything you will ever want will be yours." Lord Hammil grabbed the chair next to Miranda's and pulled it closer so he could sit next to her. Miranda slowly sank back into her chair, fixing the folds of her gown with one hand while Lord Hammil grabbed the other and held it in his.

"I know we have spent much time together but there are some things which you may not know about me. I know that I may seem weak and docile compared to some other men, but I'm really not. It may look like I couldn't protect you from harm but appearances can be deceiving. I have much power in this world of ours and I feel I could protect you and do it well. However, there are things that I expect out of my wife and these are qualities I feel you should be aware of. I enjoy the sight of you, it pleases me very much, and your demeanor and obedience is satisfying. I feel that my wife should also be trustworthy, obedient to my command at all times, and faithful. Do you have these qualities?" Lord Hammil stared into Miranda's soft brown eyes awaiting her answer.

"Of course!" replied Miranda hesitantly, feeling a little uncomfortable at having her virtues questioned, but also knowing that she wasn't quite sure if she was going to be able to live up to Lord Hammil's expectations of her. He was expecting her to be a perfect person and in this world she knew that she was not. A smile rose upon his lips as he continued.

"Good, because I feel that you do as well. I am a jealous man at times and get angry when people touch the items that belong to me without my permission. I would kill someone if they touched you where only I will be touching you." The image of Lord Hammil caressing her body and lips almost made her shiver with distaste. This feeling caused much concern for Miranda. Lord Hammil wasn't an ugly man by any means, in fact, he was quite handsome, but she still could not believe the hateful words that were coming out of his mouth. She wanted to take back what she had said to him about her father agreeing to the marriage, but knew that now she could not. Her eyes ran over Lord Hammil's form as he ran his fingers through his hair and over his mustache, as if it was a nervous habit. Miranda's eyes widened as she saw his hands shake as he spoke.

"I must have order in my life and because I am a public figure I demand perfection. Do you understand what I expect from you?" Lord Hammil grasped her hand tighter in his. Miranda almost flinched from the pain.

"I understand perfectly your expectations of me," replied Miranda as she tried to smile but couldn't quite accomplish it.

"Good, very good, I'm glad we understand each other. Now, there is another matter I wish to talk with you about. I am leaving on a ship tomorrow to go to New Providence, in the Caribbean. I have an estate down there and wish to check on it, as well as to take care of some personal matters for the queen. Would you care to join me? I know it is short notice to expect you to be ready in time, but I thought perhaps we could marry at my estate down there. I can send word ahead to make it ready for our coming. I have always wanted to get married in a tropical and beautiful place like New Providence. Would you indulge me, my sweet?" Lord Hammil stared longingly into Miranda's eyes, hoping she wouldn't say no.

Miranda was stunned by the request and yet pleased by it. She still hadn't heard from her father and was starting to get concerned for his welfare. By joining Lord Hammil to New Providence, she could find a way to Eleuthera Island to see if her father was hiding out there. The thought brought a brilliant smile to Miranda's face.

"If that is your wish, Leonard, then I will obey. I have never been to the Caribbean," Miranda lied smoothly. "You have made me very happy with your request." Suddenly, Miranda leaned forward and placed a soft kiss upon Lord Hammil's cheek. He caressed the smooth skin of her cheek and was about to partake in her lips when they heard a knock on the door.

"Enter!" said Lord Hammil, frustrated by the interruption.

"Forgive the intrusion, milord, but your guests are arriving," said a servant with short brown hair and glasses.

"Very good, thank you." He then turned to face Miranda again.

"Shall we?" he asked as he lifted Miranda from her chair by her hand, not waiting for a response from her, and walked to the door. Standing in the hallway was Davy. He followed quietly behind the pair as they entered into the Hall, their eyes falling upon the people waiting for them.

Hours had passed and Miranda was still in conversation with many of Lord Hammil's guests. He had already made the announcement of their engagement to the masses. The smile on her face felt permanent, and she would have given anything to be alone so she could act like herself instead of this stranger she was becoming. It frustrated her immensely. Miranda knew that if anyone saw her act inappropriately that she would bring shame to Lord Hammil, and from his behavior earlier, she didn't want to do that. Miranda felt her feet becoming sore in her tight shoes and knew she had to sit in a chair quickly before she lost all patience and threw them across the room. "That would surely be a spectacle," Miranda whispered to herself as she gave an unladylike snort, excusing herself from the stranger before her and sitting longfully into a chair.

Miranda could see Madam Fairaday glancing over at her from a group of women she was talking with. She waved for her to join them. Miranda stood and walked over to the group, her feet still aching.

"You all know Miss Smyth, Lord Hammil's fiancé?" The women glanced over at Miranda kindly, except for a few who snubbed her. Miranda tried not to let her smile falter.

"You are very fortunate to be marrying Lord Hammil," said a woman who had a slightly crooked nose, pale complexion and bright red lips. She also had bright colored feathers peeking out from her hair and looked very similar to a peacock in her blue dress.

"Yes, he's quite a catch. I'm indeed fortunate." The woman pressed her lips tightly as she took a sip from her drink. The rest of the women kept eyeing her tersely but Madam Fairaday guided the conversation to all of the topics she knew Miranda was aware of. Miranda seemed quite intelligent to the women before her, but soon she was getting tired and her feet started bothering her again.

"Please excuse me ladies, but I believe my fiancé is looking for me. It was nice to meet all of you." Miranda winked at Madam Fairaday and left the circle of women. She then moved back toward the hallway and sat into another chair, her hands instantly moving to massage her feet.

Davy remained in the room and watched over her as usual. There were a few times when his eyes didn't fall upon Miranda during the evening and that was because he was entertaining a beautiful woman. Her name was Lady Eleanor and Davy was quite fond of her as she was of him. He was currently leading her around the dance floor making friendly conversation, hoping that he could lure her into his bed for the night. He smiled as he remembered the last time he had done so. Though Davy was always aware of Miranda's movements, he also had needs that he had to look after as well. At that moment though, his eyes were focused on Miranda and he noticed when she suddenly rose from her chair and left the room unattended. Davy quickly made his apologies as he hastily kissed Lady Eleanor's hand leaving her on the dance floor. Not paying much attention to the disappointment that covered Lady

Eleanor's features as he left, Davy kept his attention upon Miranda. When he caught up with her he grabbed her arm in a light grasp stopping her.

"Where are you going, Miry?" Miranda turned around at the familiar voice and replied curtly, "I need to fix my appearance, but can't remember where that blasted powder room is." Irritation was in her voice as she placed her hand on her chin and looked down the hallway. "Oh, who cares where that damn room is, there are so many rooms in this house that one could get lost, and he expects me to run it?" Miranda pointed toward the large hall where she knew that Lord Hammil was entertaining his guests. "My first order of business would be to down size." Davy looked quickly around them, and thankfully saw no one who could overhear their conversation. He placed his hands upon Miranda's shoulders to calm her.

"Relax, Miry, relax. There is no reason to get upset." Miranda brought her fingers to her face as she let out a tear. She tried to regain her composure, and without looking into Davy's eyes, was able to manage it. She breathed deeply several times before her eyes found Davy's concerned ones. "What's wrong with you?" Miranda shook her head knowing that if she talked about her sorrows of the evening that she would cry full force, so she shook her head. "We will talk about this on the way home, Miry." Davy's statement brought a nod out of Miranda. "The room you are searching for is down the hallway on the left. Do you wish me to accompany you?" Davy placed his hand on her cheek and made her look at him.

"No, Davy, I will be fine. Thank you." Miranda gave her friend a quick smile before she made her way down the hallway.

"I will wait for you then," replied Davy, his voice rising slightly in order for her to hear him. Miranda gave him a wave of her hand as she moved closer to the end of the hallway. The wall, which had a beautiful painting of the house hanging on it, loomed closer and closer. She noticed that the hallway turned left, and as she made the turn, realized there was not just one room hidden back there, but six. Miranda stopped and was about to break into tears when she found her strength inside her and removed the urge to cry. She was determined not to break down over something so foolish. She took a deep breath and opened the first door she came to.

As she turned the knob, she realized the door wasn't locked—that was a good sign. But as she opened the door she realized that the room she was in was not the one she was looking for. The room was made for comfort. There were long burgundy drapes covering the windows with matching furniture and many dark wooden tables littered with tapers. Some lit, some not. As she glanced around the room the light revealed the many books that were resting upon the bookshelves on the wall. Some were dusty and some were clean from being read often. Miranda was about to leave the room when out of the corner of her eye she noticed a bright piece of parchment staring at her. She turned back around and faced the parchment laying tantalizingly on the chair to her right.

Miranda then remembered Lord Hammil telling her how he disapproved of people looking at his things without his permission. She wanted to turn and run out the door, but couldn't move. Her eyes focused on the parchment in front of her. She quickly walked to the chair and looked down at the parchment glaring at her. As she read the parchment what she learned amazed her. There was a drawing of her crystal on the page in front of her with some writing scribbled to the side of it numbered like a list. She read it to herself.

One: Captain Ditarius missing in the Caribbean

Two: Find a crystal that he has in his possession

Three: Knows where the mate of it is there are two pieces.

Four: Member of crew caught and being held at Port Royal. Might know of his whereabouts?

Five: Treasure hidden at Nombre de Dios, buried in the side of a mountain. Danger surrounds it!

Six: Cannot open the vault without the key. Needs crystal to open it, crystal is the key.

Seven: Get married!

Miranda's eyes widened with shock at the words she had read. Captain Ditarius was a name that most people called her father, especially now when his true identity was hidden. He had spent years building up the name's reputation. He was missing? The news brought instant fear to her chest. Her father always told her that if he was hiding from the law that he could be found on Eleuthera Island. He had said that it would always be his sanctuary. She must find him and make sure he was safe and unharmed. She would kill anyone who tried to harm him. So, this was the business that Lord Hammil was going down to the Caribbean to take care of? Well, it is good that she would be going with him then. She needed to find her father first and then hide him, keeping Lord Hammil away from him for as long as she could.

The knowledge that her crystal opened a secret vault hidden in Nombre de Dios surprised her immensely. She wondered if her father knew of the treasure. It didn't matter much. The fact that she knew was enough. Her father didn't tell her about the crystal when he first put it around her neck. Only that it was a piece of treasure from a ship they had plundered years ago and that she was to always wear it in remembrance of her mother. She lifted the hem of her gown and raised it to her thigh, seeing the precious stone tied there by a scarf. The neckline of her gown was too low to hide the necklace so she tied it to her thigh hoping to keep it safe, keeping her word to her father to always wear it.

She let go of the hem of her skirt and it flowed like a waterfall back down to the floor covering her legs. Her eyes then fell upon some decorative pieces of parchment. She scanned them quickly and noticed they were letters of marque. She read through the top one quickly and absorbed every word including the name of the captain which was, Riveri, and the name of the ship, *The Captain's Avenger*. She was about to go to the next letter of marque when she saw a rolled up piece of parchment with a pretty ribbon. Curious, she was about to reach for it when she heard footsteps coming down the hallway. Nervously, she looked back at the door, which she forgot to close, rose quickly and hurried to the doorway. Upon seeing no one she rushed out into the hallway closing the door tightly behind her. She moved quickly for the turn in the hallway and once she cleared the corner could see Davy waiting for her like he had said he would.

She passed by a woman in a bright yellow gown whose footsteps had to be the ones she had heard. The woman smiled at her but Miranda was too consumed in thoughts to return the gesture. Her eyes focused on Davy's until she made it to his side. When they looked at each other, Davy knew something was wrong. Miranda's chest was rising and falling heavily from almost running to him. Davy was about to speak when Miranda held up her hand to stop him. "We must speak," was all she said. Davy was about to reply when they heard a booming voice coming from the hall.

"My dove, where have you been? I've been looking everywhere for you." Startled, Miranda raised her hand to her throat feeling like she had just gotten caught for looking into Lord Hammil's private affairs. She cleared her mind before she spoke, "I have been right here, Leonard, talking with Davy."

"I believe you owe me a dance. I wish to claim it now." Lord Hammil's voice accepted no comment or discussion upon the matter as he offered his hand for Miranda to take. She smiled briefly and took it, though reluctantly. As Lord Hammil twirled her around the dance floor Miranda's mind was reeling from all that she had learned. Lord Hammil then discussed with her the time they would be leaving tomorrow for the Caribbean and other important details. Miranda kept nodding her head, showing her fake smile to please him as she listened. As the dance finished Miranda was about to excuse herself when Lord Hammil held her hand tightly, wanting her for another dance. She tried to refuse but Lord Hammil ignored her.

Miranda glanced constantly at Davy begging him to save her and when she thought that she could take no more, he did. Lord Hammil was not pleased when Davy tapped him on the shoulder, forcing him to stop.

"What can I do for you, Davy?" asked Lord Hammil angrily.

"I know you are oblivious to it, milord, but Miranda is tired, her feet ache." Lord Hammil glanced quickly at Miranda who nodded her head.

"I'm sorry, my dear, why didn't you say something?" asked Lord Hammil.

"I didn't want to disappoint you. I know how much you wanted me to dance," replied Miranda smoothly.

"You are so thoughtful, my dear, but I insist that you rest."

"I will be taking her home to rest, Lord Hammil," piped in Davy as he placed his arm around Miranda's waist and removed her from the dance floor. Lord Hammil smiled at his guests as he followed the pair. He then caught up with Davy and Miranda near the entranceway and grabbed Davy's arm to stop him.

"Don't ever take Miranda away from me again. You have made me look inconsiderate and foolish in front of my peers," spouted Lord Hammil as quietly as possible. Davy knocked Lord Hammil's hand away from his arm and glared at him as he told Miranda to go to the carriage. He waited a few seconds before he glanced and saw her step inside. He then turned on Lord Hammil and bore down on him like a fierce storm on a ship.

"You don't need me for that. You should have been more considerate toward her when forcing her to stand on her feet for most of the night just to please your peers. She's a woman, not a doll. If you wish to put her on display to impress everyone, that is your right, but I will not allow such careless treatment of her. I think only of Miranda's welfare, Lord Hammil. As her guardian I love her as my daughter, so forgive me when I say that I could care less for your pride and agenda." Lord Hammil stood fuming as he watched Davy walk the rest of the way to the carriage. He then stormed off as he heard it roll away.

CHAPTER 3

"Lord Hammil wasn't pleased with our leaving so abruptly, but I could tell that you wanted to go." Davy whispered those words as he took off Miranda's shoes and rubbed her feet one by one in the carriage as they left Lord Hammil's estate. Miranda pressed her back forcefully into the seat as she stretched her legs out to lay them upon Davy's knees, his muscular hands massaging from her toes to her heels and ankles. A sigh of pleasure escaped her lips as she rested her head against the seat.

"I made a mistake, Davy, a big one. I told Lord Hammil that father had accepted his proposal of marriage." Davy paused for only a moment while his eyes bore into Miranda's.

"If you recall, I heard the announcement of your engagement earlier in the evening. Do you feel that it was wise to speak for your father?" Was all that Davy had said as he resumed massaging Miranda's feet.

"You know as well as I that Father would accept the match, you have admitted as much to me." Davy didn't answer, he only glanced at her periodically, disapproval in his eyes. "Don't look at me that way, you know I'm right. Anyway, I took Lord Hammil for a wealthy fool, but now I've realized that he is much smarter than what I thought. You know how we talked about letting Lord Hammil show me affection? Well, I let him and I won't be ashamed to tell you that I wasn't at all impressed with his kisses. He grabbed me by the shoulders passionately but the kiss didn't show how excited he was to touch me, not that I have much experience in the matter. I will admit that it was pleasant, but I didn't feel anything in my heart and I thought I would. I am mildly disappointed with my first experience. He lacks emotion, I think. He shows no passion in the art of love, and yet he shows passion for other things." Davy raised his eyebrows at Miranda's words.

"Is this why you almost broke into tears when we were alone earlier?" His curiosity overcame him as he saw the look of sadness in her eyes.

"Yes and no, I felt overwhelmed. I would have duties, as Lord Hammil's wife, in taking care of his large estate and then having to deal with his abnormal expectations of me. He asks too much from me and I don't think I could live up to his demands. Also, he has asked me to go to the Caribbean with him so we can marry at his estate in New Providence, at least that request I would do eagerly." Davy stopped what he was doing and looked up at Miranda.

"Are you serious? What did you say to such a proposal?"

"What do you think I said? I said I would go, of course. He knows nothing of Father's identity, and I figure that if he can take us to New Providence then it wouldn't take much for us to go to Eleuthera in secret to check on Father, if he is there." Davy pushed her feet abruptly off of his knees. Miranda almost fell forward from the action, a look of surprise in her eyes.

"Lord Hammil is not a fool. You cannot treat him as such."

"Since when do you care for his feelings?" Miranda's eyes narrowed into slits.

"Watch your tongue with me child, he's a smart man. I know that you do not love him and I think deep down you fear him. Why? What did he do or say to make you distrust him?" Davy folded his arms in front of his chest awaiting his answer.

"What makes you say such things?" Miranda lowered her eyes, knowing that what Davy said to her was true.

"Lord Hammil is soon to be your husband, and yet you feel that you can dupe him to get what you want. Not a good way to start a trusting relationship. If you cared for him at all, you would never use him like you are planning to do. I was the one who told you not to share with him the truth about you and your father because the connection could be deadly, and I still feel that is the correct decision. But you can't honestly believe that we would be able to hide from him the truth of your desires to see your father. We don't know if he is even at Eleuthera. You are assuming he is because that is where you want him to be." Miranda gazed out the carriage window, a single tear falling from her eyes. She never liked it when Davy raised his voice to her. She always felt like she was wrong or had made a bad decision, even when she thought she was making the right one. It hurt her feelings when Davy yelled at her.

Davy saw the lonesome tear fall down Miranda's cheek and changed his sharp tone to one less angry. He knew how sensitive Miranda was and yet he often forgot. She had been this way since she was a little girl. It was because of this that she was rarely punished. When she did misbehave, Stratton and/or Davy had to be careful when yelling at her. The tears she would cry would bring more torment to them than they ever would her. Davy took a deep breath before continuing.

"You regret your decision, lying about your father's approval, which you never should have given without his permission. You know better, but you regret your decision now because Lord Hammil isn't the man you thought him to be. You thought he was a man you could control, who had a weak will you could convince to do your bidding. Now, because he has shown to you his true self, you have decided that you do not love him, which is not uncommon. He has wealth and power, which is both encouraged, and yet when he speaks to you of demands, your faith falters. Talk to me, Miry, what has he said for you to change your mind so quickly?" Miranda raised her soft brown eyes to meet Davy's blue ones and blurted out her answer.

"Lord Hammil can be very demanding. He told me that he expects me to act a certain way, to be trustworthy, honest and faithful. Faithful he said to me as if I was going to go and have an affair as soon as we were married. He tells me that he is a jealous man and that he will kill anyone if they touch his property and that includes me. His hands shook with his words. Yes, his actions scared me very much." Miranda intertwined her fingers together and placed them in her lap, her eyes looking at the folds of her dress.

"Then, after I saw you in the Hall and you explained to me where that room was where I could fix my appearance, I still could not find it and walked into the wrong room. I was about to leave when I noticed something on a chair. It was a piece of parchment that had a picture of my crystal on it and Lord Hammil had written a list of information on the right side of the picture. Davy, he wrote that Father was missing in the Caribbean and that a man of his crew was captured in Port Royal. It seems that Lord Hammil is going down there, not only to marry me at his estate in New Providence, but to take care of business for the queen in Port Royal. The business of finding the crystals that my father and I have in our possession.

"He had also written that the crystals open a secret vault that is hidden in the mountains in Nombre de Dios. That is why I have no faith in Lord Hammil. What do you think he would do if he found out who I really am? His love for me would crumble and fall, for I could give him everything he has ever wanted that could boost his career to a new level, as well as his greed." Davy was amazed at the information Miranda had just told him. His hand moved immediately to his chin, his fingers rubbing it in thought.

"We're in quite a predicament. You're right. Lord Hammil would use you if he knew who you really were. It bothers me to think of the possibility of him already knowing. Yet, I don't really see how he could." Davy paused in thought. "We can agree that you cannot marry him. However, your involvement in this is too deep, one way or another you can get hurt." Concern filled Davy's features.

"I would do anything to save my father, Davy, just like I would risk everything to save you if you were in trouble. I am going to play the game as long as I have to. We will use Lord Hammil to go to the Caribbean to find Father. Once there, we will need to work fast to get what we want before he does."

"If that is the risk you want to take, then you know that I will protect you. The fact that you know what Lord Hammil has planned is an advantage to us." Davy glanced out the carriage window when he said, "You must keep playing the role of the devoted fiancé. Can you do that? Any change in your behavior may cost us our lives. You must do everything he wants you to do, like it or not." He then stared at Miranda, wanting her to understand what was at stake.

"Anything?"

"Well," thought Davy, "anything within reason of course. Everything is always within reason. Do nothing you feel that you cannot handle. Always consult me first if you are unsure. I can always use the excuse that he will have to wait to touch you until you are wed but you must realize that soon he will get tired of that, and then when you are married there will be nothing I will be able to do. You will have to allow him to consummate the marriage. It is a husband's right, but before that time comes I will keep him at bay. I suggest you do the same. However, you will know when to use your wiles to get what you need from him. He's too eager to have you in his bed, but most of all he loves to have you for show. You are a trophy to him, nothing more, so we will use that to our advantage. Keep that in mind when manipulating him."

"I will continue being the obedient fiancée but it will be hard. I can't stand pretending to be something I'm not. I don't feel free when I have to act like a well born lady and not myself. Those women get tired when walking short distances, using parasols to cover their pasty complexions and their words can be evil and hurtful. To be with such company, to deal with such false mocking behavior, makes me sick to my stomach. I prefer to be open and honest, but my candor is something that Lord Hammil does not wish for. If I were mute, it would please him." Davy let out a laugh and smiled at Miranda.

"You do very well at it, I will say. Tonight you behaved exceptionally; I want you to know that. You only cursed once, that's an improvement." Miranda grabbed one of her shoes and threw it at Davy hitting him in the shoulder. He couldn't help but laugh at her. The pair talked a little while longer. Their words lasting the remaining duration of the carriage ride. When the carriage finally stopped in front of their townhouse, Davy stepped out first turning around to help Miranda out of the carriage. When both went inside, Miranda and Davy headed for the stairs and to their rooms, which were right across from each other.

"When are we supposed to leave for the Caribbean again?" asked Davy.

"Tomorrow sometime, so we better wake up early and pack so we can be ready when Lord Hammil comes and picks us up." Davy rolled his eyes as Miranda shot him a sarcastic smile.

"Goodnight, Davy!" said Miranda.

"Goodnight, Miry, and sleep well," replied Davy.

"I always do," spoke Miranda as she closed her bedchamber door, eager to get to bed.

Early the next morning, Captain Locand Riveri was standing on the quarterdeck looking down at his crew, briefing them on the day's plan. *The Captain's Avenger* was clean and ready to sail. The crew were experienced seaman. All or most had sailed under Locand's command before. Their attire, as well as their appearance, had changed since past times when they had sailed under the black flag. Now, with a letter of marque in his hand, Locand could commandeer any pirate ship within his reach and be called a privateer instead of a pirate. Those days of piracy were fading for him. He was now a man who got most of his wealth from his raids off ships who sailed by England as well as in the Caribbean, which was where he used to pirate the waters consistently. When they looted a ship, which had more wealth then they could ever dream, he gave up pirating for a time, but not sailing. *The Captain's Avenger* was his own ship. It was a three masted, square-rigged merchant ship converted for comfort and speed. It had enough guns to defend itself efficiently and take out most ships that would come up against them, and yet it was also quick enough to escape most enemies. He could easily sail away from trouble, or into it. However, today was going to be an interesting day for them all. His new life as a privateer was going to begin.

When he convinced the queen to supply him with a letter of marque, it took most of his strength and cunning. He had to bed the woman, and only afterward did she promise to give it to him. The promise, though, meant nothing until he actually had it in his hand. The queen was intelligent and wise. She knew of Locand's great sailing ability and knew that in order for her to get the treasure stored in the vault in Nombre de Dios, he would be the only man able to do it. With her Lord Hammil in charge, she was sure that she would have more money to add to her coffers and more prestige to her name in the end.

Locand looked again at the papers in his hand before placing them in a pocket inside of his waistcoat. He then placed both hands behind his back. His strong chest was thrust outward and his long, wavy, black hair, which reached to his shoulders, blew in the wind. He wore black breeches with a white linen shirt and matching black waistcoat. Inside a sheath at his waist was a dagger for protection and standing by his side was his first mate, Stevens. Stevens was an older man with long graying hair that was tied in a queue at his neck and a mustache that was shortly trimmed. His appearance was as neat and tidy as the captain's. He was almost as tall as the captain, but where the captain was muscular and lean, Stevens was fuller in the stomach and in the shoulders. He was intimidating to the crew, and as far as Locand was concerned, made an excellent first mate.

"My faithful crew," Locand began, "today is a new day for us with new rules to live by. Coming aboard will be Lord Hammil, one of the queen's favored men. We are asked to take him to Port Royal where he is to be taking care of some business and then returned safely back to England. If we do our mission successfully, we will be handsomely rewarded for our efforts." The men looked at Locand with respect and cheered. "Of course, on the way if we see anything to bring more riches to our pockets we will do so, but remember that we are privateers now, not pirates, and we must follow the rules. That has to be clear to everyone until the time is right for us to prove otherwise, if there is a time." The men smirked as they thought of fighting and cheered loudly. The noise brought a smile to Locand's face, but soon the smile began to fade. "We need to look and act differently from this point on. Our lives depend on this voyage being flawless. One error can cost us everything. Our lives—over." The crew began to sober as they understood what was at stake. Their eyes gazed upon Locand in guidance.

Locand was born in the Caribbean and his skin had a natural tan. He was tall, his shoulders broad and arms thick and strong with muscle. Underneath his partially opened shirt was a firm chest. His teeth were a bright white and shined against his complexion. Most of the crew could not say the same thing about their teeth, but they were loyal and dependable. They honored and respected the decisions Locand made, for in the past, his decisions never failed to bring them wealth and riches.

"Stevens, do we have enough supplies for our journey?" Locand looked at his men standing before him on the deck instead of in the eyes of his first mate.

"Aye, Cap'n, the men finished loading them this morning, as well as powder for the guns and some rum for the men. Food is plenty and we have enough provisions to last us until we reach Port Royal."

"Very good! Take the longboat and go ashore to greet Lord Hammil. Take a couple of men with you to load his trunks. He will be spending much time with us, make him comfortable. His safety will bring us happiness." Locand glanced at Stevens, his faithful friend was more than eager to do his bidding.

"Aye, Cap'n," replied Stevens, as he yelled out the names of a few men to come with him. Locand then told the crew to continue with their duties as he returned to his cabin to look over his map of the Caribbean and mark the route they would take.

It was midday by the time the carriage containing Lord Hammil, Miranda, and Davy reached the harbor. Lord Hammil exited the carriage as soon as it stopped and offered his hand for Miranda to take. She took it eagerly as she raised her hand to block the sun from shining in her eyes. Her attire was simple and plain. She wore a pale blue dress that revealed her narrow waist and curvaceous hips. Unlike most English women, she refused to use a parasol and adored the sun. She lifted her face to absorb as much of its warmth as she could.

As she stepped away from the carriage, her eyes scanned the many ships in front of her. She wasn't sure of the ship they would be sailing on and was hesitant to ask Lord Hammil. As she looked at the various ships tied to the dock and the ships anchored near the middle of the harbor, her eyes fell upon the name *The Captain's Avenger*. Her thoughts immediately went to its captain. Captain Riveri was the name she read on the letter of marque. She knew he must have it in his possession by now. She was curious what the other ships' names were on the other letters of marque she hadn't read.

Her eyes turned toward Lord Hammil who was in conversation with a man who had white hair and a mustache. He glanced periodically at her. Feeling uncomfortable, she turned to face Davy who was standing behind her. Davy wore tan breeches with a white shirt and matching waistcoat. The smile on his face could not hide the excitement he felt at the prospect of being at sea again. Before they could talk, Miranda noticed Lord Hammil motioning for them to follow. As they walked down the dock following the tall man with the white hair, she noticed some other men carrying their trunks. They were quiet, not even saying a word to themselves. They just held their trunks and carried them without complaint, though she did notice the looks they kept giving one another.

The wind was picking up across the water, and Miranda had to block her blond tendrils from covering her eyes many times. She refused to wear a hat but noticed that Lord Hammil wore one to keep the sun away from his face. When they finally stopped, it was in front of a longboat. The man with the white hair told Lord Hammil to step into the longboat first. He then held out his hand to help Miranda into it. As she thanked him, she glanced at his face. He was shaking his head at her as if his thoughts were occupied by something else. However, his words were a contradiction to his actions. He appeared pleasant and kind.

Miranda sat between Lord Hammil and Davy as the men with their trunks loaded the longboat with all of their belongings. As soon as the men stepped into the longboat, they started to row it to the ship anchored in front of them. To Miranda's surprise, the ship was *The Captain's Avenger*. As the longboat pulled along side the ship, Davy climbed the wooden steps that were built into the side. A member of the crew grabbed his arm and helped him aboard. Then, Lord Hammil climbed the steps, wanting to be the one to reach for Miranda and help her aboard. However, his climb wasn't as graceful as Davy's and he slipped on a step causing him to almost fall.

Miranda, who was standing in the longboat underneath him, was quickly pulled aside by the man with white hair. He held her firmly but briefly, not wanting her to get harmed in case Lord Hammil fell back into the boat. Stevens caught the scent of Jasmine coming from the woman in his arms as they watched Lord Hammil reach the top of the steps and get helped onto the deck by Davy. Miranda moved away from Stevens and started to climb up the steps. To Stevens' surprise, she did so without any trouble. He shook his head quickly, and said underneath his breath, "She's a distraction already. The Captain will not like this." The men left in the boat agreed as their eyes fell upon Miranda. Her bare legs could be seen as she pulled up her dress a little so she wouldn't trip on her skirts stepping onto the deck.

As Davy helped Miranda aboard, she caught a slight smile on his lips. She squeezed his hand tightly hoping that he wouldn't break out into laughter. She was on the brink herself. The sight of Lord Hammil trying to impress her almost made her composure *crack* . However, as he turned to face her, she could tell that he felt embarrassed. His cheeks were flushed, and as he grabbed her hand she noticed he was shaking. She smiled politely hoping it would calm him. He merely looked away from her, his eyes focusing on the man ahead of him.

"Welcome aboard Lord Hammil," boomed the voice of Captain Riveri.

"Captain, your ship is bigger than I thought it would be, but it will do nicely. Are we ready to sail?" Captain Riveri glanced several times at Miranda before his eyes focused again on Lord Hammil's.

"We've been ready since dawn. Who are your companions?" Captain Riveri was direct. His eyes again fell upon Miranda and then Davy.

"This is my fiancée, Miranda Smyth, and standing next to her is her guardian, Davy," answered Lord Hammil, his tone rising slightly and becoming defensive. Locand stared at Davy for a few minutes as recognition hit him. Davy shook his head slightly at Locand, but the action was unnoticed by anyone else.

"It's a pleasure to have both of you aboard my ship, but I must say that a woman aboard, fiancée or not, is dangerous to the crew. I cannot assure her safety if she becomes a distraction. The weeks we will spend at sea will be lonely and hard for these men. I insist that she stays behind." Locand glanced again at Miranda who glared at him in response. She was about to say something, but Lord Hammil beat her to it.

"She will not be harmed, Captain Riveri. She is to become my wife and deserves the same respect and consideration as I do!" The shout was unexpected and it startled Miranda so much that she raised her hand to her chest. She glanced at Davy begging him to intercede on her behalf. She didn't want Lord Hammil to make a scene.

"Captain Riveri," spoke Davy, "you will not need to worry about Miranda. She will stay out of the men's sight and will not cause a distraction. I will be protecting her and will make sure that she is not a bother to you or to anyone else." Locand glanced at Davy, a smile touching his lips. He nodded his head in reply to Davy's words.

"Captain Riveri, she will be with us until we reach New Providence. It is along the way. Once there, I will leave her at my estate. She will not be coming with us to Port Royal. The queen has approved of my arrangements." Miranda was pleased to find Lord Hammil speaking calmly once more. Locand narrowed his eyes at Lord Hammil, realizing the change of plan, the smile now gone from his lips.

"Very well, Lord Hammil, but if she causes a distraction to my men, I will leave her at the first island we come to." Locand glanced one more time at Miranda before turning his back toward her and yelling at his men to set sail.

Before following the men carrying her trunks down into the belly of the ship Miranda glanced on shore. She could still see the carriage they had stepped out of and something else. She was surprised to see Madam Fairaday on the dock waving at her. At least she thought that it was her, though she had no idea why she would be there. They had said their goodbyes early that morning. But none the less, Miranda was happy to see her. She would miss having another woman to talk to and confide in. It then occurred to her that maybe Madam Fairaday was waving at someone else.

She turned quickly around to see if anyone was waving at her in return, but there was no one. In fact, it seemed that she was the only one paying her any attention. Even the captain had his back toward her. Miranda briefly waved and watched as Madam Fairaday left the dock, her head bowed as she brought what looked like a cloth to her face. After several seconds, she stepped into an awaiting carriage. Miranda was puzzled by this, wondering why she would be so distraught, but overlooked it and moved toward the stairs and carefully descended. Her trunks and belongings were taken to a cabin not far from the captain's. There were bunk beds inside and Davy was to stay with her in the same room. Normally, a man would not be allowed such privileges, but because Davy was her guardian there was no better person to protect her than him.

Lord Hammil was to sleep in the cabin next to them. Inside, the cabin was small but it was neat and clean. There was enough room for Miranda to spread her clothing and some personal items out onto a table in the room. She didn't mind the cramped quarters and was used to them from spending time on her father's ship. She walked over to her trunk and opened it. She brought out her journal, which she wrote in every day and a small stack of books. She also unwrapped a piece of cloth that held two swords. She made Davy promise her that they were still going to practice fighting at sea. Somehow, she told him, they would find a way.

Miranda wrapped the swords back into the cloth and carefully laid them into her trunk. She grabbed one of her books, laid on her bed and started to read, but not before she looked out the porthole. She could feel the wind pick up and take the sails. They were traveling at a good pace now and she quietly said goodbye to England as it quickly became a speck in the distance.

Davy made his way to the deck to look for the captain. He was at the helm, overseeing his crew and making sure everything was running smoothly. He had left Miranda in their cabin, knowing she would stay down there for awhile and relax before she would make a fuss to come to the deck. He was just passing Lord Hammil, who was standing on the port side of the ship, and was about to talk to him when he noticed the man was turning pale.

"Are you ill, milord?" asked Davy. Lord Hammil placed his hand on the railing and nodded his head. Davy noticed how tightly he was gripping the railing and how his knuckles were turning white. "Do you need me to help you to your cabin?" Lord Hammil shook his head, determined not to show Davy any signs of weakness.

"I'm fine, Davy. Usually during the first week at sea I feel sick, but after that I start to feel normal again." Davy nodded his head not believing one word Lord Hammil said. All his years on a ship, Davy never once got sick, but the men he knew who did usually lasted longer than a week hanging over the side. Before Lord Hammil could say another word, he turned toward the railing and threw up. The retching sound made members of the crew stare at the person making the noise. Davy shook his head and looked up, his eyes staring into the captain's hazel ones.

Davy walked up the stairs to the helm to stand in front of Locand. Locand finished giving orders to some of his men and gazed at Davy, his black hair tied back by his neck with a ribbon.

"Where's our Miss Smyth?" Locand's gaze was strong and commanding.

"She's in our cabin, probably reading." Locand smiled, his white teeth shining brightly. "I'm going to ask you now because I know that eventually she will bring up the question. Will you allow her to come on deck if she is dressed like a man rather than a woman? She knows a dress will draw attention to her, but she does have men's breeches and a shirt to make her fit in better when she is around the crew." Locand thought for a moment, amazed that a woman who was betrothed to the man, who was at that moment heaving over the side of his ship, knew the goings on of a ship. Locand glanced at Lord Hammil and glared into his back.

"Quite a man our Lord Hammil is. You might wish to fetch Miss Smyth to have her attend to him. He's distracting my crew from their duties. For as much as Lord Hammil sails you would think he wouldn't have this retched seasickness." Locand stood staring at Lord Hammil shaking his head at the retching sound. His eyes then glanced back at Davy. "I will give you my answer later." Davy bowed his head and went to get Miranda. Locand's features still showed his dislike for Lord Hammil long after Davy had left.

Within minutes Locand saw a pale blue blur out of the corner of his eye. He knew it was Miranda coming to Lord Hammil's aid. She walked up behind him and stood there quietly. She raised a mug that she had in her hand and thought twice before offering it to him. She softly tapped Lord Hammil on the shoulder. When he looked at her she noticed that his face was a pale white and that his eyes were watering.

"Drink this, it will calm your stomach." She then handed the mug to him, which he took eagerly.

"What's in it?" asked Lord Hammil skeptically, bringing the contents to his nose so he could smell it.

"It's rum mixed with a tinge of ginger. I found some in the galley. The ginger will curb your sickness." Miranda glanced quickly at Locand who overheard her words. She noticed his eyes widened and his lips pressed tightly together. He was angry with her, she could tell, so she offered him a sassy smile.

"After you drink it, why don't you rest? Captain Riveri has everything taken care of up here. We are out of sight from our homeland and are on our way to the Caribbean. We will be at sea for several weeks, so you must relax and enjoy yourself. I am!" Miranda's soothing voice and actions brought a slight smile to Lord Hammil's lips.

"You're so thoughtful, my dear," said Lord Hammil as he drank from the mug. His stomach didn't calm immediately, but it did feel better.

"My concern is only for you, Leonard. I hate to see you this way." Lord Hammil was pleased by Miranda's concern for him and allowed her to escort him down the stairs and to their cabins. Locand's eyes followed her until she was out of sight. He then glanced back up at his crew and noticed some of their eyes lingering on the girl as well. He instantly became angry and took it out on his crew. His voice was booming as he threatened them to keep their eyes to themselves and on their duties or they would pay the price. The men instantly returned to their duties, not looking in the area of the stairs again.

Upset with the distraction and the way that Miranda mocked him, Locand aimed his sights on the stairs and started for them, passing Davy on the way. He heard Davy say to him, "Captain?" But Locand only smiled at the man not revealing to him his true intentions. Davy was, after all, supposed to protect the girl from harm, and harm was what he wanted to do to her.

Miranda finished tucking Lord Hammil into his bed and closed the door as she stepped into the narrow corridor. When she turned around, she bumped accidentally into Captain Riveri. The look in his eyes showed his displeasure as he grabbed her roughly by the arm and walked her down the corridor to his cabin. He opened the door quickly and shoved her into it ahead of him. The action almost made her lose her balance, but she reached for the bed and steadied herself.

Locand stepped into the cabin and closed the door behind him, standing in front of the door to block her from escaping. Miranda turned around and glared at the man before her, her eyes narrowing into slits.

"Where did you get that ginger? That is for the crew and should not be used for your own private uses," shouted Locand, his arms folded in front of his chest in an intimidating manner.

"I asked the cook to give me some, and he did. You of all people know that ginger can help with seasickness, but instead of helping him and easing his pain, you allowed Lord Hammil to embarrass himself in front of your crew making him look like a fool." Locand's eyes widened from Miranda's words.

"Your fiancée doesn't need much help from me to accomplish that task." Locand's gaze bore into Miranda, but she stood tall and strong, not letting the man scare her.

"He's a proud and important man, and yet you treat him as if he were an imbecile. Maybe he is, but that does not give you the right to discredit him. The queen looks highly upon him, and with the letter of marque that she gave you, I believe that you need to watch your step so you don't lose it. Yes, that would be a shame if she found out that you weren't looking after her best interests." Locand stepped closer to Miranda and grabbed her roughly by the shoulders, bringing his lips just inches from her own. Miranda could smell Locand's masculine scent as it drifted toward her.

"Watch your step, lass, for it might be your last. Don't threaten me—ever! Apparently, your lover told you of the letter of marque given to me by the queen. Which, by the way, is none of your business." Before he could continue, Miranda added in her thoughts.

"He isn't aware that I know about the letter of marque given to you, but it doesn't take a captain to figure it out. I mean, look at you. Your whole essence screams of your past and your crew looks like a bunch of cut throats. You're looking for a new path and Lord Hammil's the way to it." Locand let go of Miranda abruptly and shook his head in frustration.

"I'm surprised you have lived this long with your sharp tongue. Does your Lord Hammil know of this side of you?" Miranda rubbed her shoulders with her hands and glared at the man before her, her dislike for him growing inside her.

"What he knows about me is none of your business. You have a job to get us safely to New Providence, Port Royal, where ever, and back. Do your job and stay out of my affairs." She pushed herself past Locand and was about to reach for the door when she was suddenly turned around, her back pressed up against the door roughly preventing her escape. She tried to scream for Davy but was stopped when Locand grabbed her cheeks tightly and stopped her, the other hand placed tightly on the back of her neck. Miranda was so surprised with the action that she felt tears welling up in her eyes. Seeing that he was finally getting through to her, Locand softened his voice.

"It makes me curious how you know so much about the cure for seasickness. Only people of the sea know how to cure its ailments. How did you know about the ginger?" Miranda glanced at the ground searching for an answer, and Locand noticed her pause.

"Davy was a pirate long ago and has sailed for years. He told me about the ginger." Locand analyzed Miranda's features. She was correct about Davy, but he was certain there was more she was not telling him.

"Just so you know, your guardian cannot help you, Miss Smyth. Unlike you, he knows who the captain of this ship is and offers me the respect I deserve. You, on the other hand, haven't figured out who is in charge yet, so let me bring it to your attention. I am the captain of this ship, Locand Riveri. If you would like something, just ask me and I will make sure you get whatever it is that you desire. Go behind my back again and you will suffer the consequences. Do we understand each other?" Locand loosened his hold enough for Miranda to move her head as she nodded.

"Good! I would hate to harm your pretty features, but I will, and without much qualm." Locand moved closer and nuzzled her neck and ear, his warm breath caressing her skin. Miranda raised her hands to land on his hard chest to stop him as he whispered, "As you say, I was once a pirate. Being so you know what I am capable of doing." Locand stood back and removed his hand from Miranda's neck as he caressed her cheek, feeling her soft skin underneath his rough fingers. The smell of jasmine permeated the air as he glanced up and down the length of her body taking in her appearance. "From this day on you will be locked into my cabin until you can show me the proper respect due me. When you can obey my every command without comment, then I will let you walk on deck. Do we have an accord?" Miranda stared into Locand's beautiful green-brown eyes as she thought over her answer.

"Where will you sleep?" asked Miranda apprehensively.

"In here!" replied Locand tersely.

"Why, so I can endure your hostile and glorious presence? Davy will not approve or allow this treatment of me. He protects my virtue above all else. He will not let you touch me, nor will I allow it again without a fight." Locand slowly backed away from Miranda as if burned.

"Your virtue is safe with me. I will not touch you in the manner in which you are implying, nor am I planning to. I can go to any port and have any woman I want in my bed without a fight. Women who would be eager to spread their thighs for me to sate myself and would relish the feeling I would give them in return. I don't need some high maintenance, sassy, opinionated, demanding woman to satisfy me when I have so many others at my disposal who are easier to tame." Miranda wanted to slap Locand, but resisted the urge.

"I bet you've had many women in your bed, and that it's stained with their filth because you are definitely not the gentlemen type to have high bred ladies."

"I've had those, too." Miranda scoffed.

"You disgust me!" Locand took a step forward causing Miranda to lean against the wall for support.

"I only mean to teach you a lesson. Davy will understand that, once being a first mate to a great captain. However, I thought your first response would be to tell me how much your lover would not approve. I am surprised to hear you care more about what Davy thinks than the man you are supposed to marry." Miranda straightened from the wall and swept the blond curls from her eyes with her fingers, realizing too late he had set a trap she fell right into.

"He will not approve either, for his feelings for me are strong. His emotions will run heavy with jealousy and cause you more problems if you do this to me. I will speak for him when I say that this is what he would think of your little lesson." She could not resist this time. Without warning Miranda brought her hand back and slapped Locand across the cheek. The slap barely made his head turn. Locand's eyes filled with fury, a smile shown brightly upon his lips as he saw the smug look upon Miranda's face. He seized her by the waist, picked her up and roughly threw her onto the bed.

"I believe we have an accord. We will see how long you can last without seeing daylight for a week," Locand threatened. Miranda straightened her skirts and hair as she glared at Locand.

"Fine! It won't bother me a bit," replied Miranda angrily. Locand glared at the girl on his bed once more before opening the door.

"This would have gone so much better for you if you wouldn't have acted like a stubborn wench." Miranda folded her arms in front of her chest and looked away from him defiantly. Captain Riveri slammed the cabin door shut and locked it. Miranda could hear his mutterings down the corridor. Her eyes filled with tears as she cried her sorrows.

CHAPTER 4

"I must protest, Locand. You can't keep her locked in your quarters like this. I know she deserves it, but it's not decent." It was night now, and Davy was alone with Locand discussing the treatment of Miranda. Earlier he had seen the crazy look in Locand's eyes and knew he was angry with her. Knowing that it was not his ship, Davy knew that there was little he could do to stop him if he were to confront Miranda about her behavior. She had done what she wanted without discussing it with the captain first, as if she had full reign of the ship instead of him. Davy had to respect the captain's rules aboard his ship, if he wanted to or not, and so did Miranda. All day he had waited for the right moment to bring up the topic, but the captain was never alone and he didn't choose to make himself available until now. The night was calm, and the crew was talking quietly amongst themselves, some taking turns on deck while others slept.

Locand knew Davy wanted to speak with him, so he motioned for him to follow him into the galley where there was an empty table and a door they could close for privacy. Earlier it had been filled with food, but now it just had a bowl of apples in the center. The cook was now sleeping in his bed.

"She disrespected me, Davy. You know she did. Locking her into my cabin was the least I could do. I could flog her for the way she spoke to me earlier, or lock her in a cell. I could have given her twenty lashes for striking me alone. You know that I am well within my rights to do so." Locand sat down at the table, his hands folded together on top of it.

"I agree with you on that point, Miranda did disrespect you. She knows better than to behave the way she did. This being your ship, she should have consulted you about the ginger instead of doing what she pleased. Her words to you in your cabin—well—I can't defend those, though I am sure she was prodded." Locand glared at Davy, his eyebrows raising. "I don't disagree with you; she deserves the punishment you have given her by staying below deck until she feels contrite. But Lord Hammil will not like it if you keep Miranda in your cabin while you stay in there. It is inappropriate for her and will bring you trouble with Lord Hammil." Davy pushed the point, but knew that Locand was right. "Why don't you lock her into my cabin, I—?"

"No!" spoke Locand firmly. "It would not feel like punishment if she were to have you to save her." Davy pursed his lips together in disapproval. "Besides, I explained to you already what we had discussed when I came on deck earlier and you had approached me. I told her that I would be staying in the cabin with her, but it was only to shut her up. I don't desire her. I won't cross that line, you have my word. I will be sleeping somewhere else for the week. Lord Hammil will not press the issue, for he will most likely still be ill. If he does I will then explain to him what I have just explained to you, though I really shouldn't have to." Locand stood up from the table and moved to stand in front of Davy. Frustration showing in every movement he made.

"We have been friends for a long time, Davy. Why you didn't want me to act like I knew you earlier is beyond me, but I am sure that you have your reasons for doing so. I take it that Lord Hammil doesn't know of us being mates?" Davy shook his head; his eyes firmly upon Locand.

"He mustn't know, either. Your father and Stratton Mayne were good friends, and they sailed together often. He still mourns him and is thankful that you weren't caught in the blasting of his ship." Davy shook his head as he remembered what had happened. "You were so young when that happened, a child striving to become a man, and yet your father was so proud of you." Locand smiled slightly, his eyes becoming sad upon hearing Davy speak of his father.

"I remember it as if it were yesterday, Davy. Father was determined to overtake a frigate that was coming from Africa. He wanted to steal the slaves it contained so we could sell them over in the Americas. I protested against it, but he didn't care. He just kept telling me that it would be our biggest treasure yet and that we could retire and live off the money we would receive. He was a fool to think that only two ships could overtake it. One was ours; the other was Stratton's. Unbeknownst to us, the frigate was heavily armed, and though we had fast ships loaded with guns and were able to wound the frigate, we couldn't take the slaves and sadly, most of them drowned. They fired upon us and blew up our ship. I jumped overboard to escape it, but my father didn't make it, and was blown into a thousand pieces, sinking to the bottom of the sea with all of his sins." Locand ran his fingers through his hair at the memories he was recalling in his mind.

"Stratton saved me and took me in for a few months after that until I was ready to move on with my life. If it wasn't for him, I don't know where I would be right now. It feels like it was only yesterday, and yet it has been many years since my father died." Davy stared at Locand, his eyes roaming over his appearance. For a man who was strong and commanding, Davy remembered a boy whose heart was broken over his father's death. His black hair was shorter then, and he did not have as much muscle or well defined tone as he did now. He had grown much over the years and was now a well thought of man, a great man whom many people admired. Though Locand was hard on the outside, like a captain had to be, his insides were still that impressionable little boy Davy remembered.

"There are times when I reminisce about those days. Every once in awhile I find myself aboard his ship again, with his young daughter taking care of all the men. I think she was twelve when all of this happened. She was a pretty girl with a kind heart. I remember the crew looking upon her as if she were an angel, and they obeyed her every command without question. She cooked sometimes for them and made conversation with them all, including me. She was kind to me, well, to us and though she never spent much time with me during my brief stay, she showed me much sympathy. Her heart went out to me and she tried to heal the pain I was feeling after the loss of my father. She never realized that it was a pain she could not heal. I remember how much Stratton loved her, how we all sort of loved her. I wish I could remember her name. Do you know where she is now?" Davy smiled at Locand, realizing that he didn't know who Miranda really was.

"With Stratton's reputation preceding him everywhere he goes, she is kept safe from harm and tries to live a normal life away from all this."

"I understand completely and can empathize. I was merely curious. I didn't mean to pry." Davy shook his head and changed the topic smoothly.

"I remember those days as well, Locand. You have grown into

a fine man, your father would be proud of you for what you have accomplished." Locand snorted loudly.

"I don't know if that is a compliment or an insult, Davy." Davy narrowed his eyes as he stared at Locand.

"Your father loved you, boy."

"My father was selfish, Davy. He thought of no one but himself and what he wanted. He cared not for my mother or anyone else who should have meant more to him than some booty from a ship." Locand again snorted as he shook his head. "The man was a pig." Davy could see the pain in Locand's eyes and reached out and grabbed him into a hearty hug, catching him by surprise. Locand wasn't sure how to react at first, but then he returned the gesture. Slapping Davy's back as they parted from the embrace.

"Don't let any of my men see you do that to me," Locand sputtered as he smiled and pushed him away.

"Of course not, Captain. I rarely show such emotion to other people. I only feel the need when I see men who are young and of twenty-eight years of age whose hearts are filled with so much pain." Davy winked at Locand as he laughed aloud, though he knew it was the truth. "Now Locand, let's talk about Miranda."

"How did you get involved with her anyway?" Davy was taken off guard, not quite sure how to answer the question.

"It's a long story to be told, too long to go into it right now, but I am her guardian and protector regardless."

"Look, Davy, this woman may be in your care, but she's becoming a pain in my backside. I can't let her behave the way she did and have it go unpunished. I have killed men for less than what she has done. As the captain of this ship, I need to show the men that no one can behave inappropriately and get away with it. She needs to learn a lesson. I will not hurt or harm her, but she has to know who is captain of this vessel. Right now she thinks she is—that sassy bit of goods." Locand spurted out his last words with frustration.

"I agree and will not interfere with your command. You are, in a way, saving her from your crew by keeping her safe. She will eventually understand. I will talk to her about her behavior. She does know better, believe it or not, though she is too stubborn to admit it." Davy shook his head, his disapproval of Miranda's behavior evident. Locand raised his arm to touch Davy's shoulder.

"How is our Captain Mayne? I have not spoken to him in

months—surprisingly. The last time we were together we were arguing, and we had gotten into a fight. We usually do at least once when we are together for our opinions often clash, but soon all was forgiven. I miss sailing with him. The last time we sailed together I had joined him in the raiding of a ship. Its plunder was small, though the ship was massive. Afterward, we sailed to Tortuga and drank for days until the women had their way with us and our bellies were full and content. That was over a year or so ago. I miss those carefree days when there were no governors or laws on the islands that brought us so much pleasure." Locand turned around and walked around the room, his back facing Davy.

"Now, one of our most reliable sources for supplies and sailors is governed by someone who wishes to stop the piracy that used to go on there. Just wait, Davy, soon Tortuga will be next, then New Providence. Pirates will have no more places to go or to run. That is why we have to change our destinies now." Davy cocked his head to the side, unsure of what Locand meant by his words.

"Why must you change your destiny, my friend? You seem to be living a respectable life running errands for the queen. I am sure she pays you well to serve her." Locand placed his hands behind his back, his muscular chest pushing forward. He turned around to face Davy, a crooked grin upon his face.

"The benefits can be plentiful as long as I follow the rules. She has finally given to me what I have requested of her, a letter of marque. Now I can fight in the name of queen and country. Though if captured, it may not stop the old boot from killing me herself."

"Do you know of our business in Port Royal, Locand?" Locand walked back to the table and sat down into one of the chairs, not surprised by the slight change in topic.

"I know enough information to keep me alive. The only thing I am curious about is who they are after in Port Royal. Lord Hammil has not revealed the name to me, though I am sure he will eventually tell me more about our mission when the time is right. My concern is that our plans have been changing before my eyes. I don't like it. I feel there is a lot of secrecy about. Do you know what's going on?" Before Davy could answer the question, Stevens opened the door and burst into the room.

"Cap'n! Lord Hammil is requesting a word with you in private. He is causing much commotion and the men are displeased for being interrupted from their beds." Stevens' tone changed mockingly. "The man has only just realized that his amiable fiancée is being punished in your cabin. He says that he is in dire need of her assistance. I bet I know for what." Locand and Davy both glared at Stevens, who suddenly closed his eyes and realized the words he had let slip out. After several seconds had passed, Locand turned to Davy, giving him a roguish smile. "He must not be as ill as I thought. To be continued at another time." He then rose from his chair and followed Stevens. Davy followed them to the deck, his eyes falling upon the bright glow of the moon shining above them, illuminating their way. His thoughts were deep into the discussion between him and Locand. It was interesting to Davy, that Locand didn't know they were after Stratton Mayne. He needed to keep that information to himself for the moment. The most important thing was that he had an ally to help him when the time was right.

The week had passed slowly for Miranda. The cook would bring in her meals as ordered by Locand, but he never said a word to her, not even when she started the conversation. He merely dropped off the food and left the room. To her surprise and yet pleasure, Locand never returned to his cabin to talk to her or anything else. He kept his distance from her, which Miranda was grateful for. She couldn't stand the man after the way he had treated her. However, after having plenty of time to think about her behavior, and the disrespectful way she had spoken to the captain, she did feel remorseful. She had no right to act the way she did toward him, though he had angered her.

After Locand had locked her into his cabin, she had surveyed her surroundings. There was a table with several maps laying upon it, and a desk with a chair in the room. There was a large bed that took up a good portion of the space covered with heavy blankets and clean white sheets. The pillows were soft and yearned to be used. The first night Miranda refused to sleep underneath the sheets of the bed, but as the night became colder, she gave in and snuggled herself underneath their warmth. Her trunk was brought in and by the end of the week, she had laid her belongings all around Locand's cabin. Her books now replaced the books that were sitting on the desk, and her trunk was now at the end of the bed instead of Locand's. Some of his belongings were tossed to the far side of the cabin to make room for Miranda's.

She had figured that if she was to stay in the cabin, then it should be comfortable for her, not its captain. It wasn't painful for her to stay below for the entire week--she was used to it from being on her father's ship, but she did long to be on deck and feel the breeze upon her face. However, knowing that she could not go on deck, she had resolved herself to reading and writing. So every day she lay on her stomach upon the bed, with her thoughts consumed by the stories she read. A couple of times, out of sheer boredom, she walked around the cabin, looking into the desk and in Locand's trunk. He had only clothes in his trunk, except for a few letters she found tucked between some materials on the bottom.

Miranda had refused to invade the captain's privacy to the extent of reading his personal letters. She knew it would be wrong of her to do so. She did, however, try on some of his clothes. He had many white shirts and breeches, which were folded neatly in his trunk with a couple of different colored vests and a waistcoat for when he wished to look respectable. She started to unbutton her dress, which was light brown in color with a low neckline and thinning waist. The sleeves were past her elbow in length and the skirt was long enough to reach the floor. She brought only one corset with her and she refused to wear it underneath any of her dresses while she was at sea and aboard a ship. In fact, she refused to wear petticoats, too, and her dresses were simple, light and comfortable.

As Miranda removed her dress, letting it fall to the floor in a pile at her feet, she quickly grabbed one of Locand's shirts and held it in her hand. The fabric was soft and thin. She had felt nothing like it before in her life. She brought the shirt to rub against her face and then down her arm. Wanting to know what the material would feel like on her bare skin she removed her underclothes and slipped on the shirt. The shirt was large on her and baggy, yet the length of the arms almost fit her perfectly as well as the length of the shirt. It was long enough to cover just past her buttocks.

Miranda grabbed the collar and rubbed it against her cheeks as she pranced around the room spinning and dancing as she went. She stopped in front of the door to finish buttoning the shirt when she heard the door unlock. Panic filled her as she stood frozen to the ground not able to move.

As Locand opened the door, the sight before him made him speechless. He was so surprised, in fact, that he almost stopped breathing. After several days of Lord Hammil's pestering to let him see Miranda,

Locand finally gave in, but only when the week was up. Now Lord Hammil was standing behind him, his hand fixing his hair so his appearance would be perfect for when he saw her, but Locand was not expecting a half-naked woman in his cabin staring back at him when he opened the door.

His eyes quickly perused her appearance before Lord Hammil could see her. Locand could tell she was wearing one of his shirts; it hung low enough to cover her upper thighs but exposed everything else. Her legs seemed pale and soft, but as his eyes rose to her chest he could tell that she hadn't quite finished the task of buttoning it. Four buttons were yet to be fastened and the open shirt exposed a healthy portion of her youthful breasts, her nipples covered by the shirt. Locand saw the surprise in Miranda's widened eyes and knew it mirrored his own.

Locand quickly closed the door and pressed his back against it, his eyes focusing now on Lord Hammil. "Is she in there, Captain? I am eager to see her." Fortunately, Lord Hammil was too enthralled with his own appearance to notice Miranda's. Locand exhaled a long breath, his mind pondering what to tell the man.

"I noticed that she was just waking from a nap. She looks quite disheveled and I am sure that she would like to look her best before she sees you. You know how women can be, always concerned about their appearance." Lord Hammil nodded his head emphatically. "I will just go in and hurry her along a little bit, making sure that she has understood her punishment and will now behave appropriately." Lord Hammil nodded his head in agreement.

"I agree with your course of punishment for her. You could have done worse things to her for her behavior. I appreciate your leniency on the matter. She has never been on a ship before, so she doesn't know how to behave. I will see that she behaves more appropriately in the future. Women need to learn their place in this world. It is a shame that we have to be so cruel to them to make them see where that place is." Locand briefly smiled at Lord Hammil as he spoke, his eyebrows furrowing as he heard Lord Hammil tell him of Miranda's lack of sailing experience. By her behavior, Locand felt that Miranda had much experience on a ship; apparently, there were many things that Lord Hammil was blind too.

"Why don't you go ahead on deck. You know how women get when they are excited to see the men they care for. I am sure she will need time to fix her appearance before she sees you, so don't be concerned if she doesn't come to you right away. When she is ready, I will escort her personally to your open arms." Lord Hammil smiled brightly as he nodded his head.

"Yes, Captain, you're right. Women do take too much time in their appearance. I will be eagerly waiting for her." He then turned around and walked down the corridor to the stairs and climbed them. Locand did not move until Lord Hammil was out of sight. He then took a deep breath and opened the door again. This time Miranda was standing by the bed, her appearance not changing. Locand hastily walked over to Miranda and grabbed her roughly by the front of her shirt, closing the gaping hole that exposed her breasts. He brought her body just inches from his own.

"Cover yourself from my view, woman. Do you not care that I see you this way?" Miranda's blond hair fell forward to lie around her shoulders framing her face. Her eyes fell upon him innocently as she licked her full lips, her mouth suddenly feeling dry. The urge to grab her and throw her on the bed to ravish her body was overpowering. Locand had to fight for control. Miranda saw Locand's eyes change in color but she wasn't sure why. He was so powerful and strong. The way he brought her close to him made her want to be held in his arms. Her hands brushed over the mounds of muscle on his biceps as she tried to regain her balance.

"Thank you!" were the only words she could get the nerve to muster. Locand looked at her strangely, not sure why she was thanking him. His gripped loosened upon her shirt as Miranda brought her hand up to take their place. He then took several steps away from her as she sat on the edge of his bed.

"Why do you thank me? If you knew my thoughts you would not look so inviting and thank me for being this close to you." Miranda's forehead wrinkled as she thought about his words. She finished buttoning the buttons on her shirt before returning her eyes back to Locand's. She noticed he was watching her every move. Remembering her modesty, Miranda looked down to assess her appearance making sure that all of her body parts were covered from Locand's view.

"I thank you for protecting me from Lord Hammil. I saw him standing behind you and thought he noticed my appearance. I would have had much to explain to him." Miranda ran her fingers through her long hair. "You didn't have to do that, you know?" Locand gazed into Miranda's soft brown eyes and knew he did have to protect her. His tone changed as he turned around and faced the wall, his back now facing her.

"You need to change from my shirt back into your dress. I don't think Lord Hammil would appreciate you wearing my clothing."

"Are you not going to leave?" Miranda asked, her gaze focused on the middle of Locand's back.

"No! I told Lord Hammil that I would escort you to the deck. He would get suspicious if I did not bring you." Then he added, not being able to stop himself. "I must say, though, my shirt looks better on you than it ever could on me." A roguish smile came upon his lips as he heard Miranda cluck her tongue at his remark and remove his shirt. To bed her would be easy, Locand thought, but he knew she belonged to another. He needed to keep his attention on what was important. Instantly, Locand felt angry with himself for his behavior and lack of control. He was about to move to the door when he heard Miranda ask him, "Can you please finish buttoning these buttons for me, I cannot reach them?"

Locand turned and looked at Miranda, surprised by her request. "I will get Davy for such matters. I have never been good with such delicate things." Miranda moved to stand in front of him, her hair swept to one side.

"Please, Locand, this is the first time in a week that I have actually buttoned one of my dresses to the top. There are four buttons in the back that I cannot reach, see?" Miranda turned around so Locand could see her dilemma. With clumsy fingers Locand tried to put the buttons in the holes. It took several tries but he finally finished the task. He then grabbed Miranda's hair and moved it to cover the buttons on the back of her dress. As he touched her soft, silky hair, he could smell Jasmine permeate the air. The aroma was so intoxicating it took all of Locand's will to stop his arousal.

"Your scent could convince the most dangerous of men to do your bidding." He raised his hand to stroke her hair, but quickly retracted it. His voice was husky as he spoke his words, but suddenly his tone changed when he said, "I am sure your Lord Hammil is pleased with you." The anger in Locand's voice surprised Miranda. She turned to gaze into his hazel green eyes, but he avoided her gaze by looking at the floor. "Miss Smyth, let's not keep your Lord Hammil waiting, he is most persistent to check on your welfare."

"No, Locand!" Miranda started to say, but Locand quickly turned on her, his hands on his hips.

"Have you not learned your lesson yet? And it is Captain Riveri if you don't mind." Miranda thought about which road she was to take. As her eyes looked deeply into Locand's, she made her decision.

"I will do whatever you ask of me, Captain Riveri. Forgive my outburst, but I only wished to explain to you what I was doing wearing your shirt. I feel embarrassed and foolish for taking such liberties with your apparel."

"I am sure that my shirt didn't mind the intrusion. There is nothing to be embarrassed about. We can speak of it at a later time. Rest assured that I will hear your explanation, but from this point on please stay out of my things, unless you wish for me to go through yours?" Miranda quickly shook her head. "Good, because if I do, the fishes will be wearing that pretty blue dress of yours." Miranda narrowed her eyes at Locand's remark, but all he did was smile and nod, pleased that he got his point across. He then took Miranda's arm and escorted her from the cabin to the deck in silence.

"My dear, you look beautiful. Have you been faring well?" Lord Hammil ran his fingers through his hair as Miranda and Locand approached. Concern was evident upon his features. The sky was overcast, the sun blocked from the clouds that permeated the sky. There was a slight chill to the air, and the breeze had picked up. Miranda let go of Locand's arm and hurried to stand in front of Lord Hammil, her long hair whipping around her face.

"My concern is for you, Leonard, you look well. I am glad you have overcome your illness."

"The ginger helped," and without warning Lord Hammil raised his hand to caress Miranda's cheek. He then moved his hand to the back of her neck and drew her close to him, softly capturing her lips. The kiss was gentle and brief. Miranda was surprised by the gesture, and yet disappointed for its shortness. She leaned toward him again wanting to taste more of his lips, but he pushed her away, chastising her for her behavior. Miranda felt she had done something wrong.

"Miranda, there are sailors watching us, we are not alone. Showing affection in front of these men is inappropriate. I only wished to show you my pleasure. You have pleased me with your concern. Now, if you care to join me in my cabin we could continue this further. I have missed the sight of you, but I hope that Captain Riveri's punishment finally got through to you. I am not sure what you were thinking when you behaved so carelessly, but I hope you will be more agreeable for the rest of the journey."

Miranda turned her head away from the sight of Lord Hammil and looked for Davy. She hadn't spoken with him in the past week and knew it was upon Locand's orders that he not interact with her. Now, however, she needed to speak with her most trusted friend. Her eyes fell upon him as he stood speaking with Locand at the helm. Though he was also a guest upon the ship, he chose to help with the duties and talk with the crew. It made him feel more at home and useful.

"I am afraid that I will not be joining you in your cabin for awhile, Leonard. I have not seen the sea since we left England and wish to take in its beauty. The breeze feels wonderful against my skin and I feel free. I'm sorry, but not even you can persuade me to go below again until I am ready." Lord Hammil gazed at Miranda firmly and tried to convince her to come with him to his cabin, and even seized her arm to force her, but she stood her ground.

"You had your chance to partake in the offering of my lips moments ago. You declined, because you are so worried about propriety and what people will think. Well, I could care less." Miranda was about to move away from Lord Hammil but his grip tightened upon her arm. The action stopped her retreat and her eyes flew instantly to his as she felt his fingers dig into her skin painfully.

"Watch your tongue, Miranda. I will not tolerate such disobedience. I have not seen you in a week's time and would hope that you have missed the sight of me and would like to spend more personal time with me." His eyes searched hers for any signs of change in her feelings for him.

"Of course I have missed the sight of you. I care for you, Leonard, but I will not live my life ashamed to show my future husband affection. It would be nice if you could show me more passion with your kisses, more feeling like your words often depict." Lord Hammil gazed around the deck and noticed several pairs of eyes focusing upon them as they listened to their conversation. Miranda didn't realize she had raised her voice until she saw the disgruntled look upon Lord Hammil's countenance. In a low voice Lord Hammil said, "I am not a passionate man, Miranda, but you will get used to my touch and kisses, and learn to love them. I will make you happy."

Miranda, her chest heaving slightly from her anger, could not help but to correct the man of his assumptions. "I am a passionate woman, Leonard, and have always been. I don't want to get used to something that doesn't satisfy my needs. I want to feel cherished and adored, as if I were the air you needed to breathe. I don't want to be put on a pedestal for show as if I were some insignificant object that people should envy. I am not perfect," shouted Miranda. "Your rules are driving me mad. I could never live up to your expectations for they are too high. I am afraid to make a mistake around you. I just want to be loved, Leonard, and loved ardently. Can you do that because, if so, my heart will be yours."

"My, you've had much to think about, haven't you?"

"Well, leave a woman with her thoughts for a week and this is what you get," replied Miranda sharply. Lord Hammil didn't realize the pressure he had put upon Miranda and felt contrite for doing so. His countenance changed to one of compassion but Miranda's next words made him angry. "If you cannot give me the affection I need, then maybe you should find another bride while at Port Royal who will be able to satisfy your needs better, because I desire more than just some unsatisfactory emotion." The insult was more than he could bear and he slapped Miranda across the cheek for her impertinence. The blow surprised her and brought tears to her eyes. Her hand immediately moved to her cheek, realizing she never should have spoken her true feelings, but knew that her words had to be said.

Locand saw what happened and was about to move forward but decided against it, wondering how it would have looked to his crew if he were to protect the girl from her betrothed. He then looked to his right where Davy had been and noticed that he was already moving toward Miranda to protect her. By the time he had reached her side she was backing up slowly away from Lord Hammil, her eyes throwing imaginary daggers at him.

"I am sorry that I had to do that Miranda, but it is for your own good. I understand what you are saying, and I will try harder to please you but you, in return, will try harder to please me, for I am very disappointed." Tears streamed from Miranda's eyes as she cursed herself silently for accepting Lord Hammil's marriage proposal. Every day caused her to regret her decision more and more. "Davy, take her out of my sight, the sea clouds her judgment. Another week locked into your cabin Miranda, will be enough time for you to think about the words you have spoken to me. I have already apologized to you, by the end of the week I will expect your apology and your show of renewed adoration. Upon your behavior I will allow you to walk upon the deck as you wish, but I will be the only one to escort you." He then waved his hand for Davy to remove her from his sight, and he turned around to face the dark blue sea.

Miranda was so full of anger that she lunged forward wanting to strike at Lord Hammil, but before she could, Davy caught her by the waist, turned her quickly around rushing her from the deck to the stairs before anyone noticed what she was about to do. Locand, however, heard every word she said and saw what she was about to do. A smile rose upon his lips as he thought of the beautiful girl that brought so much pain to herself. His smile immediately vanished, however, when Lord Hammil moved to his side to speak of Miranda's punishment.

As soon as Miranda stepped down the corridor she started to run to Locand's cabin. As she opened the door, she ran inside and fell upon the bed, tears falling full force from her eyes. When Davy reached the cabin, he walked in and closed the door, shaking his head as he moved to the bed and sat upon it.

"You bring your own pain, Miry. How could you insult him like that? Your words were tolerable until then. We are going to be spending many weeks in the same company with these men. You can't behave this way and expect them to accept your disobedience. You will end up getting thrown into a cell or lashed, Miry. I could not bear to see that happen." Davy reached out and caressed Miranda's hair, but she raised her head and glared at him for his efforts.

"Why didn't you stop him, Davy? Why did you let him hurt me?" Miranda broke into heavy sobs, then started hiccupping from lack of air. Gone was the firm look upon Davy's features as he reached out and scooped Miranda into his arms, her head resting on his shoulder.

"If I knew you were going to be so rebellious, I would have stood by your side. I never would have thought you were going to act this way. You know better."

"And with Captain Riveri, did you have no pull when talking with him? You could have—"

"No, Miry, you slapped and disrespected the captain of this vessel. No man of this crew would do such a thing. He could not allow you to get away with that unpunished. You deserved his punishment. Captain Riveri forbade me to see you. He said that you would expect me to save you from him, which of course you do. He will not bring you harm, Miry, but it is you who brings yourself pain. Lord Hammil felt embarrassed from your words and it would have shown him to be weak if he didn't handle the situation well. You provoked his reaction." Miranda raised her tear stained face toward Davy.

"So, am I the only one who is to blame?" Davy caressed her cheeks as he said, "No, but you forget that this is not your father's ship. This crew is not his and they could care less for your well being. You must behave properly until it is time for you not to, but only I will let you know when that time is. Be smart, Miranda, you were never a fool. Whatever Lord Hammil said to provoke your words, forget them. He is the way he is, and we need him to get to your father, remember that. Follow his rules, and the captain's, and you will be happier in the future." Davy then held her head to his chest as he kissed it and comforted her. He could hear Miranda sighing against him as her sobs quieted.

Miranda knew that her behavior wasn't going to be tolerated much longer. She had to change, at least for now. She resolved herself for another week below deck, and actually, the thought didn't bother her. She was going to be happy to be alone for another week with no one to bother her or make demands. She would need that time to adjust her way of thinking, and the solace to collect her sanity. For one more week she would be able to act normally, without peoples' false expectations of her. The thought brought a smile to her lips as she hugged Davy closer to her.

CHAPTER 5

By the middle of the following week, Miranda was practicing with her sword. She had made a target from a sack she had asked the cook for and filled it with an old pillow making it bulge. She then hung it against the bed post and gave it a few stabs. She practiced her footwork continuously, moving back and forth in front of the sack with sword in hand. She did this for several hours before deciding to quit, hiding the sack in a secret place so it couldn't be seen. She then relaxed on the bed reading a book. She wasn't surprised when she heard a key unlock the door. As she looked up, her eyes met the blue ones of the cook.

The cook, Billy, was an older man with gray white hair and a bearded face. He was a kind man who seemed to always smoke a pipe. He was shorter than Miranda, who stood five feet and eight inches in height. His face was tan and wrinkled from old age as well as the sun. Since she had talked to him about the sack, he now felt comfortable around her to make conversation whenever he brought her food.

"How has the sack worked for you, missy?" asked Billy as he laid a tray of food on the table. Miranda rose from the bed, her blue skirts swaying around her bare ankles and feet.

"It works great, now all I need is a real target to practice on. I appreciate you not mentioning this to the captain or to Lord Hammil. I don't think they would approve of my talents." Before Miranda popped a piece of fruit into her mouth, she smiled politely to Billy. Her brown eyes expressed her sincerity. She kept her hair combed, letting it hang down the length of her back as it reached her middle. Billy couldn't help but stare at the beautiful woman before him. As she smiled, he could see the dimples that formed at the corners of her lips.

"If the captain says anything to me about it, I will have to obey him. But I don't see the harm in helping you keep busy. At least you are staying out of trouble. I will not mention what you are doing as long as I am not asked." Miranda patted Billy on the shoulder as she turned and walked to the bed, lying across it again. As Billy left the room Miranda quickly glanced at the bed post, making sure that she had put the sack away and out of sight.

A couple of hours had passed when the door to the cabin was unlocked again. It was night and Locand wanted to change his clothes, as well as get a good night's rest. He was determined to sleep in his own bed. He had made arrangements to have Miranda moved into her own cabin, but when he opened the door and found her sleeping across his bed, her hair hanging off to the side with book in hand, he couldn't wake her to do it. He decided to go into his trunk to get a new shirt but was surprised when he opened the trunk at the end of the bed and found that the clothes in it were not his.

Locand glanced around the room, the light from the candles guiding his way. He found his belongings pushed to one side of the cabin, with his books and maps. He gazed at the girl on the bed in anger, frustrated that she would take over his cabin and bed. But the sight of her lying still and peaceful changed his mood. One of her legs rose up farther on the bed, her skirt rising up exposing her bare calves, ankles and feet. Locand grabbed the blanket and wrapped it around her body, hoping it would keep her warm. As he moved to see her face, he couldn't help but to touch her soft, smooth cheek.

She looked like an angel as she rested on the bed, her right arm extended in front of her while her cheek pressed partly into the blanket. Her left arm was bent and her elbow was brought to press into her side, a red book held loosely in the palm of her hand. Locand gazed at her lips, which were full and red. They were slightly parted as she drew breath. He couldn't resist but to run his thumb across them gently. When her tongue darted out and touched his thumb, he cautiously leaned down, and while cupping her cheek, pressed his lips against hers tenderly. Her mouth was soft and warm against his. He pulled back, not wanting to be caught in the act of what he was doing, or thinking. Still asleep she angled her face up wanting more. She wanted him. He leaned down again and touched her lips. When she began to press her lips harder against his, he quickly pulled away, denying himself. He withdrew his hand and cursed himself for his weakness. Miranda returned her head to the blanket and licked her lips, sighing in peacefulness.

Locand was about to turn and leave, angry with what he had just done, when he looked again at the book Miranda held. He slowly reached for it and removed it from her grasp. When he glanced at the book, he felt a twinge of familiarity, and as he opened it, he knew what she was reading. It was his journal that he kept of all the places he had gone to and the ships they had plundered, of all the adventures that he had as captain aboard *The Captain's Avenger*.

Locand closed the book loudly and stared at the girl lying across his bed. He was angry with her for looking into his private belongings, but as he glanced around the room he noticed how she had replaced most of his things with hers, even the trunk at the end of the bed was hers. Locand roamed around the room, his hands behind his back. He wanted to wake her and yell at her for what she had done, but then he thought better of it. He realized that she never would have made herself feel more at home if he wouldn't have locked her into his cabin in the first place.

What he thought was a punishment for her turned out to be a punishment for himself. She wasn't even fazed by being locked into his cabin. Furthermore, she seemed to enjoy it. What kind of lesson was she learning? Locand wondered. It was as if she wanted to be alone away from everyone. The thought confused him. Most women he had aboard his ship, which was rare, begged to be on deck. They never wanted to stay below. But Miranda almost went out of her way to be below deck.

Locand shook his head, not being able to understand the female mind. He then turned and left the room, forgetting about the clothes he had wanted to get. He locked the door behind him, determined to change sleeping arrangements by morning. Though he wanted to discuss with her about invading his privacy, he also wanted to avoid her. He no longer worried that she would become a distraction to the crew. His new worry was that she was becoming a distraction to him. The more time he spent with her the more he thought about bedding her.

The temptation to do so was strong within him. The last thing he needed in his life was a woman. They were mere distractions, making men change their ways and lifestyles, and he wasn't ready to retire his ways just yet. Lord Hammil kept popping into his thoughts, and he knew that if he ruined his bride for him, there would be hell to pay. Locand almost didn't care, and yet, there was a feeling inside of him telling him that it was wrong to deflower a woman that belonged to someone else. The situation frustrated him, so he decided to avoid her, and avoid her he did.

For the rest of the week, he did not go back into his cabin, nor the week after. He had Billy get the clothes for him he needed, but not once did he try to get them himself again. After a month had passed, he was tired of evading his cabin on the account of Miranda, so he ordered his men to remove her belongings and place them back into Davy's cabin. He had thought that the transition went smoothly, until he heard a scream. All Locand could do was shake his head. The sun was bright, but there were clouds coming over the horizon. Locand knew there was a storm brewing.

Lord Hammil rushed below deck upon hearing the sound. When he had tried to talk with Miranda the week before, she would not speak to him. Now she avoided him completely. She even refused to take walks on the deck with him and out of stubbornness, locked herself into Locand's cabin. At night, Miranda would sometimes walk on deck, but only when she knew that Lord Hammil was sleeping, but Davy always accompanied her. She had finally convinced Davy to practice the sword with her in the hold of the ship where the storage space was located. There was enough room to move around and no one would be able to see them. However, Davy also suggested they ask Locand for permission first. He refused to practice with her until he gave it.

Now, however, Davy was on deck with Locand as Miranda was being forced from the cabin. Davy was heading for the stairs when Locand stopped him. "Let me check on her, my friend. I need a little action and I'm in a mood for a fight." Davy stopped and watched as Locand headed down the stairs toward the cabin. Davy had a smile on his lips as he turned around and headed for the helm.

By the time Locand got to the cabin, all he saw were two of his men standing in front of Miranda. She held a sword toward the men daring them to come closer. Lord Hammil was trying to reason with her, but apparently whatever he was saying wasn't working. "Everyone out!" yelled Locand, eager to solve the problem. He started to roll up his sleeves as he watched his men clear the room.

"What are you going to do, Captain Riveri?" asked Lord Hammil, mildly curious. He wanted to know what the captain was going to do to remove Miranda from the room when everything else they had tried failed.

"You might not want to see this, Lord Hammil. I have a feeling you will not approve. If I were you, I would be waiting for your fiancée in her cabin. She will be joining you shortly." Lord Hammil stepped into the corridor and out of Locand's way. He then saw Locand close the door in his face leaving him standing alone in the corridor. Lord Hammil just stood in the corridor waiting for awhile, not sure what to expect from Locand. Then he walked to Miranda's cabin and sat in a chair waiting for her as Locand had suggested, his hat in his hand.

Locand stepped farther into the cabin, his eyes never once leaving Miranda's. "What do you think you are doing?" asked Locand, his voice calm and eyes steady upon their prey. His sleeves now rolled to his elbows, his muscular forearms were ready for a fight. His long black hair hung to his shoulders as he moved, his body anticipating Miranda's next move.

Miranda watched as she saw Locand's transformation. Deep inside she felt a slight attraction for him. She found him incredibly handsome and brave. When she read his journal, she had almost wished she were with him on his adventures. He had described every detail vividly, and there were times when Miranda felt she were with him, standing by his side, seeing what he saw. Now, though, Miranda felt almost intimidated by the man. The way he was watching her made her feel like she was going to lose the fight she was about to start. She tried to stand tall and arrogant, turning her head slightly as if she were pondering her next move.

"You could have asked me to leave your cabin instead of forcing me. I would have done it, but now I'm not in the mood." Miranda lowered her sword slightly, but not all of the way.

"Will you leave then? Your punishment is over, and I wish to spend my nights sleeping in my own warm bed. You have decided to take refuge in here, but you cannot hide from your worries and fears any longer. I see what you are doing, and it's not wise."

"What is it that I'm doing?" asked Miranda, allowing Locand to move closer to her.

"This, for starters," said Locand as he grabbed her sword and threw it on the bed. His motion was so quick that Miranda wasn't fast enough to stop him. She then started backing up until her back pressed against the wall, feeling vulnerable without her weapon.

"I can use that sword, Locand. I know how," spouted Miranda convincingly.

"I'm sure you can use it well, but now is not the time to prove it. These men will one day save your life, do not end theirs because of your stubbornness." Miranda folded her arms in front of her chest as her brown eyes gazed into his.

"I wouldn't have hurt them, but I would have if they were to hurt me. I was merely threatening them. I do not wish to leave the solace of this cabin, please?" The way Miranda blinked her eyes so innocently pulled at Locand's heart. However, he knew that he should not give in to her.

"The only way I would let you stay in this room is if we were to sleep in the same bed together. I will admit that it won't be very comfortable for you. There is a reason why I have a big bed. I like to spread out and would most likely lie partly on top of you or push you from the bed. Also, I don't think Lord Hammil would appreciate our bodies intertwined in an embrace. I know for a fact that he would like to keep you for himself. However, if he asked me, I would be more than happy to share you with him." Locand lifted Miranda's chin with his hand and forced her to look at him, his body moving closer to hers pushing her farther against the wall. Locand had a playful look in his eyes, knowing that Miranda wouldn't take him up on his offer. He knew there was more than one way to get what he wanted, and he was in the mood to play the game. Miranda stood firm and unyielding until Locand grabbed her backside playfully, causing her eyes to widen and mouth to open in shock. When she saw the smirk on his lips broaden to a full smile, she merely scoffed at him and pushed him away from her.

"Fine, fine, get off me. You've made your point, I'll leave." Miranda brushed passed Locand as she made her way to the door. For a moment she thought he was going to kiss her. The prospect certainly held her attention and yet when she realized that he was only fooling with her, Miranda felt silly.

She started to shake her head, feeling foolish for thinking that a man as strong, handsome and virile as Locand would have an interest in her. Before she could open the door Locand began to speak again, "By the way, while we have this moment alone together, I would like to speak to you about invading my privacy. You were reading my journal for entertainment. Inside that book are my personal thoughts, feelings and adventures. I would appreciate it if you would be considerate enough to leave my things alone. I know that I put you in my environment, but please restrain yourself from looking through my things. You don't see me going through your belongings or trying on your clothes, do you?" Locand placed his hand on his hips, the smile once on his lips now gone. Miranda couldn't help but to smile at the thought of Locand wearing one of her dresses.

"Yes, I would love to see you wear one of my dresses. Try wearing a corset, you wouldn't be able to breathe for at least three days afterward." Miranda laughed as she moved to sit on the bed, her legs hanging off the side. "If you wish to look through my belongings by all means do so, I don't care. I have nothing to hide from you." Locand cocked his head to the side, a smirk upon his lips.

"What are you saying, that I'm hiding something from you? I am under no obligation to share with you any information involving anything. I am just a man who likes his privacy." Miranda clucked her tongue as she smiled at Locand's remark.

"Men and their privacy. I think your whole gender has some serious issues." Locand couldn't help but laugh out loud.

"Excuse me? What do you mean by that? What do you know of men, for your gender makes men's issues seem like nothing! You are more complicated than I'll ever be."

"I know enough about men to know that you are not the marrying kind, or probably even the faithful type. From your journal I have surmised that you have a great lust for life and women, but none for love. Not once did you ever speak of love with a woman or anything else, at least not yet." Miranda then pulled out his journal from underneath his pillow. "However, I haven't finished reading your entire journal yet. You may have found love on a different page." Locand looked around the room for a moment and then back to Miranda. "I found it in the bottom drawer buried beneath a bunch of things in the galley when I went in there the other day." Locand rolled his eyes and shook his head in disbelief.

"Are you a thief, too?" asked Locand sarcastically.

"When the time calls for me to be, but I will tell you this. You will be a lonely man, Captain Riveri, if you don't let love in your heart."

"And you can speak of love?" sneered Locand as he moved back and forth on the floor in a rocking motion, his weight shifting from side to side. When Miranda nodded her head, Locand laughed.

"Why do you laugh at me?" Miranda asked as she stood up from the bed, feeling mocked.

"Don't you dare tell me that you love Lord Hammil, or I will laugh in your face right now." Miranda placed her hand on her hips.

"Is it that obvious?"

"It is obvious to me, and I don't know you that well. I have spent little time with you in the past month and my thoughts about you are still unclear. However, you do not dote on the poor man like a woman who loves him would. Don't get me wrong, there are times when you appear to be very devoted, but it is only when he is partially weakened. Otherwise, you avoid him at all cost and are using my cabin as an excuse to avoid him. Do you call that love?" Locand stopped his rocking as he awaited his answer, "Because if so, then I've been behaving incorrectly all of these years. In my eyes, when two people truly care for each other, they show consideration, forgiveness, kindness, and love."

"I do not love him, but it does not mean that I don't care about what happens to him. He has wealth, power, and if you look beyond all of his strange obsessions, he's not a bad man. He deserves happiness in his life just like anyone else." Locand thought about Miranda's words for a moment, feeling they held much truth.

"Do you always look beyond what a person shows you about themselves? If so, then maybe you should take some of your own advice and treat Lord Hammil with more respect than what you have been." Miranda looked down at the floor in shame.

"I know I've been acting terribly, Locand. I'm sorry for being such a pain. I don't mean to be. There are just so many things that are on my mind and in my heart. Can you forgive me?" Miranda raised her gaze to meet Locand's, her large brown eyes and pouty lips showing her youth. Locand reached out and cupped Miranda's cheek in his hand. It was a perfect fit.

"I forgive you, Miranda, but I think your apologies should extend farther than me, don't you?" Miranda nodded her head. She then reached out her arms and stepped closer to Locand, embracing him. Her cheek rested against his broad shoulder as she held him. Locand was stunned by the action and wasn't sure how to respond. He then turned his head toward her hair and smelled her Jasmine scent. The urge to hold her against him was overpowering. But when his arms remained at his sides, Miranda pulled away from him, analyzing his features.

"Does it bother you to show me affection? I was merely thanking you for your counsel." Miranda was starting to feel that all men had the problem of showing women affection. Locand removed her hands from around his waist and stepped away from her. His eyes betraying the emotions he was feeling.

"It would not be appropriate for you to do that again. Please refrain from doing so the next time you wish to thank me. Believe me when I say that words will do just fine." The coldness in Locand's tone made Miranda feel embarrassed for her actions.

"Forgive me! I will remember that in the future to never thank you by touching you." The anger was evident in Miranda's voice. She could not understand what she did that was so wrong. Locand shook his head at her and ran his fingers through his dark hair. He then reached out and grabbed Miranda's hand, holding it in his.

"One day, hopefully when you are married and content, you will realize the effect you have on men. You are young and desirable, Miranda, and though I'm the captain of this ship, remember that I'm also just a man, and even I'm not immune to your charms. You cannot act so alluring and expect me not to notice or want you." Miranda brought her hand to her chest and stepped away from Locand, appalled.

"Do you think I am trying to seduce you? Please believe me when I say that I am not." Miranda looked around the room, her eyes wide. "You must think that I'm a strumpet."

"No!" Locand shouted and took a step toward her. "I don't believe that for a moment, but I need to bring it to your attention. This is why I didn't want you aboard my ship. It has been over a month since some of these men have had a willing woman in their beds—much longer for me. You are beautiful and tempting. Men look at you and see someone they could lie with. It is important for you to stay close to Davy and Lord Hammil when you are on deck. It is for your own safety. I trust these men with my life, but lust is powerful and a woman is easy prey here. I recommend wearing something that reveals less of you, especially in the bodice area. Davy had said that you have brought men's clothing. If that is so, then I recommend you wearing them. We already know that if you are in need of a shirt that you fit mine." Locand smiled as he turned toward the door with his intent upon leaving.

"When I walk on deck may I stay by your side?" asked Miranda lightly. Locand turned around, his arms folded in front of his chest.

"Stick to your loyalties, Miranda, you do not know me well. Davy and Lord Hammil are the ones that should be protecting you—not me."

"I don't understand, if you are the captain of this ship, then isn't it your job to protect us all?" Miranda folded her fingers together in front of her, her eyes staring at Locand intently, but he only took a deep breath, retaining his patience.

"Of course I will protect you, but you miss what I am saying. One day when you really want to, touch me again. Then and only then will you ever know what I truly mean. Trust me when I say that you should stay close to the ones who care about you, for I am incapable of doing so. It is a luxury that I cannot afford, and I will not favor you in front of these men or in front of your dear Lord Hammil." Miranda was about to ask another question, but stopped when Locand opened the door and left the cabin, leaving her alone to think about the words he had said to her.

CHAPTER 6

That night there was a storm, only one of many that they would sail into. The waves were tall and luminous as they crashed onto the deck of the ship. The crew was busy moving on deck, with Locand at the helm yelling his orders. The wind and the waves were forceful upon the ship. The wood could be heard creaking and cracking from the intensity. Locand tied himself to the helm with rope so he wouldn't be washed overboard. Most of the men did the same, depending on where they were on the deck of the ship.

Miranda was below deck attending to Lord Hammil, who had another bout of seasickness from the rocking motion of the ship. His forehead was sweating as he lay upon his bed, hunched over in pain, holding his stomach. Miranda pressed a cool cloth to his forehead as she held onto the bed for dear life, the movement of the ship nearly sending her across the room. She grabbed a bucket as she saw Lord Hammil turn to her, the pale look on his face giving away his intentions.

The storm went on for hours. Her hands and arms were sore from the grip she had upon the bed. When she was able to relax, she covered Lord Hammil with a blanket and wiped his brow again with a cool cloth. He now lay in a better position, his legs extended away from his chest, his eyes closed in rest.

Miranda had taken Locand's words to heart and apologized to Lord Hammil for her behavior. Though she and Davy were the only ones that knew what Lord Hammil's plans were, she agreed that she couldn't treat him so terribly. When she had stepped into her cabin, he had been sitting on the bed waiting for her. They talked for awhile and then he held her. As they fell asleep in each other's arms, the storm had hit. Lord Hammil insisted upon returning to his cabin, but once there fell prey to his ailment once more. She was taking care of him, feeling sorry for his condition.

Miranda quickly rose from the bed and grabbed the bucket that Lord Hammil had vomited in. She moved to the door and opened it, letting some fresh air flow through the room before she closed it. As she stepped into the corridor, she stopped by the galley to see if Billy was all right. When she stepped into the room, she saw Billy on the floor cleaning up the plates and silverware that had been tossed to the ground. Suddenly, he cursed and held his hand, blood could be seen dripping to the floor. Miranda set the bucket down and rushed over to help him. On the way, she grabbed a cloth that was piled onto the table. When she reached him, she fell to her knees in front of Billy and reached for his hand. Billy moved it away from her. His gray hair wet from the storm.

"It's nothing lass, I'm fine." His tone was curt, but Miranda didn't notice, she was focused on the wound.

"Please, Billy, let me help you." As her eyes pleaded with him, Billy gave in allowing Miranda to touch his hand. She grabbed it tenderly and wiped the blood away. The blood covered part of his hand and was running down his arm. She then grabbed a bottle of rum that was lying on the floor by her and opened it, pouring the dark liquid onto the wound to cleanse it. Billy flinched, but Miranda's calming words soothed him. She then wrapped his hand with the clean cloth on her lap and tied it. Billy looked at her appreciatively, but couldn't find the words to thank her. Noticing Billy's hesitation Miranda turned to pick up the rest of the plates.

As she worked, all Billy could do was stare at her until he saw her pick up the silverware. As she came to the knife, he yelled, "Avast, be wary of that knife—I wasn't." He then raised his hand telling Miranda that the knife was what cut his hand. Miranda nodded in understanding and stood up, placing the plates and silverware she had picked up onto the table. She then wiped her hands on the skirt of her dress and turned toward Billy. "Is there anything else I can do for you, Billy?" Billy shook his head not saying a word.

Miranda moved to the door and was about to leave when Billy stopped her. "Wait!" he said as Miranda saw him walk to a drawer and pull out a long black ribbon. He then approached her asking her to hold out her hand. As Miranda did so Billy laid the black ribbon into it. "I thought maybe you could use it to tie your long hair back." Miranda looked at the ribbon and then back at Billy. She smiled as she leaned down and kissed him upon the cheek whispering, "Thank you, Billy." Billy raised his hand in front of him, a red blush on his cheeks, feeling uncomfortable.

"No miss, thank you. Now off with ya!" Billy waved for Miranda to leave. She did so, but not before leaving him with a breathtaking smile.

As Miranda left the galley, Billy felt happy, his soul lifted. It had been weeks since he had felt good about himself. Now, with the encounter of Miranda in his head, Billy went back to work cleaning the galley, whistling as he worked, a permanent smile upon his lips.

Miranda decided to check and see how the crew was faring on deck. As she climbed the stairs to the deck, she noticed the water dripping down them. The storm was fierce, rocking them violently back and forth. She had to grab onto the railings for support. Once on deck, she could see the splashing of the waves as they crashed onto the crew forcing them to hang onto ropes that were tied to the bottom of the main mast. All that could be heard were the crew's shouts as they lowered the sails and tightened the ropes. Rain pelted her face as the wind whipped against her, pushing her toward the railing. Her eyes searched for Davy, but she could not see him. Fear filled her chest but soon she heard him as he yelled something from the quarterdeck. She quickly exhaled a breath of relief as she gazed over at him. He did not notice her, but she did see Locand as he yelled his orders. He was standing by the helm, steering the ship. His face wasn't as serious as she thought it would be. In fact, he almost looked as if he were enjoying himself.

She couldn't imagine why anyone would be pleased steering a ship into a storm that led them to nowhere. She could hardly see the prow of the ship less try steering in this weather. How Locand knew where he was going was beyond her, but he seemed to know what he was doing. Miranda looked away and focused her attention in front of her. It was then she noticed one of the men sliding across the deck careening toward the railing. He had been tied to the main mast with a short piece of rope, but it had been severed. Miranda quickly glanced around but couldn't tell if anyone noticed what had happened. When nobody made a move toward the man as he scrambled against a wave trying to find something to hold on to, Miranda reacted. She took a deep breath and ran toward him. She quickly grabbed a hold of a piece of straggling rope that was left untouched around the bottom of the main mast, wrapped it tightly around her waist and then moved toward the man. He just got finished sliding toward her when the ship lifted in the water. She thought that she had his hand, but the ship lurched again. This time both of them flew to the other side.

Miranda yelled at the man to grab her hand. She saw him hit the railing hard and was almost sent overboard when she reached out and grabbed him by the shirt, saving him. When the ship lifted again, and he was moving toward her, he reached out his hand and firmly held hers within his grasp. She then tried to pull him closer and when she did, forced her rope into his hand. She watched as his hands gripped the rope tightly, and he pulled himself toward the mast. Miranda tried to follow, but her feet slipped upon the slick surface and she fell to her knees. She looked up and saw the man tie another rope back around his waist. He then grabbed her rope and started to pull her. She could feel the rope tighten around her waist. Miranda glanced back toward the railing and watched as another wave washed over the deck. She had to hold her breath as the water drenched her from head to toe. She gripped the rope tightly as she felt the powerful wave cover her. Once it had passed, she felt again the rope tighten around her waist.

She tried to focus her attention on the man in front of her and noticed, with surprise, as another crew member came to help. Soon, she was pulled to the large mast and found herself being pushed against it as the next wave hit, her head finding some relief as she turned her cheek toward the thick wood. When the wave subsided, she turned around and found herself eye to eye with Locand. They seemed to stare at each other for some time before another wave hit and he was forced to shield her with his body as he grabbed the rope and held it, one of his arms wrapping around her holding her close. Miranda could feel the dampness of Locand's body against hers, but she didn't resist. She could feel his cheek resting against hers and heard his labored breathing as she felt his muscles flex. As she breathed in his scent, he smelled of the sea. His body produced much warmth, but she wasn't able to enjoy it for long. Soon, she saw a flash of silver as Locand withdrew a dagger from his waist. She then felt the slight tug as Locand cut the rope that was around her. He yanked her from the mast and dragged her to the stairs by her arm. Locand almost ran as he tried to beat the next wave that was about to pummel them.

As the wave hit, Miranda found herself being thrown unceremoniously down the stairs with Locand following right behind her. When she hit the floor, she spun in the water that followed them. Locand almost fell on top of her but instead of catching his breath and resting for a minute, he quickly rose to his feet as if nothing had happened. He seemed to be unhurt, but Miranda could feel a sharp pain in her backside. She winced as she moved.

"Are you all right?" asked Locand, as he reached out his hand to help her.

"Yes," replied Miranda as she readily accepted it. When she was able to stand she was about to thank him when he pulled her roughly against his body.

"What are you doing out of your cabin? I was not expecting to see you being half-drug across the deck by my men as they tried to save your life." Locand's clothes were soaked. Miranda gazed at his chest as she noticed the shirt sticking sensuously against it. She could see every curve and muscle as he stood before her with his arms folded in front of his chest. Locand was a very attractive man, and the longer she stared at him, the more she seemed to notice.

"For your information, I was up there to check on Davy, but instead found one of your men's ropes severed. He would have drowned if I hadn't helped him." Locand relaxed his body position slightly.

"Now that, I didn't see," whispered Locand.

"Of course you didn't, how could you? It would be nice for a change if you just thanked me instead of accusing me all the time of doing something wrong or inappropriate." Locand moved his hands to rest on his hips, water dripping down his face. "I am only trying to help, and when I saw one of your crew almost fall into the sea, I could not stand by and do nothing. Everyone else was too busy trying to keep the ship from falling apart in this monstrous storm. I was the only one able to help him." Locand averted his gaze to the stairs and then to the floor, ashamed for becoming angry with her.

"I don't always think that you are acting inappropriately," remarked Locand quietly. Miranda folded her arms in front of her chest as she glared at him.

"Don't you?" Now Locand's gaze focused on Miranda's features.

"No, I don't," answered Locand as he caressed her with his eyes. "What you did was heroic. You risked your life to save another." He then ran his fingers through his hair wiping the excess water from it, his handsome face covered with rain droplets. Miranda cocked her head to the side. She wasn't sure if Locand was being serious or not, but when he didn't smile, she knew that he had meant what he had said. "I find that trait admirable."

"Thank you!" answered Miranda cheerfully as she lowered her arms to her sides and smiled. She then looked at her appearance and noticed how soaked her dress was. "I am going to go and change my clothing. I'm starting to get a chill." As Locand glanced down at her he could see her nipples become hard beneath her dress. He then averted his gaze and nodded his head as he glanced down at his own shirt.

"Now, if you would be so kind as to stay in your cabin until the storm is over. We are almost through it." Miranda nodded her head as she folded her arms in front of her chest, protecting it from his gaze. "Good, now I want you to understand something. What you did is appreciated, but you also risked your life. You could have also been thrown into the sea and drowned. Did you not once think about your own safety?" Miranda's smile vanished as she thought over Locand's words. "These men are experienced sailors, and they know how to handle themselves in a storm. They know the risks. Do you?" Miranda was about to answer, but saw the look on Locand's face and decided against it as she averted her gaze. "The next time you decide to do something foolish, I want you to think about what Davy would do if he lost you. He cares for you dearly, I can tell. What you did could have not only cost you your life, but would undoubtedly affect Davy's and anyone else who cares for you." Tears sprang to Miranda's eyes. Locand saw them, but chose to harden his heart against them.

"How can you do that? You turned something heroic into something foolish and wrong. How can you be pleasant one minute and terrible the next?" spouted Miranda furiously. Locand opened his mouth slightly as he smirked.

"Practice—my dear woman—practice! I'm not here to placate you. I'm here to express to you where you went wrong. I will not coddle you like Davy does and protect you from the world. You need to hear how you put others' lives at risk for saving yours and how you put your life at risk for saving my men. I'm being realistic." Miranda glared at Locand as she wiped the tears from her eyes. "Look, I know that you did what you felt was right at the moment, and I will tell you that you probably just won over my crew for what you have done, but you also need to think about your actions in the future as well as the consequences of those actions. You never do, which is why you anger so many people. It is why you found yourself down in my cabin for almost a month. You think that you are always right when you are not. Have some humility and understand that everyone makes mistakes. It's all right to be wrong sometimes." Locand took a deep breath as he tried to calm himself. The beautiful woman in front of him was getting him frustrated.

"Do you make mistakes?" asked Miranda curiously. Locand scoffed loudly as he gazed down the corridor.

"All the time, not even I'm immune to them. However, the difference is that I accept my mistakes and learn from them. Now, be thankful that I am this way, Miss Smyth. It is for your own good. Could you imagine if I was agreeable all of the time, what would you do with me then?" Locand laughed but it did not last long for Miranda's stare quieted him.

"I would like you better for one." Miranda's words caused Locand's smile to vanish.

"I care less of your feelings, Miranda. It is better for the both of us if you loathe me." He then turned sharply and headed back up the stairs leaving Miranda staring after him.

After a few hours passed, Miranda made her way back toward the deck. She had noticed how the ship started to ease, the motion finally going back to normal, the wind becoming quieter. Once on the deck she saw the clearing of the sky as dawn approached. They had all been up for most of the night, including Lord Hammil. When she had left Locand, she had gone to her cabin and changed her clothes. She then went to check on Lord Hammil, who was still sleeping. She was exhausted herself and knew that the crew also had to be. She knew not if Davy had a chance to rest but knew that he was probably still on deck helping the captain. As her eyes scanned the crew, they fell upon him. He was drenched through, his hair wet from the storm. He was talking to some men when his eyes fell upon hers. She rushed out to him and embraced him tightly. Davy held her and kissed her on the cheek. "I am glad you are safe. I was worried about you." She ran her fingers through his wet hair holding him again.

Davy stepped away from her slightly not wanting to soak her dress. "We are almost finished here. All that needs to be done is the mopping of the deck."

"Is there any way I can help?" asked Miranda as she glanced around her.

"No, my sweet, there are enough able men here to do the job and then some. You should go back down below where you can stay dry. How is Lord Hammil?" Davy ran his fingers through his hair causing excess water to drip down his face and neck.

"He's ill again. I've been with him most of the night comforting him. He's currently resting." Miranda then thought of the bucket she had left in the galley and closed her eyes shaking her head. She was so taken aback by the cook's kindness earlier toward her, that she had forgotten it.

"I'm glad you are safe, Miry. The captain told me what had happened when you came on deck earlier. You were fortunate that he saw you before you were hurt and swept overboard." Miranda could hear the disapproving tone in Davy's voice.

"Please don't lecture me, Davy. I could not bear to hear another one." Davy narrowed his eyes as he glanced upon Miranda's youthful features. Locand had told him that he had spoken with her, but he didn't clarify what he had said.

"Well, I will be down to our cabin shortly. I'm exhausted and feel the need to rest. Why don't you ask the captain if there is anything that you can do?" Miranda glanced at the helm and saw Locand standing on the quarterdeck talking to his first mate, pointing at the deck below. His eyes suddenly found hers, to Miranda's surprise, but all she could do was stare at him. Remembering what he had said to her, she looked away from him.

"Locand can take care of himself, Davy, he doesn't need my help." Davy eyed Miranda suspiciously before telling her to meet him below in their cabin. She agreed and turned around, walking toward the stairs. Her gaze found Locand again but he refused to look at her, his attention focused somewhere else. Looking away from him she found the stairs, but before she could go down them a thin man with torn clothes and long scruffy hair, grabbed her arm. As she turned around, the man quickly let go.

"Miss?" he spoke hesitantly.

"Yes?" answered Miranda kindly. As she glanced over the man's appearance she realized that it was the same man she had saved several hours ago from being washed overboard. The man was looking around him nervously, but then focused his attention back onto Miranda.

"Thank you for saving my life, Miss," spoke the man. Miranda smiled cheerfully.

"What is your name?"

"Slim, Miss."

"Well, Slim, I was glad to help. Thank you for helping me regain my footing. The deck was so slippery. Well, as far as I am concerned we are in each other's debt," Miranda said as Slim smiled and bowed his head slightly, glancing over toward his captain.

"I better return back to my duties. I just wanted to thank you." He then bowed his head and was about to walk away when he turned back around. "If there is anything you need, Miss, anything at all, just let me know." He then walked off and returned to his duties, a broad smile on his face. Miranda quickly gazed over at Locand and watched as he folded his arms in front of his chest, a scowl upon his features. She then gave him a brilliant smile, straightened her posture to stand tall and proceeded to go down the stairs.

On the way back to her cabin, Miranda checked on Lord Hammil who was still sleeping. She then noticed that the bucket she had grabbed earlier was now placed back into the room by Billy. Miranda smiled and closed the door, heading for her own cabin. When she walked into it, she laid out a clean shirt and breeches for Davy to wear on his bed and then sat on her own. She had changed clothes from earlier, but her dress was now slightly wet on the arms and chest from Davy's embrace, but she didn't mind. She was angry with Locand for treating her so callously, but she was pleased that his crew was finally starting to warm toward her. At least one man was. She then thought again about Locand. She didn't know why he went out of his way to hurt her feelings, but he did. She then thought of a way to soften him. She quickly moved from her cabin to Locand's. She had remembered how his clothes had been soaked through so she walked over to his trunk, that was now at the end of the bed, and opened it. She grabbed a clean white shirt and laid it out on top of the chest for him to see. She then grabbed clean breeches and laid them out as well.

Miranda smiled secretively to herself. She was bound and determined to make an impression on him. She knew that Locand could be kind, but if he refused to treat her kindly then she was going to at least make him feel guilty for treating her so awfully. She quietly returned to her cabin, laid down on the hard bed and relaxed. Soon, her eyelids became heavy and they closed. When Davy walked into the cabin, he covered Miranda with a warm blanket while the sounds of her slumber escaped her lips.

When Locand was finally able to return to his cabin to rest, he was surprised to find a new shirt and breeches already laid out for him. His first thought was that Billy might have done such a thing, but when he grabbed his shirt he smelled a soft Jasmine scent linger in the air. Miranda! His eyes closed and focused in on the scent. The woman infuriated him to no end, but for some reason she was bound and determined to befriend him. He stood there and shook his head as he quickly stripped from his clothes and put the new ones on. He then moved toward the bed, eager to sleep in its warmth, but it was there he dreamt of a brown eyed beauty with soft pouty lips and long blond hair. It was there he decided to be kinder toward her, but he had to be cautious. He didn't want to lose his heart.

CHAPTER 7

Several days had gone by when Miranda decided to walk on deck again. The sun was bright, and she raised her hand to ward off the rays from shining in her eyes. The wind was warm as it touched her skin, and she felt the urge to remove her dress so she could bathe in its warmth, though she knew that it would be indecent to do so. By her side stood Lord Hammil, now fully recovered from his bout of seasickness. He was wearing a hat to protect him from the sun and often took a handkerchief out and pressed it against his forehead to absorb his perspiration. Miranda talked to him pleasantly and laughed when he made a joke. Her laughter could be heard around the ship and its pretty harmony was not lost on the crew, who occasionally glanced at the couple. It certainly didn't escape Locand, who was walking around the ship socializing with his crew. He tried to ignore the sound, but couldn't. Deep inside, he was jealous that Miranda's laughter was for someone else and not for him.

Locand remembered how he had pushed her away, and at times he cursed himself for it. He heard from Billy how she had unselfishly helped with the binding of his wound and the way she had helped him clean the galley after the storm. He also told him of the kiss she had given to him upon his cheek. The woman kept proving to be a kind and wonderful person, and yet there were times when Locand would wish that she returned to being the sassy indecent woman that had first come aboard his ship. He could have ignored her better, could have hated her more, but now his thoughts kept clouding with visions of her. The way she talked, smiled and laughed, the way she tried to be brave in front of him. It would have been easy to convince her to become his woman, but he knew he couldn't do that to her, especially when she seemed to care for Lord Hammil. It wouldn't have been right.

Miranda was pointing at a dolphin jumping out of the water

when Locand approached her. The look she had given him showed her excitement at seeing such a beautiful and amazing creature. The smile remained on her lips as she let go of Lord Hammil's arm and moved to the railing so she could get a better look. Her hair blew in the wind as she clapped her hands in delight. Lord Hammil had seen dolphins before and wasn't as enthralled with them as Miranda was.

"My dear, it's getting stifling on deck. Shall we go below?" Miranda heard the question but didn't want to leave the deck, her eyes still focusing on the dolphins as they jumped from the blue water.

"You can go below if you wish, Leonard, but I would like to stay for a few minutes more. The beauty of the dolphins amazes me." Lord Hammil thought for a moment before agreeing.

"Don't stay too long, my love." Miranda waved at Lord Hammil, her attention still focused on the water. Lord Hammil glanced at Locand before turning around and heading for the stairs.

When Miranda could see the dolphins no longer, she turned around to face Locand, who had approached her right after Lord Hammil went below deck. His white shirt was unbuttoned and she could see the dark tan on his chest. His stomach muscles were firm and rippled and could be seen through the large opening of his shirt. He looked the part of a handsome and charismatic pirate, and yet he was now a privateer. Miranda's heart fluttered as she focused her attention on his face, not forgetting how attractive he was and yet not wanting to think about it, either.

"I wanted to ask you something, Captain Riveri," said Miranda. Locand noticed how she didn't call him by his first name any longer. "Would you mind if Davy and I practiced our sword fighting in the hold of the ship. I have already found the perfect spot, but I wanted to ask for your permission first. I am rather good," she boasted as she leaned against the rail. Her blonde hair was being whipped by the wind and flowed behind her, the sun tanning her skin.

Locand stared at the beauty in front of him. Her request was a bizarre one, but one he would grant. "If it pleases you, Miss Smyth, to practice your skill then I will not deny you, but only as long as I can test them. If you are as good with a sword as you say, then I want to see it." Miranda's eyes narrowed angrily.

"Would I ask you to practice sword fighting if I knew not how? I thought I had proved my abilities earlier when your men tried to evict me from your cabin." Locand raised his hands to his hips and stared down on Miranda.

"I'm not sure, Miss Smyth, would you? Your request is an interesting one at best and one that a woman of your breeding would not ask." Miranda placed her hands on her hips ready to rebut Locand's words but before she could say a word he continued. "So, your behavior tells me one of two things. One, you are either lying about your abilities to impress me or two, you are more than what you appear to be, and I would like to mention how I saw Davy holding you back from almost striking your fiancé after he angered you. Do ladies do that? Because that is the first time I have ever seen a lady almost attack her lover. I believe that if Davy would have let you, you would have done Lord Hammil severe harm. Which, of course, goes back to our previous conversation about you being more than what you appear to be." Miranda's gaze faltered slightly as she focused her attention on the deck.

"I—" Miranda wasn't sure how to rebut the remark so she shook her head. She didn't realize that Locand had seen her anger spark against Lord Hammil.

"You, Miss Smyth, are very confusing to me, as I'm sure you are to Lord Hammil. Most women of the age act more prim and proper. They usually dislike sailing and would never be found prancing around the hold of a ship sword fighting. They would also not be on deck without a hat or parasol to cover their beautiful and yet pale features. The women I know would stay below deck, just like you do, but what differs you from most is the fact that you seem to be accustomed to life on a ship. Now, why is that?" Miranda lifted her head to glare at Locand before she pushed past him to go below. She was so angry she wasn't sure what to say. He had stopped her, however, by grabbing her arm and swinging her around to face him.

"My life and past does not concern you, Captain Riveri, and I don't have to admit anything to you, or explain. I am different than most women—so—who cares? The kind of person I am should matter to you least of all. "

"It matters if it affects me and my crew."

"I have only asked for your permission to sword play, not to go to war." Miranda and Locand stared at each other for some time, their chests heaving with their anger. Then Locand smiled mischievously.

"Should we tell Lord Hammil of your request then?" Miranda stepped away from Locand and moved closer to the rail.

"No, there is no reason to tell him. Davy and I will be practicing at night so he will not need to know. He isn't aware that I can fight and I don't wish for him to find out just yet. He would not approve of me knowing how to protect myself. He wants me to depend on him completely. He likes it when I appear weak." Miranda was about to walk away when she suddenly stopped, her curiosity peaked. "What do you think of me knowing how to sword fight?" Locand gazed out into the ocean not wanting to tell her the truth. He found her being able to protect herself quite appealing. He liked strong women, women with strength and courage.

"What I think about your skill does not matter, Miss Smyth. If you are happy pretending to be something you're not, then I am sure there is a good reason for it." Miranda gave Locand a seething glare.

"That wasn't what I was asking, was it? You know what, forget I ever asked it. I don't care what you think." Locand turned his head toward Miranda, his eyes filling with irritation. Miranda turned and walked away but not before Locand walked over to her and seized her by the arm again to stop her.

"Do you want to impress me, Miss Smyth? Then meet me tonight in the hold, alone and ready to fight. That will be the only chance you will get at a piece of me. Are you game?" Miranda stared at Locand in disbelief, her eyes widening. "If you win, I will allow you and Davy to practice whenever you like."

"And if I lose?" spouted Miranda.

"You will help with the chores on deck. I will be more than happy to put you to work to earn your keep." Miranda smiled cunningly and laughed.

"If that is your wish, Captain, then I will do as you command." Miranda bowed her head mockingly. "Tonight then?" Locand resisted the urge to choke her, though deep down he liked the challenge.

"Tonight! By the way, we are within a week of New Providence and have been on the look out for enemy ships. You better keep your skills sharp, we may need them." Miranda stared into Locand's hazel green eyes waiting to hear more, but he didn't say another word and released her arm. She nodded her head and hurried below deck. Locand watched her go until she was out of sight, then returned to his position at the helm.

Later that night Miranda showed up in the hold as Locand

requested. She was wearing a loose fitting shirt with tight black breeches she had made especially for her. It was the usual garment she practiced sword play in. She had not told Davy of where she had gone and she was thankful for it. She knew that he wouldn't approve and would probably want to witness it, and yet she also knew that he wouldn't stop them.

It was way past sunset now, and after waiting for some time for Locand to show, she had decided to give up and leave. She stopped, though, when she heard footsteps approaching. She raised her sword slightly but then quickly let it rest at her side when she saw it was Locand.

"Sorry to keep you waiting, but I was detained." Locand walked over to a barrel, unbuttoned his shirt, took it off and let it lay peacefully upon it. Miranda watched with uneasiness as she stared at Locand's exposed flesh. She was trying to deny her attraction toward him, but the more he came around her, the more she wanted him. He was in her dreams and in her thoughts. There were even times when she could smell his scent after he had left her side. Her senses were starting to be consumed with him. The feeling was definitely unnerving.

"What are you doing?" Locand turned toward Miranda, his well-formed physique causing her to stare.

"Getting comfortable; you are welcome to do the same." Locand's smile was charming, but she returned it with a smirk.

"I'm quite comfortable dressed the way I am, thank you." Miranda then added arrogantly. "Do whatever you feel will help you win for you will need all of the help you can get." Locand removed the sword at his waist and held it out in front of him.

"Whenever you are ready to begin then, Miss Smyth, by all means teach me a lesson." Locand waved her forward, but she just stood there. "What's wrong?"

"We need to discuss rules before we can commence," said Miranda matter of factly.

"There are no rules, Miranda. When you fight, you don't stop to ask your opponent which way he would like to die. You just do it." Miranda placed her sword in front of her.

"The only rules I'm talking about is with you. Do you want to include fist fighting when given the opportunity?" Locand stared at Miranda in amazement.

"You and Davy practice that as well?"

"Of course we do. Davy says I should be familiar with all of the areas of fighting." Locand laughed loudly causing Miranda confusion. "What's so funny?"

"Nothing! If you want to strike me, then you are welcome to try, but I will not return the blow, so be kind."

"Fair enough, first to disarm wins!" Miranda got into a crouching position and waved Locand to charge her. He did so gladly. Soon, all that could be heard was steel against steel. The pair turned right and then left in a rhythmical dance that caused both of them to smile with anticipation. Locand would jab, and Miranda would parry and then they would reverse. As the match progressed, both would try different moves to throw the other off their groove by spinning, ducking or something of the sort, but it wouldn't work. Locand had to admit that he was quite impressed with Miranda's abilities. She was graceful and confident with her moves as was he, but he had years on the sea for experience. In order for Miranda to be this skilled, she had to practice just about everyday.

As Locand was detained in his thoughts, he was unprepared for the kick to the stomach. He quickly bent over but not once removing his gaze from Miranda's.

"Day dreaming is hazardous to your health, Locand. Would you do that if you were fighting a man?" Miranda's arrogant smile caused him to stand quickly and regain his thoughts.

"If you were a man you would be dead."

"And if I were truly fighting an enemy, so would you." Locand's eyes narrowed as he rushed toward her, his sword slicing quickly. Miranda blocked each move but was not paying much attention to what was behind her and was surprised when Locand grabbed her by the front of her shirt and held her up against the wall of the ship, knocking the sword from her hand.

"I win!" said Locand arrogantly. The motion was quick, but Miranda's reaction was quicker. She reached for the dagger at her waist and held the tip toward Locand's manhood. She heard his quick intake of breath and noticed his eyes glancing downward.

"Wise move!" Locand smiled as he tried to catch his breath, Miranda did the same. "You are quite skilled, Miranda, I apologize for doubting you." Miranda smiled and placed her dagger back into its sheath at her waist.

"You are skilled as well. It was good competition, don't you think?" Locand stepped away from Miranda and lowered her feet to the floor. She then moved to find her sword, and both put them away. Sweat could be seen on Locand's chest, the shiny gleam reflecting off the many candles that were lit so they could see. For a while, both stared at each other without saying a word, both not knowing exactly what to say. They were satisfied with their dual, and for some reason didn't want to ruin the happy moment between them. Suddenly, the ship lurched to the side and Miranda got thrown into Locand. Locand caught her and held her to his chest. The shipped then lurched to the other side causing both of them to land against the wall. Locand protected Miranda from the blow by reversing his body so she would land against him instead.

Miranda was unsure of what was going on and gazed up at Locand in concern. He gazed back down at her and lifted his hand to her cheek. The moment was electric. Miranda's lips were now just inches from his, and she could feel his warm breath against her face. Her hands instinctively rose to caress his arms. Her soft touch didn't escape Locand's notice. He had briefly closed his eyes to enjoy the moment, but when he opened them and saw how close Miranda's lips were to his, instead of kissing her like he had wanted to do, he pushed her away from him, the ship helping with the task by lurching again to the other side.

"I need to see what is going on up there. It feels like a storm is brewing." Locand hastily moved toward his shirt, grabbed it and put it on making sure he buttoned it at least halfway. He was about to walk away when he glanced back at Miranda. She was staring at him with a perplexed expression on her face.

"You have proven yourself to me, Miranda. You can practice with Davy whenever you like, and I promise to say nothing to Lord Hammil. It will be our little secret." Miranda wanted to say something—anything—but couldn't. She was still remembering what had almost happened between them. Locand smiled and continued walking away from her until he reached the stairs. By that time, she was out of sight, he had closed his eyes tightly to think. He had wanted to kiss her desperately, and the problem was she had wanted him too, it was in her eyes and touch. It was then he decided to put distance between them and leave her alone. Locand continued up several sets of stairs until he felt the hard rain pelt against his face as he reached the deck.

The air had become much warmer during the day after the storm, and the crew often removed their shirts as they worked. Davy and Miranda frequently practiced their skills with a sword at night. They would get into mild fighting and used daggers when the swords were cast to the side. Earlier that morning, Locand had told Davy they would be arriving at New Providence by the following day. Miranda was excited about being on land but wasn't sure when Lord Hammil would be sailing to Port Royal. She hoped that he wouldn't want to marry her first. Davy and Miranda had agreed she wouldn't marry him, and that they were only using him to find her father, but if she were made to marry then there was nothing she could do about it.

That night's sleep was restless for Miranda. She was exhausted from her and Davy's swordplay, but she was thinking about what would happen when they landed at New Providence. It was also bothering her that Locand had been ignoring her all day and when she tried to talk to Lord Hammil about his business in Port Royal he had ignored her as well. Now frustrated, she found no solace in her bed so sat up and decided to read Locand's journal. She was almost finished with it and had only twenty pages left. Miranda lit a taper by her bed and finished the pages. She was absorbed with the words she was reading and at times felt like she was in a trance.

Miranda's eyes then widened when she read her father's name. Locand had described him perfectly. He had written about the last adventure with Stratton Mayne and how much he cared for and respected the man. It surprised Miranda that he even knew of her father, but as she read further she realized that several years ago Locand's father had died and it was her father who helped him get over the pain. Since that time, he had kept in contact with him and had sailed and raided many ships together in the Caribbean.

The realization hit her hard. Did Locand know that Lord Hammil was after her father? Was he going to help capture him? The thought that he would betray her father angered her, especially when it seemed like they were such close friends. She knew that she shouldn't ask him, but was not thinking correctly. She was angered and needed answers. Locand didn't seem to be the kind of man who would betray a friend, but then she remembered that she didn't know him as well as she thought she did.

Miranda quickly rose from her bed without waking Davy, who was sound asleep above her, and moved to the door. She was only wearing her undergarments but didn't remember that until she was already out the door and knocking on Locand's door. As she felt the cool breeze down the corridor, she looked down at her appearance and noticed her lack of apparel. She then decided to go back to her cabin to put on something more appropriate, but the door opened. Locand's hair was tousled from his sleep, his eyes not quite awake, as he glared at Miranda.

"This better be important, Miss Smyth. I haven't been sleeping very well lately and am in a foul mood." As Miranda saw Locand's lack of shirt, his powerful chest again revealing it's every muscle and curve, she held her breath. She was about to turn away, embarrassed for bothering him, but decided against it.

"I need to talk with you. I can't sleep and wish for your company and counsel." Miranda pushed her way past Locand into his cabin, but he merely stood aside letting her in, one of his eyebrows raised. His breeches hung low on his hips revealing the lower part of his abdomen. Locand ran his fingers through his hair as he lit some of the tapers in his cabin. When he was finished, he stood on the opposite side of the bed, his arms folded in front of his chest.

"What is troubling you so much that you could not talk to Davy about it?" Miranda thought about her answer for a moment, but could not come up with a good response.

"I am excited about being on land again and can't rest my mind. I decided to read the rest of your journal to calm me. I see that you do know how to love." Locand placed his hand partly over his lips and chin in thought, staring at Miranda.

"Does the thought of me being able to love someone, bother you? Though, most of my life has been spent on a ship, it doesn't mean that I don't know how to care for someone else." Miranda stepped closer to the bed, resting her hands upon it.

"I'm sure you are capable of love, Locand. You love your mother, she is very important to you, I can tell. You speak quite often of her in your journal, but you also loved your father. It seems that you loved your father very much." Locand moved around the bed so fast that Miranda almost let out a scream when he grabbed her by the shoulders.

"Do not speak of him, Miranda. You know nothing of my father."

Locand's tone scared Miranda and tears rose to her eyes that she could not stop from falling down her cheeks. Locand let go of her shoulders as he saw the tears, feeling remorse for causing them.

"I'm sorry, Locand!" Miranda yelled as she tried to pass him, upset that he had yelled at her, but he wouldn't let her by. Instead, he brought his hands to her face and cradled her cheeks in his palms. Miranda raised her hands up to his to remove them from touching her, but he wouldn't budge.

"I'm sorry for my tone, but I miss my father terribly. You were right. I loved him very much and yet I also hated him. He died over something foolish, and I still get upset over it. I had no right to raise my voice to you, you didn't know. But I mean it when I say that I do not wish to discuss him further." No more tears ran down Miranda's cheeks, and she regained her courage as her eyes met his. "If there is nothing more that you wish to discuss with me then I recommend you leave my cabin at once."

Locand let go of Miranda's face and stepped away from her, showing her the door with his arm. "There is one more thing I wish to talk to you about. I wish to know more about Stratton Mayne. I have read about him in your journal and am curious how you know him. You explain very little when it comes to your relationship with him." Locand eyed Miranda suspiciously before sitting on his bed to relax, his feet almost touching the floor. His long black hair fell forward as he adjusted his position on the bed, then he placed his hands behind him on the blanket and leaned back.

The pose was striking and vulnerable. Miranda couldn't help but stare at Locand's magnificent form again. She remembered how scantily clothed she was and hoped that he didn't notice. She was wrong, however, when she saw his eyes start at her feet and leisurely work their way up to her chest. Locand could see Miranda's dark nipples underneath her thin undergarment. His eyes then made it to her face, caressing her every curve and indention.

"They were great friends, Stratton and my father. They had sailed together several times and had many pleasures in each other's company. After my father passed away, Stratton comforted me aboard his ship. I sailed with him for a few months and he helped me work through my feelings of pain and loss. He gave my life meaning again and direction. I don't know where I would be right now if it wasn't for him, probably arrested somewhere and rotting in a prison, or dead. I owe him my life." The passionate way Locand spoke of her father made her want to believe that he loved him. She had assumed much from what she had read and what she knew of their journey.

"Would you betray him, Locand?" Miranda's tone was not accusing but curious.

"How could you ask me that after the way I just spoke of him?" Locand's glare shot right through her very soul.

"Because men change, Locand. Would you betray the man that saved you from a fate worse than death? What would you do to save him?" Miranda's questions brought on a twinge of anger as Locand shook his head at her.

"He is my loyal friend, Miranda, and after my father's death we have become such good friends. I would never betray him, not even if I was tortured by my enemies would I say his name." Miranda exhaled a breath but sharply took another one in as Locand jumped from the bed and stood in front of her. "What is it that you are not telling me, Miranda? Is there something I should know?" Miranda's hand flew to her chest as she thought quickly for an answer.

She watched as Locand raised his hands to his hips, his mere appearance sending shivers down her spine. She didn't want him to know yet who she really was. She wasn't sure how he would react or if what he told her about her father was the truth. She had remembered a young man aboard her father's ship whom she had tried to comfort after the loss of his father. It then dawned on her that the young man was Locand. She never would have guessed it if he hadn't told her. He had changed so much since then. She was preoccupied with the crew at that time that she paid very little attention to him, but when she did, she was always kind.

Miranda smiled briefly from her memories. Needing to change the topic, she turned her attention to Locand's muscular physique. She couldn't help but admire it. He was perfectly sculpted. Each mound of his abs was taunt and rippled right down to his hips. She knew no other man who looked as inviting as he. Curious, she reached out to touch Locand's stomach. It was smooth and solid. He jumped away from her as if she had burned him.

"What's the matter?" The concern on Miranda's face was true and innocent as Locand backed away from her.

"Why do you touch me, Miranda? I ask not for your touch." Miranda didn't know what to say to Locand. He acted as if she had hurt him.

"I'm sorry, but I couldn't resist. The action was instinctive. You are a strong and virile man. I wanted to know what you felt like." The truth startled her as she said the words. A look of surprise could be seen on Locand's features.

"You need to go, Miranda, you know not what you do. Go back to the safe haven of your bed. That is where you belong." Miranda stepped hesitantly closer to Locand and stroked his arm as he leaned slightly against the bed. His first instinct was to push her away, to not encourage the attraction they had for each other, but he could not find the strength. He wanted her to touch him.

"You are forgetting that I am a man, Miranda. A man who can feel and has desires, your touch is evoking much from me at the moment." Though Locand wanted Miranda to turn away from him at his words, she did not and instead moved closer as if he hadn't spoken at all.

"You are magnificent, Locand. I could never have believed that your skin could be so soft, yet so strong." He closed his eyes as he felt her smooth fingers roam freely up and down the length of his arm over his large bicep muscle.

"Don't do this, Miranda. Don't weaken my resolve. No good can come from it." Locand opened his eyes and stared at Miranda, his eyes soft and pleading. Miranda pulled her hand back.

"What are you resolved to do?"

"Avoid you!" Miranda exhaled sharply.

"You're impossible! All I have been trying to do is befriend you, but you are determined to hate me."

"I don't hate you, Miranda. I'm trying to do the right thing. The facts are that you belong to another man. Believe it or not, that is a big problem for me."

"I am engaged to Lord Hammil, not married to him. You are a friend. If I choose to touch my friend's arm out of curiosity, then I shall do it. I control what I do. I belong to no man," piped in Miranda. Locand shook his head and laughed.

"If that were only true!" Locand pointed his finger at Miranda with his words, then lowered his hand. "Your Lord Hammil feels otherwise, and you know it, yet you tempt his ire by vying for my attention. I'm his enemy, not his friend, and he questions your faithfulness." Miranda shook her head and blurted, "I don't care!" Locand moved closer until he was just inches away from Miranda's ear.

"You should!" Miranda could feel Locand's warm breath against her neck. It made her knees weak. The scent of Jasmine consumed Locand's senses as he pulled slightly away, but not entirely. He wasn't sure what came over him, but for the moment it didn't matter. Their breath intermingled, their mouths so close together. Both moved slightly forward and back, wanting more but not taking it. Against his better judgement, Locand hesitantly reached out his hand and moved his fingertips up and down the length of Miranda's arm. Her skin was silky smooth, it showed its pleasure as goose bumps rose to the surface. She closed her eyes as she felt his fingers trail up her arm to her neck, his hands caressing her cheek and chin. His fingers then roamed one by one over her smooth plump lips. He could feel her warm breath against his rough flesh. The sensation was erotic to Locand. His eyes clouded with desire as her tongue darted out innocently and touched him. He roughly moved his hand to the back of her neck and pulled her to him, his other hand caressing her face.

Miranda brought her hands to Locand's chest as he pulled her closer. She moved one of her hands to his face and caressed it as her other hand ran down his neck to his chest. As her fingers caressed every muscular mound and crevice, she could hear Locand's heavy breathing. He sounded as if he were out of breath as he leaned his head back to give Miranda full reign over his body. Miranda then continued to trace her fingers down his stomach until she reached the skin just above his breeches. Locand snapped his head foreword and seized Miranda's hand. He brought it up to caress his face instead, then grabbed her pointer finger and ran it across his lips.

Miranda tried to pull away, unsure of the feelings running through her, but he would not let her go. The desire she was feeling for Locand was becoming stronger and stronger as he touched and caressed her. She didn't want to stop the game they were playing and yet the urge to do so overwhelmed her. She was new to all of the pleasurable sensations running through the center of her being and wasn't sure what to do next or how to act, so she let Locand guide her.

Locand flicked his tongue out and touched Miranda's soft flesh. After looking into her eyes and seeing the desire in them shining brightly, he placed her whole finger into his mouth. Miranda gasped with pleasure. Locand's mouth was warm and moist as his tongue moved slowly around her fingertip and suckled it. Miranda removed her finger and stared at it, amazed that a man could make her feel so warm and aching inside with just the movement of his tongue. She tried to pull away from him, but Locand brought her closer until their noses almost touched. His hand was held firmly upon her lower cheeks and chin, forcing her to look at him.

"Friends?" Locand's voice was husky with desire.

"No! Friendship is not enough," whispered Miranda. As their eyes met, Miranda brought her lips closer and closer to Locand's. With eyes closed, she pressed her lips softly onto his. Locand moved his hand to caress her cheek, wanting to deepen the kiss. Miranda felt Locand's mouth open slightly and she followed suit, their kisses were soft and gentle. He then traced her lips with his tongue, and when Miranda's tongue dove out of her mouth to meet his, Locand's dove inside. Miranda's eyes widened as she felt Locand's tongue rub against hers erotically. It was a new feeling for her, one that she was slowly getting used to. As Locand's mouth slanted across hers more deeply and passionately, Miranda's arms wrapped themselves around his waist and back.

He was now cupping her face as he performed his tender onslaught upon her mouth. Miranda was sighing from the pleasure she was feeling, unconsciously rubbing her body against his, wanting to get closer. Her hands could not settle themselves, so they roamed all over Locand's back wanting more, demanding it. As her nails lightly raked down his back, Locand removed one on his hands from Miranda's face and caressed down her voluptuous body, squeezing her backside as he went. As the kiss became more passionate, more wet, Miranda could hear Locand growl in the back of his throat his pleasure. She could feel him bringing her hips closer to his. Locand's grip upon her was unbreakable.

When she was finally able to break free from the kiss, needing to catch her breath, she couldn't help but caress his large hard biceps. He was so strong, so sexy. Not wanting to change the mood, Locand made a trail of moist kisses down her neck to her shoulder. Miranda wanted to know what it was like to taste his skin so with her tongue she reached out and made a trail to his earlobe. Once there, she nibbled and licked the soft flesh. Locand opened his eyes and gazed out as if he were in a daze, rubbing his cheek against her soft shoulder. Feeling the short sleeved fabric of her undergarment, Locand smoothly grabbed it and slid it from her shoulder, leaving kisses and soft nibbles along his way, hearing a slight tear of the fabric for his efforts.

He moved to the other shoulder and did the same. As he finished, he moved slightly away to see his work. The undergarment sleeves hung at her elbow, the bodice still covering the soft mounds hiding behind it. As he gazed into Miranda's eyes, his heart ached. Her lips were swollen from his kisses and her skin was red from where he had dominated. Her long hair was tousled and her eyes held more promise than Locand was willing to accept. His hand moved to the front of the undergarment and Locand was about to rip the material from Miranda's body when he felt her hand move to the back of his neck and felt her lips covering his.

The kiss was soft and demanding. Her mouth opened and soon the kiss became rough with passion. His other arm snaked around her body as he held her to him. Soon, he broke from the kiss and pressed his forehead against hers. He could hear Miranda's rapid breathing, it was intermixed with his own. He gripped tighter to the bodice of the undergarment and was about to pull it, but couldn't find the strength. He was fighting with himself on what to do. His fingers could feel her soft breasts waiting for him behind the material but couldn't set them free. Locand let go of the bodice and stepped away from Miranda, his hands raising up the sleeves to cover her shoulders again.

As his eyes stared into Miranda's, his face looked tortured. Miranda felt the same way, a feeling of loss hit her as she felt Locand separate himself from her. She felt disappointed and wanted to continue with what they were doing.

"Why do you stop, Locand? Do I not please you?" Her eyes filled with sadness, hoping that he wouldn't say that she didn't please him. Locand raised his hand to caress her cheek, a slight laugh coming from his lips.

"You please me very much, Miranda, too much. I want you more than I have ever wanted another. What is it about you that makes me want you to myself?" Miranda smiled with hope that Locand cared for her as he ran his fingers through her hair.

"Please finish what you have started, Locand. I'm giving myself to you. I know what I'm doing. I want this." Miranda caressed Locand's cheek and was leaning forward to kiss him, but he stopped her.

"If you were any other woman, I would happily finish this. But you're not the average woman." Locand stepped away. "We were wrong, Miranda. I was wrong for allowing this to go further than it should have."

"No, Locand, this is my fault. Deep down I wanted this. I wanted you." Miranda paused. "I still do. There's something about you I can't shake, and I don't want to. You're in my blood."

"Do you know what you are doing?" asked Locand as his eyes narrowed and his forehead furrowed with doubt. As he saw Miranda nod her head he said, "I don't! I can't do this, Miranda. You deserve someone who would solely be devoted to you. I'm not that man. You don't know what you're asking of me. Trouble will come with swift wings if I make you my woman when you don't belong to me. It is wrong for you to offer me this moment." Miranda stepped away from Locand, surprised by his words.

"I belong to—" started Miranda.

"You belong to Lord Hammil and are his fiancé, Miranda, which you are determined to forget. How would it look if on your wedding night you were not a virgin?" Miranda folded her arms in front of her chest and glared at Locand, anger rising inside her.

"I don't care what he thinks. He lacks the passion that I crave to fill me. I was surprised to see that you have what I need, Locand."

"What is that exactly? What do you think I can offer you, a life of wealth and privilege? No! I can't even find that for myself, so how could I ever provide it for you? You have tried tempting me and would have succeeded in getting bedded if I didn't have the will to stop. I will admit that I didn't want to stop. The thought of being with you has haunted me these many weeks; I won't deny that. But what I feel for you is lust, not love, and you deserve someone who can love you. You are a beautiful woman, Miranda, and smart, too smart I think. Knowing that you are innocent, I am surprised to find you so skillful in the art of seduction. The way you move and touch me makes me want you more than you will know." Locand paused before saying, "I must thank Lord Hammil." Miranda's eyebrows raised in confusion at Locand's last words.

"Thank him for what?"

"For training you in the arts of seduction; you are magnificent." Miranda brought back her hand and slapped Locand across the face. The blow was expected and yet Locand knew he had to hurt her in order for her to stay away from him. If she did not then he would end up doing something he would not regret. Tears sprung to Miranda's eyes as her chest heaved from her anger.

"You are despicable, Locand. How could you say that to me? I have not known love, and I only know lust because you have caused that emotion inside of me. Who tempted who here? I will admit that I wanted this to happen. I wanted to know what it was like to touch you, to feel your lips upon mine, and I wasn't disappointed. I will not deny the attraction I have for you, but open your eyes to the fact that it was you who created this passion inside of me, you who makes me want you by my side. I have never felt this way before, and it is because of you that I feel it now. No man, including Lord Hammil, has ever touched me the way that you have. Despite what you may think or believe. But I blame you for this unwanted passion that fills my loins, these unwanted desires that only you can sate." Tears ran down Miranda's cheek as she looked at the floor and wiped them hastily away with the back of her hand.

"Fine, blame me then. That passion you speak of has always been inside of you, it just takes the right man to unleash it. I will admit that I also wanted this to happen. I can't help the feelings I have for you, Miranda. Though it would please me to make you my own, now is not the time. This is reality, a hurtful reality that we can't escape from. We cannot be together, not with Lord Hammil already staking his claim upon you. I have too much at stake to risk the agreement I have with the queen to take you from him." Miranda turned her back toward Locand, frustrated from his words.

"Am I worth so little to you that you couldn't fight for me? Some things are not always what they appear to be, Locand, and if there is something that I want bad enough, I will do anything to get it. Wouldn't you?" Miranda was speaking of the way she was using Lord Hammil to find her father, but Locand had no way of knowing her true intentions. She wanted to explain them to him, but knew that if she did, even though he was loyal to her father, she could still be used to hurt him.

"Do not want this, Miranda. I beg you. If our situations were different then, yes, I would fight for you, but now I have too much to lose. Too much at stake. I have worked too damned hard on finally getting this second chance and I will not blow it by getting involved with you. Do you understand me?" He then grabbed Miranda roughly by the shoulders, but upon hearing her soft gasp of pain, quickly loosened his hold. "I can't!" Miranda nodded her head briefly but could not say a word. She wanted to be angry with him but deep down she couldn't. She was too scared, he was acting like a wild man.

Suddenly, Locand let go and took several steps away from her. He then ran his fingers through his hair in agitation. "I'm sorry but you must reason this out. You are engaged to a man that holds my future in the palm of his hand. You may not understand about what he does, but I do. He has much power and is backed by the queen herself. With one mistake, I could end up in the stocks or worse—dead. My crew would be slaughtered or imprisoned. Tell me that you understand why I can't pursue you."

Locand reached out his hand to touch Miranda but she moved quickly away from him. His hand clenched into a fist and fell to his side. He would fight for her if he had too, but he wasn't sure at the moment what he would risk to have her by his side. Suddenly, Miranda whipped around and faced him.

"Let me ask you this, because I need to know. Do you want me to marry Lord Hammil?" Locand ran his fingers through his hair and then reached out and pulled Miranda roughly to him, but this time his fingers did not dig into her skin.

"What do you want me to say, Miranda? Would it make you feel better if I said that I don't want you to marry the man?" Miranda nodded her head in response. Locand pushed her away a little as he raised his voice. "Then feel better, for I do not wish for you to marry the bastard." His fingers gripped her arms tighter, but this time, Miranda didn't mind. The fact that Locand seemed to care for her, even a little, made her feel warm inside. Locand's tone softened.

"Miranda, understand, a man worthy of you would wait to have you in their bed until you and he were properly wed. To make love to you. I care for you too much to spoil you for another. You deserve the right to experience true love and all that it entails, not just lust. You deserve better than what I can offer you." Locand tried to pull away, not believing what he had said. He had never waited for a woman before. He always took and they always gave. He didn't like the emotions Miranda was creating inside him. He was resolved to push her away forever, but Miranda refused to let him go and held fast. She forced him to gaze into her eyes.

"If you and I could be together, and there was a chance that love could grow between us, how long would you wait for me?" Locand's eyes revealed his struggle. Seeing his indecision, Miranda began to pull away. This time Locand held fast. He didn't want to let her go.

"If there was even the slightest bit of promise for us, I would take that chance and fight for it. I would wait an eternity for you." Miranda leaned forward and pressed her lips against his. He tried to turn his head away, but once he felt her soft lips upon his, he had to give in. He passionately held her tightly to his chest and ravished her mouth one last time. Minutes later they decided to part, keeping what they had done a secret. Locand rushed Miranda back to her cabin, but with reluctance. He knew they had to be very careful in the future, for if anyone knew of their feelings for each other, it could ruin everything. They couldn't allow themselves to be alone together again. They had to deny what both of them wanted most. It was for the best—at least for now.

When Miranda returned to her cabin, it was almost dawn. She lay down onto her bed and curled up into a ball. Her eyes then gazed upon Davy, who had been sleeping in his bed, and hoped that he didn't wake while she was gone. Her thoughts immediately drifted to Locand and the precious moments they had shared together. He was right, she did deserve to know love, not just to feel lust between a man and a woman, because lust can fade, but love, love can last a lifetime. Her mother and father knew true love. She wanted to know what that felt like. Soon, she fell asleep, not realizing that New Providence was within sight.

CHAPTER 8

By early afternoon, *The Captain's Avenger* had weighed anchor and a longboat was starting to be filled with Miranda's and Davy's trunks and belongings. When Miranda walked on deck, her blue dress, which was lighter because of the warm air, revealed a hint of her breasts with a low neckline. Her sleeves stopped at her elbow and her waistline was thinning. Davy escorted her on deck and they watched as the crew hustled from one side of the ship to the other. Locand could be seen yelling his orders to the crew. He had glanced at Miranda as she walked around the deck, but kept his attention on the crew and the matters at hand.

After she left his cabin early that morning, he spent almost an hour thinking about what they had done. He had tried to go to sleep, but it kept eluding him. All he could think about was the sweet taste of her mouth as he had kissed it and the feel of her soft, silky skin upon his. It was a mistake for him to lose control and let her work her way into his heart. He had tried to deny her and yet her persistence made him give in to her will. Because of his weakness, he was falling in love with her, and as a privateer, that could be deadly.

Locand focused his attention on Stevens who was talking to him about the supplies they would need for their trip to Port Royal. Locand had picked several items that could wait until they had reached the busy port, but told Stevens to focus on the items they needed most. Lord Hammil walked up the stairs to the quarterdeck to talk with Locand. He had waited until Stevens left before speaking with him, needing privacy. His attention focused on Miranda as he waited.

"What can I do for you, Lord Hammil? We have reached New Providence in good time."

"We have, Captain Riveri, and I'm pleased. When will we be ready to set sail again? I am eager to take care of the business I need to handle for the queen in Port Royal so I can return back here for Miranda." Lord Hammil kept glancing over at Miranda, her laughter could be heard throughout the ship, the men occasionally glancing in her direction. Locand noticed the pasty white complexion of Lord Hammil's and almost grimaced as he puffed out his chest to look more important.

"I need to know what your plans are first, Lord Hammil. We'll need a day at least for my men to rest and relax before we sail again. How long will we be in Port Royal?" Lord Hammil stared at Locand. His brow was perspiring from the heat and the urge to remove his hat and fan it in front of his face was overpowering.

"We will be staying for only a few days. Your men can rest and relax at Port Royal, Captain. Port Nassau will have enough supplies for you to get what you need, but I do not wish to linger here. My estate is to the west side of the fort away from all of these foul pirates that have sailed here. I worry for my fiancée's safety. As you can see, the beautiful creature is meek and defenseless. She needs a man to protect her. I do not wish for these ruffians to harm her in any way." Locand almost scoffed at the idea of Miranda being meek and defenseless. She was far from it. If Lord Hammil knew of Miranda's ability to fight with a sword or the way she could seduce a man to do her bidding, he would probably faint. It often surprised him how blind Lord Hammil was to Miranda's true personality and nature. He wondered if it was because he was truly ignorant of them or if he just chose to overlook them.

"You are right, Lord Hammil. I will make sure she is well protected once we are on land. The longboats will take us to the island while my first mate supplies the ship with our essentials. We can leave by morning for Port Royal if that is your wish, but my men do need some time ashore." Lord Hammil nodded his head in reply, a smile upon his lips.

"Thank you, Captain. I appreciate any help you can give me on the matter. We have been sailing for months. I know how hard it can be for the men to be at sea for that long of time." Locand raised his eyebrows at the remark and smiled briefly. His feelings for Lord Hammil could be felt in the pit of his stomach. He couldn't stand the man. The mere sight of him made Locand want to throttle him, and the fact that he looked at Miranda as a type of trophy made him feel disgusted. He did not love her. He only wanted to show her off, hoping men would be jealous of his rare find. Locand shook his head trying to calm himself, taking a deep breath.

He quickly gave orders to his men. Some were to come with him to Lord Hammil's estate, while others stayed on the ship. Some were to accompany Stevens as he went into Port Nassau to get supplies. Locand warned each group to be careful, pirates were about and it wasn't time to lose sight of that and underestimate their abilities.

As the longboats were set onto the water and loaded with men, each boat went into the opposite direction. The men in Miranda's boat included Lord Hammil, who sat beside her, Davy, Locand, six other men, and their belongings. The six men oared the boat until they reached shore. The pale white sand shined like diamonds as they stepped onto it. The swords the men had tucked through their belts glistened as they pulled the longboat farther onto shore. The men then grabbed the trunks and started for the trees.

"How far is your estate, Lord Hammil? Could we not have taken a carriage to get there instead of walking through the trees?" Lord Hammil placed his hand upon Miranda's elbow to help her pass the brush in the sand.

"Do you see the rise over there under those trees?" Miranda tried to follow with her eyes where Lord Hammil had pointed, but couldn't see what he was talking about. "Hidden underneath the brush are stairs I made several years ago. No one knows they exist except for me. It is the back way to my estate. I do not wish to go through town just yet. I would like to keep your existence quiet for the moment." Lord Hammil walked ahead to show everyone the location of the stairs. When he was out of earshot Miranda said to Davy, "If I would have known I was to walk through the Amazon I would have changed my clothes for the occasion instead of wearing this damn dress." Miranda grabbed her skirts and raised them so she could walk unhindered.

"Watch your tongue, Miry, and behave yourself." Davy gave her a disapproving glare as he shook his head, but Miranda smiled when she heard a soft laugh coming from behind her. As she glanced back, she saw a smile upon Locand's face, but as soon as it showed itself, it disappeared. His face turning serious again, he focused on the hidden stairs Lord Hammil was revealing before them.

Lord Hammil removed several vines that covered the dark wooded stairs. Slowly but surely, the green trees and covering opened a pathway that led upward. He started to climb the stairs and everyone soon followed. Davy drew his sword as he led Miranda up the stairs with Locand following closely behind, his hand upon the hilt of his sword. The men followed behind with the trunks carried between them.

Sounds of wild animals could be heard throughout the trees, and the fact that Miranda could not see them made her feel uneasy. The path climbed for what seemed like half a mile. Then it leveled off to form a dirt road littered with ground cover. A few times Davy had stopped but then, after recognizing the noise, led them forward again. Lord Hammil was leading the group recklessly, not paying much attention to his surroundings. After walking it nearly a dozen times, Lord Hammil knew his way by heart and recognized every sound the woods made. His eyes focused ahead of them looking through the trees until he spotted an opening. He could feel himself perspiring and took out a handkerchief to stop the sweat from running down his face. The opening was getting closer and closer, the bright warm sunlight shining down like a spotlight upon the green grass.

Soon, the group made it through the opening only to stop to see their beautiful surroundings. The woods opened up to a road that led to a large massive white house. The grass was green around it and the doors and windows were curved which gave it a unique appeal. Stairs rose to the deck before the door and pots of pretty red flowers rose in their entire splendor reaching out for the guests. Lord Hammil waved them on and the group followed as he led them down the road and to the path that led them up the stairs. As Lord Hammil's hand reached for the door handle, a dark servant opened the door for them.

The servant addressed Lord Hammil with a smile upon his face and then opened the door wider so they could pass through. As the group walked through the door one by one, the servant eyed them with curiosity. Davy replaced his sword in the holder at his waist removing his hat as he entered into the house. His and Locand's attire was loose fitting, their shirts opened to expose their chests. Locand wore his hair in a pigtail at the nape of his neck, his chiseled features damp from the heat.

Miranda was fanning herself with her hand as she adjusted the bodice of her dress. Some of her hair was sticking to her forehead, and the need to run around naked to cool her skin was sounding more and more appealing. The house was cool inside and the escape from the heat made everyone feel better. The crew brought the trunks inside of the house and dropped them on the floor, their hands red and sore from the walk.

"Where do you want these trunks, milord?" asked one of the crew. The man's hair was soaked with sweat and his shirt had large dark spots underneath the arms.

"Follow me. Miranda's bedchamber is just up the stairs and to the left. Davy's will be across the hallway from her, and mine is at the end of the hallway." Lord Hammil led the way as everyone followed him up the staircase.

The foyer had a high vaulted ceiling and opened up to many rooms. The staircase was to the left and rounded along the wall as it led to the second floor. As the group reached the second floor, they noticed an array of tables and cushioned chairs. Many tapers lined the wall, and various vases with fresh, colorful flowers filled their vision. As they turned left and walked down the hallway, Lord Hammil opened the door to Miranda's room. He waved her in, and the men carrying her trunk followed behind.

The room was all in white with a fireplace against the wall by the bed. The bed had a canopy that gave guests privacy once the curtain was drawn around them. The floor was a dark wood that gave the room its appeal. A tall dresser could be seen opposite the bed with several drawers, and a cool breeze could be felt through the open windows. The smell of tropical flowers beckoned Miranda into the room, enticing her to stay forever. Miranda told the men where to place her trunk. Once they dropped it on the floor, they left the room.

She was so enthralled with her surroundings that she didn't notice how Lord Hammil showed Davy to his room, again, the men leaving his trunk where he had suggested. He then told Davy and Locand that he was to spend some time alone with Miranda, and that they should go back downstairs and wait for them. Davy was reluctant to leave Miranda alone, so was Locand. They had both glanced at her, but when she nodded her head in approval, they slowly worked their way to the staircase with the crew. Lord Hammil walked closer to Miranda, grabbed her by the hand and pulled her down the hallway so she could see his private chambers.

"This, my love, will be ours once we are wed," and with that Lord

Hammil opened the door. His bedchamber was twice the size of hers or Davy's. The bed was large with cushioned pillows and a billowy blanket. Colorful rugs covered the floor and pictures of the landscape hung on the walls. As Miranda stepped into the room she was amazed.

"Your estate is beautiful, Leonard. How long have you lived here?" Lord Hammil walked closer to Miranda and placed his hands upon her shoulders turning her around. Miranda's breath quickened, not liking the feeling of being alone with him.

"Many years have I owned this place. It is hidden from everyone on the island and the only way to leave is through the path and stairs. If you walk through the opposite side of the trees it will lead you into town. I like my privacy. Now you can see why I wished for us to marry here. The beauty is beyond compare to anything I have ever seen, except for you, my dear." Miranda smiled politely at the remark as her eyes gazed again at her new surroundings.

"What is meant for me here, Leonard? When do you plan on leaving for Port Royal?" Her questions were innocent enough and yet Miranda was desperate to find out when Lord Hammil would leave and return so she could leave for Eleuthera to find her father. Lord Hammil wrapped his arms around Miranda and held her tightly to his chest. As her face rose to his, he couldn't help but admire her beauty.

"I care for you very much, Miranda. I need you to know that." Miranda nodded her head slightly in reply, not wanting his face to move any closer to hers if necessary. However, Lord Hammil had other plans. He lowered his mouth to touch hers. Miranda tried to move away but couldn't break free from his embrace. As his lips pressed against hers, Miranda was determined to keep her mouth shut. But for the first time Lord Hammil caressed her cheek and opened his mouth for a deeper kiss. She opened her mouth a little, but when Lord Hammil pulled on her hair she had no choice but to accommodate him. His mouth fell upon hers and his tongue swept into her mouth. The kiss was enjoyable, but did not send shock waves to her loins. She kept trying to move away from him, but the harder she tried the more he forced himself against her.

"I need you, Miranda. I need to feel your body against mine, if only for a moment. It has been far too long since I have touched a woman like this." His fingers fiddled with the buttons on the back of her dress. He quickly turned her back toward him and in his haste, ripped her dress open in the back. Her bare skin now exposed, Lord Hammil dove one of his hands into the opening and caressed her skin.His other arm prevented her from moving as her arms were now pressed to her chest. She fought against him and looked toward the door for help but found that it was closed. When did he close it? She couldn't remember as fear filled her. Lord Hammil had a crazed look in his eyes, and she wasn't sure if she would be able to stop him if he forced himself upon her.

"Please, Leonard, stop this. I've kissed you, and I'm sorry if it filled you with desire for me, but there are some things that must wait until after we are wed. I will not let you force yourself upon me before we are husband and wife. Let me go!"

Lord Hammil forced her to turn toward him and his lips slammed upon hers to keep her quiet. The kiss lasted only for a moment before he walked slowly to the bed bringing her with him. He roughly turned her around and bent her over the side of the bed. Miranda's chest pressed against the blanket. With her hands free she tried to push away from the bed but Lord Hammil pressed his hand against her back preventing her from rising. He ripped the fabric from her dress to reveal more of her smooth skin. All the while, Miranda was pleading with him to stop.

Lord Hammil was stronger than what he appeared to be and was determined to have his way with her. She could feel Lord Hammil rubbing his hips against her backside. She could feel his hands grab her through her skirts. Miranda was pondering what to do and was about to yell for Davy when she felt Lord Hammil's arms wrap tightly around her waist and felt his sweaty brow land upon her bare back.

Miranda felt like crying. Lord Hammil had not had sex with her and yet his behavior indicated that he had orgasmed while rubbing himself against her. Miranda felt disgusted and used. She could feel Lord Hammil's heart racing against her back and wanted desperately to be away from him. He raised himself off of her and helped her from the bed. When she turned around, Miranda brought back her fist and made contact with Lord Hammil's face. Not expecting the blow, Lord Hammil took it full force on the cheek, fell, and hit his head on one of the wood posts at the corner of the bed.

As he lay sprawled out onto the floor, Miranda could see a wet spot on the outside of his breeches where she knew his manhood must lie. Tears sprung to her eyes as she screamed Davy's name. She raised her hands to her shoulders to fix her dress as she walked to the closed door. When she opened it, her eyes fell upon Davy who had run to the top of the stairs, his sword in front of him ready to fight. When his eyes fell upon Miranda and the state she was in, he immediately ran to her.

As he held her in his arms, he felt the soft skin of her back. When he turned her slightly around he saw the ripped fabric and a few red marks that he assumed to be nail scratches.

"What the hell happened, Miry? Did Lord Hammil do this to you?" All Miranda could do was nod, her voice gone from the tears she was crying. "I will kill him for this. I will kill him for forcing himself upon you." Davy pushed Miranda aside and was about to run into the room when he felt her hand upon his arm.

"Don't Davy! He did not force himself upon me. He just released himself against me. He's currently indisposed of at the moment from being punched in the face. I will say that he will have a bruise on his head when he wakes from his slumber. Please don't make this worse than it is. I hate him, Davy! I want to find Father and go away from here." Davy embraced Miranda again and comforted her. At that moment she realized that not Locand, nor his men, accompanied him.

"Where is Locand?" The question bothered Davy slightly, but he overlooked it.

"The captain went back to his ship with his men. He has done what he needed to do here. He will remain on his ship now until Lord Hammil is ready to leave." The thought that Locand left her there alone bothered her. He wasn't even going to say good bye? That fact bothered her more than anything else. She assumed from Davy's words that *The Captain's Avenger* was going to sail by morning. If that was the case, then tomorrow would be a good day to go to Eleuthera.

"Let's change that dress, Miry, and fix your appearance. It will not be long before we can be rid of him." Davy helped Miranda walk down the hallway and through her bedchamber door when she said, "Please don't tell Locand what happened." Davy helped her to sit on the bed when he replied, "Why not?" Davy wanted to see how much Miranda would tell him of the feelings he knew she was starting to feel for Locand.

"Because, I don't think he would approve and I don't wish for him to become angry over it. Or for him to do something he will regret." Davy opened the trunk and closed the door to the room, his thoughts focusing on the meaning of her words.

"It does not matter, Miry, for there is not much he can do about it. Captain Riveri has important duties that he needs to be responsible for and Lord Hammil will make sure they get done. At the moment he is at his mercy so don't think that he will be able to save you from him, because he can't. Do not distract him for any reason by tempting him. I know that you two have been arguing back and forth, but do not mistake that for feelings you think he may have for you."

"But, Davy…" spoke Miranda, but he only raised his hand for her to stop.

"No buts, Miranda. Now, let this topic go for now and get out of that dress." Miranda exhaled loudly as she watched Davy turn around, his back now facing her. She took off her dress, throwing it at Davy for his remark, and changed into the one he had picked out for her.

By sunset, Davy, Miranda and Lord Hammil were sitting at a large dining table quietly eating. There were many fruits to choose from that were native to the island as well as bread that was freshly baked. The room was filled with tension as each focused their attentions on the plates in front of them. When Lord Hammil had woken from his little nap, Davy was right by his side lecturing him about what he had done to Miranda. Lord Hammil didn't apologize to Davy for his behavior, but told him that when Miranda became his wife she would have to get used to him wanting to bed her. The topic didn't sit well with Davy, and he threatened that if he behaved that way again with her, before they spoke their vows, then he would be a man who would be missing that particular body part. Lord Hammil had acted brave, but his nerve failed him when Davy placed his dagger between his thighs proving his point as he made a slice in his breeches. He screamed in fear.

After they ate, Davy and Miranda quickly left the table and took a walk around the grounds of the estate. Lord Hammil tried to stop Miranda but she only glared at him in anger and continued on her way with Davy beside her. Lord Hammil had no choice but to let her go. He then retired to his room. The scenery surrounding Lord Hammil's estate was beautiful. Miranda had noticed it before when they had first arrived, but now she was able to focus her full attention upon it. Davy had given her space as she touched and smelled the exotic flowers that grew there. She took several sniffs of one particular flower and it reminded her of her father. It smelled like Jasmine. Her heart immediately ached as she thought of where her father could be. She hoped he was on Eleuthera. If he was not, then she didn't know where else to look.

After their walk they watched as the sun set. The sky was beautiful with its brilliant colors, the pinks, reds and yellows that splayed across the sky as if it had been painted there with an elaborate brush. As Miranda walked closer to the trees, she looked down and could see *The Captain's Avenger* bathed in the fading light. Her thoughts went to Locand.

Locand was on *The Captain's Avenger* watching the sunset as his men loaded the supplies Stevens had gotten from town. He was angry he had to leave Miranda alone with Lord Hammil, but it was expected. She was his fiancé after all. What did he expect her to do, leave Lord Hammil's side and declare her love for him? Locand shook his head at the crazy thought. He could not forget the kisses they had shared and wondered if she could not forget them as well? He cared for her, and it frustrated him. No matter what he had done to prevent this very thing from happening, it still did. His mind filled with thoughts of her. He wanted to find some reason to go up to Lord Hammil's estate and see her but knew it wouldn't have been a good idea. He wanted to touch her, to caress her supple curves, to kiss her pouty lips, but he couldn't. In frustration, he raised his hands to his head and closed his eyes. *Forget her! Forget her! Forget her!* he yelled to himself.

"Cap'n?" spoke Stevens as he walked closer to Locand. "Are you all right?" Locand raised his head and stared into the eyes of his first mate.

"I'm fine, just tired." He smiled at Stevens, who was still glancing at him strangely.

"All of the supplies are loaded, Cap'n, so we are ready to sail whenever you are." Locand nodded his head as he ran his fingers through his hair in frustration. "I heard there are some pretty women down at the local tavern. Maybe you would like to go and vent some of your frustrations on them?" Stevens had a good idea that his captain was becoming fond of Miss Smyth. He thought if he bedded another woman that she would leave his system. Locand stared at him and smiled.

"If that would help I would do it. However, there is only one woman I would like to bed and she is, at this very moment, with our Lord Hammil."

"You have sailed those waters before haven't you, Cap'n?" Stevens whispered as Locand glared at him.

"Unknowingly, and though it seems to be the case more often then not, I don't make a habit of deflowering innocent women or taking them away from their fiancés." Locand turned his gaze back to the sunset.

"She's quite a woman, isn't she? It's interesting, though, their relationship." Locand faced Stevens, his arms resting on his hips. "They are very different people. She is strong willed and smart, a woman who is self reliant depending on no one, and yet Lord Hammil acts as if she is incapable of living without him." Stevens gazed at the sunset. "I think she's using him for something. She must be, for how could a woman like that love a man like him?" Locand thought about that as well. Miranda often has proven she is capable of many things. He wouldn't put it past her to be using Lord Hammil for some other goal. It would explain her false affection for him.

"You're probably right, which makes me wonder why she is so complacent at being left behind why we go to Port Royal. You would think she would be fighting tooth and nail to come with us." Locand thought that behavior very peculiar indeed. What could be here that would keep her interest? He was unsure, but now his curiosity was peaked. Whenever he had asked her about her relationship to Lord Hammil she avoided the topic like the plague, or gave him very little information, becoming defensive. There had to be a reason why she did not want him to know what she was up to, though she had admitted to him that she didn't love him. She cared for Lord Hammil, but there was no love between them, which was why she had found him so attractive. Locand's mind raced quickly to find some answers.

"You do have a point, Cap'n. You would think she would want to come with us. I have been to Port Nassau, and believe me when I say there is nothing outstanding she would want in that town. Dangerous it is, even for us."

"Maybe here is not where she wants to be. What islands are

within reach? Close enough to sail a ship to? We will be gone for several weeks, plenty of time for her to do whatever she needs to do and return unnoticed, or not return at all." Stevens thought for a moment, but could not think of an island off the top of his head she could sail to in a few days time.

"I'm not sure without looking at a map. We are virtually surrounded by islands."

"Yes, but there must be one in particular she is fond of. Well, we will just have to see, won't we? We could be wrong as well in our assumptions, but it makes perfect sense. She has Davy, who knows his way around any ship and is good for protection. She would have everything she needed to complete her task."

"Yes, and her charms to convince anyone to help her." That comment made Locand's forehead furrow. Was she serious in her affection for him or was she using him as well for some purpose? The thought almost angered him, and yet the one thing that he knew about Miranda was that she was blatantly honest, which was why she got herself into so much trouble with Lord Hammil, and with him. She always said exactly what she thought, so the idea that she was in some way deceiving him was not a possibility. He then started to laugh.

"That minx is planning something. I guarantee it. We just don't know what it is. In time, it will be revealed."

"What of your feelings for her? I cannot blame you for desiring her, but the fact still remains that she, at least at this moment, belongs to Lord Hammil which would put her out of any of our reaches." Locand smiled as he mulled over Stevens' words.

"Yes, she is for now out of my reach, but if our luck holds out, she won't be for long," and with that said, Locand turned and walked down to the main deck with Stevens following closely behind.

That night went by slowly for Miranda. She didn't get a good night's sleep and was tossing and turning through most of it. By dawn she had managed to dress and walk quietly around. Davy and Lord Hammil were still sleeping. She did not bother to check on either of them, but noticed their closed doors. She walked down the stairs and passed several servants. They greeted her warmly as they walked around cleaning the house and adding their special touches. It was beautiful here. As Miranda stood by an open window and smelled the clean fresh air as well as felt the sun shine upon her face, she couldn't resist wanting to walk the grounds again. She immediately walked toward the front door, but as she opened it, the person she saw was the last one she expected to see. It was Locand. A smile rose to her lips, but when it was reciprocated with a frown she was confused and dismayed.

"Captain Riveri, what a pleasant surprise." Miranda reached out her hand to touch his, but he stepped away from her.

"I came here to speak with Lord Hammil. Is he awake?" Locand's tone was cold and serious.

"No, he's still resting." Miranda felt angry he did not greet her as warmly as she had wanted him too.

"Very well, then please tell him that *The Captain's Avenger* is ready to sail whenever he is. I will be waiting for him on the ship." He then turned around and started walking away. Miranda quickly closed the door behind her and followed him. She had called out his name for him to stop, but he didn't. In fact, he didn't even act as if he had heard her until she grabbed his arm forcing him to stop.

"What is wrong with you?" asked Miranda as she turned him to face her. "Why are you acting this way?" Locand folded his arms in front of his chest as he glared down on her. He could not answer. "Have you nothing to say to me?"

"What do you want me to say?" asked Locand angrily.

"Oh, I don't know, maybe that you will miss me. That you will be thinking of me while you are away?" Locand snorted as he stared at her.

"And how many times have you asked other men to do that very same thing?" Miranda stepped away and raised her hand to her chest.

"None, I have not even asked that of Lord Hammil. You are the first for that request. Is that why you are angry?"

"I am angry," started Locand, "because you have been lying to me."

"Lying to you? What are you talking about?" asked Miranda in frustration.

"I know you are here for some other reason than to marry Lord Hammil, Miranda. I know that you have been using him for some purpose. You have admitted to me you do not love him, and if that is the case, then why are you with him? Is it for wealth? Power?" Locand stopped when Miranda started shaking her head. "Give me one truth that will make sense out of all of this chaos. Give me one truth that will make me believe that you are not using me to get what you want by using your charms against me." Miranda closed her eyes for a moment, then reopened them.

"That is what your anger is really about, isn't it? You feel that my affection for you is not real, that I was pretending? Well, let me clarify it for you. You want one truth, then ask me your question, and I will prove to you that the moments we shared in your cabin were real. But first, did you mean them?" Locand remained controlled, but his features softened slightly.

"Yes! I meant every word and every action." Miranda nodded her head and smiled.

"Then ask me your question and I will tell you no lies." Locand took several deep breaths and watched Miranda as she raised her chin and breathed deeply, her features showing her seriousness. Locand grabbed her hand and walked her over to the hidden pathway and stepped inside of the trees so no one could hear or see them.

"Why are you really here? I have been wondering why you haven't convinced Lord Hammil to take you with us. He probably would, if you really wanted to go."

"Yes," Miranda answered softly, "but I don't want to go. In fact, I am quite content to stay here and admire the beauty of the island." Locand raised his eyebrows as he waited for Miranda to answer his question. "I am content to be here because I want to find my father. I haven't heard from him in several months and am concerned that he may be in danger. He usually sends me letters telling me of his welfare, but I have not received any. I fear he is hurt, or worse—dead. Lord Hammil is a means to an end. He has been pursuing me for six months now. I care for his welfare, but I am not in love with him, but you already know that. Anyway, I was asked to come on this trip and when I found out that Lord Hammil was coming to the Caribbean, I thought it would be the perfect opportunity for me to find my father and to see what has been keeping him away."

"Why didn't you tell me this sooner? I can help you, Miranda. It is within my means." Locand's features changed as he stepped closer to her.

"You are helping me. You are helping me by taking Lord Hammil away from here. It will allow me and Davy time to find him."

"Is he here, because if he is, I can send one of my men to go and look for him?"

"No!" Miranda shouted, her tone rising as she raised her hand to her chest. "No, he is not here." Locand's eyes held his confusion.

"Then where is he?" Miranda raised her finger and shook it back and forth as she clucked her tongue.

"One question, one truth! For both our sakes I cannot tell you that." Locand nodded his head though his curiosity was peaked. "Do you believe me now?"

"Yes, I do!" replied Locand resolutely. Miranda smiled as she relaxed her stance.

"Now, there is a question that I would like to ask you."

"One question, one truth!" Locand smiled as he threw Miranda's words back at her.

"Will you miss me when you leave here? Because I will miss you." Locand's smile faded as he stepped closer to Miranda and raised his hands to caress her arms. He then quickly glanced around them to make sure they could not be seen.

"Here is the answer to your question." He then grabbed her to him and kissed her. As their lips clashed Miranda wrapped one arm around his neck and held him closer as the other arm snaked around his waist, lifting his shirt and caressing his bare skin. Locand moaned as his tongue dove into her mouth repeatedly. Miranda moaned back as she felt him grab her buttocks molding her closer to his body. Soon, their passionate kisses ended when they heard someone yelling, "Miranda!" Their lips quickly parted and they both turned their heads toward the sound. It was Lord Hammil. Miranda moved from Locand's arms and placed her hand on his chest.

"Go, Locand, get out of here."

"No, I've been thinking about it and we will face this together," replied Locand strongly.

"No, we won't. Go back to your ship and know that you will be in my thoughts. Please!" she begged. "You have told me many times that you cannot afford to lose your freedom by getting involved with me. I'm going to make sure you don't. I've been thinking too and you're right about everything you said to me in your cabin. I do deserve to know love and I should not settle for less. But I also believe that you should too, and that's not lust talking." Locand shook his head, trying to shake the unwanted feelings coming over him. Miranda caressed his cheek. "I know there is promise for us and because I believe in it so deeply, I would wait an eternity for you."

"Oh, Miry!" moaned Locand as he reached for her.

"I'm protecting you, now go, and be safe." Locand moved forward, kissed her one more time on the lips, though he lingered for several seconds, before stepping away from her.

"Be careful on your errand to find your father, Miranda. I will stall Lord Hammil for as long as I can to give you time."

"Thank you!" Miranda smiled as she patted Locand's cheek and turned away from him. Locand watched her as she left the safety of the trees. Lord Hammil saw her and raised his hands to his hips.

"What are you doing over there, Miranda?" asked Lord Hammil with disapproval on his pale features.

"I was following a bird, Leonard."

"A bird?" asked Lord Hammil suspiciously. "There are many birds on this island, which one were you following?"

"A beautiful one for which I do not know the name. On my search I ran into Stevens who had told me that *The Captain's Avenger* is ready to sail whenever you are. They will be waiting for you upon the ship." Lord Hammil narrowed his eyes but did not want to push the issue for fear of Miranda becoming angry with him again for behaving badly toward her. "What's for breakfast?" Lord Hammil didn't get a chance to answer as he watched Miranda walk past him to go into the house. He then focused his attention upon the trees. When he was satisfied there was no one else there, he turned, walked inside and closed the door behind him. Locand saw the entire thing through the trees. He then worked his way down the path, his mind filled with Miranda's words.

By early afternoon Miranda and Davy had found themselves saying good-bye to Lord Hammil and the crew of *The Captain's Avenger*. They were now standing on the beach. Lord Hammil had everything he needed to take with him and Stevens was nearby to row him to the ship in a longboat. Lord Hammil turned toward Miranda and clasped her hands in his. It was the first time he had touched her since yesterday's incident in his room. Davy stood closely by her side not giving them any chance to be alone together. Earlier he had apologized profusely for not being able to stop what had happened to her, but Miranda forgave him saying that she should have called to him sooner for help.

Miranda stood as straight and cold as she could in a different dress than the one she wore yesterday. This one was cream in color and lightweight. The sleeves were shorter as well as the neckline. Her heart was pounding as she felt Lord Hammil squeeze her hands. Her face showed no expression as her eyes focused on *The Captain's Avenger*. She could see Captain Riveri standing by the helm while the men were bustling around the ship. The moments they had shared earlier were still filling her mind with pleasure. She felt better confiding in Locand about her father, though she never once mentioned his name. She knew that Locand could easily take her to Eleuthera to find him, but she could not ask him to do that. It would ruin his letter of marque by helping her find the man that Lord Hammil was supposed to be looking for. Any aid would surely mean the end of his life especially when Lord Hammil found out that her father and Locand were very good friends. He would surely accuse Locand of leading him astray. No, Miranda could not involve him in any of the things that she would need help with. Upon noticing Locand staring off into another direction, she focused her attention back onto Lord Hammil.

"Miranda, I wish to apologize again for what happened between us yesterday. I should have told you how I get after a long voyage. It would have been prudent to warn you. It was inconsiderate of me." When Miranda did not say a word he continued, "I promise that upon my return I will make it up to you—somehow." He then leaned forward and kissed her upon the cheek. He was displeased when she turned away from him.

"Very well, but upon my return I expect you to be ready for me to become your husband, like it or not. I will be gone for only a few weeks so use this time away from me wisely. My home is yours, do with it as you will, but be careful of the town. Many people have lost their lives trusting such disloyal men."

"I will use this time wisely Lord Hammil, you can count on it. And when you return, I will find it in my heart to forgive you, but not yet. The scars are too new and deep. What you have done has made an awful impression upon me. I did not realize such intimacies existed between a man and woman, and yet the shock of it all enlightened me. I am not prepared for such things and you took advantage of my innocence. I don't know what else to say other than I need time away from you to heal and understand. You used me to sate your lusts, Leonard, and though you frightened me with your aggressiveness, I wouldn't have been so surprised if you would have been honest with me about your—needs. Then maybe I could have been more prepared or something." Miranda's voice rose from her anger.

Lord Hammil instantly felt guilty again for what he had done. When Miranda was about to speak again, he raised his hand for her to stop her ranting, hearing enough. He was well aware that he had made a mistake and was tired of being reminded of it. When he saw her turn her head away from him and raise her hand in a dramatic fashion to her chest, he gave her a perplexed look and turned around, heading for the longboat. Stevens was just one of the men taking Lord Hammil aboard. Davy walked over by him and waved for him to approach. Stevens walked over to Davy, his eyes following Lord Hammil into the boat.

"Aye?" said Stevens quietly. Davy reached out his hand for Stevens to take. When he took it, he could feel a piece of parchment slide onto his palm.

"Good luck on your journey, Stevens. Please give your captain my regards." Davy lowered his eyes to their hands and raised them back up to meet the first mate's. Stevens nodded his head.

"Thank you, Davy. I will see that he gets your good wishes." Davy smiled happily as Stevens walked back over to the longboat sliding the piece of parchment into his pocket, unnoticed by anyone. Miranda and Davy both watched as the longboat reached the side of *The Captain's Avenger*. Soon the men were aboard and were watching the back of the ship as it sailed away.

CHAPTER 9

The captain of *The Captain's Avenger* wasn't able to rest until well into the night. The crew was cleaning and scrubbing the deck of the ship keeping busy. The wind had picked up and the sails were full, the ship's pace picking up considerably. The day had been beautiful and they were able to sail smoothly. When night fell, the temperature dropped slightly, but nobody seemed to mind. Locand was going over a map in his cabin, plotting coordinates to Port Royal when he heard a knock on his door. He raised his eyes from the map, focusing them on the door as he spoke his command to enter. He wasn't surprised as Stevens walked into the room, closing the door behind him.

"Everything is running smoothly, Cap'n. If the weather stays clear we should make it to Port Royal within a week or so. Also, Lord Hammil has retired." Locand looked back down at the map and drew a line marking their course.

"If that is all then return to your duties." Stevens remained standing where he was, his hands at his sides. Locand's eyes raised back to meet his. "Is there more you would like to discuss?" Stevens placed his hand into his pocket and removed the folded parchment that Davy had given to him.

"Davy gave this to me on the beach. He wanted me to give you his regards. I assumed he wanted me to give you this." He stepped closer to Locand, who met him halfway, and placed the parchment into his hand. Locand looked over the parchment curiously. He then walked over to a chair and sat into it, not sure what he was going to read. He glanced at Stevens one more time before unfolding the piece of parchment and reading the contents.

Locand,

There is much I should tell you but first there are some things I think you should know. First, Lord Hammil has made unwanted advances upon Miranda of the personal nature. In short, he almost forced himself upon her. She did not want me to tell you, for she felt that you would not approve of what he had done. Why she thought this news would bother you is something I wish to discuss further on a later date, but if you care for her, like I think you do, then you should know the truth. She does not love him and is only marrying him because she feels that it would please her father, but it will not. In fact, marrying him would bring us all down, though she had not realized it until after she had agreed to marry him. Who her father is, you will eventually find out, and when you do, you will be quite surprised. You might be the one who can save her from Lord Hammil and what he has planned for her. If I am wrong in my assumptions and you care not for her, then disregard what I have said, for it will not matter to you.

Second, you might wish to keep an eye on Lord Hammil. He has made us believe he is a weak man, but I feel strongly that he has been deceiving us. I wish I could tell you the man he is after, but I think it would be better for us all if you found out for yourself. You will find the information very interesting, as well as beneficial to you. I am sorry that I cannot tell you more, but right now it is for the better that we keep it from you. You will know why if you dig deep enough. Use any means necessary to find out the truth, your life may depend on it. Be wary, my friend, Lord Hammil cannot be trusted. I fear for your safe return.

Regards,
Davy

Locand placed the letter in his lap and brought his hand to rub his chin in thought. Stevens looked at him questioningly but Locand offered no information to the content of the letter. Then he said, "Keep an eye on Lord Hammil, Stevens. He cannot be trusted. Once in Port Royal, we will find ways to pull information from him. He has not told me anything other than that we are to take him there. I have asked him several times who we are looking for, but he will not say. I don't like waiting in ignorance while he runs the show. Are we clear?"

"Aye, Cap'n! I will keep an eye on him. I assume Davy gave us a warning?" Locand glanced back at the letter, then at his first mate again.

"He did indeed, and a warning from Davy means we should be careful. We will talk of this more when we arrive in Port Royal." Stevens nodded his head in response and left the room. Locand remained in his chair, his thoughts turning to Miranda. He had decided to go to the ship with his men once Lord Hammil had told him and Davy that he had wanted to be alone with her. It took all of his strength not to refuse and to remain by her side, but he knew that it wouldn't have been wise for him to do so.

To let Lord Hammil know of his feelings toward Miranda could be used against them. He didn't want to harm her in any way, and yet he wanted nothing more than to hold her in his arms and feel her lips pressed against his once more. Even now his loins ached from the thought of her. When they had argued he was angry at her for deceiving him, but now he knew the truth. Well, at least part of it. There were still so many questions needing to be answered, starting with who her father was. If he only knew that, he could end all the mystery right now. But she refused to tell him. Even Davy refused to tell him who her father was, which meant only one thing—he knew him.

Locand rubbed his chin. He knew many men who had daughters. Many men who he had sailed with, but who was her father? The question puzzled him, and yet the more he thought about it, the more he was unsure of who it could be. It was not obvious to him, and yet he knew it should be. Well, he would find out soon enough. Locand raised his hands to his face and rubbed his eyes. It then occurred to him that the reason why Davy could not tell him of who Lord Hammil was after was because the man was connected to her father. Or, maybe it was her father? There were so many possibilities and yet every one of them could have been the right answer. The topic was getting frustrating, but the good news was that Miranda did not have to marry Lord Hammil. With the warning he had just received from Davy, he was starting to think there was a change in the wind.

If he played his cards right, Miranda would be his woman instead of Lord Hammil's, and the thought of that brought a smile to his lips. He was indeed angry with what Davy had said about Lord Hammil's ill planned advances toward Miranda. The thought of the man forcing himself upon her or hurting her in any way disturbed him. However, he remained calm, the plan he was forming in his head would be his revenge against him. Locand couldn't wait to put it into motion.

Miranda was lying on the bed in her bedchamber at Lord Hammil's estate. Her thoughts were focused on the handsome captain who wouldn't leave her mind. Dawn was approaching, and she had awoken early in a sweat. She had a nightmare about Locand that frightened her. The dream was set in Port Royal. The governor had him locked in chains, his feet bound with rope. He had been tortured and was about to be hanged for once being a pirate and a traitor. The governor had tried to make a deal with him to set him free, but only if he would tell them where she was. He had refused, and in so doing, sentenced himself to death. She had dreamt she was standing in front of him watching. It was then she had yelled to save him.

Miranda sat up in her bed screaming and it was at that moment when she realized it was all a dream. Tears were running down her face, and her heart was beating so fast she could hear it in her ears. She was filled with relief when her eyes scanned the room, and all she saw were the white sterile walls and the curtains blowing in the morning breeze in front of the window. Miranda lay back down within her sheets, pulling them up to her neck, staring out the window hoping the sight of the lush green bushes and trees would calm her. The sound of birds waking up talking to each other was comforting to Miranda. It was then Davy had entered in a rush, his sword drawn.

"Are you safe, Miranda?" As he asked the question his eyes scanned the room for intruders. When Davy heard her scream he immediately threw on his breeches, and grabbed his sword to protect her. He had run across the hallway throwing the door open, hoping to surprise anyone who might be inside. The sound was deafening, and yet Miranda wasn't surprised by the action and remained still, her gaze focusing on the horizon.

"I'm fine, Davy, no one's in here but me. I had a nightmare again, but this time it wasn't about Father, it was of Locand. For as much as I love to come to the Caribbean, I always have restless nights. Why?"

Davy lowered his sword and set it down before sitting on Miranda's bed. He placed his hand on her arm and rubbed it gently back and forth. Miranda was turned to her side, her back toward him as she snuggled her pillow closer to her face.

"Your nightmares on the ship are because you are afraid for your father. It is understandable, for you fear for his safety. But why you dream of Locand is hard for me to say. Maybe you can tell me?" Davy's gentle words calmed Miranda, yet his question disturbed her. She rolled onto her back, Davy's hand moving to touch the bed on the other side of her stomach.

"I know not why I dream of him, but I do fear for his safety, for my dream was about him being tortured and hung in Port Royal by the governor." Davy looked deeply into Miranda's eyes as he thought over her answer.

"How many times have you been alone with him, Miranda?" His voice was not angry, but curious.

"Only a few times. Mostly it was when he wished to yell at me for behaving inappropriately. He would tell me his thoughts and give me counsel." Miranda looked away from Davy, hoping he wouldn't see her feelings for him in her eyes. Davy ran his fingers through her hair and caressed her cheek.

"Oh, Miry, you care for him, don't you?" When she didn't answer him, he continued, "Locand is an attractive man. He's brave, courageous and strong. I do not fault you for finding him desirable, especially when you compare him to Lord Hammil, who lacks those qualities for which I can tell attract you to Locand. But, Miry, there are some things you should know about him. You see—" Before Davy could finish what he was saying Miranda sat up interrupting him.

"I know he's a friend of Father's. I read his journal and he spoke of him. The last night on the ship I confronted him about it, not sure if he knew who I was or not. I wanted to know if he would use me to find him like I know Lord Hammil would if he knew of my true identity." Davy was surprised by Miranda's knowledge of Locand's and Stratton's friendship.

"What did he say?"

"He spoke highly of him to me, and told me of his loyalties. I felt foolish for assuming he would hurt Father, but I had to be sure. He doesn't know I am his daughter, and I didn't tell him. Though, he was curious of why I was so concerned about his loyalties." Davy glanced at the rising horizon, admiring its beauty before turning his gaze back to Miranda.

"He's loyal, Miranda. I've known him for years." Miranda's surprised eyes flew to Davy's.

"Why did you not tell me that you were mates? I would have been kinder to him, well, at least more respectful." Davy cocked his head to the side giving Miranda a smirk.

"You should have behaved better anyway. You know the rules of a ship, for your father taught them to you when you were young, and yet you were acting like a spoiled rotten brat. I let Locand deal with you in the way he felt was right. I thought he could make you see reason. If you were not twenty years old I would throw you over my knee and paddle that behind of yours. Be more respectful," he mocked. "You were lucky your father wasn't there, he would have been ashamed at his only child's behavior."

Davy started shaking his head as Miranda turned her head toward the window, her knees brought to her chest. A single tear ran freely down one of her cheeks. She knew her behavior of late had been atrocious, even the last night on the ship when Locand had kissed her. Wasn't she the one to provoke his reaction to her touches? He had asked her not to and yet she persisted, causing him to ravish her mouth and body with his hands and lips.

"What I want to know, Miranda, is why all of a sudden you care for Captain Riveri, especially when you have behaved so disrespectfully to him? As far as I was concerned, you two were at war with no end in sight." Davy's eyes bore into Miranda, but she kept her head turned toward the horizon, the colors of orange, yellow, and red mesmerizing her. She thought of telling him the truth, knowing that it would be the right thing to do, and yet she didn't want to see the look in Davy's eyes when she did.

"The last night aboard ship, I talked to Locand about Father in his cabin early in the morning. I woke him from his slumber. He opened the door half-naked and I found him to be incredibly attractive. Just like I told you, we talked about Father and his loyalties, but afterward," Miranda turned her face toward Davy's, taking a deep breath to give her strength. "Afterward, I caressed his bare chest and arms. I could not help myself. He asked me a question I didn't wish to answer, so I changed his mind by tempting him." Davy's eyes grew wide with surprise.

"What do you mean by tempt? What did you do?" Davy wasn't sure what he was going to hear so unconsciously held his breath.

"I tempted him to seduce me."

"You what?" yelled Davy, in shock at what he had just heard. "Why would you ever do something like that? Locand is the captain of *The Captain's Avenger* and holds much responsibility. He is one of my closest friends, as well as your father's, but he is still a man and will fall to temptation, especially if the woman who is offering her body up to him as a gift is as beautiful as you." Miranda lowered her head as Davy covered his face with his hands, shaking his head in despair.

"I don't think I'm ready for this, Miranda, I really don't. One day I knew you would become a woman and belong to someone else, but to me, you will always be the child I swore to protect." Davy paused before asking the question he knew he must ask. "Did he bed you?" Davy felt tortured for asking the question, hoping she would give him the answer he needed to hear.

"No! He found the will that I could not and stopped before we did anything like that. We only kissed and held each other, that was all, but it was enough to satisfy my curiosities about men."

"Is that the only time you have kissed him?" Davy remained still as he watched Miranda shake her head from side to side as if she were thinking of what to say.

"No! We had spent some time together before Lord Hammil left yesterday morning." Miranda's words flew out in a rush, and she glanced at Davy as she waited for his disapproving reply. Davy stood up and paced the room, his hands rubbing his stubbly cheeks and chin as he looked to the ceiling for guidance. After several laps from one side of the room to the other, he turned toward Miranda. Her innocent eyes made him feel guilty for yelling at her, but she needed to see reason.

"You are taking great risks by showing him affection, Miranda. You act as if Lord Hammil will never find out, and if he does, you will jeopardize everything Locand has worked so hard for."

"That is why we won't be doing it again. I care for him, Davy, and I don't want to see him hurt. Lord Hammil will never know." Davy smirked as he raised his hands.

"Do you see this gray hair on my head?" Davy grabbed a handful of hair to show her. Miranda nodded. "I truly believe that over the past twenty years, you are the one who has caused it. Your father has less gray hair than me. Would you like to know why? It is because he sees you less than I do, but it still comes from the same place." Miranda rolled her eyes dramatically. She had heard his words about her causing stress in his life many times over. She was not surprised to hear them now.

Miranda waved her hand at him and placed her cheek on her knees. Her arms wrapped around her legs tightly. "I do not jest, Miranda. You cause me so much grief. However, I love you too much to leave your side, so don't bother saying that sarcastic remark you always do. Now, I would like to forget about Locand for the moment and concentrate on your father. Lord Hammil said they should be gone for a few weeks, so that will give us time to find a ship that will take us to Eleuthera. He should be there in hiding—at least we hope. We will go into town today and see what we can find out. You need to don your men's clothing and find food and water to travel with us. We will need to pack light, but we need to also be prepared for the worse. Make sure you pack bandages, ointments—whatever you think we will need. God only knows what we will find."

Miranda nodded her head as she stood up from the bed. She moved swiftly to her trunk to remove a man's shirt and breeches she had made especially for her. "Make sure you bind your hair on top of your head and wear a hat. The group here can be dangerous, especially if they see a gentle woman on their grounds. Be careful today, Miry, get dressed and I will meet you downstairs in the foyer. We shall walk together. I want to make sure you are protected, but this time please, don't start any fights. To draw attention to ourselves could be fatal." Miranda turned around and put her pointer finger in the air.

"I will remind you that last time wasn't my fault. The disgusting son of a monkey kept putting his hands on me in that tavern in Spain. I had no choice but to make him see the error of his ways. I was wearing men's clothing for goodness sake."

"The man was so drunk, he didn't know the difference. I understand that, but you broke his nose, and in so doing, I had to fight off ten or so men so they wouldn't kill you." Davy placed his hands on his hips in irritation.

"I took out two of those men by the way. You didn't take them all on, so you can't take all of the credit." Miranda threw her hair over her shoulders before placing her hands on her hips.

"Oh, excuse me! You took out the man who was mauling you,

then punched another man who was blocking you from the table you were going to hide under." Davy placed his right hand upon his chest and batted his eyelashes alluringly, spouting, "My hero!" Miranda narrowed her eyes into slits as she challenged Davy. She was about to open her mouth to rebut his words, but he placed his hand over her mouth to stop her, a smile upon his lips.

"Save it for another time. You need to hurry and get dressed. I'm always waiting for you." He then removed his hand and walked out the open door. As he stood in the hallway he turned around to face Miranda, whose cheeks were now crimson from her frustrations. "I would like to also say—" But before Davy could finish his sentence Miranda rose from the bed and slammed the door in his face. He could hear her muttering words on the other side. Davy couldn't help but laugh as he returned to his bedchamber. He loved to antagonize Miranda, to see and hear her reaction to his bating was one of the best forms of entertainment. He could be heard laughing as he closed his door behind him. His thoughts focused on the days ahead.

By early afternoon, Davy and Miranda had found their way into town. Port Nassau was a beautiful town, but it was the people who roamed the streets that darkened it. Pirates! Many who wore flamboyant clothes that made them stand out. These men wore hats and pistols with swords slipped into the belts at their waists. Many had a woman on one arm and a bottle of rum in the other. The town was lawless. When a pistol shot several feet ahead of them, Davy and Miranda stopped. They watched as a man died in front of them. Miranda's arm flew to Davy's in fear. She was now wearing men's clothing with her hair tucked into her hat. Anyone who looked at her would never know she was a female.

"This town is full of vagrants, Davy."

"Yes, which is why I said that we needed to be careful. These islands are not governed, so there is no one who is going to stop these men. Port Royal has been taken over by the Royal Navy. Tortuga is being infiltrated next. These men have no other sanctuary, so they come to Nassau. Eventually, though, even this beautiful island will one day be governed and piracy will be a thing of the past down here. Men like the governor of Port Royal, and the queen, will make sure of it." Miranda stared at the sight before her in amazement and shook her head.

"What do we do?"

"Let's go into the local tavern. It will be just as unsavory as this, but we have no choice. We need to find a captain who will help us sail to Eleuthera, a captain who is a friend to your father. He has many men who are loyal to him. I only hope they can be found here." Miranda and Davy continued walking until they reached one of the taverns. The inside was filled with rowdy men who yelled at each other. Miranda was appalled at the sight. Davy would not let Miranda continue and made her stay by the door. He then made his way through the sea of men. Miranda glanced quickly about her while she placed a hand on the pistol at her waist. She had been in various types of taverns with Davy, but none as rambunctious as this, or with as many men with questionable character. Miranda tried to blend in with the wall and didn't move.

It took Davy a long time as he searched the tavern for friends. Several whores had offered themselves to him, which he passed on. Then a fight ensued in front of him, which he had to go around. Bottles flew around him smashing on the floor at his feet. It wasn't until he made it up the stairs that he spied a man who he recognized. As the man noticed him, he motioned for Davy to join him. Davy did so carefully. By the time he made it to the man's side, a mug of ale was quickly thrust into his hand. It wasn't until he drank half of its contents that the man before him spoke.

"Davy, ye old seadog, how have ye been?" The man gave him a full grin. His large looped earrings jingled as he took another drink from his mug.

"I have been well, Wallace. Staying in port long?" Wallace shook his head as he wiped his mouth on his sleeve.

"No, leaving today, actually, heading to the Pacific. You?"

"We are leaving today as well, or would like too. We are to meet someone on an island nearby, and then we are to sail north."

"North, eh?" said Wallace as he belched loudly. Davy quickly glanced around, then returned his gaze to the man in front of him. "Where is your master, Davy?" Davy knew who the man was referring to.

"He's evading the authorities," retorted Davy quietly. Wallace leaned closer to him, his long hair hanging loosely from underneath his black hat.

"He has good reason to hide. Soldiers have infiltrated Tortuga looking for him. Torturing and butchering as many pirates as they can for even a whisper of his whereabouts. Tortuga is no longer a safe haven for pirates like us to dwell. That is why we go to the Pacific. No army chasing after us." Wallace laughed loudly then regained his composure. "I hear," started Wallace as he kicked at a passing drunk who had clumsily bumped into him. The drunk turned around to retaliate but found a loaded pistol cocked and pointed right at the center of his head. The drunk's features changed several times before he backed away. When the drunk was gone, Wallace replaced the pistol into its proper place and returned his attention to Davy.

"I hear that Peter Hulms was taken prisoner. He has been taken to Port Royal for questioning. We both know what that means. It means that the words they are going to use will come from torturing devices instead of men. He's a dead man. Since Port Royal was rebuilt after the earthquake that ruined the town years ago, no pirate in their right mind would harbor there, so they now look for us at other locations. The earthquake was an excuse for them to remove piracy all together in the Caribbean." Davy closed his eyes and shook his head. "We both know that Peter was a part of your captain's crew. He will tell all where his captain's haven is. Mark my words, and if you meet up with him your life will be in danger, too."

"I'm willing to take that chance for my captain. He's a loyal and devoted friend." Wallace eyed Davy carefully and laughed loudly. He then smiled as he slapped Davy on the back.

"If half my crew were as devoted as you, I would never be caught either. Come! It sounds to me like you need a lift. The *Adventurer* is ready to sail. Fetch whoever you wish to come with us, and we will leave within the hour."

Davy thanked Wallace, finished his drink, and headed toward the front of the tavern to fetch Miranda. As he left, Wallace's first mate, Christopher, stepped up next to him.

"Do we dare go after Captain Ditarious the Brave ourselves?" Wallace took another gulp from his mug and shook his head.

"No! I know Captain Ditarious well. I respect him, even if he does have more treasure and wealth than I do. You forget that I was once his first mate. After Davy left the ship, I was the one who replaced him. Then, when we came upon the *Adventurer* and fought its crew, killing all who was aboard, he gave me the ship. And now I am captain." The first mate stared at his captain and then gazed around him.

"No, Christopher, what Davy's business is on this nearby island, is none of ours. We will aid him on his quest, then leave him be in peace. Not one member of my crew should know of Davy's true identity or who he is after. If for any reason Captain Ditarious's name is mentioned, I will know it was you who spoke it. But listen closely Christopher, for this is very important. When I hear of your treachery I will maroon you on the first island we come to, but I will not leave you with a pistol to do yourself in with and I will not push you over the side for you to swim to your safety. Oh no, that would be too kind of me. What I will do is cut off your hands and throw you into the sea eagerly waiting to watch the sharks eat you alive, ripping your flesh from limb to limb. If you survive, then you deserve the sanctuary of the island."

Wallace leaned forward and almost placed his cheek against Christopher's. "Captain Ditarious is my friend, and I will not be the scum who takes him down for their own greed. He's a vengeful man, but he is also loyal to his crew and loves them as if they were his own children. He showed me much respect and compassion the day that I became captain. I will not betray him. I would die first." Wallace paused, licking his lips. "I think we understand each other?"

"Aye, Captain, I understand and will say and do nothing. There is only a friend in need that we are helping, no more and no less. Davy and his companions will not be touched or harmed in any way." Wallace smiled approvingly and after finishing his drink and belching loudly, he pushed away from his first mate and headed for the door. Christopher took several deep breaths before following his captain, literally scared to his core. After him several other men, who were a part of the crew lounging around and drinking, followed their captain and first mate out of the tavern door.

The Captain's Avenger reached Port Royal in exactly a week's time. The weather had been warm and sunny, the wind blowing consistently in the sails. The crew let down the anchor and Lord Hammil fixed his appearance as the longboat was being lowered into the water. He wore a brown feathered hat with a matching waistcoat and breeches. Locand felt the man could have been a peacock preening itself to look more beautiful. He shook his head slightly, thinking that no matter what the man did, it would still not improve his appearance by much.

Lord Hammil turned toward Locand, his eyes filled with his joy upon arriving. "Your men, Captain, can relax for the next two or three days in port. I am to stay with the governor and will not need your assistance till then, but do stay close in case I need you for something." Locand nodded his head in reply.

"*The Captain's Avenger* will be ready to sail at any time, Lord Hammil. I am at your service." Lord Hammil placed his hand on Locand's shoulder and patted it, then walked over to the starboard rail and climbed down the steps into the awaiting longboat. Stevens walked up quietly next to Locand and stood beside him.

"He will still not tell me his plans while in Port Royal." Locand turned toward Stevens, his arms folded in front of his chest. "With that being the case, we need to find out for ourselves. He's to stay at the governor's mansion. Well, that is fortunate for us. Have a man--preferably Tom--go and find Carly. We need her to find a way to get the information we require. She has feelings for Tom, and he can convince her with ease to do our bidding. She is a maid in the governor's household and owes me a favor. I aim to collect."

"What would you have her do?" asked Stevens curiously.

"What she always does— eavesdrop." Stevens' smile widened as he stared at Locand.

"That's wise, Captain, but I'm sure Lord Hammil will not confess all of his plans to the governor, especially in front of servants."

"You might have a point there. That is why two spies are better than one and from what I hear, he is in the mood for female companionship. Let's offer him a female who will satisfy his lusts and satisfy our need for information. Find me Rose. Once she sees you, she will come running to me. Rose could torture a man with the supple curves of her body. We might need her sexual prowess to get Lord Hammil to confess to her his plans. We cannot leave this port until we know the truth in its entirety. Savvy?"

"Aye, Cap'n, I understand completely," replied Stevens.

"Good, now tell the men they are to go ashore. We must let Lord Hammil see that I am willing to do his bidding. If he thinks *The Captain's Avenger* is unmanned, then he might put his plans into motion, whatever they may be. Tell the men to enjoy themselves, but keep a handful here just in case of trouble."

"Cap'n? What if Lord Hammil is truly the fool we feel he is and is planning nothing?" Locand gazed back out toward the town of Port Royal.

"The man is not a fool, this I know. There has always been something about him I do not like. He's up to something. I would bet my ship on it. We need to find out what. Let the men know this ship will not be left unattended for any reason, those are my orders. Have them keep their eyes focused, awaiting danger. Always expect the unexpected. You will be in charge of reloading the ship with supplies, take some men with you and see that it gets taken care of."

"Aye, sir!" said Stevens as he left Locand to do his bidding. Locand watched as the longboat made it to the dock and Lord Hammil stepped out. He could tell that he had fixed his hat before walking to the governor's carriage that awaited him and stepped inside. His eyes didn't stray from the carriage until the trees and the buildings blocked his vision as it drove past them. Locand made his way down the stairs from the quarterdeck and heard Stevens address the men before he walked to his cabin to enjoy his solitude. He had to change his clothes and get ready for his encounter with Rose, but no matter how hard he tried to focus on other things, he could not get Miranda out of his mind. Toward the end of the day, he wished she were with him. Yes, she would have been an enjoyable companion.

CHAPTER 10

In was nightfall by the time Rose found Locand waiting for her in the tavern known as *The Black Flag* or *La Bandera Negra*, as the visiting patrons of the sea called it. He was waiting at a table in the corner alone, his keen eyes surveying the room for enemies. Rose had entered into the tavern, her dress dirty and torn from wear. Her cream undershirt hung from her shoulders, and her breasts nearly fell from the loosely restrained fabric. Her hair was as red as fire, and her eyes were the color of polished emeralds. Her skin was pale with freckles sprayed unevenly upon her cheeks. Her eye's searched longingly for the sight of Locand, but it was hard to find him through the crowd of men drinking and fighting for her attention.

When she did finally catch a glimpse of the handsome man, she made a path right toward him. Her short trip did not leave her untouched. Various men called out to her and tried to stroke her. A few were able to make contact as they slapped her behind in invitation. Her mind, however, was focused on the man her eyes were now set upon. The time she spent with him alone could pay her rent for months, he was worth every bit of her time, and she always made sure he was satisfied.

When Rose made it through the unsavory crowd to stand in front of Locand, he rose quickly from his seat and placed his finger in front of his lips in a show of silence. She nodded her head in understanding and followed him as he led her up the stairs to the second floor. He turned left and walked to the room at the end of the hallway. He quickly looked around him, surveying the stairs and the hallway where he saw lingering men who pressed the many strumpets against the rails and walls of the tavern, trying to get a kiss or more. Upon seeing no one focusing their attentions on them, he opened the door. After finding that the room was empty, he motioned for Rose to enter. He closed the door behind them and locked it, not wanting to be disturbed for any reason.

As soon as he turned around, Rose threw herself against him, her lips brazenly touching his as his back pressed against the door. Her arms moved instantly around his neck as she rubbed her body against his in a seductive manner. Locand could not resist but to kiss her in return. He held her close to him briefly before he moved his hands to her arms and removed them. As their lips parted, he could see the lust in her eyes. She tried to unbutton his shirt, but Locand held her hands in his to stop her.

"If this is not what you want, my love, then what do you want from me?" Rose pressed her pouty lips together as she stepped away from him.

"Your wiles are tempting, my sweet red rose, but not for me, not this time. I need you to do something for me." Locand moved away from the door and passed Rose, who eyed him saucily.

"What makes you think I will do something for you? I have not seen you in months." Rose turned toward Locand as he stopped by a chair staring at her. She saw him smoothly reach into the pocket of his breeches and pull out a pouch. He shook it at her temptingly, the sound of coins filling the air. Locand saw Rose's eyes fill with greed, a catlike smile upon her lips. She slowly stepped closer to him, her small hands reaching for the pouch. She was visibly disappointed, however, when Locand removed it from her reach.

"You didn't say you would do the job yet," Locand said, placing the pouch back into his pocket.

"Well, you didn't say what I needed to do. I'm desperate for the money, so I will do almost anything you request of me. What's the job?"

"Have a seat and rest your tired feet. I will explain to you exactly what I need you to do for me." Rose sauntered her way passed Locand to sit in the chair he offered, her face raising to stare into his.

"There's a man who is staying with the governor who goes by the name of Lord Hammil. He is thin and lanky with blonde hair and light eyes. He has some information I am interested in. He is here on business, but I do not know what kind of business. I need you to find out for me, in any way possible."

"In any way?" asked Rose as she licked her lips.

"In any way!" enforced Locand with a smile upon his lips. "The help of your brother would be most appreciated. I need you to have

Adam follow Lord Hammil everywhere he goes while he's in Port Royal. I need to know where he's going and where he has been."

"What will he get out of this?" asked Rose, her expression turning serious. Adam was a boy of only twelve, their parents were dead and she had a hard time supporting herself and could not take care of him the way that she would like to, but the love she had for him would never die. She wanted what was best for him. Rose cared not what she did to herself as long as Adam did not have to suffer from their poverty.

"His reward will be between me and him. Now, you need to clean yourself and bathe. I have purchased a dress for you to wear to lure Lord Hammil into your arms. He will not bed a whore, but he will bed a lady of decent breeding. Make him think you are more than what you appear to be. I am making plans for you to find yourself in his bedchamber at the governor's mansion. Make him bed you. I hear he's in need of a woman. You have the skill to get what I need from him. When you have accomplished what I ask and report to me, then you will be richly rewarded." Rose stood from her chair and ran her fingers up Locand's hard muscular thighs till they reached the bulge in his breeches.

"I can see you want me, Locand. Why not taste my body? I remember how to pleasure you." Rose was about to place her hand inside of Locand's breeches to grasp his manhood, when he stopped her.

"I will admit that I haven't bedded a woman in months and you are tempting, but there is another woman I wish to bed. She consumes my thoughts regularly, but for the moment she is out of my reach."

"All the more reason to let me satisfy your lusts, my Captain." Rose raised his shirt and dove her hands underneath to feel his hard, muscular, chest and back. Locand removed her hands roughly from him, kissing her quickly on the cheek.

"No, my red Rose, it is her I want and it will be her that will sate my lusts. It will be the only way for me to rid her from my thoughts. Though, I will not let you ease my lusts this day, if you do what I ask, I may let you another." The promise was enough for Rose, and she stepped away from him. Locand finished explaining to her the various steps she needed to follow in order to trick Lord Hammil, then he asked her to make sure to have Adam follow him come dawn. He told her that he would be waiting for their results aboard *The Captain's Avenger*. As Rose left the room with half the coins in her hand, Locand watched her go, his thoughts consumed in what truth he would find by the following evening.

It had taken Miranda and Davy several days to reach the glistening pink and white sands of Eleuthera. Eleuthera was a calm and peaceful island. It was also an island of many contradictions. The island stretched approximately a hundred and ten miles long, and in some areas, was no more than a mile wide. In certain areas surrounding the island there were reefs that were dangerous to all heavy ships that passed over them. There were cliffs and boulders that had protected a part of the island for years, preventing many intruders from using that side of the island to invade the peaceful occupants. Then there were the beaches that stretched for miles and miles along the shore. Now, as they stood on the warm beach with everything they owned with them, Miranda started to cry. It had been years since she had returned home. She had forgotten how beautiful the island was with all of its natural beauty. Davy offered her a handkerchief, but she refused to take it telling him she would be fine.

Once Miranda finally composed herself, she glanced quickly back at the ship that had aided them on their quest and waved to them in farewell. The ship was already sailing away from them, the longboat that had taken them to the island already being raised from the water and back into its rightful place. The sand felt warm and sugary beneath her feet as she walked through it until she reached firmer ground. They walked for what seemed like miles down a long dusty road until they reached a safe place to enter into the woods, their brows covered with sweat, their eyes falling upon one of the many pineapple plantations that existed on the calm and tranquil island. Beyond the trees on the side of a mountain overlooking a large pineapple plantation was Miranda's home where she had lived since birth. She had lived in many places, but none she would call home. Eleuthera was the only home she knew.

As the trees cleared, she saw her long missed home. Its pristine white walls with many windows overlooked the plantation. It was only one story high with many rooms and paintings inside. The greenery from the surrounding trees and plants covered most of the house. Dark green vines climbed the walls and littered it with colorful red and pink flowers, with scents intoxicating to smell. It lured Miranda and Davy into the beauty of the island. They quickly dropped their trunks and left them on the pathway, knowing that no one would bother them, and continued along their way. Soon, Miranda's excitement took hold and she moved ahead of Davy and started to run. As Miranda ran down the stone pathway leading to the door she quickly stopped and glanced to the left. There was a large stone sitting there next to the pathway. It was her mother's grave. Miranda immediately fell to her knees and started to cry, almost forgetting that her mother's grave was there. She then said a quick prayer for forgiveness and then said another for her mother.

When she opened her eyes, she made a motion to stand but then suddenly stopped. As she stared at the grave, she could tell that the spot had been maintained. The undergrowth of the plant life surrounding it had been cut away and the ground smoothed. There was also a single flower lying upon it that was now wilted. The sight gave her hope. The only person who constantly cared for her mother's grave was her father. He had always placed flowers on her grave, and Miranda often found him sitting by it and talking to it as if he were having a conversation with her mother. She had done that a few times herself.

Miranda quickly rose and moved hastily to the door, hoping she would find her father inside drinking some rum and glancing over maps looking for new destinations to conquer. When Miranda placed her hand upon the handle and turned it she found it unlocked. Before she could enter, Davy grabbed her by the arm to stop her. He then moved in front of her, his sword drawn in case of trouble to protect her.

Miranda quickly withdrew a dagger from her waist, not sure of what to expect, her eyes quickly scanning the interior as she followed Davy inside. The furniture and tables were exactly as she remembered them being placed as they stepped into the short entranceway leading into the spacious living room. The house was created to have a large room in the center with the bedrooms, kitchen and library surrounding it. The furniture was not covered with bright expensive upholstery but tasteful and delicate, just like her mother had wanted it to be long ago.

Her father had not changed a thing since she was last there, that fact made her smile. Stratton was a creature of habit, once he had things a certain way he liked, he never changed it. His philosophy was incorporated into everything in his life, whether it was furniture or food that he ate. He was predictable, rarely changing his habits. Miranda often told her father that he should change the way he did things, to spice things up a bit if you will, but he refused. Once in a while he would indulge her, but it was rare. The only thing that he did do spontaneously was pirating, which would explain why he never got caught.

They quickly searched all the rooms, but found nothing, not even a trace that Stratton was living there at all. Miranda tapped Davy on the shoulder and pointed to the library door, which was ajar. They entered into the room cautiously, but upon seeing no one, put away their weapons. Davy ran his fingers through his hair in frustration. *Where could he be*? he quietly asked himself. Miranda looked around the room filled with disappointment. She was positive her father would have been there hiding. Her brown eyes then fell upon a brightly colored parrot in a cage in the corner of the room. A smile shined upon her lips.

The parrot had a blue head with bright red wings and belly. It stood on its perch staring at her as if it tried to remember who she was. She hastily ran to it and opened the cage. The parrot was a gift from her father he had given to her in England. Knowing that he would die from the cold, she asked her father to take him home. Miranda reached in her hand, and the parrot stepped onto her outstretched finger.

"Oh, Max," she said to the parrot. "I've missed you so much. Where is Father?" The parrot rubbed its neck against Miranda as she snuggled with him. She then ran her fingers down Max's neck until he shook his head at her in pleasure.

"Cannot say, cannot say," replied the parrot. "What's the password?" he cawed.

"Password?" Miranda said aloud. She then thought for a moment and replied, "Oh I remember now—Captain Ditarious." Once Miranda said the words, the parrot replied loudly. "He's in the caves, he's in the caves." Miranda kissed the bird and placed him back into its cage. Once she made sure the cage door was locked, she turned to Davy.

"He's in the caves, Davy. Quick, behind the bookshelves, remember? Pull the dark red book that says *Freedom* on it. It will open the door to the secret passageway." Davy rushed over to the shelves and scanned them for the book. Once he saw a book with the bright gold words of *Freedom* on the spine, he pulled it partially out. The pair stood back as they heard an unlocking mechanism coming from the bookshelves. Then, in a sudden burst, the door opened slightly, its seal broken. Davy rushed forth and placed his hand upon the partially opened door and pulled it toward him.

Miranda was about to pass Davy to hurry down the corridor but was stopped by several sharp swords pointing at them. Davy put his arm in front of Miranda and pushed her behind him. They started backing up as the men moved toward them threateningly. Miranda searched from one face to the other but did not recognize any of the men she saw before her. The thought that these scavengers were looking for her father and found him in the caves, scared her immensely. The men had dirt on their faces and clothes, and the smell that emanated from them caused Miranda to look at them with disgust. There were at least five men coming from the tunnel to spill into the room before them with swords drawn.

"Who are you men?" asked Miranda while she stood behind Davy for protection. One of the men standing in front eyed her suspiciously as he replied, "And who might you be lass?" The man smiled at her showing his dark teeth with one gold shiny tooth in front. Miranda cocked her head to one side as she wrinkled her nose in distaste.

"This is my home and you are trespassing. I demand that you leave at once." The men burst into laughter at Miranda's words.

"Your home? That's not what I heard, missy," replied the man with the gold tooth.

"And what have you heard vagrant? What have you come here for?" The man moved threateningly toward them, his sword tip pointed only inches from Davy's throat. The man stared at Davy.

"You need to keep your woman's mouth shut mate, or we will make sure she suffers the consequences." Davy moved more in front of Miranda to protect her while the man with the gold tooth loomed closer and closer. One of the other men moved quietly to the other side of Davy and grabbed Miranda by the arm pulling her toward him.

A gasp of surprise left Miranda's lips as she felt someone grip her arm painfully. The man who had a hold of her was tall and lean. His hair was short and dirty, and his face was covered with dark smudges. His clothes were torn and the sword he held in his hand was now pointed at her. The man moved his grip from her arm to take a handful of her hair. He then pointed the sword at her neck, forcing her head back to expose the smooth surface. He brought his nose close to her hair to smell its scent. He closed his eyes as the scent of Jasmine filled his nostrils. Suddenly, the man let Miranda go and he pushed her away from him. Miranda immediately moved to stand behind Davy again for protection.

"What's wrong with you?" asked the man with the gold tooth.

"I've smelled that scent before," answered the man.

"What are you talking about?" the man with the gold tooth asked as he glared at his cohort, his sword still inches from Davy's throat as he tried to smell the air.

"I have smelled the scent of Jasmine that lingers in this girl's hair before. It was a gift wasn't it, the fragrance you wear?" Miranda nodded her head, her eyes narrowing into slits of confusion. "What is your name, lass?"

"Her name is Miranda, Bones, my daughter. Leave them alone or you will have to deal with me and in so doing die a horrible death." Everyone in the room looked toward the secret passageway. Their eyes focused on the man who had spoken.

"Father?" asked Miranda as she saw the man step from the shadow, a smile upon his lips. Stratton held out his arms as Miranda ran into them, the pair embracing each other tightly.

"Oh, my daughter, how beautiful you look." Tears streamed down Miranda's cheeks as Stratton lowered her to the ground and ran his fingers through her soft mane. "It has been a long time, I know, but I have good reason for staying away for as long as I have." Stratton's eyes then fell upon Davy, who pushed the man in front of him aside so he could walk closer to Stratton. The men embraced each other heartily, their smiles expressing how much they had missed one another.

"It has been too long my friend. Your daughter and I have been worried about you. Much has happened we need to discuss."

"I agree, Davy, much has happened." Stratton patted Davy on the shoulder as he held his arm out for his daughter to take.

"Father, who are these men? I don't recognize any of them. Where is your regular crew?" Stratton looked at the faces of the five men who stood before him. Their surprise at finding out that their beloved captain had a daughter was evident upon their faces, and yet their loyalty to him had also shown as they put their swords away and had nodded their heads to him in obedience and respect. Stratton focused his attention back to his daughter who was looking up at him.

"Good question, my love. All will be explained later, I promise. For now let me just spend time with you. I have missed the sight of you so much." Miranda leaned up to kiss her father's cheek and then embraced him tightly as they left the room with Davy by their sides. The men were following quietly behind, their swords put away for the moment, their minds confused with what had just happened.

CHAPTER 11

Lord Hammil had woken early the next morning and, with the governor in tow, left in a carriage to go to the fort. His first task was to talk with the man the governor had said was once a part of Captain Ditarious's crew. The carriage ride was a short one, it seemed, but only because Lord Hammil's thoughts were of Miranda. He was starting to miss her presence, and yet he found himself staring at a beautiful lady walking along the dirty streets. Her dress was clean and neat, her hair partly covered and tucked underneath a hat to shade herself from the sun. Lord Hammil watched the soft swaying of her hips and found himself licking his lips, his body filling with desire for her. He noticed the woman waving at him as the carriage had driven past; he did not return the wave, but was determined to find the woman again before he left Port Royal. Unbeknownst to him, the lady was Rose.

It was at that particular moment when Adam had grabbed on to the back of the carriage, ready to fulfill his part of the bargain for Locand. Rose glanced one more time at the carriage, her heart racing at the sight of her only brother hanging on the back for dear life. She shook her head and stepped into a building, she then removed her hat and shook out her hair. The dress Locand had given her was beautiful. It had long white lacy sleeves and a thinning waist. Rose hoped he would let her keep it when her job was finished. She never had a dress so delicate before. She then looked around and found Stevens leaning up against the wall waiting for her. *Well,* Rose said to herself, *the bait is set, now all I have to do is reel it in*. Stevens was there to tell her exactly what she needed to do to accomplish that task. Rose puffed out her chest in confidence and walked toward Stevens.

The carriage came to a stop just inside of the fort. The governor waited patiently inside of the carriage while a guard led Lord Hammil through the first floor of the fort, then down some stairs to the cells. They walked past two empty cells until they reached the third. A man, who was lying on a hard bench inside, looked up when he heard the unlocking of his cell. Chains were locked around his wrists and ankles to render him harmless. Lord Hammil walked into the cell arrogantly and stared at the man. He could tell the man in front of him had been tortured. The rips on the back of his shirt showed he had been whipped several times. Lord Hammil turned toward the guard.

"What's this man's name?"

"Peter, milord," replied the guard. Lord Hammil turned toward Peter. Peter was a man in his middle twenties. He was thin with long, dirty brown hair that hung loosely in front of his face. He was merely skin and bones, yet he survived all of the beatings he had been given, showing his strong will. The governor was insistent in finding Captain Ditarious and had used any means necessary to get the answers he sought. It would have been better if the man had given up and died, and yet he refused. The more Lord Hammil stared at the man who was sitting at his feet, the more he saw a fire still in him.

When Peter's blue eyes rose to look at Lord Hammil's, a smile came upon his face. His youthful features showed his loyalty. While there was hope still left in him, Peter would never tell where his captain was hiding.

"I've heard you were a crew member aboard the *Fighting Spur* years ago." Peter looked up at Lord Hammil but did not reply. "You should have no loyalties for your captain here. You are the one who is going to die for your silence while your captain sails freely away to train another crew member to replace you." The man looked down at the ground, then back up at Lord Hammil. "Does that not bother you, Peter?" Peter gazed up at Lord Hammil but still did not reply. "Will you say nothing to save yourself?" Peter returned his gaze back to the floor and laughed.

"Save me?" asked Peter. "No one can save me. In fact, there will be no one to save you if you find him."

"Well, rest assured that I will find him, Peter. With or without your help, your captain is doomed." Lord Hammil's words brought much sorrow to Peter's countenance.

"Does that bother you, Peter, to hear that I am going to kill your captain?" Peter suddenly raised his face and smiled arrogantly.

"The one thing I know about Captain Ditarious is that he is not easily caught." Then Peter leaned forward, "I bid you farewell and good luck on your quest, because you will get no help here." Lord Hammil smiled politely, then suddenly dove at Peter and pulled a dagger from a sheath at his waist. Peter now lay on his back while Lord Hammil sat on his chest, gripping his right hand tightly.

"Do you feel inspired to tell me anything now?"

"Go to hell," spewed Peter as he spit into Lord Hammil's face. After wiping his face with his shirt sleeve, Lord Hammil took his dagger and grabbed Peter's little pinky finger. Peter's eyes grew wide as he wondered what the man on top of him was going to do.

"I am well practiced in the art of torture. Would you like to see?" Peter just stared at Lord Hammil without speaking. "I could cut off each finger one by one and you would not feel the pain. Though, when I get to your arm you might object a little." Peter tried to remove his hand as Lord Hammil took the dagger and slightly cut into his skin.

"Wait!" yelled Peter as he stared wildly up at Lord Hammil.

"Do you wish to say something?" Peter merely nodded his head as he felt Lord Hammil rise off him. "There, see, I knew you could be reasonable about this. Now, I can make sure you are set free for your troubles, Peter, if you talk to me. I will give you my word on the matter. Remember, there are no loyalties amongst thieves."

"How?" was all that Peter replied as he rubbed his finger.

"I do carry with me some power of the queen. What does your heart desire?"

"I want to be put back onto a ship so I can sail away from here. Can you do that?" asked Peter tentatively.

"I can, Peter! Your request is within my power to grant."

"How do I know you will not betray me?" Lord Hammil looked firmly into Peter's eyes.

"You don't! However, if I am satisfied with your answers, then we will talk more about your freedom."

"What do you wish to know?" asked Peter as he stood up from the ground, his clothes hanging loosely upon his thin frame.

"Where can I find Captain Ditarious?"

"He usually sails around Tortuga between trips. Have you looked there? I have not seen him in many months, so it is hard to tell where he is now." Lord Hammil rubbed his chin in thought.

"Does he have a home away from the ship? A safe haven, as you will?" Peter looked away from Lord Hammil's gaze as he pondered the question.

"He does, but I know not where it is. I've never been there." Peter smoothly lied of course, but his love and respect for Captain Ditarious made him do so.

"I've a hard time believing that, Peter," said Lord Hammil chidingly.

"Believe it, milord. In the past few years, Captain Ditarious has changed his crew at least a dozen times. He trusts no one, now more than ever. I was not with him when he sailed to his haven." Lord Hammil looked at Peter skeptically, then nodded his head.

"Do you know of his daughter then?" Peter grew quiet, his eyes averting away from Lord Hammil. "I hear her beauty is beyond compare. She holds a special place in his heart, doesn't she?" Peter still didn't answer. Lord Hammil smiled an evil smile. "I think she holds a place in several men's hearts—including mine." Peter's eyes rose to meet Lord Hammil's.

"No, you lie!" shouted Peter.

"Oh, yes, Peter. I know who she is and where she has been hidden away."

"You lie!" replied Peter again, his voice filling with anger.

"I assure you, your master's true identity and the identity of his daughter have been compromised. Miranda Mayne is quite safe and will soon become my wife." Peter sat back down on the cold, hard, ground and placed his hands upon his face. "Does she know where her father is?" Peter glanced back up at Lord Hammil, his face turning serious as he started to laugh.

"She would be the only one who would know, except for–" Peter didn't finish his sentence fearing he would reveal something he shouldn't.

"Except for his first mate?" Peter nodded his head slowly. "Yes, her faithful guardian. He's an impenetrable wall around her. Well, that will soon change." Lord Hammil ran his fingers through his hair as he continued his questioning. "There is a little item I am looking for. Maybe you can help me find it. Captain Ditarious has a crystal which he holds dear to his heart. I need this crystal." Peter started to laugh loudly. "What is so funny?" asked Lord Hammil, his countenance showing his anger.

"I have never seen him with a crystal, you are mistaken," replied Peter.

"I was assured he has it in his possession," said Lord Hammil.

"Not in his possession," answered Peter flippantly.

"Then whose?" Realizing what he had said, Peter's smile faded. It took only minutes for Lord Hammil to take a guess, a smile of happiness shining upon his lips.

"Miranda has the crystal, doesn't she? So, she is the key to it all?" Lord Hammil turned away from Peter, his thoughts focusing on Miranda. "That was something I did not know, Peter, nor was expecting. I thank you for your help." Lord Hammil was almost out of the cell when Peter grabbed his leg to stop him.

"What of your promise? We had a deal." Lord Hammil turned toward Peter and placed a hand upon his shoulder.

"You are absolutely right, Peter. I am going to keep my word. Here is your freedom." Lord Hammil removed the dagger from his waist and thrust it deep inside of Peter's chest. Peter's eyes grew wide as he breathed his last few breaths. "I have no more use for you. My goal now is Miranda Mayne and what she can do for me. As her husband I will have rights to everything, including the treasure." Peter shook his head one last time before he died.

Lord Hammil let go of Peter and let him fall to the ground yelling, "Guards! Take care of his body. He is of no further use to me."

"Yes, milord, right away," replied one of the guards. Lord Hammil leaned down and wiped off his dagger on Peter's shirt before placing it back into the sheath at his waist. He then walked past the guard and was about to go up the stairs when a voice called out to him. Lord Hammil quickly glanced back at Peter, but then the voice spoke again. The sound was coming from a cell two down from Peter's. When Lord Hammil moved to walk in that direction, the man stood up. He was just as malnourished as Peter, and his back had also been whipped for some sin. As Lord Hammil stood in front of the man, he slightly leaned forward.

"What do you want, vagrant?" asked Lord Hammil.

"Revenge— just as you." Lord Hammil smiled and was instantly filled with curiosity.

"And what can you do for me?"

"I can tell you where your Captain Ditarious dwells, for I have been there a few times. I used to sail with him, however, he stranded me on an island when I had tried to mutiny against him. The few men who supported me died by his hand, but me, he wished to punish in other ways. He's a cold hearted bastard."

"So, where is the location?" demanded Lord Hammil, who was quickly losing his patience and tired of the talk.

"First, I would like to be set free and forgiven for my sins." Lord Hammil gazed at the man with distrust.

"That would all depend on what kind of information you provide." The man, being most desperate, gave in. Not once thinking that Peter's fate could be his own if Lord Hammil liked or disliked his words.

"He is hiding on Eleuthera Island. He has a home there which he enters through the caves on the north side of the island." Lord Hammil smiled and told the guard to open the man's cell.

"For your information, you should be allowed to go free." The man hesitated when he saw his cell door open and watched Lord Hammil step aside to let him pass, his arm extending out and pointing to the stairs. The man took the opportunity given to him and hastily ran to the stairs, but not before Lord Hammil took out his dagger and threw it at him, the blade sinking into his back. The man yelled his surprise before falling to the floor dead. Lord Hammil laughed in satisfaction as he told the guard to take care of the stranger's dead body as well, his hand reaching for his dagger as he passed it. He then hurried up the stairs, passing a boy who was scrubbing the floors. Lord Hammil hurried to the entrance where the governor was waiting for him inside of the carriage. When he stepped inside, the governor asked him what he had found out. As the carriage started rolling away, Lord Hammil relayed the information, but only the parts that the governor needed to know.

Minutes later, Adam walked to the entrance of the fort, his eyes focusing on the leaving carriage. He left the fort, throwing his pail and brush to the side of the road. Used to having boys clean the fort often, Adam wasn't stopped or questioned by the guards. He smiled as he made his way toward the harbor to find Locand. He had heard every word Lord Hammil, Peter, and the stranger had said.

Rose had followed all of Locand's instructions, and now found herself waiting for Lord Hammil in his bedchamber at the governor's mansion. A maid, Carly, who also knew of Locand's plans, had let her in and promised her that Lord Hammil would be there by nightfall. She said that he had a routine where he would eat first then retire for the evening. The maid had handed her a robe to change into, and then patted her arm in solace. She left quickly, making sure she was not noticed by any of the other servants.

Now Rose stood alone, looking into a fire that was lit in the fireplace, and held the soft robe tightly in her arms. She had quietly changed out of her clothes and put the robe on. The soft fabric felt luxurious against her bare skin. She had placed her hair seductively on top of her head with a few escaping ringlets falling to her shoulders. Her heart was racing fast, and she knew not if she had the courage to go through with what she had to do. She was used to playing with men's affections to get what she wanted, to get what she needed. But this man was different than any of the others. He was powerful and all he had to do was snap his fingers, and she could be killed. Rose's hand flew quickly to her neck as if she imagined herself being hanged for all to see.

She then shook her head, as if ridding the evil thoughts from her mind, and walked in front of one of the windows in the room. The sun was now beginning to set, and the darkness of night took its place over them. Rose turned away from the window and was about to walk around the room when she heard someone turning the door knob. Preparing herself for Lord Hammil's arrival, Rose hopped quickly onto the bed and lay upon it seductively. She turned on her side, making sure a hint of thigh could be seen between the folds of the robe. She propped her right hand underneath her head to hold it up and waited nervously for Lord Hammil's entrance.

When Lord Hammil entered into the room, he didn't notice Rose lying upon his bed. It wasn't until he removed his waistcoat and started unbuttoning his shirt that he turned to face her. When his eyes fell upon Rose, he gasped in surprise. He placed his hand to his chest and stared at her.

"What are you doing in here?" Lord Hammil asked Rose angrily. After he had composed himself, he took the time to notice the scantily clad woman lying seductively upon his bed. He realized it was the same woman he had noticed earlier walking the streets on the way to the fort. He slowly moved closer to the bed, remembering how attractive he thought she was. Now, gazing upon her face up close, she was as beautiful and charming in appearance as he thought her to be.

"I was told you wished for the company of a woman by the

governor. He hand picked me himself." Rose slid smoothly from the bed to stand in front of Lord Hammil, her hands placed softly on his chest. "Was I misinformed?" Lord Hammil wasn't sure how to react to Rose's baiting, so kept his hands to his sides.

"I mentioned nothing to him about my desires for a woman," replied Lord Hammil, his voice not angry but curious as he stared at Rose.

"If there is some kind of mistake, I deeply apologize for any inconvenience I may have caused you. I only do as I am told." Rose slid her right fingers softly to Lord Hammil's neck and caressed it. His eyes moved to stare into hers. "When I was told that I would be able to spend time with you, I felt honored. You are so handsome and strong. I could tell right away you were a man to reckon with. However, if I am not wanted then I will go." Rose raked her fingers tenderly down Lord Hammil's chest before she turned and walked toward the door. A hint of a smile rose to her lips as Lord Hammil grabbed her by the arm to stop her from leaving.

"Forgive my rudeness, beautiful dove. I was merely surprised by your presence. Please, stay for a while and talk with me. I am very interested in finding out more about you. I saw you walking along the road this morning from my carriage. You attracted my attention. Please sit down." Lord Hammil pointed to a chair by the bed and watched as Rose swayed her hips side to side as she moved past him. Lord Hammil's shirt was partly unbuttoned but he forgot as he followed Rose and sat into a chair next to her. His eyes roamed over her face and body. He saw a slight opening in the front of her robe and caught a hint of her breast.

"What is your name?"

"My name is Rose."

"Well, Rose, you can call me Lord Hammil. How long have you lived on the island? I've never noticed you before," asked Lord Hammil curiously.

"I have lived here only a few years, milord. I work at one of the local shops." Lord Hammil smiled politely as he perused her appearance again.

"Would you care for something to drink?" Lord Hammil hastily moved to the decanters of brandy on a nearby table and poured himself and Rose a drink. Before Rose could reply, Lord Hammil already thrust it into her hand.

"Thank you, milord." For the next hour they spoke about many things and Rose complimented Lord Hammil on everything she could to get him to trust her and loosen his tongue. Whenever she noticed his glass becoming empty she would fill it. After awhile she could tell that he was partially drunk. The last drink she had given him was filled with a sedative to knock him out. She had to keep him entertained until it kicked in.

Lord Hammil was laughing and relaxing in his chair. His tongue loosened so much that he was telling her things he normally wouldn't have and set his glass on the floor by his chair. Rose smiled broadly as she asked Lord Hammil the questions she needed to.

"Milord, what is your business here in Port Royal? I have not seen you before and am curious how long you will be staying." Lord Hammil leaned forward in his chair, his hand reaching to take Rose's.

"I will only be staying for one more day, then I will be returning home. I had business here, but have finished it. Now I stay only for the scenery." Lord Hammil gazed up and down the length of Rose, his eyes rising back to meet her face.

"I am flattered you have an interest in me. You are quite charming and refined. That is a rarity here." Then Rose took a deep breath. "What ship did you sail in on? I have seen so many and wonder if I have heard of your ship before," asked Rose innocently.

"I sailed in on *The Captain's Avenger*. It is a nice size ship, light, and has a skilled crew. Have you heard of it?" Lord Hammil looked at Rose almost suspiciously but changed his glare when she smiled at him, licked her lips and shook her head.

"No, milord, I have never heard of *The Captain's Avenger* before. I must admit that I talk to very few men who come off of the ships. Who is its captain, I may have heard of the name?" Lord Hammil looked away from Rose briefly as if pondering what he was going to say.

"Can you keep a secret?" asked Lord Hammil squeezing Rose's hand.

"Of course, milord. In fact, you would be pleased at what kind of secrets I can keep." Rose placed her other hand on Lord Hammil's knee and squeezed. He smiled his approval.

"Tomorrow, I will be captain. The governor owes me a favor and the current Captain, and part of his crew, will soon be locked up in the fort for whatever charges I can think up." Rose's eyes widened, but her smile remained firmly on her lips.

"Why would you do something like that, milord? What did they do to you?" Lord Hammil brought his hand up to touch Rose's cheek.

"I do so because they are of no use to me any longer. The captain is a friend of the man I am after and he will no doubt make my fiancé turn against me if he spends too much time with her. I am a jealous man, and I can't risk him interfering in what I need to do once he knows that I will force her to tell me the truth. He has already made an impression upon her." Lord Hammil's eyes wondered away from Rose's for a moment, his countenance changing. Rose's mind was filling with the urgency to tell Locand what Lord Hammil was up to, but she contained herself not wanting to ruin the moment.

"Any woman would be lucky to have you for a fiancé, milord. You're charming and sincere in your affection and devotion. You are loyal if nothing else. I am thankful just to be in your presence." Lord Hammil laughed slightly.

"Rose, I appreciate your comments. You make me feel—valued. Miranda, my fiancé, at times makes me feel unappreciated and taken for granted. I try so hard to please her, and yet I feel it is not enough. She has a strong will, but I am determined to break it." Rose pondered the name for a moment and wondered if she was the woman Locand refused her for.

"Lord Hammil, if your lover wants nothing to do with you, then let her go and find someone new. You deserve to be with someone who will please you. Who will—"

"Here is the thing about that, Rose. I am obsessed with her. She is not only beautiful, but strong. The more she refuses my advances, the more I want her in my bed. I don't know what it is about her, but I do. I know she is beyond my reach and that there are others who would fit her better, but I can't let her go. I am determined to make her love me." Rose sat in awe. Lord Hammil seemed almost possessed and what saddened her was that Miranda would never be rid of this man. He would always be at her heels.

"You cannot make a woman love you, Lord Hammil. It is an illusion, an unfair illusion for you. You can't just force someone—" But Lord Hammil leaned forward and yelled, "I can make her love me and I will. I have it within my means to force her. She will become my wife and pleasure me the way I need to be pleasured and she will love me for if she doesn't, I will kill everyone she holds dear."

Rose had leaned back in her chair in fright. As Lord Hammil realized what he had done and said, he sat back into his chair and calmed himself, avoiding Rose's gaze. As he did so he began to feel tired all of a sudden. As if all his emotions he just spent exhausted him. It took Rose several minutes to recover but when she did, she leaned forward and placed her hand on Lord Hammil's cheek. She noticed his eyes glazing. It wouldn't take long now.

"I feel that you will accomplish your goal, milord. You are a strong and virile man." Lord Hammil returned his eyes back to meet Rose's. She ran her fingers through his hair, then moved her hands to the front of his shirt unbuttoning it the rest of the way. Once she was finished, she removed the shirt and threw it on the floor. His body was lean and thin, but it did reveal muscle in his solid form. Rose stood up from her chair, Lord Hammil did the same. He grabbed her roughly and moved her towards the bed. He then began to feel dizzy. Before Rose could say anything, Lord Hammil fell forward crashing into her. Together, they both fell upon the bed. Rose let out a soft screech as she felt his weight upon her. She then used the bounce of the bed to push him off her, where he rolled over to the other side. Rose could hear Lord Hammil's snoring and was reassured that he was fine before she rose up. ,.

Her mind was trying to focus on Locand.. She covered Lord Hammil with the rest of the blankets so he wouldn't wake from the cold and find her missing, and then hurried to the window. When she opened it she saw Stevens waiting for her below. She could tell that he must have been waiting there for hours. He was almost asleep in the bushes.

She snapped her fingers to get Stevens' attention and pointed to show him where to meet her and quietly closed the window. Rose kept glancing at the motionless form of Lord Hammil on the bed and knew that he was still asleep by the loud snoring that was emanating from him. She rolled her eyes as she moved swiftly to the door, opened it quietly and stepped into the hallway, unnoticed by the eyes and ears of the many servants who were sleeping quietly in their beds.

It was still dark when Locand heard a loud rapping on his cabin door. He quickly dressed and yelled for the person to enter. He wasn't at all surprised when Stevens stepped into the cabin, his hair tousled and clothes disorganized. Locand gazed up and down the length of him before he said, “I see you found Rose.” Stevens smiled briefly at the comment.

“She said she needed satisfying. I had to oblige her.” His countenance turned serious as he gazed at Locand while fixing his appearance. “She will stay with Lord Hammil to buy us time. I’m afraid we’ll need every bit.” He quickly looked behind him where the young Adam was waiting in the hallway.

“Enter boy, I have been eager to speak with you.” Adam looked down at the floor, his hat held tightly within his hands.

“Sorry, Captain Riveri, my every intention was to speak with you first, but one of your crew said you went ashore so I waited in a tavern to hide myself. I know a girl there and she is nice to me.” Locand walked closer to Adam and patted him on the head, a slight smile upon his lips.

“Look at me when you talk boy,” Locand’s voice was gentle and firm. Adam slowly raised his youthful face and blue eyes to look into Locand’s.

“I found him walking toward the harbor, Cap’n. I knew you would want to speak with him.”

“You are correct, Stevens. Now close the door so we can have some privacy from prying ears.” Stevens closed the cabin door and stepped farther into the room awaiting Locand’s next orders.

“What did Rose find out?” asked Locand.

“She said that we are to leave port at once,” replied Stevens.

“Why would she say that?”

“She said that Lord Hammil has no more use for us. That we would get in the way of his plans, especially you. It seems he is jealous and wishes for you to stay away from Miranda. He feels that you would protect her when he tortured her to get the information he needs,” replied Stevens.

“What?” Locand almost yelled, his voice filling the room. “Why would he torture her, I don’t understand? What does she have that he wants?”

“I know what he wants from her, Captain Riveri,” whispered Adam. Locand turned to face Adam, his curiosity peaked.

“Tell me!” Locand demanded.

“I followed Lord Hammil to the fort today where he spoke to a man who was locked in a cell there. A guard called the man, Peter. Lord Hammil spoke with Peter and offered to set him free if he told him where Captain Ditarius dwelled."

"Captain Ditarius?" said Locand. "So, he is after Stratton Mayne, is he? Well, he won't find him. Mayne has always taken precautions when it comes to his hideouts. I would be surprised if the man knew."

"He didn't know. He played a fool, I think, until Lord Hammil mentioned Captain Ditarius' daughter." Locand stood motionless, his mind racing.

"No, not her! How does he know of her?" asked Locand wildly.

"I don't know, Captain, but he did say that she was going to marry him and that seemed to upset Peter." Locand turned around and placed his hand over his mouth. The only woman he knew that Lord Hammil was going to marry was Miranda. Locand closed his eyes and shook his head. It could not be her!

"What is her name, Adam? What was the name of Captain Ditarius' daughter? He must have said it." Locand's tone was sharp and commanding. Adam almost shook with fear.

"He said her name was Miranda Mayne, Captain. He said that she would know where her father would be, her and the man who protects her." Locand laughed loudly as he shook his head.

"What is it, Cap'n?" asked Stevens.

"What else was said?" Locand demanded as he ignored Stevens' question.

"Lord Hammil wanted to know where a crystal could be found that Captain Ditarius had in his possession. Peter didn't know where it was and said that he never saw any crystal belonging to Captain Ditarius, and then his daughter was mentioned again. Lord Hammil, it seems, thinks the daughter has this crystal, not Captain Ditarius. It made Lord Hammil very happy when he discovered it. Then he killed Peter." Locand's head turned violently toward Adam, his eyes boring into him. He turned the other way and paced the room, his fingers running through his hair.

"Then there was this other man. He was also a prisoner. He was a man who Lord Hammil wasn't expecting. Apparently, this man was no friend of Captain Ditarius' and was more than happy to tell Lord Hammil what he knew about him. He gave him the location of his hideout. Eleuthera was where Lord Hammil was told to go, and then he was brutally murdered as well."

"Do you know what it all means, Cap'n?" asked Stevens. Locand stopped his pacing and turned to face Stevens.

"It means we have been played, my friend, from all sides. Our Miranda Smyth is not Lord Hammil's fiancée, Miranda Mayne is. I can't believe I could not remember her name when Davy and I talked about Stratton. That was what he was trying to tell me. That Miranda was Stratton's daughter. She does not love Lord Hammil, but she thinks she can use him to find her father without his knowledge. She must know he is after this crystal and is trying to protect her father from him. However, Lord Hammil knows who she really is and is using her to find Stratton. If he thinks she has the crystal, then he will torture her into giving it to him. And now you say that Rose wants us to leave port because Lord Hammil thinks that I will protect her? He's right. She is the daughter of my good friend. I am honor bound to protect her."

Locand paced the room again, his mind racing with what he should do. "Find the crew and get them aboard ship. We will set sail come dawn. We need to find Miranda and Stratton before Lord Hammil does."

"Aye, Cap'n. Rose said she would buy us time, but she knew not how much," offered Stevens.

"Then let's not waste her time."

"Aye!" said Stevens as he turned away from Locand, opened the door, and left the cabin. Locand turned toward Adam who looked up at him admiringly.

"I am pleased with the information you have brought me. What would you like for your troubles, boy?" asked Locand. Adam wasted no time in answering, he knew what he wanted.

"I would like to sail with you, Captain Riveri," replied the shy boy.

"You would like to join my crew would you?" asked Locand. Adam nodded his head quickly, his hands wringing his hat nervously. "What of your sister, Adam. Would you leave her here to fend for herself?" Locand looked intimidating as he placed his hands on his hips.

"Captain, I love my sister dearly, but she can barely take care of herself. I have been on my own for years and crave a better life than this one. I would like to be part of your crew to become wealthy one day. Then I could come back here and save my sister from the life she is forced to live." Adam's innocence pulled at Locand's heart, and he could not deny him.

"If that is your desire then you have earned the right to be a part of my crew. However," Locand stepped closer to Adam, "I need to know where your loyalties lie. My crew obeys my every command and risks their lives for mine. Would you?" Adam replied instantly, his eyes wide with fear.

"You have my loyalties, Captain. I would never betray you. You are like a brother to me." Locand laughed and ruffled Adam's hair with his hand before he turned away from him.

"Do not expect special treatment. You will have to hold your own weight." Adam's face beamed with happiness.

"Aye, sir, I will make a good seaman. I can't thank you enough." Before Locand could reply, Adam rushed to him and wrapped his arms around his waist in an embrace. Locand couldn't help but smile and patted the boy on the back.

"Adam, you are a boy of twelve, please restrain from embracing the Captain unless absolutely necessary." Adam nodded his head as he removed his arms from around Locand. "Now, we are short on time, go ashore and pack your things." Adam looked behind him and pointed to the open door.

"My things are in the hallway. I don't have much, but what I do have is there." Locand smiled at Adam as he looked past him to his cabin door.

"In that case, find a bunk and get comfortable. Try to get some sleep before the rest of the crew comes aboard." Adam nodded his head and was about to turn around to leave, but didn't.

"You seem troubled, Captain. Is there something I can do?" Locand sat in a chair and stared at the boy.

"There is nothing you can do for me, Adam. Miranda Mayne is the only one who can change my mood now." Adam nodded his head and left the cabin quietly, closing the door behind him. Locand remained consumed in thought. He remembered the night when Miranda knocked on his cabin door, barely clothed, asking him if he would betray Stratton. He now realized why she had asked him the question. She needed to see if he would have betrayed her father by using her to find him. She thought he knew of Lord Hammil's plans so she had little trust in him. However, he had made her realize how loyal he was to her father and then she offered her body to him, but only after he had tasted her lips.

Locand closed his eyes to rekindle the memory. She had tasted so sweet, so innocent. He couldn't believe she was the girl he had remembered aboard Stratton's ship so long ago, and yet the more he thought about it, the more he became frustrated for not seeing. She had grown into a beautiful woman, with supple curves and a sassy tongue. Oh, how he longed to tame that tongue and body. Locand could feel himself getting excited and rose quickly from his chair to stand in front of the port hole. The breeze was cool and felt good against his handsome face. He willed the wind to wash away the memories, but knew it could not.

He remembered when he had talked with Miranda about deceiving him. She had told him that she was looking for her father. He knew now she was speaking the truth. She was going to find Stratton and now Locand knew where she had gone. She was going to Eleuthera to find him and now they will go there to find her. "Stratton Mayne's daughter," spoke Locand aloud as he shook his head. It explains much. Her behavior aboard ship, her temperament, and the way she bossed people around as if she were in charge. She knows much about a ship for her father taught her everything he knows. He was a master, as far as Locand was concerned, and yet her behavior could have also been her downfall. If Lord Hammil was an observant man he would have picked up on her knowledge about ships, and yet he seemed to be ignorant toward all of her strengths. Her skill with a sword was impeccable. She had a strong and courageous nature about her, as well as a passionate side. Locand shook his head again as if clearing his mind, not wanting to think any more about Miranda.

He walked over to his bed and laid upon it, knowing that in a few hours the ship would be busy with preparations to set sail, he knew he needed rest. Slowly, his eyes closed, but no matter how much he tried to block Miranda out, his mind took control and focused on its obsession.

CHAPTER 12

Miranda and Davy had spent the next few weeks with Stratton and his crew of five men, though most of the time the crew spent their days aboard the ship and out of sight until called for. Stratton had told them he had changed his crew in Tortuga before he came to Eleuthera to hide. He had spoken of his trip and how he noticed a wanted poster of himself around the town. He had decided to leave but not before he was chased through the town by half the army. At that point, he decided it was best to lie low for awhile. However, this did not end his problems. On the way to Eleuthera, pirates attacked him. Though his flag of an arrow through a heart brought fear to his enemy's hearts, the group of bandits persisted. He sunk the enemy ship in battle, but in the process lost the majority of his crew. The *Fighting Spur* had made it through with little damage, but was now left with only five crewmembers.

Though he had taken many precautions in protecting his sanctuary, there were still a few men who knew of its location. It was because of this that he spent most of his time down in the caves. The one cave in particular, though there were many caves on the island, led to the sea. If he needed to leave in a hurry he would be able to do so, leaving the beauty of the island behind him. The *Fighting Spur* was anchored not far off from the entrance of the cave and because the ship was light, the reefs didn't bother it.

Miranda had explained to her father everything that had transpired over the past few months. She talked of her engagement to Lord Hammil and why she had accepted his proposal. She then went into detail of how she found out that he was missing and why Lord Hammil was looking for him. She talked of Locand and how he had sailed Lord Hammil to Port Royal, buying them only a few weeks time to find him.

All the while, Stratton sat in a chair, with Davy by his side, listening patiently to his daughter's words. The past weeks had blown by like the wind. It was pleasant having his daughter by his side again, and yet he knew it would not last long with Lord Hammil hunting them down like dogs.

"So, Miry, you used Lord Hammil to come and find me—that was wise. The only problem is you were a fool to accept his proposal without my consent. I know you had your reasons for doing so, you have been explaining them for the past several hours, but there was a reason why I did not consent to the marriage." Miranda looked at her father curiously, her head tilted to one side.

"What were your reasons, Father? For if I would have only heard word from you, I never would have thought to accept his proposal. Besides, I accepted his proposal because I thought you would be pleased by it."

"Pleased?" asked Stratton as Miranda folded her arms stubbornly in front of her. "Pleased? Why would you think I would be pleased?"

"Because," started Miranda, "you always talk about me being happy, me being wealthy and in the highest of society. Lord Hammil will make your wishes come true."

"That is not what I want for you, Miry. I do want you to be happy, but—"

"Well, I would have been happy if you wouldn't have put so much pressure on me to be happy," shouted Miranda. Stratton rolled his eyes and raised his hands to his face.

"Enough!" spoke Davy quietly. "Miranda, your father has only wanted what is best for you."

"Don't you side with him," spoke Miranda sharply as she pointed her finger at him.

"Enough!" Davy glared at Miranda until she plopped unceremoniously into a chair with a huff.

"Miranda, I looked into the background of our dear Lord Hammil, and he has evil in his heart as well as greed. He is also not as innocent or weak minded as one may believe by his manner. He is very deceiving. I have been told that he was the one responsible for the burning of the church in Sussex years ago to flush out enemies of the crown who were claiming sanctuary. He is ruthless, almost more than me." Miranda shook her head not believing that Lord Hammil was capable of such evil deeds. "Besides, he is not fit to marry you and cannot provide you with the happiness I feel you deserve. There is someone else I think you would like better as a husband than Lord Hammil." Miranda glared at her father with a stunned look upon her face.

"Who?" she said as her eyes narrowed into slits. What was her father up to?

"He does not matter at the moment. The most important thing is that you're safe once more." Stratton smiled a catlike grin as he winked at his daughter. Miranda changed topics knowing that her father was not going to confide in her the truth of the man's identity.

"But what of Captain Riveri, Father? What will happen to him? He has helped us get to the Caribbean. I believe he is unaware of Lord Hammil's intentions, and I think he would remain loyal to you if he did know. I want to make sure you don't believe otherwise." Stratton eyed his daughter suspiciously as she spoke of Locand.

"He is not as unaware as you may think, Miranda. I left him a note telling him to be cautious of Lord Hammil. By now I am sure he knows of his true intentions, and about us," answered Davy.

"That may be so, but he will still remain loyal to us," said Miranda emphatically.

"Relax, Miry, I don't doubt his loyalties and I see that you don't either. I have known Locand since he was a boy, and I love him as if he were my own son. I do not question him," replied Stratton. Miranda took a deep breath and exhaled sharply, trying to relax. All of her thoughts of late had been of Locand and the kiss they shared. She was worried about him, and then a terrible thought crossed her mind. Would she ever see him again? The thought almost made her weep in fear, but she remained strong.

"What about the crystals? Lord Hammil knows that you have it, but he knows not of mine. There is a treasure at Nombre de Dios we can go and find, Father. Treasure the Spanish hid long ago in a vault in the side of a mountain. We can find it together before Lord Hammil does. We have the key to open it, we—" Before Miranda could finish her sentence, Stratton held up his hand to stop her.

"I am rich enough, Miry. Now all I want in my life is peace and quiet. I want you to get married and have children. I want to see them run around chasing each other like wild monkeys. The sight would bring me joy. You are getting older you know, and you need to settle down soon before you get so old that no man will want you." Miranda's mouth was agape as she stared at her father, appalled by what he said. How old did he think she was? She wasn't ready to have children yet. Miranda shook her head in disbelief and rolled her eyes.

"Oh please, Father, not another word about having children. As you can see, I am not ready to have them yet. I need to find a husband first, for that would be helpful. Now, let's go back to the topic at hand. What is the purpose of us having these crystals other than to remember mother? I wish I would have known how wonderful and selfless she was, and yet I know that she would want us to do this for her." Stratton remembered his late wife and for a moment was silent. Miranda took the crystal from around her neck and placed it into the palm of her hand to show her father. She waited for him to do the same, but he did not. Miranda furrowed her forehead in contemplation.

"We always do this, Father. Why will you not show me your crystal now?" Stratton raised his eyes to his daughter's as he heard the concern in her voice.

"It is not mine anymore, my love. I gave it to someone who I feel is better suited for it. Your mother will always be in my heart and I will never forget her, but I need to move on with my life and stop living in the past." Miranda shook her head in confusion, not sure what her father was saying.

"I don't understand. What are you trying to tell me?" Stratton looked away from his daughter to gather his nerve. He then stood up from his chair and moved to stand in front of her.

"Miranda, understand that I have been alone for many years. It has only been just within the past few years that I have met someone." Miranda stood up and moved away from her father raising her hands in front of her.

"Is that why I have not seen you in months, because you have been spending your time with another woman? Who is she, some whore on Tortuga?" Stratton slapped his daughter across the face for her impertinence. The blow surprised them both and Davy actually stepped closer to the pair to intervene. Tears instantly filled Miranda's eyes and she started to cry, she tried to run away but Stratton held her in his arms to stop her.

"I'm sorry, Miry, so sorry. Forgive me for striking you. I have never done that before." Miranda held her father tightly as he rocked her back and forth to comfort her. "This is why I have to start a new life. I am tired of the man I have become. I have become cruel and ruthless, not only to others but now to my own daughter. I want to live with you in peace, not anger. I love you Miranda. I did not mean to hurt you, but I have to find happiness, don't I? This woman has brought meaning back into my lonely life. You will meet her, I promise, and we will work this out between us. I know you want to go after this treasure in Nombre de Dios. I'm sorry that I have disappointed you, but treasure is not important to me any more. I have all that I could ever need."

Miranda pulled away from her father's arms and stepped away from him, wiping her tears on the back of her hand. "You anger me so much, Father. I'm sorry for my words but you have upset me with yours. I want you to find happiness, but you have been selfish. You could have retired when you first dropped me and Davy off in London those many years ago, but you didn't. Not wanting to give up the life of sailing, and I can understand that because I know how freeing it is, but that was when you should have retired from the life. Not now when you feel that you have seen and done enough. For years I have been without you." Miranda took a deep breath to calm herself.

"Ever since I was a child, Davy has been acting as my father when you have not been around. When is he supposed to find happiness, after I am wed and my husband takes me away from everything I love? Have you not thought of him? When I have needed guidance, it was not you who gave it. When I needed protection, it was not you who protected me. When I was sick from illness or sadness, it was not you who gave me solace. It was Davy, Father. Davy filled the void of not having a father for months on end. It was he who helped me deal with not having a mother in my life to talk to of my inner feelings and turmoil. It was he who, at times, filled that motherly void and helped me become confident and not afraid of who I was or would become. It should have been you."

"Miranda," said Davy calmly, speaking for the first time. "It was not just your father's command that made me stay with you and watch you grow." Miranda raised her sad eyes toward Davy. "I cannot have children. It is impossible for me to get a woman with child. Your father was blessing me with a gift when he asked me to watch over you. Do not blame him. For once in my life I knew what it felt like to be a father. Stratton gave me that chance." Davy walked up to Miranda and placed his hands on either side of her face. He kissed her softly on the lips, tears streaming down her cheeks.

"Did you know about Father's woman?" asked Miranda accusingly, her features filled with hurt. Davy looked into Miranda's tear filled eyes and nodded his head. Miranda pushed him away and looked back and forth between him and her father. "I love you both so much, but I can't stand the sight of either of you right now. I'm sorry, but you both disgust me. How could you keep this woman from me?" Miranda's eyes went from one man to the other.

"I had my reasons, Miranda. I knew you would not like this, but at least give her a chance, she deserves that much doesn't she?" answered Stratton. Miranda's gaze fell upon her father.

"How can you disregard what mother meant to you? For years I have only heard of how much you loved her. How can you do this to her memory? "

"Do what to her memory? She will always be in my heart. I have never once forgotten her." Stratton paused as his voice rose. "Do you think I am pleased on how little time I have spent with you over the years? I have only looked after your best interests. I have always wanted what was best for you. Do you think I have no regrets?" Miranda's head jerked sharply toward her father.

"I think that you have many." With that said, Miranda turned and ran from the room and out the front door. The bright sun shone upon her as she ran off the pathway and fell to her knees in the sand. She raised her hands to her eyes and covered them as she wept her frustrations.

When she was finished she sat in the sand, her thoughts focused on what she should do. She ran her fingers through the soft sand playfully when she noticed a shadow descend upon her. When she looked up she could not believe her eyes.

"I wish that you would have told me you were Stratton Mayne's daughter, Miranda. Again, I could have helped you." The voice was deep and husky, it matched the handsome face of Locand. Miranda stood up from the ground and smiled. She ran into his arms and he held her tightly. She wrapped her arms around his waist and placed her head upon his chest. She could hear his racing heart as he ran his fingers through her hair.

"And now that you know, what will you do with that knowledge?" Miranda asked curiously, the smile not fading from her lips.

"We will talk about that topic another time. For right now there are more important things we need to discuss, don't you think?"

Miranda pulled away from Locand and gazed into his hazel green eyes.

"Yes, there is much to discuss—and explain." Miranda placed her hand upon Locand's cheek. She thought he was going to kiss her, but he didn't give in to the urge.

"I need to speak with your father. Where is he?" Miranda's smile faltered slightly as she filled with disappointment. She wasn't prepared for the change of topic or the change of tone in Locand's voice. She moved away from him and pointed toward the door. He hurried past her and stepped into the house. He met Stratton and Davy in the hallway.

"Locand? It is so good to see you, boy." Stratton opened his arms and embraced him heartily.

"As I am glad to see you, my old friend. I wish we could talk more pleasantries but there isn't the time. I am only hours ahead of Lord Hammil who secured another ship to chase me. He's aware that you are here, Stratton. I almost did not come but I knew that Miranda, as well as Davy, would be here with you." Miranda stepped into the room and they all passed glances at one another.

"What do you know?" asked Davy, his voice filled with concern.

"I did what you had requested. I took precaution when trusting Lord Hammil. I found out he wanted to take over my ship and become its captain. Not only that, the reason he went to Port Royal was to talk with a man who was once a crewmember of your ship, Stratton. Lord Hammil is looking for you because he thinks you have a crystal, but we both know that's not true, don't we?" Stratton stared at Locand and followed his gaze to Miranda.

"So, he is now after Miranda?" asked Stratton.

"Yes, a man named Peter told Lord Hammil that she has it in her possession. Because of that, her life is now in danger as well as all of yours. Everyone needs to leave and leave now. I saw that you have five men in the caves, so I took great care to not walk through them to find you for I knew that you would be watching them and did not want you to think that I was an enemy. *The Captain's Avenger* is anchored not far from the *Fighting Spur* and my men are prepared to sail. I have spoken with your crew, and I know what happened to the rest of your men. I have given you some of mine for you to sail away with, taking Miranda and Davy with you. They are already aboard your ship. I will cover your escape." Locand looked at Miranda before returning his gaze back to Stratton.

"I will kill the man who has betrayed us," yelled Stratton angrily.

"He's already dead by the hands of our eager Lord Hammil. We need to hurry, Stratton, if we are to out run him." Stratton nodded his head and yelled for Davy to help him gather some items they would need. Miranda and Locand were left alone together.

"I want to go with you, Locand," said Miranda demandingly, but Locand shook his head in reply.

"No, Miranda! We are not meant to be together. Your place is by your father's side, not mine. Now that I know who you really are, I am honor bound to protect you, but that is all. I cannot give you what you need, and you deserve better than what I can give. A pirate's life is not destined for you. We have not done anything that cannot be reversed." Miranda stepped closer to Locand, not wanting to believe what he said.

"What if all I needed was you?" Locand could see the innocence in her eyes, then closed his eyes tightly to ignore it.

"Oh, Miranda, if only that were true. Let's not play anymore games, shall we? You have mastered the art pretty well. However, it backfired when you tried to use Lord Hammil to get what you wanted, just like you used me to get the information you sought. That was what you were telling me, wasn't it? That a person would do almost anything if they wanted something bad enough? You lured me in with your wiles and I believed you, just like you lured Lord Hammil into your bed to get to your father." Miranda shook her head in denial.

"No, that's not true. Yes, I used him to get the information I needed to protect my father, but I never allowed him into my bed, and I never used you. I merely asked you the questions I needed answers to. I needed to know where your true loyalties were, and I found out that you were on our side. Didn't I convince you when you had confronted me at Lord Hammil's estate that I was not lying about my feelings for you?" When Locand didn't answer she continued. "How could you say that I used you? I was the one that allowed you to claim my lips in an unforgettable moment. I allowed you to claim a piece of my heart." Hurt filled Miranda's eyes as her voice cracked slightly.

"I don't believe your innocence this time. Forget the kiss we shared because it meant nothing to me. You did what you felt you must do to find your father. I would have done the same, but you met your match in Lord Hammil. He's a smart man, Miranda. He's smart enough to use you to get to your father. That was what he was trying to do. You thought you outsmarted him but he knew all along who you were. He knew that if you married him, you would have to tell him where your father dwelled. He would be entitled to whatever treasure the crystal would unleash. You have the piece he so eagerly seeks, but it wasn't until now that he knew it was in your possession, and now he will show you no mercy. He wants your body bad enough, but not so bad that he could not be swayed by another woman." Miranda thought of Locand's words and anger rose inside her.

"Is that what you did to find out what his plans were? Enticed him with another woman?" Locand folded his arms in front of his chest.

"I did whatever I needed to do to find the truth. You of all people understand the magnitude of that." Locand's eyes showed his anger.

"So, you are saying that I am heartless? That the kiss and the words you said to me meant nothing?" When she didn't hear a reply Miranda spouted, "I officially hate you!"

"You are entitled, but I only did what you would have done if our positions were reversed," replied Locand, his white teeth bared with his words. Miranda glared at Locand, the anger she had for him filling her chest. Before another word could have been spoken, Davy and Stratton stepped back into the room. They could feel the tension between Locand and Miranda, but chose to ignore it.

"Are you ready?" asked Stratton. Locand nodded and watched as Stratton led the way to the library where he pulled a book from the shelf. He wasn't surprised when he saw a door in the bookshelf open. Stratton grabbed the door and opened it the rest of the way. He then started down the tunnel of rock with a taper in his hand, his extra weapons held tightly within his other arm. Miranda went down the tunnel next, then Locand and Davy. Davy made sure the hidden door was closed tightly behind them.

The tunnel was about a half a mile in length and ended in the back of a large cave that opened up to the ocean. As the group walked to the opening, they saw the *Fighting Spur* anchored in the bay with more than the five crewmembers aboard. Their eyes then fell upon *The Captain's Avenger* and noticed the crew moving quickly about on deck. It wasn't until they made it to the beach past a large group of trees, that they saw another ship anchored. They could not recognize the ship, and were about to search the beach for signs of intruders when they heard the cocking of a pistol from behind them.

Slowly, they turned around and standing in front of them was Lord Hammil with a few men with swords standing behind him. "Well, well, well, look who we have here. We have my fiancée and her father, Captain Ditarius, or should I say Stratton Mayne? Then there is Davy, and last but not least, the Captain of *The Captain's Avenger*. You are just the people I was looking for." Lord Hammil moved slightly closer to the group but not close enough to put himself in danger. Davy, Stratton and Locand were standing in a semicircle with Miranda in the middle behind them.

"What do you want Lord Hammil?" asked Miranda, the men standing quietly around her.

"I want many things, my love, but most of all I want the crystal you keep."

"I know not what you speak of. A crystal you say?" Miranda played the fool but for all of her efforts she could not convince Lord Hammil of her ignorance.

"Stop playing games, Miranda. I know what you have been keeping from me. So easily was I taken in with your beauty and innocence, but no more. You will give me what I ask for, or I will kill the men you care for one by one." Miranda was about to step forward but was held back by her father.

"She does not have what you seek Lord Hammil, but I do. However, you will need to come and get it from me." Stratton dared Lord Hammil to approach him, but he would not take the bait. Instead, the man shook his head as he smiled glowingly.

"I'm no fool Captain Mayne, and I don't believe you. I will count to ten Miranda, then you will leave me no choice but to shoot." Miranda listened to the threat but refused to give in. She glanced at the men around her one by one hoping that Lord Hammil was bluffing. She saw her father, Davy and Locand, with their hands on their swords ready to fight, but none had a pistol. Miranda waited for the count to reach ten, looking as proud as she could, determined not to show fear.

"Very well, Miranda, I have no choice." Miranda took a deep breath as she heard the pistol fire. It was pointed at her father, but at the last minute, it changed to Locand. Not wanting to see him hurt, she ran from behind him and pushed him out of the way, the bullet sinking into her arm instead of Locand's chest.

"No!" was all she heard as she sank to her knees on the beach, blood gushing from the wound. Locand had fallen to his knees from the force of Miranda's body as she moved him out from the bullet's path. When he realized what she had done he quickly rose and reached for her. He wanted to hold her in his arms, but danger was too near and she was too vulnerable, so he pulled his sword from its sheath and moved to stand in front of her to protect her. Stratton glanced at his daughter and then at Locand.

"Where was she hit?" shouted Stratton anxiously.

"In the arm, but she's losing much blood." Stratton thought for a moment while he stood next to Davy, their swords drawn and ready to fight.

"Take her to your ship, Locand. Get her away from here. Davy and I will buy you time."

"What about you?" yelled Locand, as he glanced at Miranda and watched as blood stained the sleeve of her dress.

"My life matters little when compared to my daughter's. Go!" yelled Stratton. "Get her out of here. She will be safe with you." With that said, Stratton and Davy charged toward Lord Hammil and his men. Soon, the sound of steel against steel was all that could be heard.

Locand turned quickly around and stood Miranda up so he could set her onto his shoulder. She moaned as he lifted her from the ground. He turned around and looked for a longboat set upon the shore. Once he spotted one, he rushed over to it, placing Miranda gently inside. He took one last glance over at Davy and Stratton who were still fighting. Locand could see bodies lying on the ground in their wake as they moved from one man to the other. He stared at Lord Hammil who fought Davy and stabbed him in the shoulder. However, Davy didn't falter as he returned the wound, stabbing Lord Hammil in the leg. Lord Hammil fell to the ground in pain and then turned his head toward the beach and called for more of his men to come ashore.

Locand looked toward the ship and saw six men descend into a longboat and row ashore. He wanted to stay and fight but as he turned toward Miranda and saw her pale complexion, he knew he had to leave. Locand pushed the boat from shore and jumped into it, grabbing two oars. He oared as fast as he could until he was close enough to his ship and the *Fighting Spur*. He ordered his men aboard the *Fighting Spur* to help Stratton on shore. The men wasted no time jumping into the lowered longboats and oaring to shore to fight.

Satisfied, Locand yelled for Stevens as the longboat reached the side of his ship. Locand lifted Miranda up again onto his shoulder and climbed the steps. Once he reached the top, Stevens took her from his shoulder allowing Locand to get onto the deck safely.

"Ahoy mates!" yelled Locand. "Raise the anchor, we need to leave now." The crew had already prepared the ship to sail, and as the anchor was raised from the water, the wind caught the sails. *The Captain's Avenger* was on its way.

"What do I do with her, Cap'n?" asked Stevens, as he saw the blood flowing through her dress sleeve and down her arm.

"Take her to my cabin and lay her on the bed. Ask Billy to heat water and to find me a sharp knife to remove the ball from her shoulder. Find Adam and have him look after her."

"Aye, Cap'n," replied Stevens as he lifted Miranda onto his shoulder and took her below deck. Locand yelled orders to the men until the ship was well on its way, away from Eleuthera. When Stevens arrived back on deck Locand ordered him to take over so he could deal with Miranda. Stevens nodded and took the helm asking where they were headed. Locand didn't have an answer so he told him to go south. Stevens did as he was told as Locand hurried below deck.

When he reached his cabin, he found Miranda lying on the bed holding her arm, sweat pouring from her face. Billy was in the room with the hot water and a sterilized knife as requested. Adam spoke softly to Miranda trying to calm her.

"What do we do, Captain?" asked Adam, worry for the girl in his eyes.

"Get me the bottle of rum that is sitting on my desk boy. It will help her with the pain," replied Locand. He turned toward Miranda.

"Miranda," whispered Locand as he placed his hand upon her forehead. "Focus on my eyes. Can you see me?" Miranda nodded her head in reply. "Good, now try to relax and drink this." Locand grabbed the bottle of rum that Adam handed him and brought it to her lips. She drank it eagerly, tears forming in her eyes. She then saw Locand take a dagger from his waist and cut the fabric of her sleeve exposing her arm. He tried to be as gentle as he could, but Miranda still winced in pain.

Locand grabbed the bottle of rum and poured some over the wound. He could see the liquid bubble around the red puckered flesh. Miranda moaned in pain as she tried to move her arm. Locand placed his hand upon her face and made her look at him, forcing her to stop her movement. "Don't move, Miry, it will only cause you pain. Now, I'm going to try to remove the ball. It's going to hurt so feel free to drink as much rum as you need to kill the pain." Miranda nodded her head, the agonizing look in her eyes urged him to hurry.

Locand told Adam to stand on the other side of Miranda so he could help her with the rum. Adam nodded and did what he was told, rum in hand. Locand then grabbed the knife from Billy and something that looked like a large pair of tweezers. He steadied his nerves as he dug into the wound. Miranda's screams could be heard on deck, but Adam quieted them by offering her rum. She drank it eagerly but could not resist the urge to scream her pain. When she tried to reach for her arm, Adam grabbed a hold of it to restrain her. He ran his fingers through the hair at Miranda's temple, which seemed to calm her as he watched Locand work.

Locand finally reached the ball in the wound, which he could now see. His hands were covered in blood as he worked but his eyes were focused intently on retrieving the ball. Within minutes, Locand picked the ball out of the wound with the tweezers and placed it on a plate that Billy was holding. Tears were streaming down Miranda's cheeks as Locand cleansed the wound with the rum and stitched her up. The small needle that Billy had given him did its job swiftly and accurately. Locand had much experience stitching up wounds, for he did so whenever he was injured. On occasion, he would also help mend his crew's scrapes and cuts.

"Hang in there, Miranda. Do not leave me, stay strong. The ball is removed from the wound, and I am through stitching it closed." Miranda nodded as she whispered, "Nombre de Dios." Locand leaned back as he saw Miranda's lashes falling heavily closed.

"What did you say?" asked Locand as he leaned closer to hear her better.

"Nombre de Dios, that is where we need to go," answered Miranda as her head fell onto the bed and turned away from Locand.

"Is she dead?" asked Adam with sadness in his voice.

"No, boy, she is asleep. Go and tell Stevens that our course is Nombre de Dios."

"Aye, Captain," replied Adam as he moved away from the bed and hurried out the door.

"Do you think she will make it, Cap'n?" asked Billy, concern filling his voice.

"Yes, Billy, she will live. This girl is much stronger then you or I. She is too stubborn to give up living just yet." Billy laughed as he left the cabin taking the supplies with him. Locand faced Miranda as she slept. He glanced at her bare arm and ran his fingers softly down it, remembering how she felt when she was in his arms. He then wrapped the arm with cloth and tied it tightly into a knot. The wound was just below her shoulder and was easy to wrap.

When he was finished, Locand stared at the sleeping beauty before him. The words he had said to her earlier ate at his conscience. He knew he was wrong for hurting her the way he did, but he thought it was the only way to rid her from his thoughts, especially when he resolved himself to giving her up. He had come up with the plan when they had sailed to Eleuthera. He knew that if she were to be safe, it would be away from him and with her father. However, he was not expecting the turn of events or the way she threw herself in front of him to save his life.

The action pulled at his heart and the feelings he refused to feel for her were creeping their way back into his heart. He wouldn't have known what to do if she would have died saving his life after the terrible things he had said to her. Now he had a second chance to make it up to her, and he was determined to make things right between them. Even if it meant that he had to apologize to her, he would do it. Gone were the days that they were apart. Now they were stuck with each other. Stratton put him in charge of keeping her safe and that was a promise he would not take lightly.

Locand reached over to his night stand and washed his hands with the bowl of water and soap Billy had left for him. After drying his hands on a towel, Locand reached out his hand to caress Miranda's moist cheek. The tears she had been crying earlier still hung to her lashes and flesh. After several minutes, Locand rose from the bed and grabbed the warm blanket to cover her. After several more minutes of staring at her sleeping form, Locand turned to leave the cabin, closing the door quietly behind him.

CHAPTER 13

It had been a month by the time Miranda arose from the cabin to walk on deck. She had stayed in Locand's cabin recovering from her injury, not once making an appearance until today. Miranda chose to wear Locand's black breeches, which were tied with a belt around her waist, and his white shirt to mix in with the crew. The first two weeks she could not move her arm without cringing in pain, but now she was able to move it more freely. The pain she had felt in the beginning eased up tremendously. Her wound had been covered with a cloth, which had been changed often while it was healing, but now it was removed. Miranda didn't need it any longer. As she glanced down at her arm, all she saw was a scar remaining. The stitching had been perfect, all that could be seen now was a small thin line showing where the ball had been.

Locand checked on her welfare every day by stopping in to see her. He would make friendly conversation with her but did not say anything that would upset her, keeping the personal topics to a minimum. His visits were brief. He realized that the more time he spent with her, the more he felt himself falling in love with her. The smile she gave him as he walked into the cabin made him feel warm inside, as if he were coming home. The emotion she revealed was genuine and charming. Locand found himself trying to find ways to touch her. He offered to take her for walks on deck and around the ship, but she would politely refuse, not wanting to take up too much of his time. Her thoughtfulness surprised him, and yet he found it captivating, wanting to spend as much time with her as possible. However, he knew that if he did, he would not be able to control his emotions much longer.

Locand was pleasantly surprised as he saw Miranda step onto the deck. She walked casually to the starboard side of the ship and leaned up against the railing, the wind blowing through her blonde mane.

Some of the crew couldn't help but stare at the fair woman. Her supple curves could still be seen through the tight breeches she wore. Locand wanted to talk to her about Nombre de Dios and why they were heading there, but he didn't want to bring it up. He was hoping she would tell him on her own, but as of yet she hadn't said a word about it. Within a few days, they would arrive and he needed to have answers. He slowly moved from the helm and walked toward her. Upon hearing his footsteps behind her, Miranda turned around to greet him.

"Good afternoon, Captain. Today is a beautiful day. I couldn't stay away from the sunlight any longer." Her smile was brighter than the sun, and Locand couldn't help but return it.

"I'm glad to see you on deck. How are you feeling today?"

"I feel renewed. The pain in my arm is ebbing. I can almost move it in any direction without pain prohibiting me." Miranda looked out into the ocean before returning her gaze back to Locand.

"The news is pleasing to hear. I know that you just came on deck but would you mind if we go to my cabin so we can talk in private? I promise that you can stay on deck all day and all night if that is what you wish when we are finished." Miranda was about to protest, but something in Locand's eyes made her reconsider. She nodded her head as she felt Locand take a gentle hold of her arm and guide her to and down the stairs. In the hallway Miranda led the way to Locand's cabin and opened the door. As Locand stepped inside, he closed and locked the door and moved to sit on the edge of the bed. He offered for Miranda to sit into the chair. She sat into it willingly, her hands folded in her lap.

"Miranda, I need to know why you wanted me to go to Nombre de Dios. You spoke the name the first day on my ship and because we had no where else to go, that is where we are heading. I was hoping you were going to tell me. I have waited patiently." Locand sat back onto the bed, his voice calm and kind. Miranda looked at him and knew she should tell him the truth.

"You know of the crystal I keep in my possession," started Miranda. She dipped her right hand into the front of her shirt and pulled out the crystal for him to see. Locand leaned forward to take a better look at it and at the same time brought Miranda's face closer to his. He looked at the crystal closely and raised his face just inches from hers. He was about to speak but couldn't resist staring at the fullness of her lips. The urge to kiss her was overpowering, but he resisted. He then clumsily let go of the crystal, letting it fall against her shirt, and leaned back. Their eyes met, almost uncomfortably, before Miranda started to speak again.

"This crystal, along with its brother, is a key to the treasure that is hidden in a mountain at Nombre de Dios. I don't know much about it other than that Lord Hammil is after it. That is why he is after the crystals, so he can get to the treasure. The problem that we have is that I don't know where the other crystal is. My father did have it, but now he has given it away to someone else, probably that woman he is seeing." Miranda said underneath her breath as she looked away from Locand, recalling the words her father had said to her in her mind.

"I know this treasure you speak of," replied Locand casually, standing up from the bed and looking at the mattress. He noticed how one of the corners lifted slightly higher than the other and smiled. Miranda was watching curiously as he fell quickly to his knees and lifted up one end of the mattress. He reached in and pulled out his journal.

"So that is where you have been keeping it. I was looking for some light reading." Miranda smiled as she saw Locand return to the bed, a wry smile on his lips.

"I have been hiding it from you. I knew you would want to read it again," said Locand as he flipped through the pages until he reached what he was looking for. "A year ago, before I became a privateer, I attacked a Spanish ship that was sailing past England to the New World. It fired upon my ship, we fought back killing most of the crew and holding the rest hostage. My men searched the ship and what they found was a partial map of Nombre de Dios. Now, if you look at this," said Locand as he leaned forward pulling out a map from his journal, "you can see where it is detailed. This is the town of Nombre de Dios, but through these trees there is a mountain that has a cave hidden into the side. From what I know of the town, it is only busy twice a year—once in the beginning and once in the end. At those times, the people from Panama use mules to bring treasure to the town of Nombre de Dios for the Spanish ships to pick up and take. So by the time we get there, the place should be desolate."

Miranda grabbed the map and looked at it more closely, not recognizing it. "Have you always kept the map in here?" she asked curiously, wondering how she had missed it.

"No!" responded Locand quickly, as he took back the map. He then continued as if she never interrupted him. "I didn't think much about it at the time, but I decided to keep the map anyway for future use. If you look here at the bottom, there are directions— right—left—right. This is telling us which way to turn the key once it is in the lock mechanism. I don't usually keep this map in my journal, but as of late I have been because it has been on my mind ever since you spoke of the town to me. Now, your father gave me this piece of parchment." Locand brought out the parchment from his journal and aligned it with the other piece. "If you look closely, you can see that these two pieces belong together. Your father gave me this piece a while ago. This top portion talks of a vault. As you can see, this bottom part is a detailed map of the location. Now that we have this map and the crystals in our possession, we can search and find this treasure." Miranda watched as Locand folded the map back up and placed it inside the pages of his journal.

"I don't think you heard me correctly, Locand. I said I don't know where the other crystal is." Locand reached inside the front of his shirt and pulled out the crystal. Miranda jumped forward and grabbed the crystal into her hand almost choking Locand as she yanked his head toward hers. She then lifted her crystal up and matched them together. It was a perfect fit. Miranda stared up at Locand in amazement.

"So, my father gave his crystal to you. Why?" asked Miranda angrily.

"Because, maybe he knew that I could keep it safe, or maybe he thought that I was a better match for you than Lord Hammil." Miranda leaned back, the crystals separating, her eyes showing her confusion.

"I don't understand," said Miranda in a whisper.

"Your father gave me his crystal with the words that it would bring me luck someday, better luck than it had given him. Don't you see, Miranda? Together we can find this treasure and take it before Lord Hammil can. We have the advantage. Together we can overcome all of our obstacles. You can't deny that you care for me." Miranda hurried to the door not wanting to hear any more, but Locand dropped his journal on the bed and rushed after her, grabbing her by the right arm and making her turn around to face him.

"Stop, Locand, let me go!" yelled Miranda as she pulled her arm from his grasp.

"Not until you answer my question. There has been something that has been troubling me these past weeks. I know we said some things to each other that we shouldn't have, and I wanted to make sure you know that I didn't mean them. I was cruel and unkind." Locand bowed his head as he looked at the floor. "Forgive me?" With all of her heart Miranda wanted to forgive him, but not only that, she wanted to love him. However, she couldn't. She tried to walk away again, but Locand wouldn't let her. "Why did you take the shot that was meant for me? If you hate me so much, why didn't you let me die?" Miranda was forced to stare into Locand's memorizing green eyes. She didn't want to confess to him her true feelings, not this way.

"I protect the ones I care for, Locand. If the shot was meant for my father or Davy, I would have done the same." Miranda tried to move away from Locand's arms but he would not let her go.

"Why?" Was all Locand could say, his voice soft.

"Because I love them, Locand," replied Miranda in frustration. "And please, don't give me one of your lectures about me being foolish and the consequences of my actions and how it affects others. I already know and accept my fate."

"What are you talking about?" Locand said as Miranda stared at him.

"Do you want to really know why I saved you?" Locand nodded his head emphatically. "I saved you because I love you, but I understand if you can't forgive me for the things I've done and do not share my love. But love is what I know I feel. I can't stop thinking about you. I dream of you. I—" Miranda was unprepared when Locand pressed his lips against hers passionately. The kiss was demanding and aggressive. He forced Miranda's mouth open with his tongue as he placed his hands on either side of her face. Miranda moved her hands to caress Locand's biceps and shoulders as he moved her roughly to stand against the wall. She leaned up against the hard surface as Locand made love to every inch of her mouth. A sigh escaped her lips as one of his hands moved to caress her back and buttocks. He forcefully pressed her back farther into the wall when he became more demanding with his kiss.

Miranda was taken aback by the passion and forgot where she was. The only thing filling her mind was how wonderful she was feeling inside. She wanted to please him in return so raised her hands to caress Locand's cheeks and neck, reveling in the feel of his soft lips upon hers. As she did she began to wince in pain, her wound not entirely healed. Hearing Miranda's soft whimper, and feeling her quickly remove her arm from him, caused Locand to become gentler. He regained control, but only for a few more seconds before he pulled away from her. .

Locand caressed Miranda's smooth cheek, then her wounded arm. "You are mine now, do you understand? You saved my life because you love me, and I am now protecting yours because I return that "love". The fog filling Miranda's gaze began to clear.

"You love me?" asked Miranda, a light of hope in her eyes. Locand looked deep into her soft brown eyes as he confessed his love.

"I've never said those words to another woman beside you. I've never felt love until now. You have no idea how much I love you, Miry. From the first moment I saw you, I knew you were meant to be mine. You will no longer need Davy to protect you for you are my woman now and my responsibility. My heart belongs to you and you alone."

Miranda let a few tears fall as she smiled with happiness. "I love you too, Locand. My heart and body belong to you now. Take care of them." Locand captured Miranda's lips in a tender kiss. He then loosened his hold upon her, grabbed her hand and led her to the bed.

"I thought you said you would wait for me. Have you reconsidered?" Miranda's heart began to race as Locand removed his shirt. His sinewy muscles yearning to be stroked.

"I said that I would wait for you, and so I shall. But I see no harm in comforting each other. I want to lie next to you, my love. I think that holding each other is just what we both need right now." Locand laid upon the bed first. Miranda slowly followed. She raised her left leg to lie across his. Her chest partially overlapped his as her head comfortably fit into the crook of his arm. Miranda adjusted until she could hear Locand's strong heart beat in her ear. The sound was relaxing as she snuggled in. Locand waited for Miranda to settle before wrapping his arms around her. He wanted to keep her safe, and at the moment nothing was safer than his embrace. With one hand Locand reached for the blanket and wrapped it around them. His hands returned to hold Miranda tightly as she laid her head upon his chest and fell asleep. Locand tenderly kissed her on the forehead before he closed his eyes and fell asleep from exhaustion.

The couple slept peacefully for hours in each other's arms. It wasn't until dusk when Locand rose from the bed; Miranda still sleeping serenely. He quickly put on his shirt and quietly left the room to check on the status of the ship. On his way, he stopped by the galley and asked Billy for some food and drink. He hurried to do the captain's bidding but Locand said that he was not in a hurry and would get the tray upon his return from the deck. Billy nodded his head in understanding.

When Locand stepped onto the deck he immediately walked toward the helm where Stevens was standing. They nodded at each other before discussing any problems they might be having. Stevens told Locand that all was well and that according to the map they should be seeing Nombre de Dios within the next day or so. Locand nodded his head with approval and turned to leave. Before he could, however, he heard one of his men yell from the lookout. Locand glanced toward the sky as he saw the man point to something behind him. He quickly looked toward the rear of the ship, and sure enough, there was a dark mass in the shape of a ship leagues behind them.

Locand yelled for one of his men to get his spy glass. The seaman rushed from the deck down below to fetch it. Soon the man stood beside Locand, holding out to him the item he requested. Locand grabbed it eagerly as he raised it to the north. The ship was too far away for him to see the occupants. He was unsure if it was friend or foe. He lowered the spy glass and told Stevens to tell the crew to be on their guard, there may trouble brewing. Another man took over the helm as Stevens stepped down from the quarterdeck and addressed the men.

Locand stood still, his thoughts filled with whose ship it could be. He gazed up at the sky and noticed that they still flew the English flag. If the other ship sailed closer, then he would decide what flag they would sail. Locand looked at his crew while Stevens told them the news. He moved from the quarterdeck to the main deck, hurrying below to tell Miranda of their situation.

He entered into his cabin without knocking but as he took a step, he saw the bare flesh of Miranda's legs as she arose from the bed. Surprised from the door being burst open, she quickly jumped back into the bed, grabbing the sheets to cover herself. Her brown eyes flew to the intruder in a panic, but was pleased when she found that it was Locand.

"Where have you been, my Captain? I was just about to search for you." Miranda's smile faded as she saw the concern in Locand's eyes. "What is it?"

Locand rushed to the bed but could not stop himself from wrapping his arms around Miranda and pressing his lips onto hers in a kiss. Miranda accepted the kiss eagerly as she moved her arms to wrap around his neck pulling him toward her. When the kiss ended, Locand removed her arms from around him and told her to freshen up. Her hair was askew and a few of her buttons had come undone while she had slept. Miranda obeyed him instantly, her eyes searching his for answers.

"There is a ship following behind us. It is not close enough to be identified, but it could mean danger. *The Captain's Avenger* is light and we can keep a good pace ahead of them but I will not lie and say that I am not concerned." Miranda finished buttoning her shirt and moved to stand closer to Locand.

"What do we do then?" Miranda's tone grew serious.

"The only thing we can do—we need to wait. I want to be certain before we act. We are close to Nombre de Dios. We will get there first before the other ship comes upon us. We need to set up a plan to find the treasure and leave before it can stop us. I want you to look over the map I showed you, as well as a few other maps I have rolled up on my desk over there. The maps will not go into great detail, but we need to find a trail we can use. There are swamps and natives all around, and we do not want to be hindered by them. Do you understand?" Miranda nodded her head in reply, disappointed that they could not live forever in the new world they had created for themselves.

Before another word could be said, a knock was heard on the door. Upon hearing the command to enter, Billy opened the door and brought in a tray of fruits and bread for them to eat. Miranda thanked Billy for his kindness, and Locand smiled his appreciation. As soon as Billy placed the tray of food on a table in the room, he turned around and left, not saying a word. Miranda walked over to the tray and looked at it, then returned her gaze to Locand.

"If that is what you wish for me to do, then I will do it." Miranda smiled trying to look sincere but inside she was hoping for more than just commands.

Locand could tell that Miranda was troubled about something.

He could see it in her eyes. He wanted nothing more than to spend the rest of their lives in his cabin holding each other, but he knew that it was impossible.

"I'm sorry that our brief time alone is shortened. I wish I could say that it was going to be different, but I can't. Welcome to the life of a privateer."

"Don't you mean pirate?" spouted Miranda. Locand smirked as he stepped closer to Miranda and grabbed her nimbly in his arms. He then cupped her cheek with his hand as he pressed his lips against hers in a soft kiss. "Darling, sometimes the only difference between the two is a piece of parchment. I refuse to live that life anymore and yet it brings me freedom." He then kissed her again and when the kiss became deeper and Miranda started to wrap her arms around Locand's neck holding him closer to her body, he pulled swiftly away.

"I must go, Miranda. I need to keep an eye on that mystery ship behind us. I want to be prepared if it is our dear Lord Hammil." Miranda nodded her head, her body filling with yearning for the man in front of her. For a moment, she forgot all about Lord Hammil. She had forgotten about her father and how he had stayed behind with Davy to make sure they were able to get away unscathed. A sad look appeared on her countenance. Thinking that Miranda was upset with him, Locand took his finger and lifted her chin.

"Don't think I have forgotten what we did today. The declaration of our new found love is something I will never forget." Miranda smiled as she leaned forward and kissed Locand tenderly, her thoughts now focusing on him.

"I will admit I was starting to wonder. You have turned serious since earlier. I understand your concern, but I wish we could spend more time together. Is that ship so close that you have to leave me just yet? We have only just discovered the feelings we have for one another." Locand glanced at Miranda playfully as she ran her fingers up and down his chest seductively. As she did so, she took a step back to admire him and unbuttoned a few of his buttons on his shirt to reveal his chest. He was magnificent. His upper torso was rock solid, his skin smooth and taunt. As her fingers caressed his well formed abdomen, Miranda's eyes began to fill with desire. The smile Locand had on his face broadened until she lightly dragged her fingers across the back of his breeches.

Seeing his reaction, Miranda turned abruptly around and

sauntered her way over to the bed. With her back up against it, she said, “Well, if you have to go, then go. I will be spending my time focusing on the maps doing as you requested, and will be down here all alone if you need me.” Locand’s eyes filled with desire as he saw Miranda’s tongue dart out of her mouth and touch her lips. It didn’t take much prodding for Locand to unbutton the rest of the buttons on his shirt, walking closer to her until he was only inches away. His tan, muscular chest now fully exposed, tightened as he lifted Miranda roughly, tossing her onto the bed. A smile of pleasure flew across her lips as she quickly adjusted her position, creating room for them both.

“You’re right, my love. I believe we do have some time to explore these new feelings.” Locand threw his shirt onto the floor as he climbed onto the bed. Miranda reached for him, holding him to her as he ravished her lips again and again, her hand stroking his muscular biceps.

CHAPTER 14

When *The Captain's Avenger* made port at Nombre de Dios, the mystery ship following behind had disappeared. Through the past few days, the ship did not sail closer than necessary, and when they had least expected, it had disappeared from view just hours before they had anchored. Locand was still not able to discover the flag it flew on the mast head and was curious to know why it had been following them. Though this bothered him greatly, he still ordered his crew to lower the longboats to go ashore. Half of his crew stayed behind with Stevens, as the other half filled the longboats. Their weapons were tied to their belts, over their shoulders and around their waists. Locand left strict instructions just in case the ship that had been following them suddenly returned and turned out to be Lord Hammil. The thought that it could be Stratton and Davy also crossed his mind, but briefly. Stratton knew that Miranda would be safe in his care and Locand knew that he wanted nothing to do with the treasure, so the probability that they were behind them was slim. None the less, Locand told Stevens to ready the guns and prepare for a fight. He was unsure of what to expect. The lone ship could also be a boatload of wandering pirates.

With Miranda by his side, Locand was the last to step into a longboat. Once they set off, the crew oared quickly as it tried to catch up with the other longboats ahead of them. Miranda and Locand had spent several hours pouring over the maps of Nombre de Dios and believed they knew a good route to take that would lead them to the mountain safely. As the boats made it to shore, all that could be seen were trees—miles and miles of trees. The men quickly stepped out of the boats, waiting eagerly for their captain's commands. The town could not be seen from the shore, but Locand knew which direction it was. He grabbed hold of Miranda's hand and ordered his men to follow. With swords at the ready, they descended one by one into the dark green, lush forest.

The ground was soft in some areas as they went, their feet sticking slightly in the top layer of the surface. The sounds of birds calling each other from the tall trees made them quite aware they were not alone. Their eyes searched constantly around them as they moved vines or branches out of their way so they could pass, ducking and bobbing as they went. The journey was tiresome, the heat unbearable. With every step, they felt the heat would stifle them. The humidity alone felt like a sauna, but they refused to give up, the thought of the treasure keeping them going. They risked too much to give up now.

It took hours before they could see the mountain. The men were sweating profusely from the heat and all that could be heard, besides their footsteps, were the slapping of the men's hands against their skin as they killed the mosquitoes and bugs that would bite them. Periodically, they would stop to rest, always keeping a watchful eye on their surroundings. There were times Miranda could swear that the trees had eyes. She felt like they were constantly being watched. When she had mentioned it to Locand, he said it was probably the natives. Even so, Miranda felt more and more ill at ease.

As they continued through the forest they came upon several vines that were at least a half-foot in diameter. Locand took his sword and hacked through the dangling vines that were blocking them from passing. As he removed them from their path, he noticed a small clearing. When everyone gathered into the clearing, they saw a large stream that flowed quickly before them. They could feel the warm sun shining upon their skin, making their bodies perspire with even more sweat. Their mouths were dry and parched. Miranda watched as several of the men drank from the stream's contents. As the men drank heartily, Locand motioned for the rest to do the same. They all followed and drank their fill, including Miranda and Locand, who had waited for the men to go first. Locand had refilled the empty canteen at his waist.

Once everyone's thirst was quenched, Locand told the men to keep moving, but before they could take a step forward, natives instantly surrounded them. Soon, all that could be seen were dark bodies, and in their hands they held sticks with pointed rocks at the end aimed in their direction.

The men stared at each other for some time before one of the natives stepped forward and asked in Spanish who the leader was.

The man was tall and dark. He was barely clothed, except for a loin cloth he wore around his waist to hide his most private parts. He also wore silver hoops through his earlobes and wood beads around his neck. Locand let go of Miranda's hand and moved slightly forward, answering the native in his own tongue. Miranda watched in amazement as Locand and the man had what seemed to be a calm discussion. There were even times when she saw them smile at each other. What they talked about, she didn't know, for the language was new to her. But whatever they said must have been friendly because the native raised his hand and the other natives, who were standing behind him, lowered their weapons.

Suddenly, the leader of the natives turned and waived for them to follow him. Locand told his men to follow and as they started moving forward, Miranda whispered, "What's going on, Locand? What did you talk about?" Locand reached for her hand and whispered his response as they kept moving through the trees.

"He wanted to know where we were headed. I told him it was toward the mountains. I explained how we were looking for a secret vault. He knew what I spoke of. He said that he would take us to it as long as we got what we came for and left immediately. The man said they were angry with the Spanish. Many of his men were beaten and killed when the strangers came upon them. He seemed very resentful and asked if I had the key to open the vault. When I said yes, he told us to follow him. He said that without the key, entry to the vault would be in vain, and he would have forced us to turn around. But because we have the key to open the vault, he wants us to take what is ours and leave with it."

Miranda absorbed the news as she used her other hand to swat the bugs and insects that would fall upon her. Her feet were sore and she was tired. Sweat poured down her face and her hair was moist from perspiration. They seemed to walk for miles and still could not see the base of the mountain. Suddenly, the natives in front of them stopped abruptly. Miranda tried to peak around Locand to see what was going on but she couldn't without letting go of his hand. Not wanting to be separated from him, Miranda decided to ask Locand instead, having him be her eyes.

"Why have we stopped?"

"It's hard to tell. It seems that part of the base of the mountain is covered with trees and vines. We have stopped just before it." Before

Locand could explain more, the leader of the tribe moved through his men to stand in front of him. He pointed at the gray mass before them and said to Locand, "This is what you seek. Walk straight ahead and you will see a unique shape scratched into the mountain. Below it is a hole for a key. If you are who you say you are, then entrance to the vault should be easy for you. This is where we leave you, we can go no farther. Go back the way we just came to return to your ship. Go in peace. If you or your men wander or stray from the path and decide to harm us in any way, we will kill you without warning. We have led you to the mountain and to the treasure you seek. What's inside matters little to us for our lives are simple. We do not ask for much, for our hearts know nothing of greed. Do not let me regret helping you, Captain Riveri."

The threat was real enough. Locand thanked the tribe leader for his help and bowed to him. The leader returned the bow, and before another word could be said, the tribe disappeared amongst the trees. The men watched in amazement, all of them glancing at Locand for guidance. Locand told the men to follow him, and pulling Miranda behind him, hurried to the mountain.

As they moved closer, Locand could see the markings like the tribe leader had explained to him. He removed the crystal from around his neck and told Miranda to do the same. She did as she was told and placed her crystal in the palm of his outstretched hand. He then rubbed his hand over the markings and in so doing, found the keyhole they were searching for. It was not an ordinary keyhole but was circular. Locand took the two pieces of crystal and pressed them together. The fit was perfect. He smoothly turned the crystals and placed them into the hole in the mountain. When nothing happened, he turned it to the right as the map had suggested. At that moment, they all heard a loud noise in front of them. Locand and Miranda backed away, unsure of what to expect.

There was a stone door about six inches thick in front of them that opened a crack. The air trapped inside made a hissing sound as it escaped. Locand motioned for his men to move forward and open the door the rest of the way. Five men stepped forward to do the job. When the door was pushed farther open, more of the men helped. The squeaking sound of stone against stone made the men cringe. Miranda covered her ears, staring at the large opening before her. A vault was exactly what the opening was. There was no passageway that led into it, only an area several feet away from the stone door. It was empty. Miranda took a few steps forward and stepped into the vault. Locand stood quietly behind her.

"It's empty, Miranda, though I'm not at all surprised. Who knows how long the treasure has been around?" Locand glanced back at the crystals. "We don't even know if these are the only crystals that can open this door."

"I refuse to believe otherwise. There has to be more than what we are seeing Locand— much more. I know you believe so, too, or you wouldn't have kept that map as long as you have. One obstacle is not going to make you turn back in defeat." Miranda turned briefly around to stare at Locand. "There is treasure, I was told, beyond our wildest dreams." Miranda placed her hand to her chin. She then remembered something she had read. "Danger surrounds it."

"What?" asked Locand as he took a step closer.

"Dangers surround it." Miranda said louder. "This vault should be impossible to open without the key, and if anyone tried there would be traps and dangers awaiting them. I think whoever created this vault was brilliant." Miranda turned around and faced Locand and his men. "I think whoever would hide a mountain of treasure would not do so lightly. These would have to be men who knew that one day the crystals would be found by someone else. Pirates perhaps, people with little patience and a taste for greed. Upon finding this vault empty, most people might just walk away accepting that someone else had already found the treasure. However, we are a smarter group than most and at this point have all the time in the world. Also, the map gave us three directions. It said—right, left and right. Well, the first keyhole turned right. So, there should be two more keyholes that we cannot see and the next should turn to the left." Locand smiled in understanding as he gazed back into the vault.

"What do you suppose then? That the treasure is somehow hidden in a place less obvious?" Miranda stepped farther into the vault and examined the floor. She did the same to the walls. She saw nothing out of the ordinary, and yet she knew something wasn't right. She was about to turn back toward Locand, taking several steps toward the entrance, when she saw an outline of something on the floor. She could barely see it, so moved closer. She instantly fell to her knees and used her fingers to carefully remove the dirt from around the area. Locand quickly ran forward and moved up behind her.

"What is it? What do you see?" Miranda moved from above the marking and showed him.

"Do you see this?" Locand looked down closer and noticed there was a hole in the floor.

"Yes!"

"Grab the crystals. I bet all I have that it will open the floor." Locand and Miranda glanced back and forth for several seconds before he moved toward the crystals and removed them from the keyhole. He then walked back over to Miranda and handed her the key.

"No," said Miranda as she placed her hand on top of his. "Let's do this together. Kneel down beside me. If there is treasure here, then we found it because of both our efforts, not just mine." Locand quickly kneeled, and with both of them holding the key, placed it into the hole turning it to the left. The pair held their breaths as they saw the floor in front of them move aside to expose stairs. They both moved quickly back as dirt blew from the opening smothering them. Miranda was coughing uncontrollably as Locand placed his hand upon her arm lifting her from the ground.

"Are you all right?" Miranda coughed a few more times but still could not speak. Locand handed her the canteen of water, and she drank from it eagerly. After taking several more sips, her voice returned.

"What was that?"

"I don't know, but we must be more careful when opening things in the future." Miranda agreed and walked with Locand back to the opening that was now gaped in the floor of the vault. As they stared at the stairs below, a rush of excitement passed through them.

"I don't know, Miranda, do we dare?" Miranda glanced over at Locand and noticed his mischievous stare and crooked smile.

"Aye, Captain of my heart, we dare indeed. We did not come all this way for nothing." The smile on Locand's face faltered as he stared into Miranda's youthful features.

"For a moment there you reminded me of your father, and to be honest, I don't know if that's a good thing or not." Miranda's pleased grin turned more serious.

"I'm proud to be like him, and yet there are times when I feel ashamed."

"Don't judge him so hastily, Miranda." Miranda's gaze flew quickly over to Locand.

"You know too, don't you?" Locand didn't reply. "You know that he has been seeing a woman behind my back? Well, she cannot replace my mother."

"You never knew your mother, Miranda. You know not what having one is like. Wouldn't you like to?"

"No, you know nothing—"

"I know that he has found love again. Look at us, Miry, we found each other. Why can't your father—"

"Our situations are not the same," snapped Miranda.

"Aren't they?" Locand's eyes narrowed, knowing that their situations were very similar.

"No!" Miranda bowed her head thinking over Locand's words.

"You cannot fault him for finding happiness—for finding love."

"Yes, I can, especially when he sacrificed my happiness and our time together to do it. You cannot possibly understand how I'm feeling."

"Actually, I do!" Miranda's head lifted sharply.

"Really? How?" Locand looked quickly around him and noticed how his men were paying them much attention.

"This discussion will have to wait for another time. Now is not the place to dip into my past." Miranda and Locand stared at each other for some time before they spoke again.

"Did your father—"

"Let's just say that I have a sibling from the ordeal," Locand hastily whispered. Miranda gazed over at the crew and nodded her head in understanding.

"At least I feel a little better." Locand cocked his head to the side and wrinkled his nose while shaking his head in confusion. "I'm still an only child. I have no other siblings to worry about."

"At least not yet," teased Locand. "You haven't met her. She could be a little older than you and may be able to have a plethora of children." He knew his words would spark Miranda's temper. Miranda gave him a scathing glance before shaking her head.

"Don't even suggest such a thing. It's a repulsive idea," hissed Miranda as she grabbed some dirt and threw it at him. She then decided to change the topic slightly, though her next question still concerned her father.

"Do you think Davy and Father are safe?"

"If I know those two, I would say they are. Don't worry. I'm sure they are well." Though Locand's smile was sincere, he also had his doubts, but in no way wanted his concerns to show. He knew Miranda depended on him to keep her safe and protected. If that meant to keep her ignorant as well, then so be it. "Now, can we please focus on the treasure?" After hearing Miranda's frustrated, "Fine!" Locand turned around and ordered some men to find some wood for torches. When the men returned, Locand grabbed a short broken piece of wood for himself and, while the crew watched, wrapped the tip of it with a torn piece of fabric he had taken from one of his men and used flint to light it on fire.

"Well, it's now or never!"

"Wait!" Miranda hastily ran to the crystals and removed them from the keyhole on the floor.

"What are you doing? What if the door closes, locking us in there?" Locand saw Miranda shake her head as she held up the crystals and placed them both around her neck.

"Impossible! The keyhole on the wall to open the vault proved that the key is needed to both open and close it. Don't you see? That is why these crystals are so important. Without them you cannot enter into the vault nor can you leave it. I am bringing them just in case we need them, and I have a feeling we will, for there must be at least one more keyhole to find." Locand nodded his head as he gave Miranda a crooked smile. Yes, she was definitely like her father.

Miranda quickly followed Locand as he moved toward the stairs and went down them. Half of the crew was ordered to wait behind, while the other half followed their captain and Miranda with their torches in hand.

As Locand descended the stairs slowly, he could feel them slightly give way as loose sand gathered at his feet. He took several deep breaths to calm his nerves as he reached behind him to grab Miranda's hand. She gave it willingly, her eyes wide with fear and curiosity, though the warmth of Locand's touch soothed her. She could hear the members of the crew behind her drawing their weapons with anticipation of the unknown. The room below the vault was dark, and it was hard to judge exactly how deep it was below the vault or how wide. Their torches brought them much light, but as they stepped farther and farther below ground, they suddenly felt chills of cold air wash over them. Soon, Locand could feel solid ground and pulled Miranda with him as he stepped into another area. What he saw amazed and yet confused him.

There was a clear, blue pool of water at the end of what appeared to be a large deep tunnel. Light seemed to illuminate from its sides, but Locand couldn't detect where the light was coming from. The inside of the tunnel appeared to be smooth and shiny like glass. A rainbow of colors could be seen the closer they walked toward it. As they entered the tunnel, they realized water was running down the sides of it. The floor of the tunnel was rocky and covered in water, and each of them had to be careful as they walked through it so they wouldn't fall. As they entered an area on the other side, they saw stalagmites coming up from the ground. One in particular stood right in front of the pool of water with several smaller ones circling it. Miranda and Locand separated while they each stepped closer to inspect the pool.

"There almost seems to be a light coming from within the water. It's amazing how clear and beautiful it is." Miranda bent down to feel the water but didn't lower her hand any farther as she saw a small fish come to the surface, then another. Locand reached down and grabbed Miranda's arm, pulling her roughly up before her fingers could touch it.

"The water is beautiful all right—beautiful and deadly."

"What are you talking about?" Miranda pulled her arm out of Locand's grasp.

"You said yourself that danger surrounds the treasure; well, here it is."

"Possibly, but fish—dangerous? Please, Locand, you go too far. Besides, I don't even see the treasure. We don't even know if it's down here. This may just be a wild goose chase making us look like fools." Miranda raised her arm. "Behind these walls, as well as the walls behind this pool, is solid rock. Within the pool is nothing but—" It was then that a light of some kind, coming from within the water, caught her attention. It was almost like a reflection. Miranda quickly fell to her knees and leaned closer to the water, but did not touch it.

"Locand? I think I know where the treasure is."

"I was afraid of that." Miranda turned her head toward Locand as he rubbed his chin in thought. "This makes no sense."

"No sense?" piped in Miranda as she stood up from the ground and dusted off her breeches. "What is the problem? The treasure is in the water. All we have to do is go in and get it out."

"Do you honestly believe it is that simple?"

"How can it not be?"

"I will show you." Locand turned toward one of his men. "Mikal, come forward." Mikal, who was a small man with thinning hair and partially bad teeth, stepped forward. Miranda could tell he was nervous, for there was sweat on his brow and his mouselike nose kept twitching.

"Aye, Cap'n?"

"Could you show our dear Miss Mayne your right hand?" Miranda instantly looked down and waited for Mikal to bring his right hand forward from behind his back. When he did so, the room filled with Miranda's intake of breath. Mikal had two fingers missing. Miranda's eyes stared at Locand's wildly.

"Who did that to him? What cruel, sick man?"

"'Twas no man, missy," answered Mikal, but before he could elaborate Locand interrupted.

"Can you tell me what kind of fish these are, Mikal?" Mikal nodded his head as he stepped forward. However, no fish could be seen. He then hesitantly reached out and brought his three fingered hand to touch the water. Miranda leaned forward and silently watched him. Soon, several fish came to the surface, and as they did so, Mikal jumped back, his arm flailing to the side, hitting Miranda square in the chest sending her backward.

"Sweet mother of pearl, those are piranha! Piranha!" yelled Mikal as he moved quickly back to stand with his shipmates, his body shivering uncontrollably from what he had just seen. Locand rushed quickly over to Miranda and placed his hand upon her shoulder.

"Are you all right? I should have warned you not to stand so close to him. Years ago we had an encounter with this barbaric fish. Mikal knows it well." Miranda winced in pain as she placed her hand on her back. Mikal had sent her right into one of the stalagmites. Miranda could have been hurt worse, but was thankful that a sore back was all she felt.

"Danger surrounds it! Well, piranha would make sure that the treasure was kept safe. It is quite brilliant, actually. I forgot all about that kind of fish. The question is, how are we supposed to get it out without being eaten alive first?" She then placed her hand on the stalagmite for support and caressed it. It did not feel quite like the others she had touched, and as she ran her fingers up and down its length, she discovered a hole. "I think I just found the answer." Locand walked around the stalagmite and saw what Miranda had found. It was a circular hole similar to the ones used to open the vault and the trap door that led them underground.

"Quick— the crystals!" Locand held out his hand as Miranda removed the crystals from around her neck placing them into his palm. Locand grabbed the crystals with his opposite hand and placed them into the hole turning them to the right this time. Nothing happened at first but then a loud–almost deafening–noise came from the pool. The water seemed to drain but it only appeared that way because of the rock emerging from it. Miranda and Locand stared at the water in amazement. Sitting on a mound of rock were several wooden chests with doubloons and various other gold items piled high. Jewels were also hanging out of them, the size of which no man had ever seen before. Locand quickly motioned for the men to move forward and collect the treasure.

"Look at all of that treasure, Locand. It's incredible," oozed Miranda in astonishment. Her eyes grew wide from the sight before her, and she was so taken with what they had found that she could not move.

"I think I know what the vault is used for, Miranda." Locand turned toward Miranda with a crooked smile on his lips. "It must have been used by the Spanish when they would come here and load up the treasure from Nombre de Dios. The ships only came twice a year to pick up the mighty loads, and if something ever happened to one of the ships, they would have nothing left to take back to their homeland and to their king. I bet they would save some for themselves in case it was ever needed in the future. This is probably what they stored for safe keeping."

Miranda thought deeply about what Locand had said and knew it could be a possibility. She then heard Locand yell to Mikal to inform the rest of the crew to come down and help retrieve the treasure. She watched in silence as the men left to do Locand's bidding. Soon, the men who had been waiting by the entrance of the vault descended the stairs and ran to them, a few sliding on the loose sanded steps and almost falling to the bottom. Once through the tunnel, the crew moved stealthily to the heavy chests, being careful not to step into any of the surrounding water. Locand had warned them about the fish as they passed him. Then they all started loading the loose treasure into the chests, which took quite a long time to do.

When that task was completed, they lifted and carried the chests away from the pool and through the tunnel. Locand had removed the crystals from the stalagmite and the stones lowered back into the water. Locand and Miranda were the last to enter back into the tunnel and watched as the treasure was taken up the stairs and out of the vault. The men set it down and rested, waiting for everyone to follow them. When all of the treasure and crew were removed from the stone vault, and no one was left behind, Locand took the crystals and closed the door in the floor and then closed the main door in the mountain. Miranda could hear the vault door squeak and heave its heavy burden as it sealed itself again. Locand removed the crystals from the hole and placed them around his neck. Feeling satisfied, he turned around and walked back toward Miranda, who had been waiting with the crew in the trees, grabbed her hand and led her down the path. They watched as the men carried the treasure in their arms before them.

Hours had passed by the time the crew made it to the longboats. Their bodies were covered with sweat and their arms were fatigued from the load they were made to carry. As they stood on the warm beach, their feet covered with sand, they noticed an eerie silence from the woods. The men dropped the treasure into the longboats and stepped into them. One by one, the longboats were pushed into the water and the only noise that could be heard was the lapping of the water as the men oared toward *The Captain's Avenger*. Locand gazed around at the trees trying to figure out what could be wrong. Everything looked the same as it did before, but something didn't feel right. The birds were not singing their merry song, and it felt to him like they were being watched from somewhere above.

As the boats drew closer and closer to the ship, a man called out to the crew that was left behind to help them. When no one came, the man turned toward Locand for direction. He nodded his head for him to try again. The man yelled louder to the crew, but again no one answered or came to the railing. Miranda's chest filled with dread. *Why did no one come?* She was not the only one to think the question. Locand was asking himself the same one. He had left half of the crew on the ship. Where were they?

After several moments of analyzing the situation, he waited until the longboats were alongside *The Captain's Avenger* before telling the men to board with caution. The men withdrew their swords from their waists, placed the blades between their teeth and started climbing up the steps. The first man stepped onto the deck. Several more followed. It wasn't until most of the crew were on deck that Locand felt it safe enough for Miranda to board. He was following behind her when he heard some of the men shout out, "Begad!" one man said, "For all that is holy!"

When he reached the deck, he saw Miranda cover her mouth with her hand and scream. As he looked before him, he saw the slain bodies of the rest of his crew scattered about the deck. Blood was everywhere. The crew walked around the deck identifying what they could of the bodies. Some of the men had remained quiet and some spoke angrily about what had happened, talking of revenge. Miranda almost refused to move forward and thought she was going to be sick by what she saw. As she gazed among the slain, there was one body that wasn't accounted for. It was Adam's. She hoped beyond hope that he was able to escape from what happened.

"Locand?" Miranda whispered as she turned around to face the railing, not being able to look at the sight of the bodies any longer. Locand had moved passed her and ran up the stairs to the quarterdeck where he found Stevens lying on the ground stabbed in the heart. He touched his hair with his hand and stared into the dead eyes of his friend. "What happened here, my friend?" Locand acted as if he were waiting for an answer and felt foolish when he realized that Stevens could not give him one. He then raised his eyes to the sky and closed them.

He was about to look back at Stevens when he heard Miranda yell his name. Her voice sounded as if she were in a panic. When he stood to face her, his eyes fell upon Lord Hammil. He was unprepared when the man punched him in the face. Locand fell to the ground next to his dead friend and placed his hand on his jaw. It was sore. Anger filled his eyes as he rose back to his feet and stared at Lord Hammil.

"Did you do this to my men, you son of a bitch?" Lord Hammil glanced quickly behind him not taking his eyes away from Locand for too long.

"Yes!" was all that Lord Hammil replied, his eyes falling upon Miranda. "I am glad to see that Miss Mayne is not dead. I was disappointed when she took the shot that was meant to kill you." Locand could not resist the urge to return the blow that he had been given. Lord Hammil fell backward but was caught by one of his men. He was about to launch forward to attack Locand, but the man behind him held him back. "All right!" Lord Hammil shouted to the man behind him. "Let me go, I have composed myself." The man let him go as requested, and he ran his fingers through his hair in frustration. "Now is not the time to start this. I have another way to get back at you for taking my woman."

"Your woman? You can't talk and walk at the same time without concentrating too hard, and you call her your woman? I find that amusing. What rights do you think you have to her? I'll be damned if I will let you harm her in any way." Locand brought back his fist and made contact with Lord Hammil's jaw. The punch forced him to step back, and Lord Hammil lost his balance and fell down the stairs, taking his man with him. Locand stood watching as Lord Hammil's body almost rolled down the steps, hitting the railings, to land in a heap at the foot of the stairs. As soon as Miranda saw what had happened, she moved closer to Lord Hammil's body, but stopped when she heard Locand yell her name telling her to stay away. He started to descend the stairs moving ever closer to his target. On the way, Locand checked on the other man and knew that he was dead as he saw the angle of his neck.

Miranda stared at Lord Hammil's limp body on the deck. She then noticed his hand flinch, and saw his head move. Before she could get a breath out to warn Locand, Lord Hammil rose quickly from the deck and grabbed hold of her, wrapping an arm around her neck. Her hands flew to his arm that was slightly choking her. Locand jumped forward and leaned against the stair railing.

"No!" he shouted as he saw the blood pour forth from Lord Hammil's forehead, flowing like a stream down his face. He raised a dagger toward Miranda threateningly.

"Thought that you had killed me, eh? Well, no such luck Captain Riveri. There are two things that I will be taking from you today. One is the treasure. My men have already taken your longboats with the treasure that you worked so hard in getting back to my ship. You can take a look if you like." Locand didn't bother looking; he cared not for the treasure, but for Miranda.

"And the second?"

"Miranda will be coming with me. We have some unfinished

business to attend to. It will be unfortunate that you will not be able to join us, but I think you have helped me enough." Locand's eyes narrowed, not sure what Lord Hammil meant.

"How have I helped you?"

"You have helped me find the treasure I was searching for and the man I needed to kill." Miranda took a sharp intake of breath as she listened intently to Lord Hammil's words. "I picked you for a reason, Locand. You are one of the most talented of captains I have ever heard about. You are resourceful, strong, and handsome. I knew Miranda was Stratton Mayne's daughter. It was the only reason why I brought her along on your ship. I was also aware of your standing relationship with him. Sooner or later, I knew it wouldn't take long for you to seduce his only daughter and turn her away from me. It was what I counted on. I played sick long enough to throw her at your feet." Locand gazed at Lord Hammil in amazement. "It took you long enough. I was sure that you would fall prey to her charms, but I thought you would have succumbed to them sooner. Your will is stronger than most men's."

"I don't understand. Why would you play these games with us?"

"The answer is simple, I needed the treasure and there was no way I would have been able to get it on my own. Miranda and Stratton were the only one's to have the crystals to open the vault. Though, I will admit that I was taken by surprise to find that Miranda had the crystal in her possession. If I would have known that sooner I could have taken it from her when I had the chance, and believe me when I say that I had every opportunity. I was equally surprised to find that Stratton gave his crystal to you, but in the long run it was to my benefit. You apparently trusted Miranda enough to go after the treasure with her, so I can assume that my plan worked out perfectly thus far."

Lord Hammil laughed as he continued, "When I left for Port Royal it was to talk to one of Mayne's old crew members. I needed to know the location of his hideout. Eventually, the dolt gave me the information that I needed, but it wasn't exactly what I was looking for. Then, to my surprise, an enemy of Stratton's filled in the blanks. I was thrilled because I never would have known of Stratton's hideout if it wasn't for that man. Low and behold, the safe haven is Eleuthera Island. I never would have guessed that on my own, not in a million years."

"What of my father, you bastard? What of Davy? Did you kill them?" Miranda's words were tortured as she tried to speak against the pressure of Lord Hammil's arm against her throat, her feet almost not touching the ground.

Lord Hammil leaned forward slightly as he whispered in her ear, "You shall find out soon enough, my love, and though they did fight admirably, they failed in their attempt to stop me. I'm sorry!" Miranda screamed as she fought against his arm, her nails clawing at the exposed flesh. Lord Hammil lowered his dagger to stop her, and at that moment, Locand lunged toward him. He was caught off guard, though, as he felt two sets of hands suddenly reach out to hold him back. The men pulled him down to fall back against the stairs, their muscular arms restraining him.

Locand looked quickly around at his surroundings, his eyes falling upon half of his dead crew lying on the deck and then on the rest of his men who were standing in a circle surrounded by Lord Hammil's men, swords pointed at them. Was this how their lives were to end? Locand refused to die this way. At that moment, he noticed the uniforms of the English army. These were Port Royal soldiers. Locand scoffed loudly. Lord Hammil must have made a deal with the governor. He then noticed several of his men staring in his direction, waiting for the cue to fight back. Locand looked straight ahead at Lord Hammil, a smug look upon his face. Lord Hammil had underestimated him severely.

"What's it to be then, Lord Hammil? Are you to stay and fight against me like a man? Or will you run away with your tail between your legs like the weak, pathetic, coward I always thought you to be? Because believe me when I say that I will not let you take Miranda without a fight." Lord Hammil gazed at Locand arrogantly.

"Does she mean that much to you that you will sacrifice your life for hers?" Lord Hammil's lips quivered as his temper rose, and though Miranda's eyes searched Locand's for help, he did not once glance in her direction.

"She means more to me than she does you. Look how you treat her!" Lord Hammil glanced briefly at Miranda and slightly loosened his hold. "And they call me barbaric?"

"Brave words from a man currently being held captive by my men. Who do you think is to stop me from doing whatever I want with her—you? I think not my valiant Captain, but I do agree that it is our time to leave. I am too smart of a man to fall prey to your baiting."

Lord Hammil moved closer and closer to the port side of the ship with Miranda in front of him. As he gazed down below to the clear blue water he saw the last longboat waiting for his escape. One of his men waved at him from it, giving him the signal.

"Till we meet again, Captain Riveri." Locand watched in amazement and anger as Lord Hammil grabbed Miranda tightly around the waist and stepped off of the ship. He heard Miranda's screams echoing off the water.

"No!" was all Locand yelled before he fought against his captors with renewed vigor. He was able to free his arms and punch the men that were holding him in the jaw and stomach. He then reached for the sword at his waist and stabbed it into one of his assailants, then turned and did the same to the other. Their bodies fell on the stairs as blood poured out of them. The surrounded crew took the cue from their captain and began to fight the men before them. Locand ran to the railing and saw his longboat start to oar away from his ship faster and faster with Miranda and Lord Hammil inside. The pair had landed in the water, and their clothing was soaked and clinging to them.

Locand punched the railing in frustration and stared at Miranda. His eyes meeting the ones of the woman he loved. They gazed at each other until the longboat was out of sight from the cover of trees and undergrowth. The longboat headed with determination toward Lord Hammil's anchored ship, which was hidden outside of the bay that protected Nombre de Dios. Locand turned around and spent his frustrations on the men who were left behind to defend themselves. A few of Lord Hammil's men jumped over board, but the rest stayed to fight. It did not take long for the deck to be covered with more dead bodies, but this time they were the dead bodies of the enemy.

The men cheered aloud in victory, holding their swords in the air with excitement. Locand didn't want to ruin the moment of the men's success, but knew that if he wanted to save Miranda, they needed to leave now and close the gap between his ship and Lord Hammil's. Locand yelled for his crew to throw the bodies of the dead overboard and clean the deck of blood. He spoke to his men and promised them revenge. They were going to go after Lord Hammil to get Miranda and the treasure back.

The crew quickly did as they were told. Half of the men cleaned the deck while the others prepared the ship to sail. Locand looked in the direction of where Miranda once was one more time before he went below deck in a rush. His mind was focusing intently on his revenge. He tried to forget about Miranda and knew only one way for him to do that. He needed to think like the ruthless pirate he once was. He changed his ways, yes, but there was more at stake than some treasure. His future with the only woman who could tame his heart was on the line, and he needed to win this battle. He had to.

CHAPTER 15

When Lord Hammil stepped aboard the *Flying Wasp*, which was a large Naval vessel, with Miranda by his side, he ordered the rest of the crew to set sail. A man named Lieutenant Mansfield stepped forward. He wore a plain coat in full dress with white cuffs. His waistcoat was laced around the edge and his pockets were surrounded with broad gold lace. His hair was pulled back away from his clean shaven face and tied at the base of his neck with a black ribbon. He looked neat and orderly.

"Yes, Lieutenant?" asked Lord Hammil, who was glaring at the man impatiently. He quickly pushed Miranda toward Lieutenant Mansfield, and watched as he gripped her arm, tightly pulling her to stand closely by his side.

"What of my men, milord? Are we to leave them aboard the enemy's ship to get slaughtered?"

"Your men were dead, Lieutenant, as soon as the captain returned. We will join them if we don't leave this forsaken place immediately. Captain Riveri is very angry with me for taking his treasure and woman." Lord Hammil pointed toward Miranda. "Trust me when I say there is nothing that you can do to save them. Right now all we can do is save ourselves." Lieutenant Mansfield stared at Lord Hammil with a stupefied expression

"Captain Riveri? He is the pirate we're after?" asked the lieutenant angrily. When Lord Hammil didn't reply he continued, "And I bet that ship we are staring at is *The Captain's Avenger*." The lieutenant shook his head and cursed to himself.

"Who cares who the vagrant is, Lieutenant," shouted Lord Hammil.

"He's a man who shows no mercy to his enemy and is almost as bad as Captain Ditarius. You fed my men to the wolves when sparking his temper and killing his crew."

"The man is a pirate and deserves to be punished for betraying me—for betraying the crown. I did what needed to be done. If lives were lost, then that is the price of war." The lieutenant was about to speak again, but couldn't because Miranda spoke.

"He's a pirate no longer. He has changed his ways and is now a privateer. You label him wrongly. He has done nothing but follow your orders to the letter. He is a saint compared to you." Lord Hammil reached forward and grabbed Miranda's cheeks painfully. Tears sprang to her eyes.

"You would like to think so, wouldn't you?" asked Lord Hammil as he let go of Miranda's flesh. "Now, shut up! I don't want to hear one word out of your treacherous mouth." Miranda tried to be brave but failed miserably as more tears fell down her cheeks. Lord Hammil ignored Miranda's tears and turned his attention toward the lieutenant. "Your governor loaned his best ship and crew to me for a single purpose. Did your men unload the treasure from the longboats like I requested?"

Lieutenant Mansfield stood quiet for a moment before answering the question. His mind was still mourning over the deaths of the men he had unfortunately lost in a battle that could not be won.

"Yes, milord, the treasure is aboard and is safe and sound in the hold. I checked on it personally." He then glanced over at the beautiful woman by his side, tightening his grip upon her arm. "What shall I do with her?" Miranda winced from the pain in her arm, waiting to see what Lord Hammil would say.

"Take her below and lock her into a cell until I have need of her. My mind is too preoccupied to deal with her right now." He gazed at Miranda's wet shirt as it clung to her breasts. Licking his lips he added, "Make sure she's not harmed, Lieutenant. She is a prized possession." Lieutenant Mansfield nodded his head, pulling Miranda roughly with him toward the stairs.

Miranda narrowed her eyes and glared at Lord Hammil until she was almost to the stairs, then she looked straight ahead. Out of the corner of her eye, she saw a white blur near the deck. From curiosity, she turned her head to the right to see what it was. Her eyes fell upon the small body of Adam. His wrists were bound with rope and tied to the large wooden post of the mainmast. He was sitting on the ground staring at her. His face had many small cuts upon it and was bruised. From his saddened features, she caught a glimpse of a smile. His eyes seemed to light up from the sight of her.

"Miss Mayne?" was all that could be heard from the boy's lips, his voice soft and quiet. Miranda tried to go to Adam but was quickly pulled back into reality by Lieutenant Mansfield. He then pulled her violently down the stairs by her arm until everything on deck was soon out of sight.

As Miranda was being pulled down another set of stairs and through the hold of the ship, her eyes memorized every space and crevice. She saw the treasure that was chained securely toward the prow as well as the cargo and extra rations that were stored there. She was taken to the cells that were built into the side of the ship. There were two cells, one across from the other, and two men already occupied one of them. Miranda barely glanced at the men as Lieutenant Mansfield opened the cell with a key and pushed her inside. Her hands were not bound, and Lieutenant Mansfield felt there was no need to tie them. Where was she going to go?

Miranda heard the loud clank of steel as the door closed and locked. She saw Lieutenant Mansfield place the key inside of his front pocket and walk away, glancing at her periodically before he moved out of sight. Miranda started pacing her cell, her mind filling with thoughts of escape. She then remembered she was not alone. She paced some more before she could muster the courage to glance at the men in the cell across from her. The men were lying down on the uncomfortable flooring of the ship sleeping, tired with boredom from being locked in their cages for so long. Miranda stepped closer to her cell door to try and get a better look at them. As one of the men moved from the shadows, she saw his face. Her features lit up with excitement when she recognized who the man was. "Davy?"

One of the men heard a woman's voice speaking to him and sat up to see where it came from. When Davy's eyes fell upon Miranda, he quickly stood up and moved to the cell door. "Miry, is that really you?" He rubbed his eyes, not believing what he was seeing. He had thought she was dead. He had hoped that Locand found some way to save her from the bullet she had taken. But even with the faith he had in Locand, he knew the decision of her living or dying was not up to him. Davy was filled with relief when he heard the child he had helped raise talk to him. She was partly his daughter, too.

"Yes, my faithful friend, it is I. I have been so worried about you. What happened?"

"It is simple really. Lord Hammil's men bested ours. We had no choice but to surrender. It was either that or die, and frankly, the hope that you were alive was enough for us to give up our swords."

"What happened to Father's ship?" Before the question could be answered, a moan came from the man on the ground. "Is that Father with you?" Miranda pointed toward the man. His face was covered with shadow, and she could not see him clearly. "Why does he not wake from the sound of my voice?" Fear filled her chest as she hoped the man was not dead. At that moment, she heard a weak and cracking voice coming from the motionless body.

"Miranda, my daughter, is that you?"

"Father?" Stratton tried to rise from the floor but could not do so without help from Davy. "What happened to you?" Miranda's features filled with concern from the sight before her. Stratton gazed at his daughter as he leaned against Davy for support.

"Thank Lord Hammil for what he has done to me." Stratton turned slightly to show Miranda the whip marks on his back. She gasped in horror.

"Why would he do that to you, Father?" Stratton faced his daughter again and shook his head.

"He's upset I outwitted him. His goal was to capture me and steal the crystals. He wanted the treasure that only the crystals could reveal to him. I assume you and Locand found it?" Stratton didn't wait for Miranda to answer. He knew what she would have said. From the sounds that he had heard earlier, it was already onboard. "Well, it does not matter, does it? He wants it for his own gain. He cares nothing for the crown, nor for any of us." Miranda absorbed what her father said and narrowed her eyes in anger.

"I will kill him, Father, for what he has done to you. This, I promise." Davy glared into Miranda's stubborn features and shook his head.

"You will not, Miry."

"Just watch me, Davy. He has it coming. I do not fear him," said Miranda with determination in her eyes.

"You need to fear him, child, for he is not who we thought him to be. He is worse." Several seconds passed before he spoke again. "He has fooled us all. Talk sensibly, will you? He could have any one of us punished just for being who we are. We need to find a way to get out of here." Miranda stared at her father and then looked back at Davy.

"What can we do?"

"He still cares for you, Miranda. His feelings, as well as his desire for you to marry him, are strong. He was not pretending or lying about that. If you can convince him that he is the better man than Locand–and that you desire him–then we will have a chance to live and be set free." Miranda turned away from the cell door and stared at the wooden wall behind her.

"You can't ask me to do that. I don't love him. I love Locand and will not betray him for our freedom. Besides, I don't think that lie would pass twice." Davy was about to speak, but Stratton raised his hand to stop him.

"We are not asking you to betray Locand. In fact, I'm quite thrilled that you care for him, for it is what I wanted. He's the man I hoped for you to love. However, now is not the time to discuss such things. What we are asking you to do is to buy us time to get out of this cell. I think I have a way we could accomplish it." Stratton proceeded to explain to his daughter his idea. At first, Miranda felt mixed feelings, but then she realized that it would be the only way for them to be set free. She agreed to the plan without hesitation.

Days had passed by slowly. The lull of the ship made it hard for Miranda to stay awake. Her eyelids were falling heavily, and it took all of her strength to keep them open. She almost gave in to the temptation when she heard footsteps approaching. Her eyes then flew open, and her heart began to race. Moving to stand in front of her was Lieutenant Mansfield. He took the key out from his front pocket and unlocked her cell.

He opened the door cautiously, not sure what to expect from the quiet beauty who was sitting on the wooden floor before him. He didn't bother to glance at the men in the cell behind him. When he walked slowly to Miranda's cell, he noticed the men were lying in the same fashion as when he last saw them. They were no threat to him.

Lieutenant Mansfield opened the steel door and motioned for Miranda to come to him. "Lord Hammil wants to see you. I recommend coming quietly. He's in a foul mood, but I think you might be the one to cheer him up." Miranda obeyed, nervous about what she was about to do. She didn't want to spend time with Lord Hammil, but knew she must.

As she stepped through the cell door, she noticed the key was still being held captive in Lieutenant Mansfield's hand. She pretended to trip and fell forward. She threw herself against Lieutenant Mansfield who had fallen against the other cell and let go of the key to catch her. The key was on its way to the floor, but before it could reach its destination, Davy reached out his large dirty hand and caught it. He then lay back down quietly, the key tucked safely in his palm.

"I'm sorry, Lieutenant. I didn't mean to trip. Are you all right?" The lieutenant gazed into Miranda's warm brown eyes, then at her round tempting lips. Her body felt soft underneath her clothes, and the lieutenant couldn't help but notice it as he held her against him. His mind was reeling, trying to think of the last time he had a woman in his bed. It had been months. His hold on her began to loosen, and he started to caress her back unconsciously. Miranda had moved a step closer until her lips were only just inches from the lieutenant's. As she gazed up at him innocently, he lost control and tasted her lips. The kiss was brief but Miranda encouraged him by rubbing her supple curves against his. He bent low to kiss her again but then stopped and closed his eyes. Suddenly, he shook his head roughly as if to clear it. His hands moved back to her arms and he gripped her brutally. Miranda's face showed her pain.

"I have to take you to him. He wants you for his own purposes. I have my orders and can't stray from them." Miranda opened her eyes wide, giving him, again, the impression of innocence.

"I said nothing to imply that I don't want you to take me to him. I'm clumsy, that's all. Forgive me if I gave you the wrong impression. I'm nervous and afraid, for I know that he will hurt me for betraying him. I feel so alone." Lieutenant Mansfield loosened his painful grip and brought one of his hands to caress Miranda's cheek. "For a moment, in your arms, I felt safe." The lieutenant smiled as he held Miranda briefly against his chest.

"You are a tempting delight, woman. I will also say an innocent one. You are here for revenge only. Some of my men were killed today because of Lord Hammil's stupidity, and that angers me greatly. He showed them no compassion and didn't think of the consequences of his actions." Lieutenant Mansfield averted his eyes away from Miranda's for a moment, and then returned to them when he felt more calmed. "I will not let him harm you while I'm by your side, this I swear. But I can't stop him when you are away from me. I'm sorry, but this is the governor's ship, and though I find you desirable and wish that you were a woman destined for me, I do have my orders to abide by. I am a Lieutenant in the Royal Navy and have my loyalties and future to think about. I cannot mutiny against Lord Hammil. Understand that even though it would not bother me to do so—I cannot."

Miranda nodded her head and felt Lieutenant Mansfield's hand grip her arm once more. They quickly straightened up their positions, turned and moved forward, walking back through the belly of the ship to the bottom of the stairs. Miranda turned her head away from the lieutenant's and smiled. Her father's plan worked after all.

CHAPTER 16

The Captain's Avenger was several leagues away from the *Flying Wasp*. Locand stood on the quarterdeck and stared at the ship in front of him. He had changed his attire after the fight with Lord Hammil's men. He now wore a clean, billowy white shirt with a short jacket, pistols, wide dark breeches and a sword at his waist. His hair was tied into a queue at the base of his neck with a ribbon. The look upon his face held no warmth or laughter like it did in the past days when Miranda stood by his side. Now his face was stern and cold.

The crew even noticed a difference in their captain's behavior. Locand would shout his orders relentlessly, not giving the crew much time to rest. Having only half of the crew still alive, the men understood the urgency and followed their captain's orders without question. However, some men were exhausted and lacked food and drink. A couple of the men had fainted from fatigue and when another man dropped on the deck, Locand knew he had to do something.

He immediately walked to the railing and shouted to get the men's attention. He ordered half of his men to rest while the others remained on deck. Every couple of hours he told the crew that they would switch roles. Half would sleep while the others worked on deck. However, when the occasion arose and they were ready to fight, Locand said that he would wake them in advance and prepare them. The men nodded their heads in approval of the order. Each one of them was exhausted and drained of energy. He told the men to get back to work, dividing them up equally and excusing the men who he decided should rest first.

As the rest of the crew moved back to their positions on deck, Locand heard his stomach rumble. Not being able to remember the last time he had eaten, he knew the men were feeling the same pains of hunger he was. Not having Billy around to cook the meals, he yelled instead for another man named Tom, who was cleaning the deck intently. Tom could cook just as well as Billy, and sometimes better, and had helped him on many occasions prepare the meals. As Tom had stepped toward him, Locand ordered the man to prepare enough food and drink to replenish the men's spirits. Tom bowed his head and replied, "Aye, Captain!" Tom took a few steps and then turned around suddenly. Locand stared at the man in surprise.

"Captain? If you don't mind me saying so, you could use some rest before we continue farther. You, above anyone else, have seen more danger and battle. You must be weary." When Tom didn't hear a response, he quickly excused himself and went below deck to the galley to prepare the food as he was told.

Locand stared at the retreating body of Tom for some time before casting his gaze back again at the *Flying Wasp*, which was quickly moving farther and farther away from them. His ship was moving as fast as she could go, and yet she couldn't keep up with the *Flying Wasp*. His hopes of getting Miranda back were fading, and yet he knew he must keep trying. For their love, he knew, he must not give up.

Now, more determined than ever, Locand ordered his crew to tighten the sails. They needed to catch the wind better if they were going to save Miranda. The crew did as the captain requested and tightened the sails, pulling on the ropes as hard as they could and tying them to the posts. Locand steered the ship into the wind and to his delight, the wind filled the sails fuller and he could already feel the ship's pace quicken. A devilish grin crossed his features as *The Captain's Avenger* sailed closer and closer to its target.

Miranda took a deep breath as Lieutenant Mansfield placed her in front of Lord Hammil's cabin and knocked on the door. It didn't take long for him to answer. Lord Hammil opened the door with a sly grin. His clean white shirt was partially open to expose his pale bare chest. The blue waistcoat was discarded and all Miranda could see in the room was food on a table with a few tapers lit. Imagining what Lord Hammil had planned for her, Miranda returned the grin with a smirk.

"Here she is as you requested, milord. Would you care for me to stay?" Lord Hammil gazed into the lieutenant's face and laughed.

"No, Lieutenant, I will not need your services for what I need to do. Go back on deck and let me know when we are in position. How are the other prisoners? Well, I hope?"

"They haven't moved since I've seen them last. The one is still in pain from the lash." Miranda gazed back and forth from Lord Hammil to the lieutenant, her eyes glaring at them with interest.

"You better send someone down there to clean Captain Ditarius' wounds." Miranda's eyes flashed angrily at Lord Hammil, but his eyes only returned her stare unwaveringly. "I would hate for them to get infected before he gets a chance to hang for his crimes in Port Royal."

"No!" Miranda yelled. She glanced quickly at the lieutenant for help, but saw him barely shake his head at her unspoken question. He then focused his attention on Lord Hammil. Miranda turned toward him and did the same. "Is that where we are going, to Port Royal?" Lord Hammil ignored Miranda's question and looked toward the lieutenant.

"That will be all, Lieutenant. Again, let me know when everything will be in place. Several days have passed. We should be meeting up with the fleet soon." Miranda, not sure what Lord Hammil was talking about, was furious that he chose to ignore her. To get his attention, she brought back her hand quickly and slapped him across the cheek. The look upon Lord Hammil's face showed his surprise.

"I'm asking you a question, don't you dare ignore it." Lord Hammil sneered at Miranda.

"You want my attention, you've got it." His reactions were like lightening as he grabbed her roughly by the wrist, pulling her into the room. Miranda was so surprised by the action that she lost her balance and fell onto the floor in a heap. The lieutenant stepped forward to help her, but Lord Hammil blocked him.

"I said that would be all, Lieutenant." Lieutenant Mansfield shook his head defiantly but proceeded to back off. His eyes fell upon Miranda's form and saw the look of fear in her eyes.

"It would not be right for any of us to harm her, milord. She is our prisoner, but as you said before, she's also very valuable. Her virtue tarnished would not be wise from you." Lord Hammil looked threateningly at the lieutenant.

"What I choose to do with her is no business of yours. I have conversed with the governor, and we have come to an agreement of sorts. She is not your concern. Now go to the deck or I will inform the governor of your lack of respect, and he can punish you in the way he sees fit." The lieutenant hesitated for a moment before he glared at

Lord Hammil and made his way to the deck, his heart aching from the promise he did not keep.

Inside the room, Lord Hammil closed the door and turned on Miranda. He loomed toward her menacingly as she raised herself from the floor and stood up, dusting off her clothes from the fall and running her fingers through her hair. "You wanted my attention, my sweet, now you have it. But I bet you are asking yourself if it is the attention you are looking for." Miranda straightened her back proudly and glared into the evil eyes of Lord Hammil.

"What did you want to see me about, Lord Hammil? I liked my cell and am angry that you disturbed me from my solitude." Miranda's voice remained cool and aloof, but Lord Hammil was not fooled.

"You're angry that I disturbed you because you realized that your father and Davy were in the cell across from you. I'm not daft, child. I know what you are truly feeling about what I have done to your father." Miranda smirked at Lord Hammil, resting her hands on her hips.

"Then you will know how much I detest the sight of you." Lord Hammil shrugged his shoulders in reply. "Is that all you have to say for yourself?" asked Miranda heatedly.

"No! I have much more to say to you."

"Then say it and stop playing these games. If it helps, I will start. How long have you known that I was Stratton Mayne's daughter?" Lord Hammil stared boldly at Miranda, his eyes not wavering from her face.

"I have known since just before we left for the Caribbean. It was a shock to me for sure, but a pleasant one. Why else do you think I would ask you to come with me? I might add you were more than willing. I was hoping for your eagerness to travel. I knew that if no one else could find your father, you could. You are his daughter and Davy his faithful first mate." Miranda's eyes widened from what she heard.

"Yes, Miranda, I knew of Davy's loyalties to your father. He's a very devoted man to watch over you as if you were his own blood. I was sent here from the queen to get the Spanish treasure and bring it back to her. I will in fact do that, but not before the Governor of Port Royal takes his fair share of the cut and I, mine. I also wish to fund a little war against our fair queen. The treasure will help me do that. Her enemies are great, and combining them will overthrow her."

"But that is treason!" yelled Miranda not believing what she had heard.

"Yes, it is. I am no fool, Miranda. I have many connections. The queen has made it so. I'm only using them to my advantage." Miranda shook her head in disbelief.

"Why involve Locand? What has he done—" Before Miranda could finish, she heard Lord Hammil laugh.

"I knew where Captain Riveri's loyalties lied. That was why he was picked for this journey, as I know you must have heard when I told him aboard his ship. I knew if I made myself unavailable long enough that you would fall for him, and that, my dear Miranda, is what I needed you to do."

Miranda could not believe what she was hearing and shook her head yet again. She remembered vividly the words he had said to Locand, and yet at the time, they didn't sink in.

"But why? Why would you want that?"

"Because, I knew that if you could not find your father, then Locand would be able to. Either way, I was determined to find the crystals and knew that I would eventually need you or him, at some point, to get them and find the treasure. I took a chance thinking that your father had the crystals in his possession. I was amazed that your father gave the other crystal to Captain Riveri. That, I was not expecting, and yet deep down it was what I wanted. Who else to help you find the treasure in Nombre de Dios but your savior Captain Riveri? I knew that if you got under his skin like you did mine, he would do anything to help you. Besides, his loyalty and devotion for your father would have forced him to protect you. I was surprised to learn that he didn't recognize you when we first came aboard *The Captain's Avenger*, but that did not matter. Eventually, I knew he would remember or would be reminded by Davy of your existence—therefore of his oath."

Lord Hammil gazed briefly around him before turning his attention back on Miranda. "You have cost me much in this little venture, but I am willing to overlook it." He slowly reached out his right hand and caressed Miranda's smooth cheek. She didn't back away from him, but didn't enjoy the caress either.

"And why would you overlook my involvement in all of this?" Miranda was curious about Lord Hammil's intentions. She now realized that he was a very intelligent man, and her future was clenched tightly in his fists.

"Because, my sweet, before I knew of your true identity, I was in love with Miranda Smyth. To be honest with you, I still am. You are a magnificent creature Miranda, and I would still like you to become my wife. You have shown me much courage and strength these past months, and my love for you has only gotten stronger with each passing day. I am willing to forgive all transgressions on your part and allow you to live freely and happily by my side."

"What of my father? What of Davy? Does your forgiveness pass down to them if we marry?" Miranda held her breath hoping that he would tell her what she needed to hear.

"If you marry me willingly, Miranda, I will extend my forgiveness to them. However, you must realize that the governor wants your father to hang in Port Royal as an example that no pirates belong there. It is part of our bargain, but there might be ways around it if I am persuaded."

"I beseech you to find them!" Miranda looked away from Lord Hammil and glanced around the room in contemplation. "I will do whatever you ask." As she looked past the bed, that was only a few feet from her, she noticed the room was much smaller than Locand's had been. There was a desk against one of the walls and tapers that gave off much light. She noticed a brown, medium sized trunk that was locked, lying against another wall. It was at that moment Miranda realized how hopeless her situation was. She hoped that Locand was following their ship, but what if he wasn't? What if he gave up on her?

No! Miranda thought as she shook her head in anger. He cared for her, she knew that. That thought brought her to another— their love. She refused to think of how loving and passionate Locand was. His soft mouth covering hers as they kissed. His strong arms holding her as if they were a shield. When she felt Lord Hammil's hand upon her shoulder, she screamed in surprise.

He had woken her from her thoughts and for his efforts jumped back several feet and raised his hand to his chest. "Don't worry, my dear. I will not strike you again." Miranda placed her right hand over her eyes and composed herself, the fright almost making her cry. As her racing heart began to slow she knew what she must do.

"Where would we marry, Lord Hammil?" Miranda raised her eyes to stare into his.

"At New Providence, of course. I was not lying when I said that I always wanted to get married there. It is my family home."

"When would we marry?" Lord Hammil walked up to Miranda and placed his hands upon her shoulders again.

"We will wed after we make our delivery to Port Royal and the governor gets his share of the gold. After that, we will head for New Providence, wed, and then go back to England. I will have a new bride and new wealth, and you will have your faithful servant and father." Miranda's thoughts were in turmoil. To marry Lord Hammil would make part of her family safe, but her heart would be lonely, for she did not love him, she loved Locand.

"What of Locand?" The mention of Locand's name made Lord Hammil flinch. Miranda could feel the brief movement in his hands.

"He will be taken care of. At Port Royal I had planned for him to be taken by the guards and put into the cells at the fort until he was hanged for piracy, and I was to use *The Captain's Avenger* as my ship to find the treasure. How he knew of my plans to capture him, I will never know, but he outwitted me and left the harbor before my plans for him could be set into motion. I had to instead make a bargain with the governor to borrow his ship and crew to find you. He cost me some of my fortune and will pay for it with his life."

"Locand is a pirate no longer but a privateer, given a letter of marque from the queen. You cannot hang him." Anger rose in Miranda's chest as she fought to defend Locand.

"Oh, my dear, but I can. Once I tell the queen how Captain Riveri turned against me, she will condone any course of action I decided to take. The letter of marque was his last chance to become respectable and he knew it. He was to do the queen's bidding with the understanding that if he ever went against the crown again, he would be hung for his past transgressions. I have no problem turning him over to the governor to deal with."

Miranda ran her fingers through her hair as she realized exactly what Lord Hammil had used her for. "You used me to make Locand break the contract, to break the letter of marque given to him by the queen? It will be my fault then if he is hanged for piracy. He took his last chance and threw it away to help me, by going against you. It's my fault."

"Yes, Miranda, it is. But let's not forget the fact that he helped a wanted pirate escape. He went to Eleuthera, not just for you, my dear, but to tell his faithful friend that I was coming. He warned your father about me. To me, that goes against his letter of marque. He only betrayed himself." Miranda raised her fingertips to her lips and stared at Lord Hammil with disgust.

"Why do you despise him so much?" Lord Hammil lowered his eyes before he could answer.

"I despise him because a few years ago he took my bride away from me." Miranda's eyes opened wide in amazement.

"What?"

"Don't look at me so surprised, my dear. Your Captain is capable of much trickery and deception. He met my bride when she was at a celebration. I was late doing some business for the queen. More to the point, I didn't show. She was there, and he had kept her company in my stead. The following morning, I went over to her townhouse to apologize, but instead of finding her I ran into Captain Riveri who was leaving. She heard me arguing with him, and she came out and explained to me what had happened. She said that she had seduced him, but I don't believe her. He charmed her, seduced her into his bed where he soiled her for me. He probably doesn't even remember her name, that was how important she was to him." Miranda was in awe of the story she had just heard, and though she knew that she should be angry at Locand for what he had done to another man's woman—she couldn't. The woman was years before her time, but it did explain the tension between the two men.

"What was her name?"

"Her name was Lucy, and she looked very much like you."

"I am sure that Locand wasn't aware that she was to become your wife."

"I don't care! The point is she went willingly into his arms. If he didn't use his pirate ways to lure her to him, she would be my wife at this moment, and I wouldn't be searching around for another bride." Miranda's eyebrows lowered in thought, glaring at Lord Hammil and feeling like a used towel.

"So, why do you want to marry me then? To get back at him for what he had done by making me your bride? It doesn't make sense, Leonard. You threw me into his arms, you admitted as much to me."

"You're right, I did push you toward him, and I can tell that you care for him. But the one thing that is different between you and Lucy is that he cares for you in return. Because of that, I will use you to make things even between us. By marrying you, it will hurt him, and that is precisely what I aim to do. I want to hurt him as much as I was hurt when I found out my bride betrayed me by bedding another."

"Where is she now?" asked Miranda curiously.

"Married to Lord Havenor. They are a good match, though, an informant and a whore." Lord Hammil said his last words so carelessly that fear crept into Miranda's chest.

"So, it is vengeance you want? Then why put the effort into chasing my father?"

"Why not? He is the notorious Captain Ditarius the deadly. I want the prestige when the masses hear how I captured him. No man has been able to do that before."

"And me?"

"Miranda, your beauty could make the strongest of men do your bidding. I can offer you much wealth and freedom. To have you on my arm would make the men of the world green with envy. I am a man who has little of love, beauty and power. Now that I have the chance, I wish to have it all." Lord Hammil leaned forward, his lips just inches from Miranda's. "I will admit that you are my one weakness."

Before Miranda could say another word in reply, Lord Hammil grabbed her firmly toward him and placed his lips upon hers in a passionate kiss. He gripped her tightly in his arms and forced his tongue into her mouth. Miranda's eyes grew wide as she felt his tongue mate with hers. She tried to pull away but couldn't. The kiss was pleasant but did not have the same effect on her as Locand's had. His kisses could light a fire so hot within her loins she needed to use his body to quench it.

As Miranda slowly moved her face away from Lord Hammil's to end the kiss, she felt his grip tighten around her forcing her to move closer. When he decided to finally end the kiss, Miranda could see his eyes cloud with lust. Though her lips were red and moist, her eyes or body showed no affect. However, Lord Hammil didn't take the time to notice that fact as the smile on his lips grew wider with satisfaction.

"I have longed to kiss you, Miranda, thank you for allowing me the pleasure." Miranda resisted the urge to roll her eyes, like she had much of a choice to stop him from forcing his lips upon hers. "I told you that I would try harder to please you. I hope this kiss was more to your liking."

"Yes, it was. It was much better in fact." Lord Hammil smiled arrogantly. "Now what?" added Miranda.

"Now, my sweet, you will be staying in my cabin with me until we reach Port Royal. I will allow you to go on deck and move around freely to stretch your legs, as long as you behave properly."

"Can I go on deck now without your company?"

"You can only go in my company or the Lieutenant's," clarified Lord Hammil. "Does that satisfy you, my love?"

"For the moment," replied Miranda as she moved past Lord Hammil and reached for the cabin door handle. "Shall we go then?"

CHAPTER 17

Locand was in his cabin poring over his maps when he heard a knock on his door. He chose to ignore it as he moved his finger down an imaginary line and stopped. Locand stared at the map in disbelief and shook his head. No, his calculations must be off. But when he looked at the coordinates again, he looked up and stared at the wall. They were headed for Port Royal, but why? Locand's thoughts started to fill his mind with all sorts of reasons. Lord Hammil was taking him to Port Royal which meant that the governor was involved, which he had known from the army men that filled Lord Hammil's ship, but what did he want with him? Before Locand could entertain another thought, he again heard the knock on his door.

"Enter!" he almost yelled in frustration. He took a deep breath and tried calming himself.

"It is Tom, Captain. I'm sorry to disrupt you, but we have a problem. Ships have been spotted coming toward us, and they carry the English flag." The man hesitated before continuing, "The ships are part of the governor's fleet. I remember seeing them when we were in Port Royal. What are we to do? Do we fight?"

Locand placed his hands on his desk and stared at the map. Lord Hammil arranged for the governor's fleet to come after them? He planned things perfectly, didn't he? There was not much they could do to save themselves. They were extremely outnumbered and could be over taken with ease. Locand looked back up at the wall and made his decision.

"This is what we will do, Tom. If we are to go down, then we will go down fighting. I want you to raise the flag with the red scarf." Tom stared at Locand as if he hadn't heard his words correctly, and then said, "So, it has come down to this. Alas, pirates we are again. Nothing can save us from the noose this time."

"We have no choice, Tom," said Locand. "We have tried to change our ways, but Lord Hammil is determined not to let us forget our pasts. There is no other way but to fight. Lord Hammil will show us no quarter, so we must not be afraid to offer him no mercy as well. This ship is all I have. I will not relinquish it into the hands of the devil." Tom nodded his head in agreement. Locand proceeded to explain the rest of his intentions. After Tom left his cabin, Locand punched his fist into the wall in frustration, then buried his face in his hands. Everything he had worked so hard to achieve, in a single moment, was gone.

Miranda was the first one to spot the ships that were sailing in their direction. She was walking the deck watching the many men of the crew moving about and doing their duties, when she spotted something in the distance. She walked closer to the railing and raised her hand to block the sun. She saw the flags immediately and realized what they were. It was the governor's fleet. The fleet contained many ships but only three were sailing toward them. She quickly turned to find Lord Hammil. He had his back toward her talking to a member of the crew.

Miranda remembered what he had said to Lieutenant Mansfield about letting him know when the fleet had arrived. Why did Lord Hammil require the governor's fleet to sail with them? Many thoughts were flowing through her mind, but none that made sense. She was about to stand by the railing and wait for Lord Hammil to notice the ships, but by then, they would already be upon them. She turned around and walked swiftly toward him. Before she reached him, one of the crew yelled from above that three ships were approaching.

Lord Hammil hurried up the stairs to the quarterdeck and looked toward the southeast. Sure enough, he saw the fleet approaching. A wide smile fell upon his lips as he looked down toward the deck and spotted Miranda. Her hands were on her hips and the look upon her face was one of irritation. Lord Hammil descended from the quarter-deck and walked toward her.

"So my dear, what do you think?" The smile on his pale face beamed at her.

"What do I think about what? I don't understand what you wish to accomplish with the governor's fleet by your side. Why are they here?" Lord Hammil placed his arm around Miranda's shoulders and turned her around, walking her to the railing from which she just came.

"Those ships are not for me, nor are they for you. They are here to capture Captain Riveri. Brilliant, isn't it?" Miranda turned sharply and stared into the merry eyes of Lord Hammil.

"No!"

"Oh, yes! His ship has only half a crew. I have made sure of it. He will have no choice but to surrender himself and the ship to the fleet. Captain Riveri is an intelligent man and knows that it would be futile to fight. Now, if he had a full crew on board, I would be more concerned. But I know he will make the right decision and yield. He will not risk the rest of the lives of his men in a battle he knows he would not be able to win." Miranda turned back toward the fleet and then toward *The Captain's Avenger*. A tear escaped her eyes as she saw Locand standing strong and proud at the helm.

"Now, my dear, there is no reason for you to cry. This will be over soon." The urge to punch Lord Hammil in the face was overwhelming. Lord Hammil walked away from her and left her by the railing as he instructed his men on what to do. She stood by that same railing until the fleet sailed close enough to Locand to demand him to give up his ship. There was a moment when Miranda thought that he would fight the ships now surrounding him, but instead he yielded, and *The Captain's Avenger* was boarded. Long wooded planks were dropped, landing on the railings, and grappling hooks were tossed over with men swinging on them, landing on the deck. To her pleasure it was then that Locand and his men started to fight. Miranda watched in anticipation, and Lord Hammil in horror, as the men of *The Captain's Avenger* fought for their very lives. Few of Locand's crew perished in the battle, but when one of the other ships drew close enough to board, the fight was futile and they surrendered, soon becoming outnumbered. She then saw two men grab Locand and tie his hands behind his back, pushing him aboard one of the ships. Tears of sorrow fell down her cheeks. There was nothing she could do to stop it.

Locand stared in Miranda's direction until he was made to go below deck. He did not want to surrender but thought it would be better than risking the lives of his crew when he knew they were too exhausted to fight more than three dozen men. Locand also knew that he would not be able to save Miranda if he were dead. He needed to stay alive for her if not for himself. His future was uncertain, but Locand was determined not to give up. He needed to stay strong to withstand whatever peril was destined for him. If the governor was this determined to have him, then Locand knew his fate would be worse than death.

As the fleet ships pulled away and veered off into another direction, *The Captain's Avenger*, in all its glory, was left behind. Miranda stared at the ship in revelry remembering the special moments that Locand and she had shared upon it. Then, before she knew what happened, she heard loud cannon blasts and watched in shock as several cannon balls hit *The Captain's Avenger*, damaging her. Pieces of wood flew everywhere, and the main mast had been broken. The ship slowly started sinking to the bottom of the sea as water moved quickly over it, wiping away all existence. Miranda's mouth was agape as she saw the ship disappear. With the sinking of the ship, she felt her hopes and dreams spiraling down with it, lost in destruction.

It took several weeks before they reached Port Royal. Lord Hammil's ship was casually following the three fleet ships that was now several leagues ahead of them. Miranda had spent most of her time below deck in Lord Hammil's cabin crying her sorrows. She was not allowed to go to the hold where she knew her father and Davy were kept prisoners. She had almost hoped they would have freed themselves by now, but knew it would be foolish for them to do so. Where would they go? Her father's plan was to wait until they reached their destination before acquiring their freedom, until then he said they would remain in the cell.

Miranda's thoughts often fell upon Locand and what would happen to him. She knew there was not much she could do to help, but it didn't stop her from wanting to try. She then remembered that Adam was still tied to one of the masts on deck. She spoke to Lieutenant Mansfield, and requested that Adam receive water and food. He told her that Lord Hammil had other orders, so she softened her features, blinking her youthful eyes alluringly until eventually he gave in to her demands. He still felt bad about not coming to her aid against Lord Hammil like he had promised. Miranda made sure she used his feelings for her as an advantage.

Miranda stood in front of the porthole in Lord Hammil's cabin when she heard him come in. He refused to knock when she was in the cabin and made the habit of just walking in unannounced. Miranda turned around briefly. She saw Lord Hammil unbutton a couple of buttons from the top of his shirt and wipe his face with a towel. For all the time he spent in the sun, one would think he would be tan, but he was not. He removed a large hat from the top of his head and tossed it upon the bed. His pasty white complexion almost looked paler as he wiped the sweat from his brow.

"Are you still down here sulking?" Lord Hammil's words caused Miranda to turn back around to face the porthole, her back fully facing him. "I will take that as a yes." He then walked up to her and placed his sweaty hands upon her shoulders.

"Do not touch me!" Miranda remained stiff as Lord Hammil tightened and then loosened his hold upon her.

"Will you not let me kiss you?" Miranda turned around quickly. Lord Hammil had no choice but to remove his hands from her.

"When we are wed, I will have no choice but to allow you those pleasures, but not yet. I am furious with you and will not indulge your fantasies." Lord Hammil narrowed his glance as he stared at Miranda. Then without warning he grabbed her roughly by the shoulders again and forced her toward him. Their lips met forcefully, but Lord Hammil did not mind. As Miranda tried to pull away from him, he moved his hands from her shoulders to cup her face. She could not stop his tongue from pushing its way into her mouth no matter how hard she tried. He held her face tighter as his tongue moved rapidly inside. It was hard for her to enjoy the kiss, for his movements were too fast and she could not keep up.

Miranda tried to push herself away from him again and this time he let her go. She stumbled back several feet as she wiped the wetness from her lips. "I must say, my dear, there is just something about you that fills my blood with desire." *I wish I could say the same*, thought Miranda, though she dared not speak her words aloud in case Lord Hammil punished her for it by hurting her father or Davy.

"I have something for you." Lord Hammil ignored the scathing looks he was receiving from Miranda and stepped closer to her, placing a dagger in her hand. Miranda looked at the weapon and then back at Lord Hammil suspiciously.

"You have much faith in me to give me this."

"My gift to you is the freedom of the boy on deck. I believe my starving him of drink and food might have nearly killed him. Why don't you go and take care of him. Mind though, that he will not be set free, just temporarily released until he gets better." Miranda glanced back at the dagger before placing it through the belt at her waist. "Lieutenant Mansfield knows that you have the dagger and that you are only supposed to use it to cut the boy free. If by chance you use the weapon on one of my men, rest assured that you will join the boy and be tied up next to him. Understand?" Miranda nodded her head in understanding and walked toward the door.

"You can use one of the cabins next to mine. There is a spare bed in there." Miranda heard Lord Hammil's words and chose to respond by only nodding her head, but then she reconsidered, deciding that she would like to leave him with a parting remark.

"Thank you for this! I appreciate you allowing me to care for the boy."

"See, I am not as heartless as you may think. I do hope this proof of faith will allow you to accept me for who I am, and hopefully one day— love me?" Miranda stared at Lord Hammil, not quite sure of how to answer his question and, yet, thinking that he was asking too much from her to assume there could be love between them. As far as she was concerned, he was heartless. His one moment of kindness toward her was only because he thought he had killed Adam.

"Only time will tell, Leonard. We will have to see how many other good deeds you can do for me. As far as I am concerned you have much to make up." Miranda gave Lord Hammil a small smile before turning around, opening the cabin door, and walking out into the hallway. She closed the door loudly behind her as she made her way to the stairs that led to the deck.

Lieutenant Mansfield met her at the top of the stairs and pointed her toward Adam. She quickly moved to him and dropped to her knees before him. Adam's head was lying on his chest. His eyes were closed and his lips were slightly cracked. His arms were dangling slightly above his head and his wrists were red and raw from the rope digging into them.

Miranda grabbed the dagger and cut through the thick rope. It was not an easy task, and took her a little bit of time to accomplish it, but suddenly she heard the ropes give, and Adam fell in a pile on the deck. "Please, help me carry him below, Lieutenant." Miranda was about to grab Adam's arms to lift him, but Lieutenant Mansfield quickly scooped up the boy with ease and carried him below deck for her. Miranda placed the dagger back at her waist and followed quietly, glancing periodically around to see if any of the crew was paying her any attention.

Once below, she hurried in front of Lieutenant Mansfield to open the cabin door that was next to Lord Hammil's. Inside, the lieutenant walked slowly to the bed and laid Adam's limp body upon it. The boy's head turned to the side, his lips slightly open with his arms by his sides.

The lieutenant stood close to Miranda's side as she hurried toward Adam. He watched her carefully as she felt the warmness of his face and arms. "Can you please fetch me some water, food and a cloth? The boy is parched and will surely die if he does not get water soon." The lieutenant stared at Miranda for a moment before hurrying to do her bidding. When he left the room and closed the door behind him, Miranda exhaled a deep breath. She then focused her attention back onto Adam, concern filling her features. She touched his forehead briefly as she whispered his name.

"Adam?" He didn't answer. She noticed the rise and fall of his chest and was thankful for it. She tried again and this time she saw his eyelids flutter. Miranda grabbed his arm with her hand and squeezed. "Adam? It is me, Miranda."

Adam turned his head toward the feminine voice that seemed to call to him out of the darkness. His eyes opened slightly as he quickly scanned the room. Finding that they were alone he opened his eyes wider and smiled. Miranda leaned back and cocked her head to the side in confusion.

"I knew he would send you to save me from those unbearable ropes if he thought I was dead. That miserable cur has no pity." Adam started to sit up, but Miranda placed her hand on his chest and pressed him back onto the bed. It took her a moment to realize that Adam had been pretending. A slight smile crossed her lips as she thought about how this young boy outsmarted the prestigious Lord Hammil.

"You must keep pretending, Adam. It will be the only way I can detain you from being tied up again. Lord Hammil told me that as soon as you are better you must return to the ropes, but I will keep you from that fate as long as I can. He thought you were ill or near death."

"That was the idea, Miss." Miranda shook her head as she heard the cabin door being opened. Adam turned his head to the left and lay quietly upon the bed, his eyes closed and peaceful as before.

Lieutenant Mansfield stepped into the room with a tray filled with all of the items Miranda had requested of him to bring. He gently laid the tray upon a table in the room and walked closer to Miranda, his hand holding a cup of water for the boy.

"Has he moved at all since I left?" Miranda could hear the concern in the lieutenant's voice.

"Unfortunately not. I was hoping he would have by now, but I think the water will help. Thank you." Miranda turned briefly and grabbed the cup out of the lieutenant's hand. She carefully turned Adam's head and brought the cup to his lips. He drank the contents slowly, his mouth and lips feeling dry and parched. Miranda laid Adam's head back down onto the pillow and ran her fingers through his hair.

"Thank you for your help, Lieutenant, but you can return to your duties. I can take care of him from here." The lieutenant hesitated, his lips opening slightly wanting to say something.

"I'm sorry, Miranda. Sorry that I couldn't be more help to you." Miranda kept her attention toward Adam as she spoke.

"Don't worry, Lieutenant. Your career is more important than saving someone in need. You have made that quite clear."

"Miranda!" The lieutenant grabbed a hold of Miranda's arm, but she just glared at him in response.

"You owe me nothing, sir, so do not pursue this course."

"I will make it up to you. I feel ashamed of myself for what has happened to you, for how you have been treated." The lieutenant paused for a moment and let go of her. "For what is going to happen to Captain Riveri. I see that you care for him and that Lord Hammil is using him against you." Miranda reached for the lieutenant, her hand grasping his arm tightly.

"What is he planning, Lieutenant? Please, you must tell me. He has told me very little about his plans." The lieutenant glanced at the boy on the bed, then returned his gaze to Miranda.

"The fleet is to take Captain Riveri to Port Royal where he will be hanged. Your father and friend will be by his side in the gallows."

"But Lord Hammil said that if I marry him, he will spare their lives." The lieutenant raised his eyebrows skeptically as he shook his head.

"He is after one goal and lies to get what he wants. I've overheard his plans and know what he's doing. His intentions were to sail to New Providence and not see the hangings, but his curiosity has gotten the better of him. He wants to make sure it is done. We all sail for Port Royal, and I guarantee that your wedding will be there as well." Miranda's hand dropped to her side as she stared across the room blankly. "We are getting closer and should be arriving by early morning." Lieutenant Mansfield placed his hand on Miranda's shoulder. The action forced her to look at him. "I should leave you alone now. You need time to think." He spun around and headed for the door. Before opening it, however, he walked back to Miranda and removed the dagger from her waist, "Just in case!" He again headed for the door, a smirk upon his lips. When he reached it, he turned to face Miranda one more time.

"I would lock the door to give you more privacy, but I seem to have lost my key. You wouldn't happen to know where it might have gone, would you?" The lieutenant's question caught Miranda by surprise as they shared a knowing glance. What shocked her more was the fact that he seemed not to care. "Oh, well, it will turn up eventually. Until then I'm sure that it found itself to be in a safe place and will be used wisely when the right moment arises." Miranda narrowed her eyes at the lieutenant. She glanced at the cabin door and realized there was no lock on it. The lieutenant knew exactly where the key had been lost and wanted to make sure she knew it.

"I will see you are not disturbed." Lieutenant Mansfield glanced at the boy on the bed, smiled, opened the door and left. Miranda turned around and faced Adam, who was now sitting up, his legs hanging carelessly over the side of the bed. His eyes were wide with youthfulness and curiosity.

"What was that all about?" Miranda stared at the blanket on the bed and raised her hand to her face in concentration.

"I don't know, Adam, but I believe the Lieutenant is giving us time to find a solution to our problems." Adam jumped up from the bed and stood in front of Miranda.

"If what he says is true and we are sailing to Port Royal, then how are we going to save Captain Riveri and his crew? With the governor's men watching over them, the task would be close to impossible." Miranda's mind was swimming with possibilities but none she thought would work. Then all of a sudden, Adam snapped his fingers. The action caused Miranda's head to jerk up forcefully. A smile was evident upon the boy's lips.

"We will save him the same way we helped him when Lord Hammil was staying with the governor. I will ask my sister, Rose, for help. She will be able to help the captain escape again."

"What are you talking about, Adam? What do you mean, again?"

"My sister distracted Lord Hammil long enough for Captain Riveri to sail away from Port Royal and the trap he was setting for him. I, of course, also helped which is why I am a part of his crew now. I earned my place. I was the one who found out the truth of your identity, as well as other things of course. But if it wasn't for my sister's help, the captain would have been captured by the governor's men and hanged, along with his crew." Miranda's brow furrowed with confusion. She wasn't quite sure what his sister did to distract Lord Hammil.

"I'm sorry, Adam, but what exactly does your sister do?" Adam's smile faded slightly as his gaze flew to the floor.

"She's a woman of the night, Miss, a common whore." Miranda whispered a silent, "Oooh!" But as she thought more about the words Adam had just spoken to her, she spoke more loudly, "Oh!" Now everything Adam had said was making sense to her as well as what Lord Hammil had confessed to her. When they spoke earlier he had wondered how Locand could have known about his plans to capture him and take over his ship. Now Miranda understood how Locand had known. It was because of Adam and his sister. Adam's sister had seduced Lord Hammil, and there he confessed to her his plans.

She, in return, told Locand–allowing him to sail away from Port Royal unscathed. The information he received from Adam must have been enough to direct him to Eleuthera. However, Locand and her father had been close enough friends that he would have known exactly where to find him. She then remembered what Locand had said to her on Eleuthera. He had said that Lord Hammil was in need of a woman. That he was not immune to seduction—essentially. Knowing that little bit of information, Locand must have sent Adam's sister toward Lord Hammil for a reason. He must not have trusted him to begin with and, with their past history, she could not blame him. She then remembered that Davy had also said that he warned Locand not to trust Lord Hammil.

The complexity of the situation awed Miranda. But it seemed that, though Locand was able to sail away from Lord Hammil once, he would not be able to do so again, at least not without help. What bothered Miranda the most was the fact that Locand knew what he was risking for her. He knew that his life was at stake for getting involved with her, and yet he still did it. Why? Because he loved her? She hoped with all of her heart that his feelings for her were pure and true. It was because of her faith in Locand that Miranda felt the need to save him. The need to help him escape. She loved him too much to let him die for her. By any means necessary, she would try to save him.

If Adam's sister could make Lord Hammil trust her enough to confess his desires, then maybe she could get him to do it again, or at least be enough of a distraction to him so it would give Miranda time to free Locand. A quick thought ran through Miranda's mind. It was an unwanted curiosity. She was curious how well Locand knew Adam's sister? The question that haunted her was if she ever seduced him into her bed? That particular thought caused the briefest hint of jealousy, but she cast the feeling aside immediately. The past did not matter to her, only the future. She did not care if he had gone to her bed, only that he wouldn't be revisiting it. Miranda returned her focus back on Adam. She could tell he was ashamed of what his sister did for a living.

"I can see that you are uncomfortable talking about your sister's occupation."

"Only in front of you, Miss. I do not wish for you to think ill of her. She does what she can to protect me from the world, as well as herself. We were not blessed with much and my sister can barely take care of herself. I know I was a burden to her but she still gave me some of the money she earned so I could eat every day." Miranda's heart went out to Adam. She now knew why Locand had let him join his crew. It was so he could provide him with a better life than the one he was living.

"Your sister loves you, Adam, and she is willing to sacrifice herself for your safety. She wants a better life for you. There is much honor to be found in that." Adam's chest seemed to puff out a little as a smile shown upon his lips. "Now, let's talk about your sister. I think you're right. We will need her help again if we are to free Locand. I will take care of my father and Davy. They already have a key to free themselves. They will only need to know when to use it." The pair talked for hours before settling on a plan that was tangible. Miranda only hoped their plan would work. She prayed they could pull it off. All of their futures depended on it.

CHAPTER 18

Miranda stayed with Adam in his cabin for most of the night. She wanted to keep up with the façade they were creating of Adam's illness. She didn't want to bring on suspicion from anyone, especially Lord Hammil. He would arrive every few hours into the cabin to check on her welfare as well as Adam's. He had pleaded for Miranda to return to his cabin to sleep next to him, but she had refused. It was during these visits that Adam would lay upon the bed motionless. A few times he would move his head or arm, sighing as he made the motion, but mostly he would remain still.

After Lord Hammil felt his efforts were in vain, he would leave. But not before giving Adam a scathing look when Miranda wasn't looking. He missed having Miranda's attention focused on him. He almost craved the touch of her hand upon him when he had felt ill. He missed the nights when her body would lie against his when he fell asleep.

By morning, Port Royal was in sight. Miranda had decided earlier to go on deck to check on the activities above when she saw an island mass through her porthole window. She was hoping she would be able to find out more about what was going to happen to Locand by listening to the crew and watching the other ships ahead of them.

When Miranda stepped onto the deck, she was immediately accosted by Lord Hammil, who, it seemed, was waiting for her arrival. Her eyes remained focused on the ships ahead of them, and she watched eagerly as they sailed into the harbor and dropped their anchors. Longboats were soon lowered and were then filled with members of the crew. Locand and his men had been tied to the mast for the past few days, and it was there where they were forced from their broken sleep and into the boats. A tear almost escaped her eyes as she saw how her lover was brutally treated.

Lord Hammil, not wanting Miranda to see too much of the goings on around them, grabbed her elbow and turned her toward him.

"I missed you last night, Miranda, and now that we have reached Port Royal my spirits are lifted." Miranda's mood had plummeted to beyond sadness.

"Is that where we are, Leonard, Port Royal?" Miranda scoffed loudly. "It's amazing to me how you can be so different. I thought you to be at least compassionate toward others, but I was wrong." Miranda thought of a question that had been bothering her. "Was it you who burned down the church in Sussex, killing all of those innocent worshippers?" Lord Hammil took several steps away from Miranda and stared at her as if she were deformed.

"I would hardly say they were all devoted to God. I did what I needed to do, what no one else had the stomach to do." Miranda thought for a moment that he was going to deny it, but instead he smiled broadly and folded his arms in front of his chest. It was at that moment she saw him for what he really was, a ruthless and callous man who cared for no one but himself. He was a monster.

"I couldn't picture you doing something as brutal and inhuman as that, and when I was told that it was you, I didn't want to believe it." Lord Hammil took several steps closer and leaned toward her.

"And who told you that, your beloved father no doubt?" When Miranda didn't answer he continued, "Yes, our wonderful Captain Ditarius, we know he has a spotless record. I have heard of him killing hundreds of men, and yet his sins do not bother you." Miranda's gaze bore into Lord Hammil's. "I would call that hypocritical."

"Actually, his sins do trouble me, as do yours." Miranda paused as her gaze moved up and down Lord Hammil's length. "You appear so weak. I never would have thought you could be so merciless."

"That is why I'm so valuable to the queen. No one else would suspect it of me either." He then kissed her cheek and spoke softly in her ear. "Sometimes, the quiet ones are the most dangerous of men." Tears sprang to Miranda's eyes as she realized, again, how hopeless her situation was.

"You deceived me so smoothly, Leonard. You deceived us all. You are much wiser and more powerful than I ever could have thought." Lord Hammil smiled as he cupped Miranda's cheek in his hand and kissed her lips. Miranda didn't pull away but let him have his way with her for the moment. She knew it wouldn't last long for they were on deck where the crew was watching them, and she knew how

Lord Hammil lived and died with the rules of propriety. When the kiss ended, he quickly glanced around and kissed her lips again before pulling away from her. "You are also cruel and barbaric," Miranda spouted off as she stared at him.

"Now, would I deceive you, my darling? I think you better look in a mirror before you start judging me so harshly, don't you think?" Lord Hammil's tone was rough and angry. "I know I have kept you in the dark, but it is for good reason, just as good of a reason as it was for you to keep me in the dark about your identity." Miranda rolled her eyes and pursed her lips.

"Where are they taking Locand?" Miranda raised her arm toward the ships in front of them.

"You must face the reality that he is going to die for his sins, Miranda. He's not an innocent pirate. In fact, he has taken many lives and some of them were with little care. The governor wants his head, and I am more then willing to give it to him."

"Yes, and you're just as innocent as he is." Miranda didn't bother to turn her head and instead kept her attention focused on the ship ahead. When she didn't hear a reply she asked, "And me? What is to be my fate?" Miranda's voice broke slightly but she lifted her head high. Lord Hammil caressed her cheek with his hand and forced her to look at him.

"I told you of your fate, Miranda. We are to be wed."

"I thought we were to marry in New Providence. Why are we here?"

"There is a slight delay in proceedings. Our stay will not be as short as I had originally made you believe. The truth would upset you, my dear, so I will not indulge your curiosity, but I will tell you this. The governor now owes me a favor and will marry us up at the fort instead of in New Providence. Though the change of location disappoints me, the governor has made it worth my while to stay. The look upon your face shows of your concern, but there is nothing for you to be concerned about. I promise we will discuss this topic further, but for right now, we have other things to take care of. For instance, we need to go ashore and find you an appropriate dress to wear for the occasion."

"Will we be staying here on the ship? I need to keep an eye on Adam." The smile on Lord Hammil's face started to fade.

"You will stay by my side from now on and not by that boy. We will be staying at the governor's mansion and will have all of the luxuries that you deserve." Miranda became instantly alarmed. If Lord Hammil would not let her out of his sight, then how could Adam's sister distract him? She also needed time to free her father and Davy. She needed time to free Locand. A bright smile rose upon her lips as her mind was spinning.

"Leonard, I cannot leave Adam's side. His condition is critical. He needs my full attention for the moment and cannot be moved." Lord Hammil squeezed Miranda's arm as he was trying to control his temper. She winced slightly from the pain.

"I insist that you forget the boy. I have more important needs for you to tend to." Miranda's eyes grew wide as she saw the desire in Lord Hammil's eyes.

"I will not satisfy you in that way, Leonard." Miranda lowered her voice so the crew could not hear what she was saying. "We are not wed yet. I will not let you take me before you become my husband. Afterward, you can do what you like with my body, but not before." Lord Hammil became frustrated and squeezed Miranda's arm more painfully. "You are hurting me!" yelled Miranda as she looked around for the crew to help her. A few of the governor's men stepped forward, not liking to see any man harm a woman. When Lord Hammil saw some of the men's expressions, he loosened his hold.

"You and I not being wed is a problem I'm going to shortly remedy. I will not have you in my bed, that's fine for right now, but you are going with me ashore. There are some things I want you to see, and I need you to be seen." Lord Hammil let go of Miranda's arm in distaste.

"What of my Father and of Davy?"

"I would not worry about them. Half of these men are going to stay behind to guard them. And I wouldn't get any ideas about trying to free your father. The men have orders to kill him if he surfaces. If you make a wrong move Miranda, then neither Stratton nor Davy will be around to see us wed. In fact, their lives will end sooner than you think." The threat was made clear to Miranda, and yet she knew that she had to do something to help them. She needed to at least give them time to free themselves. That was where Adam came in. If he stayed aboard the ship, then he could at least sneak out and warn them.

Miranda took one last look at the longboat that carried Locand to shore and stared at the awaiting carriage. She knew from the seal on the side that it was the governor's carriage waiting for them.

"If you would like me to come with you ashore then I will go. But remember, I am free to do as I like. I will not be held captive in your room or anywhere that I don't feel is suitable." Miranda poked her finger at Lord Hammil's chest. The action did not win her points with Lord Hammil as he stood in front of her in silence, glaring at her in disbelief of her boldness. "I will go and pack. I am assuming you would like to go ashore immediately?" Lord Hammil nodded his head as he clenched his fists in frustration. "Then I will return on deck shortly." Miranda spun around on her heel and headed for the stairs to go below deck. As soon as she walked down them, she immediately headed toward Adam's cabin. Instead of knocking on the door announcing her presence, she opened the door quickly and stepped inside, closing the door behind her tightly. As she turned to face the room, her eyes immediately found Adam who was sitting on the bed. She quickly moved toward him explaining in detail what had just conspired between her and Lord Hammil.

Adam was concerned about the change of plans, but after talking quickly over what needed to be done, the plan became simple once again. Instead of Adam talking with his sister and enlisting her help, it was now up to Miranda to find her and explain to her the situation. Adam would then stay behind on the ship and take care of freeing her father and Davy. The plan seemed effortless, and yet the risks scared them. They could not fail in what they needed to do.

Miranda left Adam's cabin hastily and headed toward Lord Hammil's where her belongings were left untouched. She grabbed a couple of necessary items she had left there and snatched her hat. She then placed the hat on her head and walked down the hallway to the stairs, climbing them confidently. Lord Hammil was again right by her side grabbing her elbow possessively in his hand. "Once ashore we need to find you more appropriate apparel. Those men's breeches do you no justice." He then steered her to the portside of the ship where one of the longboats had been lowered. Lord Hammil proceeded downward. Miranda stealthily climbed down the steps and into the longboat after him. As her mind raced with the many unknowns, the longboat was rowed to shore, and before she knew it, she was inside of a carriage and on her way to the governor's mansion.

The governor's mansion was beautiful to behold. Miranda had never seen anything so big and pristine white. Their carriage passed through the large black gates that kept the mansion safe from intruders. When the carriage stopped, Lord Hammil was the first to step out. He reached his hand into the carriage for Miranda to take and helped her down the narrow steps onto the brick pathway he was standing on. Miranda gazed at the beautifully scented flowers before her surrounding the mansion. The morning light and the soft breeze that blew against her face were enough to give her confidence and hope.

Lord Hammil swiftly escorted Miranda into the mansion while a short, homely looking servant followed behind them. Miranda had thought the outside of the mansion was beautiful, but the sight of the interior made her catch her breath. Before her eyes could gaze upon everything she was eager to see, the governor walked up and greeted them. The governor wore a dark blue waistcoat with white breeches. He was an older man with a gray wig upon his head. His features were pleasant with pale white skin and a clean shaven face. His blue eyes gazed at her kindly as they approached each other.

Though the governor's countenance appeared kind and gentle, there was something in his eyes that told of his ruthlessness. There was a coldness there that seemed to linger in his heart. At the sight of Miranda, the governor instantly grabbed her hand and bowed to kiss it. He then quickly stood erect and shook Lord Hammil's hand in greeting. The men talked absently about the weather and their voyage in front of Miranda as she gazed admiringly at her surroundings. When there was a pause in the conversation, the governor asked Lord Hammil to follow him into his study to talk of certain matters of state. The governor turned toward Miranda and politely bowed, excusing himself.

"It is a pleasure, Miss Smyth. Now, if you will excuse us for a moment. My servants will supply you with all that you will need, including a more appropriate outfit. I have dresses a plenty, please pick out a few that you feel are worthy of you. I know you have spent much time at sea so if you would like a bath or anything, just ask." Miranda bowed her head slightly and smiled at the governor's graciousness. It was then that she noticed him staring at her. He had cocked his head slightly to the left as his eyes roamed over every curve of her face.

Miranda was about to say something, but stopped when she saw a crooked smile ease its way onto the governor's lips. He then gave an inelegant snort as he turned abruptly away from her, turning his head only slightly toward Lord Hammil as he passed him. Miranda was confused at what she had just seen but didn't have much time to ponder it. Lord Hammil turned toward her, blocking her view of the governor's back.

"We might be awhile, my dear. A servant will show you to your room. When I'm finished, we will go and look for a wedding dress for you." Lord Hammil stepped closer to Miranda and placed his hands lightly upon her shoulders. He then leaned down and kissed her softly on the lips. His hand gently cupped her face before he turned quickly on his heel and headed toward the study. Miranda looked toward the servant on her left and started to follow him up the stairs, her mind reeling with what she needed to do.

As soon as Lord Hammil stepped into the study and closed the door behind him, he heard the governor laugh, "How clever of you, Leonard." Lord Hammil's expression turned serious as he walked toward a chair and sank into it. He knew exactly what the governor was talking about. When he noticed the governor staring at Miranda, Lord Hammil knew that he recognized who she was.

"I don't know what you mean!"

"Don't play those games with me. You know exactly what I mean. If I am not mistaken, your Miss Smyth is Captain Ditarius' daughter. She looks just like him." Lord Hammil gazed keenly at the governor.

"You are very observant indeed, sir. She is Stratton Mayne's daughter and my future wife."

"So, you have Mayne in custody then?" The governor gave a catlike grin when he saw the nod from Lord Hammil. "Two gifts for me you bring. Not only do I have the infamous Captain Ditarius, but Captain Riveri, too. He's a special favor for you." Lord Hammil folded his hands onto his stomach and gazed silently at the man before him. "You have been wise to hide Mayne's daughter's identity from me, and yet foolish. My interests are for Mayne alone, not for his daughter. Her fate does not concern me. I do, however, find it quite devious of you to use her to find her father only to turn him over to me."

"It's a job, nothing personal. I do what the queen asks of me, without condition. She does not care what happens to Mayne, she only wants the treasure. I have spent months in trying to find him, and I knew that Captain Riveri was the key. Having sailed on his ship before, and Mayne being almost a father to him, it seemed only natural to get him involved. I did what I had to do to get what I wanted—what I needed." The governor glared at Lord Hammil, who returned his stare unwaveringly."

"But you forgot one thing in your so carefully laid plans. You forgot the friendship that once existed between Captain Riveri and your betrothed. You would have to have known that he would help her and not you."

"Governor, it was their relationship I counted on."

"Oh!" The governor thought for a moment before realizing what Lord Hammil had confessed to him. "That's brilliant, I must say, and I can see you are a devoted man, but that is not what I question."

"What concerns you then?"

"You have feelings for Stratton Mayne's daughter, Lord Hammil. Which is compelling and yet most inconvenient. You must realize that her heart will never truly be yours. Your deceit has made sure of it. She is at this moment no more yours than she is mine." Lord Hammil turned his head and gazed out the window. "She's a beautiful creature to be sure, but none the less, she can't be trusted. You know this, for you are not an imbecile." Lord Hammil's eyes snapped sharply back to the governor.

"I will not harm her! Not for you and not for anyone!" The governor held up his hands in a surrendering motion.

"I'm not asking you to. Though I'm glad to hear you have given your future bride some thought. I'm merely suggesting to you that I have men who could take care of her for you. With a snap of my fingers, I can make her not exist." Lord Hammil narrowed his eyes as he leaned forward toward the governor.

"I have given her much thought, but her fate lies with me and no other." Lord Hammil leaned back into his chair, his hand running through his hair in anger. "Now, what is my reward for giving you what you most deeply desire? I am handing you the notorious Captain Ditarius to humiliate and torture at your will, as well as some gold for lending me some of your finest men and ships. And let's not forget Captain Riveri and some of his crew. What am I to be given in return?" Lord Hammil's true nature was showing itself as his eyes narrowed in on the governor.

"What we had agreed upon, naturally. I will marry you and Miss Mayne up at the fort, it is the least I can do. I will then hang Captain Riveri shortly afterward so you can watch him die— per your request. You will then be furnished with a strong ship and crew so you can sail back to England, giving the queen my highest regard, while Captain Ditarius' fate will be left up to me to decide. Drawn and quartered sounds like a pirate's death to me. Will that satisfy you?" Lord Hammil nodded his head in approval. "Good! Now, I'm eager to see our dear Captain Ditarius. Where is he?"

"You will see him soon enough. He's still on the ship with his loyal friend and first mate, Davy. I've made sure they cannot escape. Half of the crew was left behind to see to it. Also, Riveri has been taken to the fort with what is left of his crew. I will happily say that he is a broken man." The governor smiled his pleasure at the news.

"Good, very good, but be kind when torturing him. He must be alive when he is hung, it exudes more excitement from the crowds." He then rapped his fingers several times on his desk. "I will be stopping by the ship to visit Captain Ditarius. I want to see him with my own eyes before I give in to your demands."

"Of course! I would expect no less," said Lord Hammil cheerfully.

"I will also be visiting our Captain Riveri. I want to make sure he's comfortable. Both of these men have caused me much trouble, Lord Hammil. It will be a pleasure to end their lives. Now, if you will excuse me, I need to take care of some business, as do you." Lord Hammil stood up quickly, nodding his head in agreement. He glanced at the governor one last time before opening the door to the study and heading toward the stairs.

As Lord Hammil and Miranda went from shop to shop looking for a wedding dress for her to wear, Miranda spotted the place known as The Black Flag. Adam had told her that his sister could be found there. How she was to get inside without Lord Hammil noticing her was going to be the problem. He had been keeping a watchful eye on her all day, not letting her out of his sight.

Miranda was currently wearing a pale blue dress that snugged her torso tightly. Her sleeves were shortened and her underskirts were white. Miranda would have preferred wearing men's clothing, but Lord Hammil had made her change before they left the mansion. Her long hair now blew in the breeze as she pondered what to do. As her mind raced from her troubles she heard a carriage approach them and stop. They were walking the dirt streets of Port Royal, every now and then gaining a view of the ships in the harbor, when she heard a familiar voice behind them.

"Lord Hammil, the governor has requested for you to meet him up at the fort. He wishes to speak with you. I am ordered to take Miss Smyth back to the governor's mansion until you return for her." Lord Hammil turned around and saw Lieutenant Mansfield standing by his side. The lieutenant did not, at any moment, turn to gaze at Miranda but kept his eyes forward and focused on Lord Hammil.

"I will take her back to the mansion first, then I will go to the fort."

"No!" insisted the lieutenant, almost too forcefully. Lord Hammil stared at him skeptically. "The governor needs you right away, milord. He was most persistent in his command." Lord Hammil narrowed his eyes sharply.

"Very well, Lieutenant. Take the carriage. I will walk the rest of the way." Lieutenant Mansfield reached for Miranda's hand. Once he felt her fingers gripping his, he led her to the carriage and inside. "I will see you soon, my dear," spoke Lord Hammil as he walked over to the carriage, placing his hand upon the door. Miranda nodded and smiled. Lord Hammil grabbed a hold of the lieutenant's arm and pulled him aside. "Keep her safe, Lieutenant. If any harm befalls her, you will have to deal with me." The lieutenant bowed his head in obedience and stepped inside of the carriage. Lord Hammil watched as the carriage drove away, dirt flying up after it.

Inside of the carriage Miranda gazed at the lieutenant in surprise. Before she could say a word, however, the lieutenant turned to face her. "I hope you know what you are doing, Miranda." The couple stared at each other for several moments before Miranda responded.

"You hope I know what I am doing? Did the governor actually send for Lord Hammil?"

"Yes! He has already visited your father on the ship. I will admit that he did not look well. The governor was quite pleased and sent me to get Lord Hammil to meet him up at the fort. Your Captain Riveri is there awaiting his fate in a cell." The lieutenant glanced quickly out the window and withdrew a sigh of relief when Lord Hammil was no longer in sight. "Stop!" yelled the lieutenant to the driver. Miranda held onto her seat tightly as she felt the carriage come to a complete stop. Her eyes gazed questioningly up at the lieutenant.

"What are you doing?"

"I'm trying to help you. The governor, unknowingly, bought you some time. Now, I have spoken with Adam. He told me that you have a plan, though he didn't trust me enough to tell me what it was."

"Why am I supposed to trust you?" Lieutenant Mansfield stared at Miranda, admiring her features.

"Look, I know I let you down before. I promised I wouldn't let Lord Hammil hurt you and he did. It is traitorous what I am doing, and yet I am willing to do it. I have spent years of my life watching men like Lord Hammil and the governor destroy people's lives. They take and take and take until there is nothing left. There are things that I agree with, of course, and things that I do not. But I have watched countless, innocent men be persecuted and punished for things they did not do just to be made an example of. I don't agree with that. Your Captain Riveri has a letter of marque from the queen. Lord Hammil has seen fit to ignore that letter, all in the name of jealousy. Fair? I think not. Captain Riveri's past transgressions are not on trial here. I am determined to see that he is set free." Lieutenant Mansfield ran his fingers through his hair as he glanced out of the carriage window.

Miranda was amazed on how much the lieutenant knew about Locand. She then remembered how she had defended him on Lord Hammil's ship when she was first brought upon it. She had said that he was a privateer but she didn't remember mentioning anything else in front of the lieutenant about him. Miranda shrugged her shoulders and dismissed it thinking that Lord Hammil must have said something. She then noticed how the lieutenant glanced back toward her. "So, you have a plan to free Captain Riveri and his crew. Let's get on with it."

Miranda wasn't sure if she could trust Lieutenant Mansfield, but when she glanced into his eyes, they held no deception. There was no trickery hidden there, only good intentions. She also knew that she was running out of time and needed to find Rose fast. The lieutenant's help would be most appreciated at the moment.

"I need to also free my father and Davy," spouted Miranda freely.

"I can help with that. I am assuming you left Adam on the ship to free them? I can buy him time by causing a distraction. Will that be enough to prove my faithfulness?"

"It will indeed. Now, I need to get to The Black Flag. There is someone inside I need to see."

"Done! However, you need to know that The Black Flag is known for its terrible reputation of hosting whores and disreputables. It is the only tavern here that will do so. It tries to cater to the various sailors who come here. I have never gone inside but I am sure that it will not be safe for you to go alone."

"That is why you are coming with me. I need to find someone who will be able to detain Lord Hammil long enough for us to free Locand and his crew."

"Who have you chosen to do that?" The lieutenant asked as he opened the carriage door and helped Miranda step back out onto the dirty street.

"A woman, of course!" The lieutenant said no more as he reached out his hand to clasp Miranda's arm and led her to the tavern. As they reached for the door, Miranda took a deep breath before stepping inside.

The Black Flag was as dark as its name. When the lieutenant had said that the tavern hosted many disreputables, it was an understatement. When Miranda and the lieutenant walked through the door they barely missed a dagger that was thrown near their heads and embedded itself inside the wall beside them. Miranda's eyes grew wide as she saw several men fighting in front of her. As she looked around she noticed several men standing around cheering for their best fighter while there were some who were drinking ale and conversing loudly.

Miranda's feet moved slowly forward as the lieutenant grabbed her hand and pulled her farther into the room. She was receiving several glances from men who were sitting at tables and watching them closely. One of them twirled his mustache as he smiled a dark and almost toothless smile, his tongue licking his lips. Miranda stepped quickly behind Lieutenant Mansfield and brought her hand to his waist grabbing the back of his shirt. She wanted to make sure that through all of their weaving and bobbing through the crowd of miscreants that he didn't lose her.

Lieutenant Mansfield and Miranda finally made it to the bar that was across the room. As the lieutenant tried to yell over the noise of the room to the barkeep, Miranda glanced at her surroundings. She had no idea which one of the willing women, who were walking around showing off their breasts to whoever wanted to look, was Rose. As her eyes searched the room, she saw a couple of women with red hair and pale skin, but she could not see any of their faces. One woman in particular straddled a man's thighs who was sitting in a chair and brought her hand to rub against his manhood. At the sight, Miranda quickly turned her head away, her cheeks becoming flushed with embarrassment. As she turned her attention back to Lieutenant Mansfield, she overheard the conversation he was having with the barkeep.

"I'm looking for a woman named Rose. I'm in need of her assistance with a delicate matter. We are old friends," added the lieutenant smoothly as he brought out a bag of coins and shook them in front of the man. Miranda saw the barkeep turn away in a disgruntled manner and walk over to a plump woman who was serving drinks to some men at a table. The woman glanced over in their direction with a disgusted look upon her face and nodded her head to the barkeep. The woman then walked off to a room on the lower floor. She was gone for only a few minutes.

"This is a pleasant place isn't it?" remarked Miranda as she moved closer to the side of the lieutenant after she felt a man brush her shoulder as he walked by with a girl on his arm. She raised the lieutenant's arm and placed it slightly around her. She heard the lieutenant replace the coins in his pocket while he held her tightly against him showing ownership and comfort.

"You can't say I didn't warn you. Just remember that you were the one who wanted to come in here." She felt the lieutenant's breath on her face as he leaned down and whispered in her ear. Miranda rolled her eyes as she focused her attention back to the room where the plump woman had gone. A few minutes later, a beautiful redhead in a loose fitting dress appeared in the doorway, the plump woman following quickly behind her. At her appearance into the room, a few men hollered for her to come over to them, jingling coins to get her attention, but she only smiled in their direction and waved, lifting her breasts through her dress roughly making the men yell more loudly for her. She immediately turned her attention toward the bar and leaned back to hear what the plump woman behind her was saying.

The lieutenant quickly moved Miranda behind him and focused his attention elsewhere when he saw the woman look toward him.

Rose nodded her head as she saw the plump woman point to the man who had asked for her. Rose quickly ran her fingers through her hair and down her dress to try and fix her appearance. She didn't recognize the man who had asked for her, but she didn't care. Money was money and he asked for her personally. Rose proceeded to walk alluringly toward Lieutenant Mansfield.

Miranda saw Rose approach them as if she were approaching her next prey. There was a glint in her eye, and her supple curves moved side to side in exaggeration as she placed one hand upon her hip. She could see why Locand had used her before. Most of the women in the tavern had runny make up, their clothes partially torn and disheveled, but not Rose. She kept up with her appearance, her dress looking almost brand new and shiny as she glided slowly toward them. When Miranda was able to look away from the beautiful woman, she was about to say something to the lieutenant, but before she could say anything to warn him, Rose walked up to him and placed her hand upon his arm.

"You asked for me, lover?" The lieutenant turned his head toward the silky voice. His eyes roamed over the red headed beauty standing beside him.

"Are you Rose?"

"I am indeed. What can I do for you?" Rose's eyes slowly perused the lieutenant's features.

"I am in need of your help. Is there somewhere we can talk in private?"

"We can do more than talk if that is what you wish?" Rose leaned forward and brushed against the lieutenant's manhood, her eyebrows rising in emphasis. The lieutenant jumped back suddenly and almost knocked over Miranda who was standing close behind him listening to their conversation. Miranda had to grab a hold of a chair to stop from hitting the ground. After realizing what he had done, Lieutenant Mansfield turned quickly around and reached for her. When Miranda was finally steadied, he quickly apologized and placed his arm around her shoulders. Rose saw the exchange between the two and narrowed her eyes.

"Who is she?" The bitter tone in her voice did not escape Miranda's ears. Lieutenant Mansfield turned quickly back toward Rose.

"This is a friend of mine. She would also like to speak with you." Rose quickly scanned Miranda's features.

"Follow me then. I know where we can go." Miranda and Lieutenant Mansfield turned around and followed Rose through the sea of vagrants to the stairs. Once up them, they turned left, walking to the end of the hallway. The short jaunt was not uneventful. Several times Miranda had to move out of the way of couples who were barely clothed as they groped and kissed each other eagerly. Her eyes would widen and color rushed to her cheeks as she felt embarrassed for seeing the vulgar display. As she again caught up to Rose and the lieutenant, they quickly walked into a room Rose had opened with a key.

As they stepped inside, Rose closed the door behind them and locked it. She swiftly moved over to stand in front of Miranda and Lieutenant Mansfield staring from one to the other, her hands placed on her hips. "So?"

"Your show, Miranda," said the lieutenant. Miranda nodded her head as she gazed at Rose.

"You look just like your brother." Rose's hands went to her chest as her mouth dropped open. Her manner immediately changing.

"You know Adam? How?"

"He was aboard Captain Riveri's ship. I am a friend of Captain Riveri's and your brother's. He told me where to find you. I was assured that you can help me with our little problem." Miranda proceeded to explain to Rose what had happened to Locand and why she needed her help.

"Let me get this straight. You want me to entertain Lord Hammil while you go and set Locand and his crew free from the fort?" Miranda nodded her head. "I did this for Locand already, but it was to get information. I don't know if the lie will fly twice."

"You must try, Rose. I'm to be Lord Hammil's wife. I do not wish to marry him, but he is insisting. The governor also wants my father and Locand dead. He is quite persistent upon it. If you do not distract Lord Hammil, then Locand is as good as dead, for I will not be able to help him. The lieutenant is risking his career to help us. He has offered to cause a distraction so Adam can free my father, who is the notorious Captain Ditarius. You see, if we can't make this work, then we will be doomed, and Lord Hammil will have won. Your brother's life is also at risk here. He idolizes Locand. I have done what I can to keep him unharmed and safe, but I don't know how long that will last if we fail. I can only control Lord Hammil to a point, beyond that my opinion and will does not matter."

Rose paced the room as she thought about what Miranda said. "He wishes to bed you doesn't he? Lord Hammil?" Rose was wise to the will of most men.

"Yes, he does, but I have been holding back. It is the only leverage I have over him." Rose smiled as she nodded her head.

"You're lucky. Your Lord Hammil is a powerful man, a very disturbed man, and one I fear you will never be rid of." Miranda was concerned over Rose's words but chose to say nothing about them. "Now, Locand is the complete opposite of Lord Hammil." That comment caught Miranda's attention. She often wondered what kind of relationship he had with Rose, but she had decided not to care, saying that the past was the past. Now, however, because of Rose's comment, Miranda was curious.

"So, you have been with Locand?" Miranda was almost not able to ask the question. Her voice squeaked, and she had to clear her throat. Rose glanced up and down the length of Miranda, realizing that she could easily tell her any lie she chose to upset her, but instead Rose wanted to tell her the truth. She liked Locand too much to destroy the feelings she knew he had for the girl, for Miranda must have been the one he refused to bed her for.

"I have, but it has been a long time since he has warmed my bed." Rose raised her smooth eyebrows as she waited for an answer.

"Locand is a grown man and can do whatever he wants. I was merely curious."

"Is that so?"

"Of course," replied Miranda smoothly.

"Well, to be completely honest, when I saw him last he denied me his bed, though I offered myself to him willingly."

"Really?" Miranda couldn't help but ask, as she felt somewhat relieved.

"Yes! I will admit that I was disappointed, but he made it clear that I wasn't the one he wanted." Rose saw the slight smile that came to Miranda's lips. "Does that please you?" Miranda was very much pleased with the news. Locand could have bedded Rose in a heart-beat, but chose to save himself for her, which meant that he truly did care for her.

"That news pleases me very much, Rose. As you probably can tell, I have feelings for him.

"I know, as he does for you. Now, I will do what I can to distract Lord Hammil, though it will not be easy. I will also buy you as much time as I can, but you must move quickly." Miranda nodded her head as she thought about what she had to do.

"I greatly appreciate the sacrifices you are making for us, Rose." Miranda placed her hand upon Rose's arm and smiled sweetly. Rose returned the smile.

"I know that you must think me a terrible person for sleeping with men who pay me for my services." Miranda was stunned by Rose's words and her features softened. "But I want you to keep in mind that I do what I do out of necessity. It is not who I am, but only what I have become." Rose's gaze moved quickly to the lieutenant's and then back to Miranda's. "I would like to settle down one day, away from here. Possibly marry a kind man and have children."

"I do not doubt that Rose. I don't judge you. From what your brother has told me, you have a good and selfless heart. You have done what you had to do in order to survive. That takes courage." Miranda removed her hand and paused. "I will do what I can to help you attain your goals, to help you start a new life. I want you to come with us when we leave." Rose's eyes met Miranda's and she immediately felt a special bond between them. Her eyes showed her appreciation. Miranda quickly wanted to change the topic before she started to weep from the sentimental moment. "What do you need me to do?" Roses features turned serious again, more professional.

"I need you to deny Lord Hammil your bed again, but only after you put him into the mood. He will get frustrated and will want some release. I will make sure that I am readily available. He knows that I am interested in him. Do you understand where I am going with this?" Miranda nodded her head quickly.

"Yes, but I am not sure how—"

"All you have to do is arouse Lord Hammil enough to want to bed you. Sway your hips, touch your body, whatever he likes. Pretend he is Locand, and you are trying to seduce him into your bed." Miranda could do that for she remembered vividly how Locand had made her feel as he had touched her body. How she tried to make him feel as he ravished her lips and she had caressed his body. "You must make him so filled with desire that he can taste you, but you must be careful. If you stop too soon, his passion may fade, and if you stop too late then he will take you. Believe me when I say that he will take you and use your body to satisfy his lusts. He is an aggressive man and will not have the self restraint or wisdom, not to rape you. He came upon me swiftly and without care. I will also warn you this, if he takes you, he will be finished within fifteen seconds and you won't know what happened. Let's just say that it will not be enough time for you to pleasure yourself." Rose nodded and then shook her head in disbelief. Miranda remembered what Lord Hammil had done to her at his home in New Providence. She hadn't thought much about it since then, but as she brought up the memory she did realize how quickly Lord Hammil pleasured himself.

Miranda's eyebrows rose when she heard Lieutenant Mansfield whisper, "I can last longer than that." The lieutenant snorted loudly, but when he noticed the women staring at him, he cleared his throat and said, "Sorry!" and focused his attention on another part of the room.

"I will work closely with the lieutenant. He must cause a distraction after I have gone to Lord Hammil's bedchamber and while he is preoccupied with me. Once I am there, you will only have so much time. Does that work for you?" The question was directed at Lieutenant Mansfield by Rose.

"Don't worry about my part. I will fulfill my end of the bargain." Miranda and Rose nodded their heads quickly while they continued to discuss in more detail what was to be done to ensure victory. As the lieutenant heard the plan unfold, he decided that it wouldn't work. It did not allow them enough time. "Ladies!" the lieutenant said loudly, interrupting their discussion. "I have another idea, listen to this."

When evening fell, Miranda was in her bedchamber at the governor's mansion and was standing by the window glancing out toward the water. She could almost see the ships that were harbored in the port and wondered if Lieutenant Mansfield's plan for Locand's rescue would work. After she was finished talking with Rose, Lieutenant Mansfield had walked her safely back to their carriage and took her straight to the governor's mansion. It was there she waited by herself for almost an hour before Lord Hammil and the governor had returned from the fort.

When Lord Hammil arrived he had searched her out and brought with him a white box wrapped in a red ribbon. Miranda had accepted the box with reluctance, already having an idea of what it could be. When she opened it, she found a beautiful cream colored dress. As she raised it from the box she noticed the intricate detail around the bodice and wrists. The dress was truly magnificent. She was excited to try in on, and yet not for the occasion for which she knew it was meant for, so she laid it gently back onto the box.

Miranda thanked Lord Hammil for the dress and spent the rest of the evening by his side talking with him about different topics. The one topic she wanted to discuss, but Lord Hammil didn't, was Locand. She wanted to know how he was faring in the cell she knew he must be in. Every time she brought up the topic Lord Hammil would conveniently change it. As darkness came, Miranda decided to retire, trying to figure out how to go about seducing Lord Hammil, but before she could, Lord Hammil started what she could not.

"My dear, would you be so kind as to try on the dress and see if it fits? If it doesn't, then I want time to get it altered before our wedding." Lord Hammil walked over to the box, grasped the soft fabric and placed it into his arms, bringing it back over to Miranda.

"If it will please you, just give me a moment, and I will return shortly." Miranda was about to turn around when Lord Hammil reached out his hand.

"No!" he almost shouted. "Change in here so I can see you. If you will not let me touch you at least allow me the sight of you. You bring me much pleasure. I promise that I won't touch you." Miranda didn't like the idea but knew she had no choice. She briefly nodded her head as she moved far away from Lord Hammil to the other side of the room. She then placed the beautiful dress down upon a chair and started undoing the buttons on her dress. As she disrobed, she tried not to stare at Lord Hammil, but couldn't resist. The man almost fell to the ground. His mouth was agape and his features were filled with lust. It was as if he were in a trance as he watched Miranda step into the cream dress and lift it to cover her breasts and shoulders. She could not reach the back buttons so Lord Hammil offered his services eagerly.

As he approached Miranda and reached her back, he could not find it within himself to button the buttons. He felt Miranda's back stiffen beneath his hand as he caressed her skin. Then almost forcefully did he remove the fabric from her shoulders wanting more from her.

"You promised me, Lord Hammil," reminded Miranda as she endured his touch. Miranda wasn't surprised when he turned her around and kissed her lips passionately. Remembering what Rose had said to her, Miranda returned his kisses convincingly but did not give him the pleasure of seeing any more of her nakedness. She forced one of her arms to hold the dress tightly against her breasts. With the other hand, Miranda stroked Lord Hammil's arms and face as she kissed him, her body wiggling seductively against his. Her hand then moved dangerously close to his inner thighs separating their bodies, and felt a hardness there that spoke of Lord Hammil's feelings.

When she could feel his fingertips digging into her shoulders demandingly, Miranda knew it was time for her to go, so she ended the kiss and pushed away from Lord Hammil. Lord Hammil was frustrated with her decision to stop and seized her arm tightly to prevent her from leaving. When Miranda was forced back into his arms, his lips gently kissing her neck, she could also feel the hardness of his manhood against her backside. He moved his hips against her body.

"No!" she shouted as she fought him, but surprisingly, Lord Hammil grabbed her roughly by the back of the neck and forced her toward the wall where he moved his grasp to the front of her throat, slamming her up against it. Her hold on her bodice had loosened as she fought Lord Hammil's hand. Desire filled his eyes, and something else that she feared the most.

"You see how much I desire you, Miranda. I am this way because of you. Touch me!" Miranda shook her head in refusal, not wanting to indulge him. "I command it you ungrateful tease." Lord Hammil reached up with his left hand and grabbed her wrist, forcefully bringing her hand to the bottom of his shirt, encouraging her to take it off. Reluctantly, she did as directed tossing the shirt on the floor.. Lord Hammil slightly leaned forward as if he were to satisfy himself right there. Miranda's smooth hands now raised in front of her as she tried to keep him at bay. She felt disgusted. Lord Hammil lowered his right hand from Miranda's throat and grabbed the bodice ripping it from her grasp. With her smooth large globes finally exposed, Lord Hammil pressed his bare chest against hers. It was almost his undoing.

"I—almost cannot— contain myself— when I'm— around you— Miranda." Lord Hammil's eyes closed as he reveled in the softness of her skin. Tears began to fill Miranda's eyes with what she was being made to endure. Then his eyes opened sharply. "I want more of you!" he blurted, his hand ripping at the front of the dress to remove it. "I want to take you here and now!" Miranda had enough. She pushed him away from her so forcefully that he fell backward landing on his back on the floor.

"I will not indulge your fantasies tonight. Tomorrow, when we are wed, I will let you take me, but not now. No!" Her head was shaking so vehemently that she could not stop until she yanked open the door of the chamber, raising the bodice of her dress to cover her bosom, slamming the door behind her.

Lord Hammil was burning with desire for her but let her walk away from him and run to the safety of her room. Giving himself solace, he decided that her leaving would be for the best. She would be his bride tomorrow and then there would be no excuse she could give that would make him stop. After several minutes had passed, Lord Hammil was debating on sating his lusts with another woman. He felt the pulsing of his manhood between his thighs. He needed satisfaction. His decision was made. He sent a message for Rose to come to him immediately.

When Miranda returned to her room she watched out the window for a messenger. Sure enough, she saw one leave the front door and head down the hill toward town. So far everything was going as planned. Rose would be coming soon. Miranda had been afraid that Lord Hammil was going to force himself upon her. She was convinced that he would have if she hadn't stopped him. Tears flowed down her cheeks freely now as she let the dress fall at her feet, feeling used and disgusted.

Miranda immediately grabbed fresh clean clothes, feeling dirty in the beautiful dress she was forced to wear. As the task was completed, she decided to stand again by the window. She now wore a plain nightgown that covered her body all the way to her feet, just in case Lord Hammil came to her during the night. It was imperative for him to believe that she was in her room the entire night and not responsible for anything that was going to happen.

Miranda again reviewed the plan in her mind. Lieutenant Mansfield had changed their plans considerably. He had told her and Rose that he would be the one to free Locand. How he was going to be able to manage that was beyond her, but his concern was of time. Earlier, when they were alone in the carriage, he said that he cared for her and wanted nothing to happen to her. If she got caught, he knew that she would be tried for treason and would most likely hang. Though Miranda appreciated his concern, she had told him that he was putting his life in the same danger. But when she said this, he only told her not to worry and that he would be fine. What that meant, Miranda didn't know. Did he have a plan for that, too?

Miranda shook her head as she gazed out the window hoping to see some kind of sign that everything would work out. Her heart was racing from all of the unknowns. She not only doubted herself, but also the plan she was now a part of. After taking several deep breaths to calm her nerves, she made a motion to turn away from the window, but before she could she saw a soft flicker of light and then a flash of red blowing in the wind. A sign had revealed itself. Rose was coming!

CHAPTER 19

As darkness fell, Lieutenant Mansfield was trying to think of a way to cause a distraction. As he turned toward the harbor and saw his fellow soldiers aboard the ship guarding Captain Ditarius and the gold, it hit him. Slowly, the lieutenant made his way to the fort. He had no problem getting in and at this time of night, though it was guarded, no one bothered him. He quickly walked inside and down several hallways until he reached the staircase that led down to the cells. Surprisingly, no one was guarding the captives. Each of them sat quietly, some were asleep on the ground while others were trying to find a means of escape by pulling and pushing on the cell bars. As they saw the lieutenant approach, the men stared at him with hatred. Their gazes changed, however, when he withdrew a key and unlocked the door.

"Where is your Captain?" asked the lieutenant eagerly.

"He is not with us. Lord Hammil took him somewhere else." Concern filled the lieutenant's features as he again scanned the contents of the cell. "Wake your friends!" the lieutenant ordered quietly. The men did as they were told. The ones that were sleeping stood up and rubbed their eyes. A few grabbed for a dagger at their waist but forgot that their weapons were taken from them and only wrapped their hand around air as they cursed to themselves. "Listen to me, all of you. I am here to free you."

"Why would you free us?" asked one of the men. It was Slim.

"Because, I made a deal with Miranda Mayne or as you may know her to be, Miranda Smyth," answered the lieutenant. "Lord Hammil's beautiful bride to be." When he spoke his words, a smile rose on some of the men's lips. "However, this is how it will go. I will show you a way out, but in turn you will need to flee. You cannot go back to the ship and to your Captain. I was planning on freeing all of you, but now I need to search for him and cannot guarantee success."

"We will help you find him!" spoke one of the men.

"No!" replied Lieutenant Mansfield sharply. "I am risking much to help him, but I can get out of here with little to no problem. It will be harder for me to do so with a handful of men by my side." The men looked at each other and then nodded their heads.

"Fine!" spoke Slim. "We will do as you say."

"Good!" spoke the lieutenant as he waved the men to follow him. With all of the men behind him, he walked silently back up the stairs and took a left toward the back of the fort. There were several doors that led to the trees that surrounded the fort but they were hidden from view. He had used them several times with no one noticing they were there. As he glanced all around them, he opened one of the doors. After staring into the trees and listening to the surrounding sounds, he told the men to go. A few of them hesitated but then, once one went, they all followed. Slim looked back hesitantly; not wanting to leave his captain in the hands of the lieutenant, but with a reassuring nod he followed his friends into the trees.

Lieutenant Mansfield closed the door and walked cautiously through the fort past several rooms and doorways. The rooms were empty. Most of the men were walking the walls above him as they watched for intruders. As he worked his way back out into the courtyard, he thought again of what he could do for a distraction, though at the moment it almost didn't matter. Without Locand, it would be pointless. As he looked around, he noticed some barrels. It was the powder for the guns and bayonets. It was stored in barrels to keep it safe. Seeing the pile of barrels and a long roll of fuses lying next to them, he quickly grabbed the roll and placed it inside of his waistband, his waistcoat covering it from view. He then grabbed the top barrel and moved it carefully, by rolling, toward a dark shadow by the wall. It was at that moment, as the lieutenant stared out into the open courtyard, that he realized where Captain Riveri was. He was in the middle of the courtyard.

As the lieutenant blinked several times to adjust his focus his eyes again fell upon Locand. His back was placed against a large wooden pillar and his arms were tied behind his back to it. His head was bowed, and he could tell that Locand was asleep by his posture. He was bent slightly over and his chin was almost touching his chest. Not quite disregarding his train of thought with the barrel, the lieutenant quickly looked around the courtyard for fellow soldiers. In the distance he could see two, but for the moment they weren't paying any attention to him. Instead, they were looking out into the harbor.

He quietly walked up to the still form of Locand. As he looked again toward the guards who were still looking away from him, he raised his arm and was about to touch him when he saw a red mark by his neck. The lieutenant leaned forward to look at the mark and realized there were more. Locand had been whipped. Anger instantly filled him as he shook his head. He then raised his hand and tightly covered Locand's mouth.

When Locand felt a hand covering his mouth, his eyes instantly opened. He tried to stand straight but was quickly reminded of the lashings he had received by Lord Hammil's order. His eyes were still heavy with sleep, so he tried to shake his head to regain focus. He instantly remembered being in the fort courtyard for hours. After he had received several lashings with a whip, Lord Hammil and the governor had told him that he was going to be the focus of a grand occasion. He was to watch as Miranda and Lord Hammil wed and then, he was to be hanged in front of them along with his men as a wedding present. The thought saddened him and yet he did not resolve himself to death.

As he gazed around him, he noticed the man holding his hand over his mouth. As recognition set in, the lieutenant removed his hand and placed his pointer finger to his lips. Locand nodded in understanding and smiled.

"Brother?" Locand whispered. Lieutenant Mansfield smiled, his white teeth shining brightly in the dark. Lieutenant Mansfield was a half brother to Locand. They had the same father but had different mothers. Their father introduced them to each other when they were children, and because their father was a notorious pirate, the lieutenant took his mother's last name. Even after their father's death, his legend preceded him and it was because of this that they avoided seeing each other. They didn't want anyone to put two and two together, and yet they would frequently find ways to be together.

Stratton Mayne was the only one who knew the truth, and he raised Locand as if he were his own son aboard his ship until he was ready to be on his own. The lieutenant lived with his mother at the time, and it wasn't until they were older that the brothers rekindled their lost sibling relationship. Though the brothers lived very different lives they looked similar in appearance. The lieutenant was the spitting image of their father. The last time they had spent time together was two years prior in Spain before the lieutenant sailed to Port Royal and joined the Royal Navy.

"Yes, Locand, it is I." Locand smiled with joy, but as quickly as the smile came, it vanished.

"Lyle, it has been too long."

"It is always too long, Brother, but we are together now. I need to get you out of here. I knew that one day this would happen."

"What! You knew one day that you would save my life?" Lieutenant Mansfield raised the corner of his lips into a smirk before he removed the dagger from his waist.

"You have taken our father's path. You are more of a man than I am. You were always the brave one."

"No, Lyle," Locand interjected as he stared into his brother's eyes. "I was always the foolish one. If I would have settled down and made a new life for myself long ago like you did, I wouldn't be here now. After I am freed, everything is going to change, I promise you," both men smiled at each other. The lieutenant was about to cut the rope that bound Locand's wrists when he heard a voice from behind him.

"What are you doing, Lieutenant?" The voice startled him, but the lieutenant quickly regained his composure. When he turned around he saw the two guards that were once in the distance.

"I was merely checking on the prisoner per Lord Hammil's request. I brought out a dagger for protection. It was hard to tell if the prisoner was asleep or not and I didn't want to take any chances." The guards looked from one to the other skeptically, but nodded their heads in understanding.

"Be careful, Lieutenant, this bloke is a slippery one," said one of the guards. "He should be moving a lot slower now since he has been whipped. The look on that Lord Hammil's face when it was done was almost sickening." The guard shook his head from the memory. The lieutenant hid his anger inside as he smiled at the two guards, replacing his dagger into its sheath at his waist.

"Have your replacements come then?" asked the lieutenant coolly.

"Yes, they are already in position. We are going to get some rest so we will be ready for tomorrow's festivities, but first we were going to get some food. Care to join us?"

"No, I still have work to do. Lord Hammil is quite adamant that I remain here for another hour or so to watch over the prisoner. It will be a boring task for sure, but one that I will gladly take. Scum like this should be punished, and I am here to make sure that it is done." Lieutenant Mansfield glanced at Locand who narrowed his eyes and glared at him as he pulled aggressively at his restraints.

"I don't envy your job, Lieutenant. Well, goodnight then." The guards grabbed their bayonets and walked away until they were out of sight inside of the main building of the fort. After some time, Lieutenant Mansfield withdrew a breath and again retrieved the dagger from its sheath, cutting Locand's ropes.

"Scum?" breathed Locand softly, "That was harsh." But the lieutenant chose to ignore his brother's comment.

"That was close, Locand, too close." Locand almost fell to the ground as pain shot through his arms and back. The lieutenant quickly reached out and caught him before he hit the ground. "Can you walk?" Locand quickly nodded his head as he felt his brother's arm around his waist.

"I'm fine! What do we do now?" The lieutenant carefully moved Locand into a shadow by the inner wall of the fort. He then waited and watched as the guards walked the outer walls of the fort but paid no attention to the courtyard. He quickly let go of Locand and told him to stay where he was. He then moved quietly to the barrel of powder he had grabbed earlier and quickly rolled it to the place where Locand had been tied to the post and stood it up. After wiping the sweat from his brow and glancing in Locand's direction, he grabbed the roll of fuse that was tucked into his waistband and removed the cork that covered the entrance to the barrel. He placed one end of the fuse into the open hole and walked silently back toward Locand, unrolling it as he went.

"Now, my Brother, we are going to cause a distraction."

"A distraction for what?" asked Locand curiously.

"We need to buy some time for Adam to free your friend Captain Mayne. From what I understand, he already has my key to open his chains but there are guards aboard the ship. We need to get them off and you on. The gold is aboard the *Soaring Eagle* and was transferred there shortly after our arrival. Neither Lord Hammil nor the governor have decided to remove it to their own coffers just yet." Lieutenant Mansfield was about to move forward, but was stopped by Locand's hand upon his arm.

"Where's Miranda, Lyle? I need to know. Is she safe?" Though there was no moon that shined in the dark, Lieutenant Mansfield could still see the look of concern in his brother's eyes.

"She is with Lord Hammil in the governor's mansion. She is detaining him with the help of Rose."

"I'm going to find her!" As Locand moved forward, the lieutenant grabbed his arm and held him back.

"No, Locand, you mustn't. The three of us planned your escape. Your women need to do their parts before they come to the ship and to you."

"The only woman who has my heart is Miranda. Rose is a friend and does not belong to me." The comment made Lieutenant Mansfield look at the ground and shake his head.

"Your remark almost saddens me." Locand narrowed his eyes at his brother's comment.

"What do you mean by that?" The lieutenant stared at the entrance to the fort and knew that once they crossed it, they would be free.

"Nothing! Miranda is an extraordinary woman, and I can tell that she cares for you very much. I will tell you more about everything later, but what I will tell you now is that she does not know that I am your brother. I told her that I was helping her because I care for her, and believe me brother when I say that I do. Her and Rose are risking much to save you, and it was Miranda's idea to use Rose to distract Lord Hammil just like you had done before. He has been trying to bed her for some time and is determined to have her, but for the moment it will be Rose who will be sating his lusts while I free you." The lieutenant glanced at Locand and saw his hardened features.

"I'm sorry, Brother. I didn't realize how much you cared for Miranda, but I care for her, too. However, she can only give her heart to one of us, and I know at this moment that it is not me." He took a deep breath before continuing, "I will stand down, Locand. She's yours." With that said, Lieutenant Mansfield lit the fuse and helped Locand to the fort entrance and out through the gate undetected.

Rose knocked softly on Lord Hammil's door as she placed her hands on the front of her dress and smoothed the wrinkles. She knew she only had so much time to entertain him, but she hoped that it would be long enough for the lieutenant to free Locand. Before Rose could think any more about Locand's escape, Lord Hammil opened the door.

"You sent for me, milord?" Lord Hammil hastily reached out his hand, grabbed Rose roughly by the arm and brought her into the room closing the door loudly behind them.

"Did anyone see you?" Lord Hammil asked impatiently. His still naked chest was labored from his words.

"No, I don't believe so. Why, is something wrong? You seem so agitated tonight." Lord Hammil ran his fingers through his hair as he paced a circle around Rose.

"No, nothing is wrong. I just need some special attention from you. My mind is filled with many worries, and it won't be calmed until tomorrow." Rose waited a moment to see if Lord Hammil was going to tell her more, but when he didn't speak further she brought up the question.

"And?"

"And get undressed or I will do it for you. I need to see you naked. To finish what my love has started but left in wanting. I need to be satisfied!" Rose wasn't prepared to begin so quickly. When she didn't move fast enough, Lord Hammil stopped his pacing and glared at her. He then rushed over to her threateningly. Rose began to back up, her fingertips raising to unbutton the front of her dress, but Lord Hammil lost patience as he took both his hands and ripped at the fabric, making a large tear from the dress's neck to the waist, exposing Rose's full mounds. His eyes grew with excitement as he lowered the dress to around her shoulders, pinning her arms at her sides. Her breasts were his for the taking. His breathing sounded labored as he pressed his body against hers. .

Wanting more, Lord Hammil removed his breeches, his manhood standing erect. He grabbed the fabric of Rose's dress pulling her with him as he began to back up until his legs pressed against the bed. He quickly stripped Rose of the rest of her dress. Her lush curves causing Lord Hammil's gaze to fill with desire.

"Milord," Rose began, but was quickly silenced.

"Don't talk! Just let me have my way with you." Rose had no choice when Lord Hammil sat on the edge of the bed pulling her with him. He had his way with her several times. But it wasn't like before when he had woken up from being drugged. Then he was quick and selfish with his commands, not once thinking about her needs, he only sated himself. He was still forceful and demanding, yet this time he helped her find her way until both of them were sated.

"You're just what I needed Rose," panted Lord Hammil. Out of breath, Lord Hammil moved Rose up more on the bed, then covered her body with his as he partially laid beside her.

Rose was impressed with Lord Hammil's stamina, but was on edge, knowing what was to come. She could feel Lord Hammil's breathing begin to calm as he fell asleep with his head on her chest. Then it happened, the sound she was expecting to hear. A loud noise came through the window. Lord Hammil's eyes instantly opened and he rose from the bed. He didn't care that he was naked as he approached the window.

"What was that?" asked Rose as she laid her hand upon her chest in false curiosity, knowing the noise had to have been caused by the lieutenant. Lord Hammil grabbed his breeches and put them on. He saw smoke coming from the fort. He instantly gritted his teeth.

"Miranda!" Lord Hammil yelled as he headed for the door. He opened it forcefully, walked through the door, and down the hallway toward Miranda's chamber. His chest exposed to the cold.

Miranda also heard the explosion and immediately went to the window. She could not see the fort clearly but did see the smoke billowing from that direction. Her heart raced as she heard footsteps. Knowing that it was Lord Hammil didn't ease her sense of surprise as he forcefully opened her door.

"Where are you?" yelled Lord Hammil as he stepped into the room. Miranda touched her hand to her throat as he stepped closer.

"I'm right here, Leonard. Why do you approach me so menacingly? What was that noise?" Miranda couldn't help but step farther away from Lord Hammil as he kept looming toward her. When he reached her side he roughly grabbed her by the arms and pulled her to him. Miranda's face wrinkled as she felt his nails dig into her skin.

"Did you do this?" Lord Hammil asked, his tone filled with anger and suspicion.

"How could I? I have been in this room ever since I left you earlier. What are you accusing me of?" Lord Hammil eyed Miranda distrustfully before he let her go. Miranda could see the slickness of his skin and knew that Rose had just finished satisfying him. A look of disgust covered her features. "I see you finally were able to satisfy your needs." Lord Hammil glared at her.

"If you were to satisfy me in the way I need you to, I wouldn't have to turn to other women to do the job. In fact, I should have had you in the room to watch so you would know how I like to be pleasured." Miranda was appalled.

"I know all too well how you want to be pleasured," she spouted in return. Lord Hammil raised his hand and caressed Miranda's hair and face.

"No, my love, you don't. You think I'm incapable of satisfying you." He then seized her arm and brought her just inches from his lips. He smelled of sex. Miranda tried to pull away. "But tomorrow, you will learn how generous a lover I can be. I can be very generous." Lord Hammil lowered his lips onto Miranda's. She returned the kiss convincingly, though she felt disgusted how Lord Hammil could move from one woman to the next so easily. When Lord Hammil went to partake of her lips again, his hands now cupping her face, Miranda quickly turned and focused her attention back to the window.

"What happened?" Her question brought him back into reality.

"There was an explosion at the fort where your darling Captain Riveri is being held captive." Miranda quickly lunged forward toward the door but Lord Hammil stopped her by the hair. Pain filled her features.

"Let me go! I want to know if Locand was killed in the explosion." Overwhelmed, Miranda fell in a heap to the floor with her hands covering her eyes sobbing loudly. Lord Hammil took a few minutes to evaluate the situation before reacting.

"You will stay here, Miranda. I will check on the situation for you. It would be a pity if the dear Captain perished in the explosion instead of by my hands." With that said, Lord Hammil turned away from Miranda and headed out the door. After several minutes Miranda rose to her feet and ran to the window, wiping the forced tears away from her cheeks. Within minutes, she saw a carriage pulling Lord Hammil toward town and to the fort.

"Was that Lord Hammil leaving?" The voice behind her caused Miranda's heart to beat quickly.

"Rose!" Miranda said loudly as she placed her hand upon her heart. "You scared me. Yes, it is him."

"Do you have another dress for me to borrow? Lord Hammil destroyed mine." Rose had come into the room with just a blanket around her.

"Of course, take this one." Miranda handed her a dress from the closet, then turned her back toward her so she could put it on.

"I overheard what he said, Miranda. Lord Hammil was a surprising man tonight in bed. He actually pleasured me and not just himself. To be honest, he was probably practicing for you. His actions made him almost likeable." Miranda wrinkled her brow in disgust. "I said—almost."

"I don't care about Lord Hammil. He's still a monster underneath it all. I am more concerned for Locand and what might befall him. Do you think that explosion was created by Lieutenant Mansfield?" Miranda began to take off her nightgown and put on a dark dress.

"It must have been him. Regardless of who did it, the explosion is giving us time to leave. Are you ready?" Miranda nodded her head quickly and followed Rose out the door to set the next part of their plan into motion.

Adam also saw the explosion. He quickly moved to the cabin door and opened it. Above deck he could hear the guards running about frantically. Then, just as he had hoped, he heard one of the men in charge tell everyone to hurry and save the fort. It took several minutes, but soon the deck was emptied. Adam opened the door farther and walked down the hallway to the stairs that led to the deck. As he carefully mounted them he quickly looked around and saw no guards left behind. With excitement filling his chest, Adam ran back below deck to where Captain Mayne and Davy were kept prisoners.

When Stratton heard someone coming, he began to unlock the cell door. Lieutenant Mansfield had visited them hours earlier and told them briefly about a distraction. From the noise that could be heard from outside, Stratton knew that it was time to leave. As Stratton moved quickly from the cell, Davy was not far behind him.

Adam was hurrying through the belly of the ship to free Stratton and Davy when he noticed them coming toward him. He quickly stopped as they came to stand in front of him and explained himself. "I am Adam, Captain Mayne, and am here to free you. Lieutenant Mansfield said that he explained to you what is supposed to happen?"

"He did indeed, boy, he spoke to us earlier today and told us everything. I am assuming the noise we heard was the distraction he spoke of?"

"Yes, Captain! There was an explosion at the fort, and all of the guards left to assist their fellow officers. Also, as you can tell, they moved the treasure over to the *Soaring Eagle.* They have it minimally protected, and those men also left to go to the fort to save it from the fire. Miranda and the lieutenant know about the treasure and will meet us over on that ship." Adam felt uncomfortable being so close to a man who was infamously known as Captain Ditarius the Deadly. He had heard many stories of his ruthlessness and courage, but as he stood now only a few feet away from him, he was amazed to find that he wasn't scary at all. In fact, he seemed almost ordinary.

Stratton and Davy hurried past Adam to the deck where they saw for themselves how desolate and alone they were. Happy to finally be free, they almost became careless with their freedom until they heard men rushing through the streets of Port Royal to the fort. It was at that moment they crouched down by the port side railing and looked at the scenery around them.

"It looks as if the *Soaring Eagle* is ready to sail. Once everyone is aboard we will be able to sail out of here with no disturbance. I just hope they come soon." Stratton didn't express his fear for Miranda's safety or Locand's, but his eyes did. Davy could tell his good friend was worried. In truth, so was he. All of their lives were at risk if they were caught. Smoothly, the three of them left the *Flying Wasp* and made their way over to the *Soaring Eagle*. They thought it best to swim there instead of using the dock to walk all the way over to it and get spotted. Once they made it to the ship, they climbed onto the dock just in front of the plank and boarded the ship swiftly. Their clothes were soaked, but they didn't care.

The trio crouched down on the deck for some time watching the action going on around them, their eyes frequently watching for signs of Locand or Miranda. They were so consumed with what they saw that they didn't notice when Locand and the lieutenant climbed the rope that was hung over the side of the ship and landed onto the deck, their clothes dripping with water.

Lieutenant Mansfield reached for Locand as they stepped aboard deck. He could see him hunched over in pain, the marks from his lashings shining brightly with renewed blood. Locand winced as he felt the lieutenant's arm wrap around his waist helping him move forward. As he gazed ahead his stare fell upon Adam, who was the first one to notice their presence.

"Locand!" yelled the boy as he stood up and ran to him. Locand placed an arm around Adam briefly and embraced him.

"It is nice to see you, too, Adam. You look well." Stratton and Davy also stood and moved toward the lieutenant and Locand.

"My boy," said Stratton with joy. The two men embraced each other and yet both of them winced with pain. As Stratton removed his left hand from Locand's back he noticed fresh blood upon it. He quickly placed his right hand on Locand's shoulder and turned his back toward him. Sure enough, bright rich blood could be seen through his dirtied shirt. "Oh my God!" said Stratton as he started to fill with rage. He had personally been whipped five times by Lord Hammil and his back was still not healed from those wounds. Locand had been whipped more times than that, there had to have been at least a dozen marks upon his back. Before Stratton could say anything to Locand, a voice from behind him spoke.

"Look! There is Miranda and she is coming with another woman. Come on, Miry," said Davy quietly as he encouraged her to come to the ship. Locand, as well as Lieutenant Mansfield, turned their heads and watched as Miranda and Rose paddled a longboat toward the ship. Once they reached the side and were out of sight, Locand could hold on no longer. Miranda was safe. That was all he cared about. As he heard her voice talk to him as she climbed over the rail, a slight daze came over his eyes. Locand tried to blink several times to regain focus, but it didn't work. Soon he became limp in his brother's arms.

Deep into the night, the governor, with Lord Hammil by his side, was standing around the outer wall of the fort. The fire had finally been put out but not before the other kegs of powder had been ignited too. It wasn't until now that they looked over the harbor and noticed that a ship was missing. The governor knew that the fire was no coincidence with the missing Captain Riveri. He had somehow escaped with a ship, Captain Ditarius, and the gold. It wouldn't have surprised him, either, if the beautiful Miranda Mayne were missing, too.

Lord Hammil was absorbed in thought as well. When he saw the fire, his immediate thought was that Miranda had somehow started it, but now he realized that she wasn't involved at all and the fact the Locand had left without her made him smile. But as quick as his smile came, it vanished. Was she still waiting for him to return? The thought made him instantly worry, and he left with the governor to go back to the mansion. Hours had seemed to pass as Lord Hammil sat in the carriage impatiently tapping his hands upon his knee.

When they arrived, Lord Hammil jumped out of the carriage, ran into the mansion, up the stairs and down the hallway to Miranda's room. When he threw open the door he realized with sadness, that she was nowhere to be found. Lord Hammil quickly checked his room. Rose was gone, too. In frustration, Lord Hammil hurried downstairs and asked to see the governor. A servant directed him to the study. As Lord Hammil came to the door, he didn't bother to knock, but barged in.

The governor was just taking off his gloves and threw them on his desk when his eyes met Lord Hammil. "She is gone too, isn't she?" Lord Hammil nodded his head in response and stared at the ground.

"What are we going to do to get them back, governor?" The governor laughed as he moved silently to the door and closed it, his back still facing Lord Hammil.

"Get them back? Nothing!"

"Nothing!" Lord Hammil yelled as he snapped his head up in anger. "We must get them back. I can take another ship and track them." Before Lord Hammil could continue, the governor raised his hand to stop him.

"You have cost me much in this little venture of yours. Not only did I lose Captain Ditarius, but the prestige that he was going to bring to Port Royal and to me. I wanted to be known as the governor who killed the most notorious pirate ever. I don't even have the gold you promised me to console my anger and disappointment. Now Captain Riveri is missing as well as Miss Mayne. So tell me, my dear Lord Hammil, what I have to be joyous about?" Lord Hammil lowered his head and stared at the dirty floor knowing that everything the governor said was true.

"We are going to forget about both pirates for the time being. They are no longer our problem. You, on the other hand, will always remember what a fool you were to trust a woman. You must realize by now that it was because of her that this happened. I told you not to trust her and for your stubbornness they all escaped with the gold. I will admit that I feel sorry for you, for when the queen finds out what happened, you will surely lose your head," said the governor brusquely. He then slowly reached inside of a hidden sheath at his waist and pulled out a dagger. The governor quickly glanced at the blade before he focused his eyes again on the door in front of him, his hand tenderly caressing the smooth handle. "Now, let's discuss what happens when a man betrays me! Yes, let's have a brief discussion about that."

CHAPTER 20

Stratton Mayne sailed the stolen ship to Eleuthera Island. Fortunately for them the weather was breezy and dark. They had sailed for hours. Stratton was tired as he steered the ship, unwavering on its course. Several times he had looked behind them to see if another ship was following, but each time he did he saw nothing. Though the sight pleased him, it also made him feel tense with worry. He frequently spoke his concern with Davy.

"I keep looking back to see if Lord Hammil is following, and each time I do, I am surprised that he's not." Lieutenant Mansfield walked up the stairs at that precise moment and overheard Stratton and Davy's conversation.

"I wouldn't worry too much about that, Captain Mayne. The governor does not take betrayal lightly," offered Lieutenant Mansfield. All eyes were then focused on the lieutenant as he stood confidently in front of them. The lieutenant looked tired as he ran his fingers through his hair and scratched his chin. "He lost much today. He will be quite angry with Lord Hammil for all of us escaping with the gold on one of his ships. You see, Lord Hammil was supposed to give a fourth of the gold to the governor for aiding him in the retrieval of it, as well as of Captain Riveri and yourself. He was then going to bring the rest of the gold, as well as the assurances of your deaths, back with him to England. The queen wanted the gold, which is why he was sent down here in the first place, and he was supposed to use you and Captain Riveri to get it, knowing the relationship that you two had.

"Yes, the governor will be quite angry with Lord Hammil, and I am sure that he will not forgive him. The prestige of your name alone spread on the streets of Port Royal, and to all of its visitors, would make the governor quite famous. He has dedicated his life to removing pirates from the seas and hanging their broken or hung bodies by the harbor to let all know that pirates are not welcome at Port Royal. Your death would have made him all but unstoppable. You are well known for your cunning and ruthlessness, Captain Ditarius, and I will almost guarantee that Lord Hammil is dead for his mistake in underestimating Miranda. He let his lust for her consume him to the point that he became blind. He will not be coming after us, nor will the governor send any more men. Lord Hammil and I are the only ones who know where your hideout is. The rest of the crew was kept ignorant of it, so you should not fear anyone bothering you again." A smirk rose on the lieutenant's cheeks as he smiled confidently at Stratton and Davy.

"How do you know this, Lieutenant?" asked Davy as he eyed him with amazement.

"I spoke often with the governor and was one of his most trusted men. That is all gone now though." The lieutenant's voice held no regret but held a hint of sadness. Davy and Stratton glanced quickly at each other.

"What I would like to know," said Stratton with curiosity. "Is why you decided to help us? For all the times you came to us in the cell, you were never friendly, nor were you this eager to help. I don't understand the change. You weren't the one to hurt us, but you did not try to stop it, either." Lieutenant Mansfield took a deep breath before he answered the question, his eyes looking out into the sea.

"You must understand, Captain Mayne. That if I, in any way, showed compassion for you, then I would be found out. Lord Hammil was already suspicious of me because I tried to protect Miranda from him. I knew what I was sent on this ship to do and that was to help get the gold and capture a pirate. That was my order from the governor himself. However, I took the order lightly when I found out that Lord Hammil was after Captain Riveri."

"Why would his name prevent you from doing your duty?" asked Stratton.

"Because, Captain Mayne, blood is thicker than water. Wouldn't you agree?" Davy narrowed his eyes as he pondered what the lieutenant had said. Stratton opened his mouth slightly in surprise.

"Blood? You are a relation?" asked Stratton.

"The only one he has, Captain Mayne. Locand is my half-brother." Stratton could not believe what he had just heard.

"Lyle?"

"At your service, Captain," replied the lieutenant as he bowed his head in respect.

"I knew of you, Lyle," admitted Stratton.

"And I knew of you, Captain. Locand always spoke so highly of you. After Father died he said that you helped him move on. It was hard for the both of us to deal with, but I had my mother to give me solace where Locand had no one, except you of course, and his mother. Though, she was in no position to really help him. He always said that you treated him as if he were your son. He was very fortunate in that respect." Stratton patted the lieutenant on the arm and then, after telling Davy to grab the wheel, embraced him. The lieutenant was surprised by the action but relaxed and returned the embrace.

"Speaking of Locand, how is he?" asked Stratton as he stepped away from the lieutenant acting like nothing had happened between them.

"Miranda is with him now, he will live. The lashings he received were most painful, but he has a strong will. When I left him, Miranda was cleaning the wounds again. I haven't seen her for some time now." As the lieutenant looked around, he heard Davy say that he would check on her. Stratton took over the wheel and watched as Davy walked down the stairs to the main deck and went below.

The lieutenant's eyes briefly fell on Rose and Adam as they stood by the portside rail of the ship and looked out to sea. He focused his gaze again on Stratton and returned to their conversation.

Rose had her arm around her brother's shoulder and held him tightly to her side. A few tears escaped her eyes as she felt freedom wrap around them like a protective glove. She had risked much to help Miranda, but it was worth it. Locand was always a good friend to her and had given her many coins in the past to help her and Adam get by. She knew he had pitied her, but she didn't care. She willingly accepted his help because they needed it. She was far from proud when it came to their situation, and Locand was the only one who had ever wanted to help them. For years she had sold her body to the highest bidder to put food on the table. Sex was a tool to get what they needed, and it didn't mean anything to her. It was only a job.

She hoped her life was going to change. She glanced quickly at Lieutenant Mansfield as she kissed her brother on the head. Yes, a new life with one man to love would be gratifying indeed. She always hoped she would one day have children and a loving husband, but her dreams were smashed to pieces when her parents died, leaving them nothing. They had become so much in debt there was no way for them to get out of it. No one would hire her, and then one day when she went into the local tavern, she instantly got hired to be a waitress when one of their girls walked out on them.

The money was slim. It wasn't until a rich man came into the tavern and saw her, requesting her to bed him for a considerable amount of money, did she consider prostitution. She had bedded him for several days and made enough money to pay off all of their debt, yet they were still barely getting by. The tavern decided to use her as a whore for all of their upscale clientele, the problem was that The Black Flag rarely brought in decent people with lots of money to spare so she had to do other things. However, she had made a name for herself around Port Royal and was used for many services, all of which she was willing to do for the right price.

Now those days were hopefully over and she could start a new life, a blessed life. Her only goal now was to find an honorable man to settle down with. Her eyes again stared at Lieutenant Mansfield. He was pleasant looking, and she was attracted to him. The fact that he knew of her past and what she had done made him more desirable to her. She knew that she had nothing to hide from him. At that moment, the lieutenant glanced at her and smiled. Rose smiled in return and turned her head quickly away from him. Her thoughts then turned to Locand. When her and Miranda boarded the ship all she saw was Locand going limp. Concern filled her chest, but in her heart she knew he was going to be fine. He had to be for Miranda's sake.

As soon as Locand had passed out, Davy and the lieutenant had both carried him down below deck and placed him gently on a bed in one of the cabins. Miranda quickly followed them, and once Locand was settled onto a bed, she removed his shirt carefully and tended to his wounds. It wasn't long after that she had felt the ship move forward. Soon the lights of Port Royal became dimmer and dimmer until there was nothing left to see. Miranda jumped up to the porthole and glanced out it, a smile on her face as she felt a loosening in her chest. She had been so stressed about Lord Hammil and Locand that she wasn't able to relax, yet now she felt again a tightening in her chest as she glanced back at Locand.

Quickly she hurried back over to the bed and gently turned Locand to his side and cleaned the marks upon his back with a rag and some rum she had found by the bed. Her eyes welled up with tears from the sight of the red welts. Her heart ached as she imagined the pain he must have endured by Lord Hammil's hands. Instantly, she felt rage and pressed harder into the wounds as she sterilized them. She didn't realize what she had done until a soft moan escaped Locand's lips. Miranda immediately felt contrite. "Lord Hammil indeed," Miranda spoke as she tried to cleanse the wounds more gently.

Locand remained with his eyes closed for most of the trip to the island. Davy would visit her below deck to check on both of them. Miranda would also go above deck to help her father periodically, but mostly she spent her time by Locand's side taking care of him. When they finally reached Eleuthera Island and anchored the ship by the hidden entrance to Stratton's home, they were all able to relax. Miranda had been curious as to what had happened to her father's ship, but her curiosity was appeased as she saw it in pieces and partially sunk in the water. Lord Hammil had destroyed it.

As Miranda regained her focus, she noticed a longboat being lowered to the water. Everyone on the ship climbed down the rope ladder and loaded into the boat. Locand received help from the lieutenant and was carried down on his back. Once the longboat reached shore, everyone moved quickly inside of the cave. Locand had needed help walking and leaned on his brother and Miranda for support. His eyes were now open and alert. They walked through the dark tunnel for quite awhile before it led them to the secret door in the library. Not until all of them stepped into the room safely did Stratton exhale a sigh of relief. Home!

The library looked as disheveled as it was the last time they were there. Nothing had changed, and it would have been surprising if it had. As everyone made it out of the library door, a few of the men disbursed to see if there were any intruders about. Within minutes, they returned not having found anything. Stratton could not stop smiling as he breathed in the air and patted his stomach happy to be home. He told Miranda and the lieutenant to take Locand to one of the bedchambers, but Locand refused.

"I'm fine. I need no more coddling." He tried to stand by himself and did so, but not without wincing in pain first, his hand moving quickly to his back. Miranda gave Locand a questioning glare, but he refused to look at her.

"Well," spoke Stratton as he lifted his arms. "I must say it feels great to be back home." Davy smiled and nodded his head as everyone else looked around them. "Lets disburse! Everyone find a chamber to call home for the duration of our stay and let's get some much needed rest." Everyone agreed readily and separated. As everyone left the room, Miranda stayed behind to help Locand, but when she reached for his arm he moved it away from her grasp.

"Are you all right?" Locand walked out of the room with Miranda staring after him in confusion. She followed him into a small bedchamber down the hallway and watched as he walked to the window, his head bowed and resting in his hand.

"I'm fine, Miranda. I'm sorry, but my back still aches."

"All the more reason for me to help you. Why will you not let me?" Locand turned around slowly.

"I have spent the past week lying in bed dreaming about what could have happened to you." Locand again touched his head. "I missed you, Miranda. I have missed you so much." Miranda ran to Locand and caressed his cheek.

"I have missed you, too. Forgive me for not being able to save you sooner. I—" Locand stared at Miranda in amazement.

"Don't ever apologize to me. You and Rose risked everything to save me and you shouldn't have done it. You could have been killed."

"But I wasn't!"

"I will say this for you. You did choose your allies wisely." Locand tried to calm, changing the topic slightly. He was angry that she had risked her life for him and yet he was pleased by it.

"Were they not the same allies you chose to find out about my father and Lord Hammil?" asked Miranda.

"They are the very same, except our Lieutenant Mansfield," replied Locand. Miranda smiled proudly as she admitted, "I was able to charm him into helping us, though there were times he did volunteer his services. I am not exactly sure why he wanted to help." Miranda thought about her own words for a moment and it caused her forehead to furrow.

"I can help with that. You see, there is something about the lieutenant you are not aware of." Miranda looked up innocently at Locand and folded her arms in front of her chest.

"Oh?"

"He is my brother!" Miranda's arms fell to her sides as her mouth opened slightly in surprise.

"Your brother?"

"Yes! Do you remember when I had told you that I had a brother?" Miranda nodded her head. "Well, the lieutenant and I have the same father, and we are close to being the same age. I am older, but not by much. No offense to your feminine wiles, but he helped you because of me." Suddenly, it all made sense. It explained the lieutenant's reaction when Lord Hammil told him they were going after Locand. He was not pleased because they were brothers.

"That explains much!" Now it was Locand's turn for his forehead to furrow.

"What do you mean by that?"

"Your brother was angry when Lord Hammil told him that he was going after you. It was then he became almost a different person." Locand smiled arrogantly, but then it faded.

"I'm still angry with you for doing what you did. Lord Hammil is not a man to trifle with, and yet you decided to take it upon yourself to use him again. It was not wise and could have back fired on you."

"What did you want me to do, let you die?"

"I expected you to do whatever you needed to do to save yourself," shouted Locand. "I wanted you to be safe and unharmed."

"I did!" shouted Miranda. "I saved myself from living a life without you. I had too much to lose to do nothing. I had to do something. My father and Davy could have died along with you, and Lord Hammil and the governor wanted you dead. There was no way I could have let them do it. Not to any of you. I love you!" Locand reached out and pulled Miranda to him, tears streaming down her cheeks. He held her until her tears were spent.

"I love you too, Miry. I truly do!" He then reached down and brushed his lips against hers softly. However, Miranda wanted more. She wrapped her arms around his neck and opened her mouth slightly for him to access. He did so without hesitation. Soon their lips ravished each other until they were begging for more. Miranda pulled away.

"What about your back?" Locand stood straighter and winced. He wanted nothing more than to hold Miranda, ravishing her lips like before, but knew it would not only be difficult, but painful as well.

"It hurts terribly." Miranda caressed his cheek, wishing she could take away his pain. "Will you stay with me? I need you by my side."

"Of course! There is no other place I would rather be than by your side." Miranda helped Locand over to the bed and helped him to lie on his side. She then crawled in next to him, snuggling into his chest, his strong arms surrounding her.

"Are you comfortable?" asked Miranda, hoping she wasn't hurting him. Locand's back ached, but he didn't care. He had everything he could ever want lying next to him. He then smiled.

"I'm perfect, my love, just perfect." Soon the pair closed their eyes and fell asleep. The tension in their bodies ebbing as they, for the first time in a long time, felt safe.

Chapter 21

Several weeks passed and everyone was more at ease and rested. The fear that Lord Hammil or the Governor of Port Royal were to come after them was no more an issue. It would have happened by now. Rose and Adam were getting more acquainted with Lieutenant Mansfield. A few times someone would catch Rose and Lyle holding hands when they thought no one was looking. The first time Miranda had seen it she had smiled and encouraged their feelings for each other. Davy and Stratton had been able to recover from being in the cell aboard the *Flying Wasp* and had been spending time fixing the house and walking the beaches. Miranda and Locand had been helping them with whatever they needed done but also tried as much as possible to spend quality time alone together.

They were frequently keeping to themselves and could be found many nights just sitting outside under the moon and talking. Their love for each other had grown. Frequently, Miranda and Locand would sleep in the same bed, though Locand still honored what he had said. Though they were both ready for that next step in their relationship, Locand held fast to his promise. He wanted to bed her, but knew the right thing to do would be to wait until they were wed. He wanted to be her husband, never losing her again.

That night she had joined him in bed. His shirt was removed as usual so Miranda could feel his warmth against her. They had snuggled together, now comfortable in their positions more than ever. By the next morning, Davy had found them still in bed together. He had been looking for Miranda, but when he had checked her bedchamber, he could not find her. Knowing that she had been spending a lot of time with Locand, his bedchamber was where he had checked next. He was hoping she wasn't in there, but when he knocked and opened the door he saw her form still sleeping while Locand stealthily moved from the bed.

Locand had been up from the pain in his back when Davy had entered. He was resting on his arm staring at Miranda's serene features when the door opened. Davy gazed at Locand with disapproval as he saw him raise his fingers to his lips and point toward the door. Davy led the way as Locand followed. Once they made it into the hallway and the door was closed behind them, Davy spoke.

"Stratton will not approve of this, Locand. You were lucky that I was looking for her and not him." Locand was only wearing his breeches as he ran his fingers through his disheveled hair and yawned. He was not self conscience about how his scars looked and in fact, would have forgotten all about them if it wasn't for the pain and bruising he still constantly felt.

"I think he can say nothing about it, don't you? For that would be hypocritical of him." Davy raised his hands to his hips and shook his head.

"Do not go there, Locand. We are talking about you and his daughter. Is this the first time you—"

"No!" answered Locand quickly as he looked around them to see if anyone else was up, but there was no one that could be seen. "No, this is not our first time sleeping together, nor will it be our last. Though to reassure your mind, I have not bedded her. " Davy pursed his lips tightly in disapproval.

"I promise to say nothing to Stratton about this, but—"

"I love her, Davy! I—love—her." Davy could not believe what he had heard and opened his mouth slightly in surprise.

"I will admit that I was curious, but I had no idea." Locand bowed his head slightly to the ground and raised his hands to his face.

"I know this is hard for you, you are like a father to her but I want to be with her. I want her to be my wife. I cannot live one more day without her near me." Davy slapped his shoulder hard and smiled. Locand looked up and had to regain his balance, his face wincing from the pain in his back. When Davy noticed what he had done, he apologized.

"Sorry about that, but your response pleases me, Locand, as I know it will please Stratton."

"What would please me?" Stratton had just turned the corner when he had heard Locand's and Davy's voices. He was fully dressed and it seemed as if he had been up for some time. Dawn had already come and gone, and though they usually slept in, it seemed like everyone was off to an early start that morning. Stratton moved to stand by Davy's side, his hands casually placed on his hips. His gaze moved from one man to the other, but no one answered him. "Well?"

"I was discussing with Locand the treasure and what he was going to do with his share." Davy did not want to admit they were talking about Miranda and the fact that she was at that very moment asleep in Locand's bed. He knew well the tension that it would cause between them.

"And what did you say?" Stratton's handsome features were relaxed, his smile and curiosity genuine. His eyes fell upon Locand as he waited for his answer.

"I have been thinking. I cannot hide here forever. I love this place, and I have never felt so relaxed anywhere else, but the queen has given me a letter of marque, and I must honor it. If I don't return with about half of the treasure, then the next time I get caught I will surely hang, and there will be no second chance for me. I love being a captain. It brings me freedom. I like the new life that I have started for myself, becoming a privateer. I have worked hard to erase my sins and move on. However, because of certain circumstances, I have fallen back into the path for which I am trying to avoid. I have become the pirate I once was, and I will be damned if I will remain this way. I want a different life, and I am willing to give up everything to attain it. But this time I have a new reason. It is not just to save myself this time, but the love I have for someone else. For her I would do anything. I would renounce my life as a pirate forever, and even a privateer if that is what she wanted from me. All I want is her in my life and in my heart." Stratton narrowed his eyes as he folded his arms in front of him.

"Who do you speak of?" Stratton almost held his breath as he waited for an answer. He knew how much time Locand had been spending with Miranda, and he was hoping that Locand was going to say that she was the woman he was talking about.

"I love your daughter, Stratton. I love her so much in fact that I would be willing to give up everything I own to have her." Locand took several deep breaths before he continued. "She loves the sea, and I know that when I tell her about what I need to do she will not understand. She loves sailing too much, but I will not deprive her of that. What I am saying is that I am asking you for permission to marry Miranda. I want her as my wife, by my side always." Locand's features were young and yet experienced. It meant a lot to him to have Stratton's permission.

"How will you support my daughter if you give up pirating?" Stratton's voice was soft and curious.

"You mean— we! How will we be supporting our wives?" Stratton's features hardened, he had not realized that Locand had known he was married. "By taking half the treasure back, I will be doing the queen a favor. I should then be rewarded by keeping my privateer status, for that is what I will be requesting of her for bringing more gold to her coffers. With that comes wealth and with your help and Davy's, we can start a business of our own that will keep us closer to England and to the ones we love." Stratton did not miss how he was being included in Locand's decision to retire. "I am hoping that Lyle will join us along with Rose and Adam, too. We could all start over again."

"And what about me? The queen is not just going to forgive me for my past transgressions." Stratton's tone turned deep and angry. Locand stepped forward.

"She will and the reason is because she has never seen you before. I will tell her that you died, and she will never know the difference. Then, you will be able to live freely as well. The only thing the woman knows about you is your name, that is all. So change it, shave your face, cut your hair, it will not matter, for in her eyes you will be no more." Stratton lowered his gaze and stared at the floor. "You have an obligation to spend more time with Miranda. You have deprived her of having you as a father. Davy has done a wonderful job raising and taking care of her, but it is you who should have done it."

"Don't tell me of my responsibilities, for I know them well," shouted Stratton.

"Do you?" Locand moved several feet closer to Stratton, "Because if you did, I wouldn't have to be standing here reminding you that you now have an obligation, not only as a father to your daughter, but as a husband to your wife." Locand saw the disgruntled look on Stratton's face but he did not ease up. He was determined to tell him how he felt.

"Is that what this is really about? Are you angry that I married your mother?" Locand glared at Stratton as he closed the gap between them.

"Angry does not seem to sum up how I feel."

"When did she tell you?" Locand looked away briefly.

"On the day I left London, before I boarded *The Captain's Avenger*, she told me that you two were wed and have been husband and wife for a couple months short of a year. At the time, I was still angry with her from when I had first learned of your relationship." He then scoffed loudly. "She said that I needed to use this trip to look inside my heart and find forgiveness for her."

"And have you?" asked Stratton eagerly.

"Yes, but before I left we came to an understanding of sorts. She's worried about you, Stratton, and she made me promise to find you and bring you home. Though, to be honest, I did not realize that I was going to have to keep up my end of the bargain this way. I figured that you would eventually return, and I wouldn't have to bother. I didn't realize that I would have to help save you." Locand paused for a moment. "Don't you realize how important you are to my mother? You have to return with me. She deserves to have happiness."

"This is my fault," piped in Davy. Both men looked toward him. "Madam Fairaday wanted to tell Miranda about your relationship, but I beseeched her not to."

"Why?" asked Locand before Stratton could even open his mouth. "It would have been better if she knew the truth."

"Because, I felt the news would be better coming from her father, not from her, but she had already told you about the marriage, Locand. She said that she had mentioned it to you." Locand shook his head vehemently while Stratton buried his face in his hands. He then composed himself and grabbed Locand by the shoulders.

"We had discussed this—you and I. You had said that our relationship didn't bother you?"

"Your relationship doesn't bother me. What does is the fact that you had gone behind my back and wed without even the courtesy of considering how I would have felt, or Miranda, for that matter. Your decision was rash and ill planned. My mother is my world, I am all that she has left and yet you not once confided in me your intentions. Did you not think I would be hurt?" Stratton stared into Locand's eyes and saw the tears welling up inside. For years, all he saw was a strong man and illustrious pirate, a friend to the end. But now he saw a child who loved his mother. "I just asked you for permission for me to marry your daughter. I gave you that respect and consideration. Did you not think I deserved the same?" Stratton closed his eyes tightly, the feeling of remorse filling him.

"I had no idea this would bother you so much. I did not mean to hurt you. I love you, Locand. You are like a son to me."

"That is why it hurts so much." Locand's eyes filled with hurt, and he was about to turn away when Stratton grabbed his arm to stop him.

"Don't walk away from me. We need to talk about this." Locand stopped but turned his head away from Stratton's gaze. "I'm sorry for the pain I have caused you. When Miranda introduced me to your mother, I did not realize who she was, how could I? Miranda didn't even know. We have discussed this. You know all of this. Your mother befriended Miranda for years, helping her fit into society. She invited me over one evening for supper when I was visiting Miranda, and we had a wonderful time. I saw how amazing and kind she was, and the more time we spent together, the more I realized how much I wanted to be with her. So, whenever I visited Miranda, I stopped to visit her too. The night you walked in on us was the first time I realized who she was. Did you not think that I was surprised to learn that you were her son? I could not believe it, and when you stormed out of her bedchamber your mother was in tears and she begged for me to talk with you, and so I did.

"It was fate that I met her, fate that I fell in love with her. When we married, it was out of spontaneity. I am getting older, Locand, and am often lonely. I have Miranda but knew she was being taken care of by Davy. I didn't want her to share in the life I lived. I promised her mother when she was born that I would keep her safe, that I would show her another world, but living in London was a life I couldn't live. I was a pirate after all, a rogue of the sea. What we do is not a life for a daughter. So what I did for her was in her best interest, though it saddened me to leave her." Locand slowly turned to face Stratton.

"Do you understand where I am going with this? Eventually I knew that our two worlds would collide and now you know the truth. However, you must realize that our marriage couldn't be publicized. Your mother, the queen's friend and confidant, marrying a pirate, not just any pirate mind you, but Captain Ditarius the Deadly? We both know that it wouldn't do well for either of us. So, we had to keep it a secret, even from the ones we love. Your mother knows everything there is to know about me, about Miranda, and she accepts it. She loves me. I am just sad that you had to find out this way."

"What of Miranda, when were you going to tell her? You cannot keep the truth from her for too much longer, for when she finds out, it will devastate her."

"I told her that I was seeing someone. She knows that, but I never mentioned that we were wed and I know I should have."

"Yes, Father, when were you going to tell me that you had a wife?" All three men turned to look toward Locand's bedroom. There was Miranda, her beautiful features hard as she stared back at them. She had been sleeping in Locand's bed when she heard voices coming from the hallway. She had quickly dressed and slightly opened the door to hear what was being said. It was then she learned that her father was married and the woman was Locand's mother, whoever that was, for she did not hear the name. The shock nearly caused her to lose her balance. Why had no one told her? But the more she listened, the more she found out why. She was angry that everyone seemed to know about her father's marriage except her. She was also hurt and disappointed that she couldn't have been trusted or even blessed with the information.

"Miry!" said Stratton, but she held up her hand to stop him.

"Don't talk to me unless it is to explain yourself and your actions. I cannot believe you are married, Father. I think that I should have been the first one you told, not the last.

"It is not like that, Miranda," said Locand, but Miranda turned on him next.

"Not like what? Did you not care for me enough to tell me that the woman my father has been seeing is your mother? More importantly, that she is now mine?" Miranda shook her head as if to clear it, her chest rising heavily from her anger. "I feel betrayed by the both of you." She then glanced at Davy. "By the three of you."

"How can you say that, Miranda? I would never intentionally hurt you," said Locand as he moved toward her. Tears started to fill Miranda's eyes, but she refused to let them fall.

"I don't know if I will be able to trust any of you again. The fact that you all have been sheltering me from the truth angers me greatly." Then, when Miranda was able to control her emotions she said, "I want to meet her." Locand and Stratton both glanced at each other in surprise, and then at Davy.

"You will, Miry, I promise you. As soon as we return to London we will search her out, and I will introduce you."

"She's in London?" The smile on Stratton's features dimmed slightly. "You mean to tell me that your wife lives in the same city that I have been living in these past years? Oh, how convenient it must have been for you to spend time with us both and yet you never once thought to introduce us?" Before Stratton could say another word Miranda broke into tears and ran down the hallway toward her bedchamber slamming the door behind her. Locand was about to go after her, but stopped when he felt Stratton's hand on his arm.

"Let her be. There will be time later to explain it."

"What are you talking about?" asked Locand.

"We are going to set sail today. I have been up preparing the ship since early this morning with Lyle, Rose and Adam. They are still down there working. I wasn't going to admit it to you, but I have already thought about your mother and returning to her. I just let you get your feelings off your chest. I know that you have wanted to do so for some time now. I just merely gave you the opportunity. You have to learn to do that more often, boy." Stratton smiled and turned to leave, but before he did, he turned quickly back around. "Oh, you have my permission to marry my daughter, and because you will be her husband soon, you can deal with her." Locand glared at Stratton, a frown upon his face.

"Oh no, you will not drop that responsibility on me."

"Fine," spouted Stratton angrily. "By the way, while I'm thinking of it, what was Miranda doing in your bedchamber?" It was Locand's turn to smile as he saw the expression upon Stratton's features.

"We were talking."

"Talking?" Stratton's eyes narrowed as he shook his head. "Were you whispering because I heard not words coming from there?" Locand shook his head and exhaled sharply.

"Fine! I will deal with Miranda. She's my woman, after all, and my responsibility. When I'm her husband I will be taking care of her and will have to deal with emotions like this."

"Good, I'm glad we see eye to eye on this. Now, what I really want to know from you is the truth. What was Miranda doing in your bedchamber? Is her virtue—intact—or have you…" Before Locand could answer Stratton retorted with, "Never mind. I would rather be ignorant for the moment, but I promise you, this topic of her virtue will come up again." With that said, he walked the rest of the way down the hallway while everyone else dispersed.

Chapter 22

In the days that followed the men of the *Soaring Eagle* made a stop at New Providence to pick up a crew. They could make it to London alone, but if by chance the queen's officers met them in the harbor, they had to make sure their story was sound. Stratton had done as Locand had suggested and cut his hair with the help of Miranda, though she barely talked to him. When she did, she made sure the topic was something other than his new wife. The topic still infuriated her and the longer she avoided it, the happier she was, at least for the moment, though her father did explain to her the exact information he had told Locand. Stratton had also shaved his face, which gave him a smooth and youthful appearance. He couldn't remember the last time he had seen his chin, and it felt strange when he glanced into the mirror and saw a stranger staring back at him. The one thing he refused to remove was the loop earring in his right ear. He had removed it upon occasion, but it was now the only evidence left of who he was and he didn't want to erase himself completely. However, when Locand had seen it, he had quickly exchanged it for another less obvious earring. Though Stratton didn't like it, he trusted Locand's judgment and watched as Locand placed the earring into his pocket.

Locand took over as captain with Lieutenant Mansfield by his side as first mate. Everyone else helped with the ship until they reached New Providence. While they were anchored there, Stratton and the lieutenant went ashore for provisions while Davy found them a respectable crew. The pickings were plenty for Port Royal had repelled many of the pirates that would have normally retreated there. When Davy lined them up on the dock for Locand's inspection, he approved every choice and after a long and meaningful speech telling them of there destination, welcomed them aboard the *Soaring Eagle* and set sail. Half of the treasure had been hidden in barrels that the crew could have mistaken as gunpowder for they were lined up by the cannons. The other half had been divided equally amongst them and hidden in a place where each thought it would be safe. The dividing had been done prior to them leaving Eleuthera Island.

It took months to finally reach London. Beside a few storms, their journey was pretty much uneventful. They did have to careen the ship and beached it on an island to clean and scrape the barnacles from the hold. It was a laborious task indeed, but one that needed to be done to help the ship go faster and to prevent rot caused by the teredo worm. If they wouldn't have had it done, the ship could break up and sink to the bottom of the ocean, and no one desired that. Locand had noticed that the job needed to been done and did it on an island where they would be safe.

During that time Stratton and Davy helped with the chores of the crew and kept to themselves, not wanting any of the them to suspect who they were. Rose and Miranda spent most of their time below deck and became good friends. Often, Miranda would see the lieutenant and Rose behave lovingly toward each other, and it was during this time she ached for Locand's touch. He had angered her by not telling her that her father was married to his mother, and yet Miranda was having a hard time hating him for it. In fact, the first moment he had come to her to apologize, she had grabbed him to her, not letting him finish his words and kissed him hard upon the mouth. After that she refused to mention his betrayal as long as he didn't bring it up and they spent his brief visits just talking and holding each other.

The day the *Soaring Eagle* made port in the London Harbor, Miranda stepped onto the deck and watched as the men hastened to do their work. Each of them was excited to be in a different place. Though Locand had told them he would be in need of their services again, for now they were to go ashore and enjoy themselves. The men were eager to do just that. Miranda was watching the docks with anticipation, wondering if the queen's soldiers would be waiting for them, but the more she looked, the more she was relieved there was no one standing on the docks waiting for their arrival. Locand walked silently up to her and wrapped his arms around her waist, kissing her cheek.

"Do you think this will work, Locand, because I cannot bear to be without you if it doesn't?" Locand caressed Miranda's cheek with his hand and forced her to look at him.

"It will work, trust me." Miranda smiled weakly, but her mind was still in turmoil. Locand gazed at the beautiful, clear, morning sky surrounding them, and though he felt joy at being able to see his mother again, his heart felt heavy. Not once did Miranda allow him to talk about her. She didn't even want to know her name, and this troubled him deeply. He knew when she found out that his mother was Madam Fairaday she would be furious with him. Miranda would also be angry with his mother for not telling her who she really was, and yet how could she? His mother didn't go around telling everyone that she was the mother of a rogue pirate.

Though she was certainly not embarrassed of his career choice, her position as the queen's confidant would be in jeopardy, as well as her future and title. She had worked too hard to forget her past to make a mistake like that, but would Miranda understand their situation? Locand did not know but could only hope that she could. They had spent years hiding from everyone their true identities. No one suspecting they were the wife and son of the legendary Logan James, the black scourge of the sea for which he was unpleasantly known. Though Stratton and his father were friends, he also went under an alias, which was why he had taken the fear inflicting name of Captain Ditarius the Deadly, but now Stratton wanted to change his ways, as did they all. Yes, he knew well the dangerous waters for which they were headed. Stratton, his mother, and himself were in danger, at least until he could speak with the queen. He knew that once he had done that task, they could all breathe a little bit easier.

"Miranda?" spoke Locand quietly, he had to at least warn her of his mother's identity but before he could say another word Miranda had prevented it by speaking.

"I don't want to talk about it, Locand." Locand released his arms from around her and ran his fingers through his hair in frustration.

"Are you not even the slightest bit curious of who my mother is?"

"No, Locand, and I don't care."

"But—" Locand tried to plead with her but it did no good. She was being stubborn. Miranda raised her hands to her hips and stared at him in anger.

"I already told you. I've been thinking a lot about what you said on our way to Nombre de Dios. My father does have a right to be happy, but so do I. All I care about is you, Locand. Who your mother is doesn't concern me. I have already decided to give her a chance.

She deserves that much from me. I have been acting childish and I want to make it up to you." Locand raised his eyebrows skeptically but Miranda just gave him a winning smile and turned away from him, walking below deck to pack her belongings.

By midday, Miranda, Davy, Lyle, Rose and Adam had all made their way to Miranda's home, for which she had taken residence for years. It was still in the same condition which they had left it and the servants greeted them at the door, taking everyone's belongings and placing them into one of the many available rooms. *It was nice to be home*, thought Miranda, though her heart still missed the beauty and calm of Eleuthera.

She glanced at Davy and smiled at him as he walked by her, heading toward his room on the first floor. As she walked toward the living room area, she remembered fondly how her and Davy used to sword play for hours, but then another thought crossed her mind, an unsettling thought. Once she was married to Locand, would he still embellish her with the attention and guidance that she so desperately needed? It was then she realized that her father would be spending more time with her now that he had returned for good, and though his attention was what she truly craved, it was going to be different not being able to rely on Davy to keep her out of trouble, or to help her say and do the right things. Her childhood was rushing behind her and it scared her. She was a child no longer but a grown woman now.

Miranda heard her name being called by Rose and turned regretfully away from the room and walked up to her grabbing her hand in reassurance. She knew that Rose was concerned about her future. Though Lyle had accepted her for who she was and cared for her, would everyone in London look at her the same way as her new friends? Or would they just label her as a whore and use her as such? Rose was determined to change her life. She wanted to live respectably, and now that she had her portion of the gold she could do just that. She could finally start a new life. In her mind, London was the right place to do it.

While Miranda was busy with her new guests, Stratton headed toward Madam Fairaday's estate which stood on the outskirts of town. She had twenty acres or so and a house that could probably be home to half the town. He had missed her terribly, though he would not admit it, especially to Miranda and Locand. When he arrived by carriage, he was informed that Madam Fairaday was still at the palace having tea with the queen. Though he was slightly disappointed, he decided to stay and wait for her to return in her bedchamber. Before he left the ship, he told Davy to have everyone meet them at Madam Fairaday's estate for introductions in a couple of days. He would let them know exactly which day by a note. Until then, he was to watch over everyone. Davy was glad to do it, for it gave him purpose again.

For years he had been like a father to Miranda, but now it would all change. Once Locand and Miranda were married, she would not need him anymore and the rest of them could handle themselves. He had decided that is was time to find his own happiness. He needed a wife to focus on and adore. Being that there were no outstanding prospects at the moment, he had decided to discuss the topic with Madam Fairaday. She did have a friend, Lady Eleanor, who he had spent time with several months earlier but had ignored when she had tried to move their relationship to the next level. She was a fine woman, an upstanding aristocrat, and yet she was also very down to earth. She had cared for him. She had even told him so, but at the time he had wanted nothing to come between his duties or loyalties. His first priorities were to Miranda, but now he was free to do what he wanted. He was now free to love. After his discussion with Stratton, he had promised himself that he would go and search her out.

Stratton had been pacing the floor in front of the fireplace in Madam Fairaday's bedchamber for what seemed like hours. He had wanted to prepare her for what he knew would come— the truth. He had to talk to her about what had transpired between him and Locand, as well as Miranda, and what had happened in the Caribbean. Stratton then breathed in a long worried breath. Yes, the night was going to be a very stressful one indeed. He knew that Madam Fairaday would be upset with the truth he was going to tell her. He had been gone for several months in hiding. He had not once sent word to her just in case there was trouble. What angered him the most was the fact that he had not once given her the consideration due her. She was his wife now and deserved better from him. His memories then dwelled on the past when he had been married to Miranda's mother. A tear came to his eyes. In his heart he had felt like he had betrayed her somehow but then he knew she would want him to be happy, and now he was. His thoughts then turned toward Locand. At that moment he was on his way to the palace to speak with the queen. He hoped their plan would work.

Locand had just arrived at the palace when Lord Havenor met him at the entrance.

"Captain Riveri, how pleasant it is to see you again." Lord Havenor's false politeness and smile annoyed Locand, but still he smiled back and extended his hand in greeting. He was wearing a clean white shirt under a beautiful bright blue jacket. His hair was combed and he had taken a bath.

"It is a pleasure too see you again, Lord Havenor. How is your wife?" At the mention of his wife, Lord Havenor's smile faltered slightly. Locand had met Lord Havenor's wife once. She was a youthful creature in her thirties who had an exuberant personality and was fondly thought of by many. Years ago, before she had been married to Lord Havenor, she had seduced him into her bed.

"She is well, thank you. It is thoughtful of you to ask," replied Lord Havenor wanting to change the topic quickly. "Where is our Lord Hammil?" He then said slyly, "Kill him did you?" Lord Havenor laughed as if he were jesting but the smug look on his face told of his true feelings on the matter.

"I am afraid that Lord Hammil had an accident and will not be joining us— ever."

"I'm sorry to hear that, however, I see that you have found the treasure?"

"That is for me and the queen to discuss. I believe she is expecting me."

"I'm sorry to say," started Lord Havenor, "that the queen is undeniably detained and will not..." Before Lord Havenor could finish his sentence a feminine voice could be heard coming from the large open hallway where pictures of the queen and her predecessors were hanging on the clean whitened walls.

"I think that her majesty can find time for news about what Captain Riveri can bring to her coffers, don't you Lord Havenor?" The voice came from Madam Fairaday as she walked stealthily toward them, her golden white dress swishing back and forth in the latest London style.

"Captain Riveri," greeted Madam Fairaday as she bowed her head slightly toward her son. A secretive smile spread across Locand's lips as he stepped forward and grabbed Madam Fairaday's hand, kissing it in greeting.

"You look as young and beautiful as you did when I saw you last, Madam Fairaday. You are in good health I trust?" Madam Fairaday smiled broadly as her cheeks rose into a flushed state.

"Shameless flatterer!" chastised Madam Fairaday as she started to laugh. "The queen is in her private chambers. She wanted to rest after her long meeting this morning and is quite fatigued. I will be more than happy to take you to her."

"Your kindness would be appreciated." Locand stepped forward, smiled an arrogant smile at Lord Havenor who glared at him, and followed his mother down the hallway. As they walked silently together Madam Fairaday glanced quickly behind her to see if anyone was following them, but there was not. Lord Havenor had hastily stormed off and there was no one else in front of them or behind. Madam Fairaday quickly guided Locand to a private room on the second floor where she knew that no one could overhear their conversation. When they both stepped into the room, Locand quickly surveyed their surroundings and when finding that no one was in there, closed the door. As soon as he did, Madam Fairaday rushed over to him and wrapped her arms around Locand's waist tightly.

"I was so worried about you, my son." Tears sprang to Madam Fairaday's eyes as Locand wrapped his arms around her.

"Mother, I just want to say that I'm sorry for being angry with you. I never should have—" Madam Fairaday raised her fingers to Locand's lips.

"It does not matter, you are the world to me and if my marriage bothers you…"

"No!" spoke Locand determinedly. Madam Fairaday stepped away and eyed her son skeptically. "You have a right to be happy. I was being selfish and angry when we spoke last, though you have to agree that I had good cause." Madam Fairaday nodded her head and bowed it slightly. "But it does not excuse my words toward you. You are my mother and deserve respect as well as happiness. For a short period of time I forgot that." Madam Fairaday caressed her son's cheek and smiled.

"Oh, Locand, I am glad that you have taken my advice and thought about your actions and words, for I have thought about mine. I should have been more considerate toward you. I am in love with Stratton, though at the moment I know not where he is, but I should have told you about our feelings for each other. I should have discussed it with you to see if it bothered you that I was to wed another man. I am a grown woman and did not think that it would bother you so. We have been a team for years, you and I. I did not mean to put him between us." Madam Fairaday stopped when she saw her son shake his head.

"That is not why I was angry with you." Madam Fairaday's eyebrows furrowed as she thought of what another reason could be. "Stratton Mayne was one of Father's oldest friends. He helped me get through some pretty rough times when Father died. He is like a father to me. That is what bothers me. The two people that I respect and care for the most are married to each other. Does it please me? Yes, in a way, and yet it bothers me, though it is hard to explain why."

"I knew that a pirate helped you get over your father's death, but I didn't know it was Stratton."

"Well, now you do, but rest assured that we have talked about our feelings on the matter, and we now accept each others views." Madam Fairaday turned her head slightly to the side and narrowed her eyes.

"You have talked with him? Recently?" Locand smiled as he bent down and kissed his mother's cheek affectionately.

"He should be at your estate as we speak. You made me promise to bring him back and so I did. He is waiting for you." Madam Fairaday's eyes began to water and she could not hide her excitement.

"Really, Locand, he is here?"

"Yes, now as soon as you bring me to our queen, I want you to go to him. He has much to explain to you." Locand's mother nodded her head, and she let him guide her to the door, but before it could be opened she placed her hand upon it.

"What did Lord Hammil want you to do for him? The queen never said other than that she was after some treasure." Locand was reluctant to tell his mother the truth but knew that it was the right thing to do.

"We were to get something from Stratton, a crystal of sorts, but I want you to understand that I did not know of our purpose beforehand. You know that I wouldn't harm him in any way." Madam Fairaday nodded her head and Locand continued. "I was also a target on Lord Hammil's dart board, and I didn't find that out until later as well. Stratton and I were to be both executed in Port Royal for pirating." Madam Fairaday's eyes filled with concern.

"There is nothing to worry about, Mother. We are both finally home and safe." Locand had raised his hand quickly to stop his mother from worrying. "I am going to fix this. Once I talk with the queen I am going to get our freedom back. This I promise you. No more worrying about us on voyages again, at least not for awhile." Madam Fairaday nodded her head, wiped the tears from her eyes and opened the door. She was eager to get this over with and talk with Stratton. She wanted to know the whole story of what had happened, and she knew that he would tell her. Locand was her son and though she knew that he told her the truth, she also knew that he was protecting her. More happened that he was not telling her. Madam Fairaday squeezed Locand's hand tightly and then let go as they reentered the hallway where several people were walking ahead of them.

When they finally reached the queen's chambers, Madam Fairaday knocked on the door. "Yes?" said a soft voice coming from behind a beautifully adorned white door. Madam Fairaday knocked on the queen's private door and a pretty girl with brown curls answered it. "Madam Fairaday, I thought you had gone?"

"Hello, Tara, I had almost left the palace when I was fortunate enough to run into Captain Riveri from the ship *The Captain's Avenger*. I thought that her majesty would like to see him. She has been eager for news from the Caribbean." Tara stared at Locand for several seconds and smiled. Locand smiled and color immediately rushed to the girl's cheeks.

"I will wake her, Madam Fairaday, if you could wait right here for a moment."

"Of course!" Madam Fairaday knew well how the queen would react to being disturbed. Terribly! But she also knew that it would be worth the interruption. Several minutes passed before Tara answered the door again to let them in. The poor girl's hair was tousled from what Madam Fairaday knew was probably a pillow being thrown at her head.

"She is ready to see you now, Madam Fairaday." When they walked into the room, the queen stood near a table in the corner. Her appearance was slightly disheveled, but she still appeared to be in good form. She was wearing a casual but elegant blue gown that fit her snugly in the chest and loosely around the waist and legs. On her ears hung large gaudy pearl earrings and around her neck a thick matching pearl necklace. Her fingers were also laden with many rings of various gems. The queen was a plump woman, but she held her figure well and her gowns were always made to flatter her. Her dark auburn hair was up in a braid that crowned her hair and her pale and pasty complexion was covered with several layers of makeup, her lips and cheeks a bright rouge.

"Emily, I thought you had left to return home? After Lord Barrington's lengthy discussion about politics, and his wife's views on the upcoming gala for my birthday, I was sure that you could use a rest as well," said the queen in a tired voice as she took several steps closer to Madam Fairaday. "Especially since you had to deal with that woman yourself. Handling Lord Barrington is easy compared to dealing with that snappish little pincushion he calls a wife."

"They think only of your best interests, Your Highness." The queen rolled her eyes as if she were used to hearing those same words being told to her quite frequently. "I am quite fatigued and was leaving the palace as you had suggested when I noticed Captain Riveri talking with Lord Havenor in the foyer. I knew that you would be interested in knowing of his arrival so I took it upon myself to bring him up here to see you. I apologize for the disruption." The queen waved her hand carelessly as if saying that it was no bother.

"You are a good friend, Emily, the best. You know my desires well and always indulge them." Madam Fairaday smiled politely and bowed her head. "Now if you will excuse us..."

"Of course, Your Highness," said Madam Fairaday as she bowed her head again and curtsied. She knew the queen well, for they had been friends for years, and with that friendship came a way of handling her. Madam Fairaday knew well how to handle and manipulate the queen, and the fact didn't go unnoticed to many of the aristocracy. If anyone wanted something from the queen, they would usually go to Madam Fairaday first to see if they could convince her to fight for their cause. Though they knew that the decision was ultimately up to the queen, it never stopped them from trying.

Madam Fairaday's smooth demeanor and considerateness toward the queen pulled much weight in her decision making. The queen often asked her for her opinion, and she would give it freely and unbiased. She always treated the queen with the utmost respect and was rewarded often for it. Sometimes the queen would do as she suggested and sometimes she wouldn't. Her relationship and guidance had given the queen much success and brought much money to her coffers, so her ideas and suggestions were often listened to. Because of this, she was the reason that Locand was given the letter of marque and pardoned for his past transgressions. Locand's charms helped, too, but she was the determining factor convincing the queen that she could not do without him and now it was proven that she was right.

Madam Fairaday smiled politely and turned around, not once looking at her son. Once the doors to the queen's chambers were closed, the queen took several steps closer to Locand, eyeing him skeptically. "So, you have been talking with Lord Havenor. What about?"

"You, Your Majesty. He didn't want me to come and see you. I was fortunate that Madam Fairaday came when she did for I don't think he would have let me in. I have just arrived in port and wanted to make sure that I saw you right away." The queen smirked as she folded her hands to rest in front of her.

"He does not like you, Captain Riveri. Do you happen to know why?" Locand knew exactly why there was tension between them, but he did not speak of it. Instead, he remained still, his hands behind his back. "Don't pretend to be a fool for I think you know exactly why he hates you. It has something to do with his wife, doesn't it?" Locand focused his gaze upon the queen and nodded his head. "Pretty little thing she is, young too. Did you bed her?" The question was direct and to the point, the queen never sidestepped anything. She was too impatient to do that.

"Years ago, before she had become a lady." Locand was starting to feel uncomfortable but still remained strong and confident in appearance.

"Wasn't that around the time that she was going to wed Lord Hammil?" Now the real reason came out. Lord Havenor's wife, Lucy, had once been engaged to Lord Hammil. When Locand had met her he did not know of who she was. He had met her at a celebration his mother had at her estate. During that time he was taking a rest from pirating to enjoy some time with his mother after being away for several months.

There were many women and men at the celebration, and when

his eyes fell upon Lucy, he found her breathtaking. She had short mousy brown hair with innocent blue eyes and a pale, clear complexion. They had danced several times together and when the night was over he had taken her home. Lord Hammil was supposed to meet her there but had never shown, so he was her escort for the evening. When he had taken her home she had invited him inside. It was then that she had come on to him. Being a man who didn't want to deny a beautiful woman, he bedded her, several times in fact. It wasn't until the next morning that he found out she was engaged to Lord Hammil. He had met him at the door and saw him leaving. Lucy had to explain the truth to the both of them when Lord Hammil lost his temper and started to argue with him.

Since then, Lord Hammil and he had a strained relationship and one that never had to be dealt with until they were put together on *The Captain's Avenger*. The queen was a smart woman indeed. It had been months after the confrontation with Lord Hammil that Lord Havenor had taken Lucy for a wife. At their marriage celebration, he had kissed her on her cheek and had congratulated her. It was then that Lord Havenor started to dislike him for he knew that they had once been lovers.

"You are correct, Your Highness. She once belonged to Lord Hammil." The queen smiled knowingly and clucked her tongue.

"It must have bothered you to know that."

"Not really," replied Locand smoothly. "I cared not at the time and now she matters nothing to me so Lord Havenor's hatred of me is unjustified. I have no interest in his wife any longer."

"Whose wife are you interested in now?" Locand's eyes narrowed, but he revealed nothing.

"No one's!" The queen laughed loudly and raised her hands to her hips.

"I am sure that you comforted Lord Hammil's betrothed some time during your voyage and no matter how much you reassure me that you didn't, I know the truth. You are a handsome man, Captain Riveri, and your charm could swoon even the most prudent of women, so for her to deny you would be all but impossible. Am I right?" Locand just raised his eyebrows and smiled causing the queen to raise her right hand to her chest and laugh loudly again.

"Ah, Captain, I am sure that you had her too, probably to Lord Hammil's dismay. Now, let's move on shall we? Where is our dear

Lord Hammil, I thought he would be coming with you to see me?"

"He was lost at sea, Your Highness. Upon our return, my ship was attacked and the gold was taken. Most of my men were killed or wounded, including Lord Hammil, and yet I went after the ship and took her for you. However, *The Captain's Avenger* is now sunk. I lost my ship in the battle. My men and I fought bravely and though we were able to retake a good portion of the gold back before my ship had sunk, there was nothing more that we could do. I have six barrels filled with gold and jewels for you to keep. I am sorry there is not more." The queen steadied her gaze upon Locand and searched his features for a lie, but there was none. His face was stone and revealed nothing.

"You have fulfilled your part of the bargain, Captain Riveri, but did Lord Hammil?"

"I am not sure what you speak of," replied Locand smoothly.

"Come, come, did he not tell you why you were sent to Port Royal?"

"Not until later did I find out our true purpose."

"He can be so childish. I thought that he would have explained it to you for it was your help he needed to find the treasure. I see that you did find it, so you were aware that you were after Captain Ditarius the Deadly?"

"Yes!"

"And did this bother you, for you two were friends at one time weren't you?" Locand stared at the queen in anger, yet held back his true feelings.

"Of course it did, but as you said, we were friends. I have not seen him in years and he has changed considerably since then, as have I."

"Is he dead then? I can tell in your features that you still care for him, but I don't care about that. Do you understand what I am saying? I need him to be dead. He has stolen much from my ships, and I aim to have his head for it. The Governor of Port Royal promised me this." The queen clenched her fists in anger, then quickly composed herself.

"Then you have your wish, Your Highness, because he is." The queen's gaze grew wide.

"What proof do you have of this or do you expect me to just take your word on the matter?" Locand reached into his pocket and took out Stratton's looped earring.

"Here is my proof!" He reached out his hand and the queen extended hers. When the earring dropped into her palm, the queen smiled greedily.

"So, it is true." The queen held the earring up and analyzed it. "I have been waiting for years to hear of that man's death and now I finally have the assurance." The queen walked swiftly past Locand to one of her dresser drawers and placed the earring inside. After she closed it, she walked back to stand beside Locand.

"What of Lord Hammil's betrothed? Does she live after all of this?"

"Yes! I have brought her back with me and she has now returned to her home." The queen nodded her head and clucked her tongue.

"So, they were not able to get married after all then?"

"No, unfortunately not."

"I have never met the girl. I was planning on it, but then plans changed. Is she pleasant?"

"She is and was very much in love with Lord Hammil. They were supposed to wed on New Providence before we were to return home, but it didn't work out. She is still saddened by his death." The queen's eyebrows rose, as she smirked.

"I must send her my condolences then. He was a good man that Lord Hammil, always did everything I wanted him to do to the letter. Ah, well, such is life, yes?"

"As you say, Your Highness." The queen moved closer to Locand and placed her hand on the lower part of his back.

"Now, what do you want for your efforts, Captain Riveri? You have made me a very happy woman." The queen tried to look alluring but Locand had no interest in her.

"I wish to keep the ship that I currently have to replace the one I lost."

"Done!" replied the queen quickly. "And?"

"I wish to also keep my privateer status, for I think that I have proven my abilities to you. My pirating days are over, unless it is for the crown, and I would like to move on with my life. I would like to open a business of sorts and remain in England a free man. I feel that I have earned it for what I have done for you." The queen remained quiet as she eyed Locand leisurely.

"You have thought much about this, Captain."

"Yes!" said Locand quickly as he looked down at the queen. Her hand was now caressing his back, but he only remained still not encouraging her affections.

"Is this what your heart truly desires?"

"It is!" Locand answered firmly. The queen stepped away from Locand and walked to the window. Locand watched her as she folded her arms in front of her chest, her back now facing him.

"You ask much from me, Captain." Locand lowered his head thinking that the queen would not give in to his demands. "But nothing that I wouldn't do or haven't done before. Men have asked more from me— much more." She then turned around and stared at Locand. "If your freedom is what you want then you shall have it, but on one condition." Locand was ready to agree to anything, but then eyed the queen skeptically.

"What would that be, Your Grace?"

"I will free you from your past sins allowing you to have a clean slate as long as you sail for me whenever I wish for you to under your privateer status. And that is on my convenience— not yours. You will be able to choose your own crew and do as you like, but there will be times when I will want you to do things on behalf of the crown. Tasks that will be similar to the ones that you have just returned from. Are you willing to do this for your queen and country?" Locand was thrilled with the queen's conditions. He did not want to give up his sailing ways completely, and yet he wanted to remain here in England with Miranda. The queen was offering him exactly what he wanted.

"If that is what you desire from me, then you have my ship at your disposal." Locand raised his hand to his chest and bowed his head. The queen smiled her approval.

"I will make sure that you are fully pardoned. Now, I want you to listen closely because I want you to understand this. If you, for any reason, go against the crown and return to your pirating ways stealing against me, I will cut off your head and take everything that is dear to you. Am I clear?" Locand took several deep breaths before answering.

"Crystal clear, Your Highness!" The queen smiled as she understood the pun and took several steps closer to Locand.

"Good, then we are in total agreement. I will be sending Lord Havenor to your ship to collect my treasure. Make sure it is ready for him."

"Of course, Your Highness. I will see that it is done."

"Excellent! Now, I believe that we are finished here. I will update Lord Havenor, and he will be giving to you, when he retrieves the treasure, updated letters of marque of your privateer status and other things. Guard it well for you have earned every bit of your freedom. You are free to start a business of your choosing with whomever you like, but choose your allies well."

"That will not be a problem, Your Highness. I have close friends who will serve me well and are devoted."

"I am glad to hear it. I will send word when I am in need of you. Until then, I will assume that you will be enjoying your freedom. However, never forget what we have agreed upon, because I won't, and you and your crew will be at my beck and call regardless if your will desires it or not." Locand nodded his head in understanding. "Now, if you will excuse me I would like to get some rest before I am disturbed again for another meeting." Locand walked up to the queen, kissed her jeweled hand and turned swiftly around, exiting the room in great haste.

When Locand returned to his ship, he had found his brother there waiting for him. The barrels of treasure had been brought on deck and were sitting by the gangplank waiting for Lord Havenor to come and take them. As soon as Locand boarded, his brother walked toward him in greeting.

"I trust that everything went well with the queen?" Lyle's voice was filled with concern. Locand smiled broadly as he slapped his brother on the shoulder.

"Of course!" Locand could hear his brother's exhaled breath of relief. "I was worried myself, but the queen believed every word of what I said and now all of us have our freedom."

"In return for what?" Lyle knew there had to be a catch.

"For sailing for her whenever she needs my services as a privateer. I'm not concerned, however, for I'm one of many men that she has at her beck and call, and all of whom want to bring glory to their names. I will not vie for her attention, so I will most likely be one of the last ones that she will need to help her. That, I think, she forgot about when she proposed the idea to me."

"Miranda should be pleased," spoke Lyle casually. Locand cocked his head to the side and stared at his brother.

"I did this for all of us, Lyle, not just for her. I want us to be a family again." Locand and Lyle embraced heartily, then quickly separated. “Where is Miranda, anyway? I thought that you were with her?”

"She’s with Rose and Adam. The women decided they needed new dresses, and I think that Miranda wanted to help Rose find some pretty ones that will help her fit in better. I had no desire to go with them, so I made Adam go.”

"Punishing the boy, are you? You realize that when they return he will be traumatized by the female mind, and yet will be no closer to understanding them than we are now.” The men laughed as they walked to the port side of the ship and leaned against the railing. “Speaking of Rose, how are you two getting along?” Lyle gazed out at the harbor.

"Good! Better than I would have expected, actually.”

"Have you…” Locand didn’t want to ask the question directly but Lyle understood what his brother was asking when he had raised his eyebrows.

"Yes!” Lyle gazed at the ocean again but not before saying, “She’s good!”

"Isn’t she?” responded Locand quickly without elaborating. Lyle narrowed his eyes on his brother, concern filling his features.

"Do you think she will be happy here? She’s worried what people might think about her past.”

"What do you think?” asked Locand. Lyle rubbed his chin, letting out a long breath.

"I would like to say, yes. I mean, so far she seems happy here. I just don’t want these snobbish English women to look down upon her for what she has done.” Locand raised his hand for his brother to stop.

"It matters not what other people think. Rose did what she had to do to survive. Any woman here would have done the same if they were in her position. Who cares about her past, do you?”

"No!” Lyle almost shouted. “I care not about her past. I only care for her future. I forgive her for what she has done and don’t look at her differently for it. I am falling in love with her, Brother. She is an amazing woman—clever and strong. Stronger than anyone I have ever known. She impresses me.”

"Well, then there is your answer. Look—” said Locand as he placed his hand on his brother’s shoulder. “Rose has friends here. Her and Miranda seem to be enjoying each other’s company, and you know that she will look after her and help her adjust to English life.

My mother will also guide Rose, just like she has done for Miranda, and help her fit in. Trust me, my Brother, Rose will be just fine. There is nothing for you or her to worry about. Besides, soon we will be living together." Lyle folded his arms in front of his chest in curiosity.

"What are you talking about?"

"I have spoken with the queen and have told her that Miranda did not marry Lord Hammil. That frees her from that bond, and on the way here I ran into Alexavier and Samuel LaRoice. They have a shipping business just up the road a ways. I talked to them a year or so ago about helping them out. Anyway, they wish to expand their business, but need the financial backing to do it as well as additional experienced help. They are master craftsmen of ships, and in addition to building them, they also maintain them–keeping all of these ships you see in the harbor in good sailing condition. These past years have brought much fortune to them. They have been so busy, in fact, that they now just want to spend more time with their wives, Isabelle and Rochelle. The demand from the crown, as well as from other sailors, has kept their business flourishing. I have sometimes even seen Isabelle and Rochelle working to help keep up with the clients.

"We have talked, and they agreed to have us as partners. We are to discuss the details and sign a contract next week. With our partnership you, Stratton, and Davy will all have equal shares, and we will therefore spend our time together making money, working hard and staying out of trouble. With all of our knowledge combined we can triple their business enough for them to open up another shop at another port. They know this and are excited about it. As duty calls and the queen wishes for me to sail on her behalf, I will do so, and we will take that as an opportunity to make more money for ourselves. So, while we are working hard our women will have plenty of time making names for themselves in society, like my mother has, and raising our children." Locand's idea seemed logical and as he glanced at the sunset heard Lyle ask, "Where will we live while we make a respectable living for ourselves?"

Locand returned his glance to his brother. "We shall stay at my mother's. She has a large estate, and I am sure that she would not mind all of us living with her. She has often talked of grandchildren running around and such. I wish for my future children to be able to live on many acres surrounded by trees. I want them to run wild and carefree." Lyle laughed as he stared curiously at his brother.

"All you have been speaking of lately is children and family. Has our lonely and disturbed childhood made you this hard pressed to start a family of your own?"

"I have gone so long without it in my life that it is what I long for the most. Do you not feel the same way that I do?" asked Locand as he placed his hands on his hips. His tone had turned slightly serious, though he tried to smile to lighten its impact.

"Yes, of course I do! I have thought of having children and a wife. I have dreamed of not living a life on the sea or in the army. I want all of the things that you do, Brother, so do not take offense to what I have said. It is just comical how much of a husband you truly sound like though you haven't taken the vows." Locand smirked slyly at his brother and turned his gaze toward his ship.

"I know, but that is how much I wish to be with Miranda. I would do anything to keep her. In fact, I would like us to get married on this very ship surrounded only by our loved ones and friends. Yes, that would be my idea of a perfect wedding, not in some stuffy church with hundreds of people or crew. No, something simple, like me." Lyle patted his brother on the shoulder and laughed loudly causing Locand to glare at him. Just then Locand thought of something and quickly changed the topic. "Lord Hammil is dead, isn't he?"

"I can guarantee it. The governor has killed men for less than what Lord Hammil has done against him. He's dead."

"Good, because it would be inconvenient if he decided to arrive and tell the queen exactly what happened between all of us. His contradictory words would put my life in jeopardy as well as anyone who is near me." Locand thrust his fingers through his hair in frustration letting the topic go. "So Lyle, what do you think of my idea?" Lyle smiled as he slapped his hands together.

"I think it sounds wonderful. Out of curiosity, though, what will be done with Miranda's place when we move in to Madam Fairaday's? Will Stratton take it over since it is probably in his name?"

"Actually, the house belongs to Davy and Miranda jointly. I have already talked with Davy about it, and he is going to take it over. He will still live there once we have moved out. He has helped Stratton raise Miranda and has been by her side since the day she was born. Though the task will be a hard one for him, he says that he trusts me enough to turn her over to my care. This I appreciate immensely from him." Locand then started to chuckle as he recalled Davy's words.

"He has said that he is looking to finally settle down so it would be a good place for him to have a wife. If it is not, then he will sell it."

"It seems that you have planned everything out perfectly," spoke Lyle.

"No, not perfectly, there is still one more thing that needs to be done." Lyle gazed at his brother as he turned his head to gaze out at the neighboring ships in the harbor. "Miranda still has to confront my mother, which is Stratton's new wife. I don't know how she will take the news."

"Didn't you tell Miranda who your mother was on the return journey?"

"That is the part that is so frustrating to me," spoke Locand, irritation ebbing into his voice. "She will not listen. I have tried many times to tell her, but she won't let me. It is like she would rather not know. She will be angry when she finds out the truth." Locand focused his attention briefly toward the water below before he glanced back at his brother.

"Then she can only blame herself, Locand, and no other. Miranda is stubborn. If she chooses not to listen, then she cannot be angry with you, only at herself. You have told me before that she is friends with your mother and has been for years, so I really don't see what the problem is."

"The problem is the fact that she does not know that Madam Fairaday is my mother. She has absolutely no idea, and when she finds out that my mother has been keeping the truth from her all this time–well, it will not be pretty." Locand ran his fingers through his hair, then covered his face with them.

"Everything will be fine. It is not your responsibility to tell her anyway. It is Stratton's, but it will not matter. For a short period of time she will be angry, but then she will understand and accept it. I have a feeling that you will make her see reason, and if she loves you, then her anger with you will be short lived."

"I hope so," replied Locand as he cut their conversation short and turned toward the prow. It was then that he watched Lord Havenor, with several officers by his side, step out of a large decorative carriage and walk down the dock toward them. Lord Havenor's expression seemed crestfallen as he withdrew from his pocket letters of marque wrapped securely in a leather binding. Locand smiled broadly as Lord Havenor approached. Freedom!

CHAPTER 23

Several days had passed when they finally received word from Stratton. However, the note came from Madam Fairaday requesting all of them to visit her at her estate for supper. Miranda was excited when they received the invitation. She had not seen Madam Fairaday since she had returned and was anxious to tell her all about her trip and what had happened. The day she had returned she had written her a note letting her know of her arrival, but she did not get a response in kind. Miranda did not worry, however, because she knew of the queen's hold on her and knew that Madam Fairaday had many responsibilities that came before her. The entire day, all Miranda could talk to Rose about, and anyone else who was in earshot of listening, was Madam Fairaday and how wonderful a woman she was and how close of a relationship they had. Miranda then talked about how she thought that Madam Fairaday was perfect for Davy, who she thought had a crush on her, and though Madam Fairaday denied having an attraction for him, Miranda still thought she could picture them together.

Though the house was full of men, they all had decided to turn the other way when Miranda got close enough. Locand and Lyle had disappeared as soon as she started talking about how trustworthy and honest Madam Fairaday was. Adam was willing to listen and was the only one wanting to hear every word that Miranda had to say about the wonderful woman. As soon as Davy passed by, she started to sing Madam Fairaday's praises more loudly, but instead of getting a positive reaction from him she only got a cold glare and a lecture correcting her of her assumptions about his feelings for the woman. Davy then quickly walked to his room on the second floor, slammed the door and locked it so she couldn't come in after him.

The only one missing was Stratton, and Miranda knew that he was spending time with his wife like he should. There were times when

Miranda wanted to beg Locand to tell her who his mother was, but pride prevented it. He had tried to tell her many times, but she had refused to listen to him and now that she wanted to know, she didn't think that he would tell her. It didn't matter, though, because she was still determined to do right by Locand and her father and accept the woman as a part of the family. At least that was her goal, but in her heart she had her doubts. She hadn't realized it, but not knowing who her father's new wife was bothered her tremendously.

The day was a long one for sure, but the night was getting better. By dusk everyone was dressed elegantly and riding in two separate carriages that had picked them up and took them to Madam Fairaday's. Miranda, Locand and Davy were sitting in one carriage while Lyle, Rose and Adam sat in the other. Locand was wearing white breeches with a dark navy jacket and gold buttons. Miranda dressed to match him in a dark blue dress that hung slightly from her shoulders, caressed her breasts and waist firmly and then billowed luxuriously from the waist down. Her hair was up and decorated with small red flowers. When Locand had first seen her, he had almost decided not to go to his mother's but to spend the rest of the evening making love to her in his arms, but Davy brought him swiftly back to reality as he half dragged them out the door by their elbows. The ride was silent, except for the sound of the wooden wheels crushing over dirt, and all eyes seemed to be focusing on the many things that were going on outside of the square windows of the carriage. They were intently watching the final settings of the sun; the beautiful red-orange hues mesmerized all who gazed upon them.

When the carriages finally pulled up to Madam Fairaday's and stopped, Davy was the first to step out. He had then raised his hand for Miranda to take but Locand stopped her from accepting it.

"I need a moment alone, Davy," said Locand. Miranda glanced over at Locand in curiosity then glanced over at Davy. She could see the indecision in his eyes.

"Make it quick, Locand, we are expected." Locand nodded his head quickly and waited for Davy to close the door of the carriage for privacy. When he did Locand quickly turned toward Miranda.

"What's wrong?" asked Miranda as she placed her hand upon his knee.

"I haven't gotten the chance to tell you how wonderful you look tonight." Miranda smiled broadly as a flush grew on her cheeks.

"Thank you. You look quite dashing yourself." Miranda leaned forward seductively, her hand caressing up to Locand's thigh, and gave him a healthy glance at the top parts of her breasts. "I miss you by my side. I would have liked nothing more than to stay at home with you tonight and—" Before Miranda could finish her sentence, Locand raised his finger to her lips and shook his head not wanting her to continue. It surprised him when she playfully darted her tongue out and licked it. He needed very little encouraging. He swiftly raised his hands and grabbed a hold of her shoulders, leaning forward and pressing his lips against hers passionately. The kiss was deep. When Locand heard Miranda sigh her pleasure he instantly pulled away.

Locand could see the passion filled eyes of his love and knew that his held the same emotions. Miranda was disappointed when he pushed her gently away from him.

"What's the matter?" she asked innocently as she tried to catch her breath, her chest rising and falling heavily. Locand ran his fingers through his hair and took several deep breaths to calm himself.

"Nothing, I just don't think that now is the time to do this," but then he leaned forward, wrapped his fingers quickly around the back of Miranda's neck and pulled her close to him. "But I promise you that we will finish this later." He then kissed Miranda one last time before he let go of her and sat back into his seat adjusting himself. Miranda's smile was mischievous and pleased. She then took a quick glance at her appearance, and seeing nothing out of place, relaxed and sat back into her seat.

"If you didn't want my affection, then why hold me hostage in this carriage?" asked Miranda as she smiled slyly, her arms rising. Locand hastily moved to the edge of his seat and glanced at the floor.

"There is something that I wanted to discuss with you." Seeing the serious expression on Locand's face, Miranda moved to the edge of her seat as well.

"Yes?"

"It has been pleasant living together these past few days. I have had a chance to see you in more of your natural surroundings, though there are times when a ship could be mistaken for your home because of how relaxed you are upon it." Locand laughed briefly, then continued. "I feel at home with you, Miranda, and truly believe that I could be happy anywhere as long as you are with me."

"Oh, Locand..." began Miranda, but Locand stopped her.

"It is because of this that makes what I have to say next even more important. On Eleuthera, when you overheard me and your father talking, I had asked him for your hand in marriage." Miranda had missed that part of their conversation but was no less excited by his words.

"Locand," started Miranda with tears in her eyes. "I would be honored to be your wife. I assumed that we would one day marry but—" Miranda's sentences came out jumbled but Locand didn't mind. He raised his right hand and caressed her cheek affectionately.

"I love you, Miranda. I need to make sure that you know that."

"I do, Locand, just as much as I love you. You know that you have my heart and always will." Locand's hand lowered as his forehead furrowed.

"Would you care for me no matter what might come between us trying to push us apart?" Locand stared at Miranda for several seconds before she responded.

"Regardless of what adversities we might face, I will not let them tear apart the love we have for each other. We will work through them, whatever they may be. Believe me, there is nothing—" Locand raised his hand to stop her from speaking.

"Betrayal?" The mere word caused Miranda to sit back farther into her seat.

"Yours?" she asked firmly, her voice rising slightly. She relaxed when Locand shook his head.

"I would never intentionally betray you." Miranda nodded her head as she scoffed loudly. She then raised her right hand to her face and touched her cheek.

"Are you referring to your mother's betrayal?"

"Miranda, listen—"

"No, you listen," chimed in Miranda as she pointed her finger at Locand. "I don't even know who your mother is so—"

"You know her better than you think you do." Locand moved back into his seat and smacked the back of his hand against his leg in frustration.

"Fine, you win. Who is your mother?" Locand gazed at Miranda and started to shake his head.

"It does not matter now for you will find out soon enough, but I want you to promise me something." Miranda's eyebrows rose.

"Yes?"

"When you finally meet her, whenever that may be, you must promise to not take your anger out on me for I have been trying to tell you for the past few months who she is, you have just been too stubborn to listen." Miranda and Locand's eyes clashed for some time before she finally nodded her head.

"I promise to not be angry with you, but I want you to understand that it is not you who I want to hear the truth from. I want my father and now my—"Miranda exhaled sharply before she continued, "my new mother to explain to me why they did what they did. That is why I have been so stubborn. You could tell me of your mother's identity, but it wouldn't solve the problem. It is not your responsibility to explain anything to me. All I want from you is your love, and I have it. That is the most important thing to me." Locand smiled as he leaned forward and quickly kissed Miranda upon the lips. Before they could finish with their conversation, Davy opened the door. Locand quickly got up and stepped out of the carriage. He then reached in and held out his hand for Miranda to take. As she descended the steps and touched the ground, the pair followed Davy down the lit stone pathway that led to Madam Fairaday's front door where a servant was waiting for them.

Upon entering into the great hall, they were greeted warmly by several servants and then had to follow one of them down a hallway to a smaller, less intimidating, sitting room. The house was magnificent with its freshly polished wood floors and its many tapestries. On the walls hung countless pictures of sceneries and sea landscapes but none of family portraits. The hallway was lit brightly from the numerous candles that hung from the wall. Locand had wrapped Miranda's hand around his arm to rest on his bicep as they walked together with Davy closely behind them. As the servant stopped by the sitting room, Miranda was surprised to see her father step out of it. He was dressed handsomely in a pair of cream breeches and dark jacket with a white shirt underneath. He held a glass in his hand that he swirled frequently which looked like it had Bourbon in it. He gently sipped at it as his eyes fell upon his daughter and Locand.

"Locand," said Stratton in greeting.

"Stratton," replied Locand casually.

"And how are you, my daughter?" asked Stratton as he moved

hastily forward and placed a kiss on Miranda's cheek.

"Well, thank you. I didn't know that you were going to be here. Did your wife come with you or did you decide to leave her at home?" Miranda's tone was flippant and her remark did not go unnoticed by her father. Stratton narrowed his eyes and smiled as he saw Locand squeeze her hand in warning.

"I was invited here, just as you were, and to your chagrin I did bring my wife and your new mother, so you better watch that tone. It makes you appear quite ugly, my dear. Besides, you promised me that you were going to give her a chance."

"Yes, well that was before you decided to wait until now to introduce us," replied Miranda seethingly. "And at Madam Fairaday's estate, too, have you no shame?" she continued on, but before Stratton could reply Davy placed his hand on his chest and pushed him slightly back and away from Miranda while Locand gripped Miranda's hand to keep her under control.

"Stop it, both of you," spoke Davy as he glanced from one to the other. "Now, we are in the presence of other people so save this argument for later before you hurt more than just your feelings." Miranda and Stratton both glanced around them and saw the looks Lyle, Rose and Adam were giving them from the doorway. Neither of them could see Madam Fairaday or anyone else watching them argue from inside of the room. Miranda quickly apologized to everyone, but still glared at her father in anger.

"Madam Fairaday has already been introduced to everyone so I think that now would be a good time for you to speak with her, Miranda," encouraged Davy. "She has been eager to see you." Miranda ran her fingers along her brow and nodded her head. She then quickly moved away from Locand and her father, walking into the sitting room. She was worried about who she might find standing next to Madam Fairaday, but when she glanced ahead of her the only woman she saw was Madam Fairaday, which puzzled her greatly. As she stepped closer, she glanced around the room and noticed two long sofas with several chairs surrounding them that were light and dark in color. There were also tables littered with glowing tapers and two windows against the wall that let in plenty of light during the day with heavy dark curtains that were currently hanging down in front of them.

Madam Fairaday stood restlessly in the center of the room by a couch clenching her fingers together nervously, her burgundy dress billowing around her as she moved. Her hair was curled and hung loosely around her shoulders. She looked beautiful, beautiful and for some reason anxious, thought Miranda as she slowly approached her.

"My dear, Miranda, I am so glad to see you," spoke Madam Fairaday with false confidence.

"Madam Fairaday, it has been too long. I am glad to see you, too." Miranda then rushed quickly forward and embraced her. The embrace was heartfelt, but when Miranda tried to pull away, Madam Fairaday almost couldn't find the strength to let her go. When she finally was able to, Miranda glanced at her strangely but said nothing to her about it. Miranda felt the whole situation was bizarre. When she glanced around her, she noticed how everyone was hanging back as if they were waiting for something to happen. It was at that moment that she saw Locand standing several feet inside of the room. She smiled pleasantly as their eyes met. She then waved him forward to join her, and Locand didn't hesitate. When he reached her side, he wrapped his arm around her waist possessively and pulled her close to him. Madam Fairaday didn't miss the action but held back her emotions.

"I want to introduce you to Captain Riveri. He is the Captain of the ship *The Captain's Avenger*, well, now the *Soaring Eagle*." Miranda squinted her eyes at Locand, not quite sure how to explain the change of ship, but he only shook his head at her as if telling her not to pursue the topic further. She then smiled proudly at Madam Fairaday and continued. "I have so much to tell you about our voyage and other topics." Madam Fairaday saw the glance shared between Miranda and Locand and knew that much had happened between them. "I have some very exciting news to share with you."

"Well, my dear, I am anxious to hear all about it." Miranda reached for Madam Fairaday's hand. She eagerly gave it and Miranda squeezed it gently, the women smiling at each other. Before Miranda could say another word Locand blurted out, "Miranda has agreed to be my wife." The look of shock could be seen on Madam Fairaday's face and a cough—from Stratton--could be heard from the back of the room. When Miranda turned around, she could see her father approaching them with another glass in his hand and he moved to stand next to Madam Fairaday, handing her the glass filled with Bourbon. She hastily let go of Miranda's hand and eagerly accepted the glass. She then quickly downed the contents. Miranda's eyes grew wide with surprise.

"Are you all right?" asked Miranda. Madam Fairaday raised a hand to her chest.

"Fine!" she said though her voice was quiet and cracked. Stratton had neglected to inform her of that news. She was quite surprised by it. Miranda could see the glares that Locand and Madam Fairaday were now giving to one another and realized that they were almost hostile.

"Do you know each other?" asked Miranda wearily for she could think of no other reason why two strangers would give each other such scathing looks. Madam Fairaday turned her gaze upon Miranda and then again to Locand. Within seconds, Locand could feel Miranda moving away from his arms and out of his grasp.

"I am glad that you asked the question because we do know each other." Miranda was unsure of how they knew each other so took a big step away from the both of them. "He is my son!"

"What?" Shock crossed Miranda's features and then horror, soon the expression changed to one of betrayal.

"How can that be?"

"It is a long story at best, but the truth needs to come out. I am your father's wife and have been so for almost a year now! I know that we should have told you this sooner. Believe me when I say that I would have liked to but…"

"A year?" Miranda's eyes turned to her father's but he only looked away from her. "Should have told me sooner? In all of the time that we have spent together you couldn't have told me the truth? Months ago would have been better than a year later. Days afterward would have been better." Anger now filled Miranda's voice. "How could you do this to me? I trusted you!" Miranda yelled her words loudly as tears filled her eyes. Tears filled Madam Fairaday's eyes as well. "I can't believe you kept this from me. You were like a mother to me!" Madam Fairaday reached out her hand to grab Miranda's but she held hers out in front of her to stop her, tears streaming down her face. "Don't touch me!" Madam Fairaday quickly withdrew her hand and covered her mouth with it. Miranda glanced at Locand, but refused to find comfort in his arms. Instead, she turned and ran from the room.

Rose was the only one who wanted to stop her and knew that she must have been hurting. "Miranda!" she yelled but as soon as she made a motion to go chase after her, Lyle quickly stopped her by placing his hands upon her shoulders. “Let me go!” Rose yelled as she fought against Lyle.

"This is not our fight, Rose. Do not interfere.” Rose quickly spun around in Lyle’s arms and stared at him as if he were a monster.

"How can you stand there and do nothing?” Lyle had also felt the urge to go after Miranda but knew that it wouldn’t have been wise so he turned and stared at Davy, who focused his gaze upon Stratton, and as he did so, shook his head in disapproval. Stratton knew what his old friend was trying to tell him, but focused his attention on Locand instead. Locand turned angrily at his mother and Stratton and raised his finger toward them.

"Damn it, she’s right! You should have told her the truth months ago instead of waiting a year later.” Locand took a deep breath to calm himself, but it was hard. “I found out about your relationship a long time ago and we all know how that ended. I am still not over it, but I did choose to accept it. Granted, it took me months to do so, but I had decided that your happiness was what was most important. How do you think Miranda feels to know that the person she has trusted over these past few years married her father without consulting her, and then told her nothing about it until today? You would be crushed, too.”

"Locand—” started Stratton, but before he could say another word, Locand cut him off.

"Don’t you dare try to justify this by telling me that you were sparing her the blow for that is what you have done with her her entire life, sparing her from all that is bad in this world. She is stronger than what you think she is, and no matter what your reasoning was, you were wrong.” Stratton took a threatening step toward Locand but Madam Fairaday pressed her hand against his chest to stop him. Angry, Locand turned swiftly on his heel and followed Miranda. Davy was about to follow too, but Stratton stopped him.

"Let Locand deal with her. At the moment I think that he will be the only one she will listen to.” Davy nodded his head though his heart ached for not being able to stop the pain he knew she must be feeling. Stratton raised his arm around Madam Fairaday, but she pushed it away, tears running down her face.

"You are losing your daughter and I my son. What have we done?” Stratton closed his eyes and remorse hit him full force.

"I will fix this, my love, we will have our children back," and with that said he left the room with Davy by his side leaving Lyle, Rose and Adam to fend for themselves. Adam however, after waiting for such a long time, had found his way into the kitchen and was eating some food that had been prepared leaving Rose and Lyle in the hallway by themselves. After everyone had gone, Madam Fairaday sat into a chair and raised her hands to her eyes, weeping loudly. Rose glanced into the room wanting to find some way to help.

"You need to do something," demanded Rose.

"Me? What am I going to say to her?"

"I don't care what you say, but say something. You are Locand's brother; it is your obligation to help him." The couple bickered for several more minutes until Rose just grabbed Lyle by the arm and shoved him into the room. He would have turned around, too, but couldn't when he noticed Madam Fairaday's gaze upon him, her makeup now running slightly down her face. He quickly took a deep breath and fixed his appearance as he slowly approached her.

"Do you mind if I join you?" Madam Fairaday shook her head as she blew her nose into a white handkerchief that she had removed from the sleeve of her gown. When she was finished she concentrated on her lap.

"Madam Fairaday—"

"Please, call me Emily, Lyle."

"Of course, Emily." Lyle took a deep breath, not sure of what he was going to talk about. "I know that everything seems cloudy, but with every dark day there is a silver lining." Madam Fairaday gazed up at Lyle and smiled.

"Your father used to say that all the time." Lyle smiled and nodded his head.

"I know!" At last the tension between them had been broken.

"You look just like him, even more so than Locand. I know I say that to you every time we meet, but it still holds true. So..." Madam Fairaday paused as she blew her nose again. Lyle had met her many times before in Spain and in other places when she would go on vacation away from prying eyes to spend time with Locand. Locand would usually invite him to join them, seeing that his mother had long past been dead. "So, what do you think about all of this?" The dreaded question was finally asked.

"Well, it is a problem for sure but one that has been somewhat solved. Miranda knows the truth and now it is up to Locand to deal with her. I could tell that you were unaware of his feelings for her." Madam Fairaday raised her eyebrows.

"Do you think he is planning on marrying her just to spite me?" Lyle laughed loudly which caused Rose to glance into the room out of curiosity.

"Locand is no longer a child, Emily, he loves her. I never would have thought it possible from him, and yet his heart has always been warm and kind, just like yours. On the sea there is no room for error. When you get into a fight with another ship it is kill or be killed, but to a point Locand always showed mercy, unlike our father. I think that it always bothered him that father was so cavalier with other men's lives. He did not care and when killing, never once gave it a second thought. Locand, on the other hand, never killed unless it was necessary and yet he was well respected by his crew and other pirates. It is amazing to me to see how loving he is toward Miranda. I have never seen that side of him before. I hope that one day you can look at him and see what I see because if you could, I know that you would understand how much he needs her. He just wants to be happy, same as you."

"Oh, Lyle," said Madam Fairaday as she brought the handkerchief up to dab at her eyes. Lyle leaned forward in his chair and grabbed Madam Fairaday's hand.

"Trust me when I say that everything will be all right. All of the truths are out in the open and now there is no room for deception, no more room for lies. Locand will make her see, trust me in that. You and Stratton, then, will still have some mending to do in the family relationship, for I don't think that either of them will be able to place their trust in you for a while."

"I know, but I will do what I can to get that trust back. I cherish every moment that Miranda and I have had together and I don't want to lose that bond. Now that you are here our family is complete." Lyle smiled as he leaned back into his chair.

"I have already told Locand that I would stay here with him. His wishes are the same as yours. Thank you for them."

"I loved your father, you know, but it just became too hard to be with him. Your father cared for two things and two things only—his ship and his sons. You and Locand were all he cared about, not his lovers or his wife. He cared naught for us. We were only a means to an end as far as he was concerned. The last time that I saw him, he told me how proud he was of you and Locand, how he wanted to teach you both the ways of the sea. He confessed to me many times of his unfaithfulness, of which I could never forgive him for, but he was not remorseful about it. In fact, all he talked about were the two of you. His betrayals angered me so much that I left him, but I really had no choice in the matter. Men from all walks of life wanted to use Locand to get back at Logan for what he had done. His treacherous deeds were known throughout the seas as well as his love and devotion to his sons.

"We were barely surviving, running from place to place when too many people came into towns to ask about us. Then one day he had come and given us a chest full of gold to help. He then wanted to take Locand with him to sail the seas. You were with him. I don't know if you remember, but it was the very first time I met you. I refused him, for Locand was all that I had left, but he didn't care. He was determined to take him from me, and he did. Locand did not want to go, but Logan dragged him from my arms. He was about fifteen then. It was the last time I saw him for a long time. A year went by and then two. Locand would send me letters telling me how he was fairing and the places he'd been. I was happy for him. He would often send me gifts. I cherished every one of them for each time I received one, I knew that my son was alive.

"And then one day Locand wrote telling me of your father's death. I was sad, but by then I had established a new life, a life I could be proud of. A life that Logan James could not run, but Locand needed me." Tears filled Madam Fairaday's eyes. Lyle leaned forward. "I know that you have had no easy life as well, especially when he gave you his namesake, Lyle."

"It was hard indeed, that was for sure. Having his name kept me on the run as well, until I had changed it to Lyle Mansfield. At that point I became a free man, for Lyle Mansfield was a man that no one knew and who had no past, where Lyle James was someone people wanted to capture. My story is similar to yours except that my mother was sick; she died when I was younger. A friend of my mother's took care of me until I was old enough to be on my own and look for work. Because of Father and Locand's decisions to become pirates, I knew that one day they would get caught. It was just a matter of when. After Father died, I wanted to protect Locand from having the same fate. It was then that I enlisted in the Governor of Port Royal's Army. Locand was not aware of my decision for some time. I had decided not to tell him just in case he ever needed me. I wanted to keep the truth a secret, at least until he needed to know. Even when we would secretly meet, I never said a word.

"I had worked hard and became a Lieutenant. I had a roof over my head and food in my stomach and at that moment, it was all I cared about. I often kept track of what was going on by conversing with many of the pirates that came into port. It wasn't until Lord Hammil asked for help from the governor that I was told to assist him in the capture of a Spanish treasure and to deal with the pirates responsible. At the time I thought nothing of it and was surprised to find that Locand was the man they wanted to capture. I could not reveal myself to anyone and had to do as I was told, but when the time came, I aided Miranda and Rose with the freeing of Locand and Stratton. It was then that he knew what I had done." Lyle smiled reminiscently to himself and then refocused his gaze upon Madam Fairaday.

"He was fortunate to have you to guide him through his life. He always spoke so highly of you, and I think it is a shame that you are letting what happened between you and Stratton divide you. Your relationship is too strong for that. I know that it saddens him, as I know it saddens Miranda to find out the truth. I owe Locand much for when I had no one he was always there. He took responsibility over me and helped me to survive. He's a good man—a good brother. I want nothing more than to see us reunited for good, but if that is to happen, we need to work through this together." Lyle stopped and took several deep breaths. He watched as Madam Fairaday nodded her head several times in agreement.

"He is fortunate to have us both, for we all need each other now," replied Madam Fairaday. She then smiled and swiftly rose from her seat and gathered Lyle up into a long embrace. Lyle only laughed as he placed his arms around her and kissed her cheek, the mood of the room becoming much lighter.

When Miranda had left the sitting room she had charged down the hallway toward the front door. The servant had opened the door for her and she was out it in a flash and heading toward one of their awaiting carriages. The stone pathway's light shone upon everything and Miranda barely made it halfway before she broke down and cried full force. Over her sobs she heard her name being called. When she turned her head she noticed Locand approaching. "Leave me alone!" she yelled as she lifted the skirts of her dress and tried to run, but she was not fast enough. Locand was soon upon her and grabbed her by the arm.

"Miranda, stop!" yelled Locand but Miranda kept trying to pull away from him. "You promised me!" was all that he said. Soon Miranda stopped fighting and stood staring at Locand. "You promised me!" This time his tone was softer and tears flowed like rivers down her smooth cheeks.

"Did you know about this, Locand?" her voice was quiet and accusing.

"I had an idea that they were going to tell you tonight."

"Which was why you were trying to warn me?" Locand nodded his head briefly. Miranda wiped her tears away with the back of her hand and glanced toward the carriage.

"I feel like such a fool. Part of me is happy to find that Madam Fairaday is your mother and yet a part of me doesn't want to believe it."

"Now you know how I have been feeling. I have had mixed emotions."

"But on your ship you convinced me that their happiness was more important than—"

"Than your feelings. Well, that goes the same for mine. While I was convincing you to forgive your father I was also convincing myself to forgive my mother. A hard task to say the least." Locand smiled and reached his hand out to grab Miranda's. "Come, I want to show you something." Miranda didn't have a chance to refuse as Locand pulled her back toward the house. Once inside he pulled her up the stairs and down a hallway to the right. The house was massive with several different hallways and corridors to walk down. Miranda almost felt lost for she was looking at doors of rooms that she had never seen before. Soon Locand stopped at a room with double doors. He hastily let go of her hand and opened them. Once inside, their attentions fell upon a large bed in front of them not that far from a burning fireplace. The room was warm and cozy. The bed was covered with a dark thick blanket with a matching canopy that surrounded it for privacy. The drapes were currently tied back and all that could be seen were the many pillows lying perfectly on top of the blanket. There were two white dressers on either side of the room with matching chaise lounge chairs in the center. A padded table was put in between them and lying upon it was a man's shirt thrown carelessly across it. There were two windows on the opposite wall with curtains that matched the bed. A large square rug covered most of the floor and was hidden partially under the bed.

"Whose room is this?"

"My mother's!" Miranda's eyes grew wide as she stood still not wanting to step any farther into the room. Locand, however, walked quickly to his mother's bed and knelt down looking underneath it.

"What are you doing?" whispered Miranda frantically.

"I am looking for—aha, found it!" Locand withdrew a large bundle of something white that was tied with a long dark black ribbon. He placed them on top of the bed and watched as Miranda hesitantly moved to stand by his side.

"What are those?"

"These are letters that I have written to my mother whenever I was at sea. They usually accompany a small gift from a place where I have traveled. She is wearing a handkerchief that she always puts into the sleeve of her dress. I got it from Spain, it was hand-woven."

Miranda gazed at Locand in amazement as she saw the letters. "Why do you show me these?"

"Because, you've read my journal, you know how much I love my mother for it was you who brought up the fact." Miranda nodded her head. He had spoken often of his mother in his journal and was always affectionate toward her. "Then you also know that there cannot be a drift between you? Not between the two people I love. I will not be forced to choose between either of you, and I will not be made to take sides." Miranda glanced toward the ground.

"I would never force you to choose. It would be like asking me to choose between fathers, I wouldn't be able to do it." Locand felt relieved. "How long have you known of their relationship?" It was Locand's turn to look away.

"For several months now." Locand shook his head and pushed the letters away from him. "For some reason you seem to think that I am not bothered by their relationship, but let me explain to you how I found out. I have been trying to tell you this for months but you never wanted to listen. Will you listen to me now?" Miranda quickly nodded and Locand raised his arm out and pointed to one of the chairs for them to sit in. Only after they moved to one of the chairs and sat down did Locand speak again.

"Several months ago, before leaving with you and Lord Hammil on my ship, I was doing a special favor for the queen. I cannot mention what I was doing, but I was on my way back here to visit with my mother after months of being away. When I had arrived in port I came straight here. I had looked for her everywhere and upon not finding her, thought to look in her bedchambers thinking that she might be taking a nap or something. That was a big mistake on my part." Locand ran his fingers through his hair and took several deep breaths. "When I had walked into this very room I found her and your father—" Locand had a hard time continuing.

"Found them what?" Miranda could only imagine but still needed to hear it.

"I found them in bed together." Miranda's features showed her surprise and disgust. Making love was a beautiful thing, but picturing her father and Madam Fairaday doing such an act was unthinkable.

"What did you do?"

"I did what any person would do in my situation. I turned around and walked back out the door. I was furious. I have seen Stratton many times when I have returned home, in port or at any one of the local establishments, but it never occurred to me that you were here and that you were the reason why he was in England. I didn't think that at all." Locand shook his head and gave Miranda a half smile. "Well, it didn't take long for your father to follow me out the bedchamber door, probably on the urgency of my mother. We had a long discussion and many truths came out. He had no idea that I was Madam Fairaday's son and though that pleased me it also angered me because he had said that they had been seeing each other for some time, though he didn't go into further detail than that. I had found out that they had been seeing each other ever since you had introduced them." Miranda's mouth opened slightly, her forehead creasing in thought over what she had heard.

"They have been together for that long? I never realized it."

"You were not supposed to." Miranda laughed loudly as she covered her face with her hands.

"And all this time I thought that it was Davy who was in love with her." Locand shook his head and scoffed loudly.

"I don't know what made you think that." Miranda shrugged her shoulders and shook her head. "Anyway, afterward I left my mother's estate and headed for the harbor but it was only to find myself clamped in irons by the queen's men who were waiting for me there. She was ready to hang me too, that cow, but had then thought better of it. With the help of my mother I was freed, but only to find myself at the queen's mercy.

"After some time had passed, the queen met with me and with the help of my mother again, and my charm, persuaded her to give me a letter of marque. It wasn't until later that I was needed to find your father and would be the captain who would sail Lord Hammil to Port Royal. The rest you already know except for this. After I was freed, my mother and I had a lengthy discussion and it was then that she had told me of her feelings for Stratton, how she loved him and how they had been married for several months. I was not ready to accept it and was furious with her about it. I was right in everything I had told you about your father. He deserves to find happiness and from what I see they are happy." Locand's words penetrated Miranda's brain. It all started to make sense now. The way Madam Fairaday had been acting before she left for the Caribbean. It seemed like she had wanted to tell her something too, but had restrained herself. Something then flickered in Miranda's mind, and she gazed at Locand curiously.

"So, it was you that Madam Fairaday was waving at down at the docks."

"Yes!" replied Locand curtly.

"I thought that she was there to say goodbye to me. I was curious to know why she was there, and when I looked back at you, you hadn't paid her any attention. Why?"

"Don't you think it would have looked strange if I were to wave at her in front of my crew?"

"No, she is your mother, Locand. It is not like…"

"Nobody knows that she is my mother, Miranda. Not even the queen herself."

"But why?" Miranda was confused. Locand rubbed his chin with his hand and gazed into the fire.

"Look, there are some things that you need to know about me, secrets that need to be kept." Miranda was unsure of what Locand was talking about. Everyone knew of Madam Fairaday, how could no one know she had a son? Her question was soon answered.

"You know that my father died when I was young, but I don't think that you know who he was." Miranda shrugged her shoulders.

"I have no idea who your father was. When you were aboard my father's ship, I was only told that your father had died. How, it didn't matter to me and I never thought to ask. I was taking care of many of my father's crew at the time, keeping them fed and such. Who was he?"

"My father was Logan James." Locand could hear Miranda's sharp intake of breath and watched as she raised her fingertips to her lips.

"The scourge of the sea? There is no way you could be his son." Locand smiled and raised his arms, his palms up.

"I am, and so is Lyle." Miranda could still not believe what she had heard. Logan James was often confused with Blackbeard. He was ruthless and yet wise to the ways of the world. He was the only pirate whose bounty extended to his family. She had remembered her father and Davy talking one evening about it. She had not realized until now that the reason why her father had kept Locand with him on his ship was not only to help him with the loss of his father, but also to save him from others. When she raised her eyes to meet his, Locand looked away from her.

"I don't want your pity, Miranda, so please don't look at me as if I were some weak and defenseless babe." Miranda instantly stared at the ground, feeling almost ashamed for what she had done. "Do you have any idea what my childhood was like? My mother had to change her name, as did I, as did Lyle. None of us were safe. Men from all walks of life wanted a piece of us, and some were close. We were all ashamed to know my father. I was ashamed to have his blood running through my veins, and yet as a child I envied him, envied his lifestyle. I thought it was fascinating the way he could sail a ship, even in the most terrible of storms. He rose above it. He had taken me away from my mother when I was fifteen, taught me the ways of the sea and how to depend on no one. Lyle was with me, and though we both enjoyed sailing, we were nothing like our father. He loved to fight, loved to kill. There was one time when his crew fought against a Spanish Galleon. I will never forget this. After my father and his men won the battle, he ruthlessly decapitated men's body parts and then threw them into the sea where awaiting sharks devoured them.

"He never showed any remorse over what he had done, and in

turn, that night I remember throwing up over the side of the ship, with Lyle by my side comforting me. At that point I hated him, hated the kind of man he had become. It literally sickened me. Many times I had wanted to go home to my mother, but he would never allow it telling me that I needed to be a man and forget her, but I couldn't. It was her love that kept me sane. I had sailed for years with him and through all that time I had fallen in love with the sea and often did I see its beauty bring out something good in my father. It was that part, that emotion that brought me closer to him. When he died, I was in some way relieved, and yet I knew that I would miss him for he was the only father I knew. It was then that Stratton took me under his wing, guiding me, protecting me. After the time I spent on his ship, I finally was able to go home. By the time I returned, my mother had evolved into the woman she is today.

"While I was away, she had taken her mother's name and in so doing found herself to be associating with people who were in the highest of society. It didn't take long for her to meet the queen, and when she had done so, captivated her. They have been friends now for many years and she has often asked my mother for advice. She does not know of her true identity nor does anyone else, except for all of us. No one else knows that I am her son, and I prefer it to be that way. Even though years have passed, we still cannot take the chance of someone finding out the truth about who we really are. Do you understand, no one can know?" Miranda reached out and caressed Locand's cheek.

"I promise that I will not say a word to anyone. Your secret is safe with me." Locand grabbed Miranda's hand and kissed it, then held it in his lap.

"Miranda, I love you more than anything in the world, and it is because of this that we need to accept the love that our parents have for each other. They are happy and no matter how we might feel about it or how they went about their relationship, it doesn't matter. My mother has been through hell for so long that I am finally happy that she has found happiness, that she has found the love I know she deserves to have in her life. Can you accept this, because you really have no choice in the matter? They are married and there is nothing we can do about it." Miranda let go of Locand's hand and gazed at the bed in front of them.

"I just can't believe that they would do this without telling us about it. I had no idea they were seeing each other. I feel like such a fool. They should have at least consulted us."

"They are not children, Miranda, they do not have to tell us anything. I agree with you, they should have at least said something so it wouldn't have been such a shock to us, but again, they did what they thought was right. They did what their hearts were telling them to do just like our hearts are telling us because we are in love, they got married. Can we blame them for finding happiness?" Miranda shook her head.

"No, I cannot blame them. I want them to be happy. I do. I am just surprised by all of this." Locand raised his hand and again caressed her cheek. "When did you decide to lose your anger for what they have done? I know that you said that it was on our voyage, but when did you finally come to terms with it?" Locand withdrew his hand and smiled.

"The first time I kissed you. That moment was a culmination of many things. Suddenly, my mother's deeds were not as important as her happiness, and you were all I could think about. When you jumped in front of that bullet to save me, it was then that I could not deny my feelings for you any longer. You sacrificed yourself for me. It was then that I sacrificed my freedom and all that I held dear for you, knowing that my life could be over if the queen, or any of her men, wished it for going against the crown by helping you. When Lord Hammil's intentions to destroy us all failed, it was you who I wanted to be with, you who I wanted to love for the rest of my life and couldn't live without. You had made me satisfied and content, and I knew there would be no one else who would be able to fill that void inside of me. Then, when you risked your life to save mine again at Port Royal, I became speechless and filled with joy again for your selflessness. Don't you realize what you have done?" Miranda was speechless over Locand's confession. Inside, her heart ached, and tears sprung to her eyes. She could only shake her head in answer.

"You have changed my life forever with your love. Now I can never go back to being the man I once was and now all I want is for you to become my wife and have our children. I want a family I can love and learn from, and I want it with you. I love you so much."

"Locand—" Miranda started to say but was interrupted.

"And I know that you love to sail and we both share that love, and I wouldn't dream of asking you to not do it, so, I have decided that whenever I am sent by the queen to wherever she needs me to go, you will join me. I could not bear it if I had left you for months at a time." Locand's forehead furrowed as he waited to hear Miranda's thoughts, but instead of words she started to cry. She then leaned forward and wrapped her arms around Locand's neck.

"If forgiveness is what you want from me, then you shall have it. Anger should not separate us for any reason. At this point you can have anything you want from me. Your words were so beautiful and heartfelt." Miranda then kissed Locand and between kisses she said, "I will talk to your mother—I will talk with my father—I will beg them for forgiveness—Oh, you taste so good." The kiss then deepened until Miranda could speak no more. Locand ran his fingers through her hair and pressed her closer to him. Their tongues clashed wildly as they yearned for one another. Soon, Miranda had forgotten where she was until she heard someone in the background clearing his throat.

Miranda was startled and broke the kiss. She had not realized it but her and Locand had been lying down on the chair wrapped in each others arms. Both of them immediately sat up and were surprised to find Stratton standing several feet inside of the room with Davy just behind him. Miranda and Locand quickly separated and stood up from the chair. Miranda's appearance, now disheveled, didn't take away from the flush on her cheeks or the smile of content on her lips.

"Miranda," started Stratton, his voice serious, but Miranda stepped forward and stopped him before he could continue.

"I am so sorry, Father, for my behavior against Madam Fairaday and you. I should have embraced your union instead of criticizing it. Though, you have to admit that you should have handled it better." Stratton nodded his head though his eyes fell upon Miranda skeptically. "Good, now that the truth is finally out of the way I can rekindle my friendship with the woman I have trusted for years."

"Oh, Miry," said Stratton as he caressed her cheeks with his hands and kissed her. "I promise that from now on things are going to be different between us. No more lies, only truths." Miranda smiled and embraced her father again. When he let her go she quickly moved to Davy's outstretched arms and felt him kiss her on the cheek.

"That is my good Miry." Miranda smiled and returned Davy's kiss.

"Is she still downstairs where we left her?"

"Yes, why don't you go ahead. We will be right behind you." He then kissed Miranda again on the cheek and let her go. Miranda turned quickly toward Locand who she thought was right behind her.

"Are you coming?" Locand ran his fingers through his hair and adjusted his shirt.

"I will be right there, my love. I think your father wishes to speak with me." Miranda nodded her head and glanced at everyone in the room one last time before leaving it and heading down the hallway toward the staircase.

Locand was left to stare at the befuddled eyes of Stratton. "How did you manage to do that? I was all ready to come in here and argue with her, but instead you have it all under control." Locand moved swiftly toward his mothers bed, grabbed the letters that he had written and returned them from where he had retrieved them. He then turned toward Stratton and Davy.

"It is called the power of truth. I know that you are not familiar with it but I told her everything about me and my mother, the same things that I know she has told you."

"I hardly believe that she could have changed her mind just because of that? I know my daughter and..."

"Why not, our lives are very compelling, yet pathetic. I knew she would feel sorry for me. Besides, I do have my masculinity and I know exactly what she desires from me, so I just used it to my advantage." Stratton glanced at Davy before taking several steps toward Locand.

"This is Miranda you speak of so freely, not a whore."

"Don't ever speak your daughter's name and that word in the same sentence. She is an angel." Locand and Stratton were almost nose to nose.

"Have you bedded her? I am her father, and it is time that I know the truth of what is going on between you." Locand stood his ground and narrowed his eyes.

"You know the truth, Stratton. I love her and we are to be married, you gave me your permission, remember?"

"Yes, and I see that you threw it into your mother's face. I didn't get the chance to tell her about that yet. Now she will be angry with me for keeping it from her. She was quite surprised, did you notice?"

"Yes, I noticed, but I wanted her to know exactly how I felt about your daughter, and now she does. I have no doubt that she will be discussing the topic with me later." Stratton and Locand glared at each other menacingly.

"You still have not answered my question. Does she still have her innocence or not?"

"How dare you ask me? I thought you knew me better," replied Locand convincingly.

"I can't believe that I have to ask you, but I see the way you look at each other and I can see the desire that she has for you in her eyes. For my own sanity I have to ask it."

"What do you take me for, Stratton?"

"A pirate, an opportunist like me," spoke Stratton angrily. Locand only laughed as he shook his head.

"That is quite ironic, isn't it? Do you not remember the girl in Barbados?" Stratton thought for a moment before answering.

"You're talking about that young—"

"Aye," replied Locand quickly.

"Now, that girl was before I met your mother so there is no reason to bring her into this."

"No? She was a virgin, yes?" Stratton closed his eyes briefly.

"Yes, but that girl did not have the body of a virgin," defended Stratton.

"She was nineteen," answered Locand mockingly.

"Twenty, actually, but she did look older!" Locand laughed as he clenched his fists.

"You were three sheets to the wind that night, of course she looked older. For all you knew the child could have been an old spinster. I tried to warn you, too, but you didn't listen, and you have the audacity to accuse me of taking your daughter's innocence?" Davy stepped in between Locand and Stratton and shook his head.

"What is wrong with the two of you? You should be ashamed of yourselves." Both Locand and Stratton glanced at Davy quickly before focusing their attention back to each other.

"Do you want to know the truth, Stratton, because I know it?" Davy stared in frustration at Stratton as he awaited his answer.

"Aye!"

"She still has her innocence!" Stratton closed his eyes and exhaled briefly. Davy glanced at Locand quickly and raised his eyebrows imploring him to agree. When Stratton again looked at Locand, he smiled. “I have been probing her about this very topic and she has assured me that nothing has happened between them—at least not yet.”

"I’m sorry, Locand, I should have known. No hard feelings, eh?” Stratton reached out his hand for Locand to take, when he did he pulled him close and embraced him.

"I do think though,” started Stratton, “that we are due for a fight, don’t you?” Locand smiled broadly, his white teeth shining brightly against his tan face. He then removed his jacket and handed it to Davy. Stratton did the same.

"I thought that you would never ask. We are definitely due. We have been bickering back and forth like children and I only know of one way for us to relieve the stress.”

"Not here,” replied Stratton quickly. “The last time we fought you landed on one of your mother’s tables and broke it. After you left she threw the leg at me. It hurt, too. She hit me in the head.” Stratton rubbed the back of his head in emphasis. “So, this time we need to be much more careful.”

"Where then?” asked Locand eagerly.

"Outside, that way it will be harder for us to injure ourselves and the furniture.” Locand readily agreed and the trio left the bedchamber. On their way down the hallway Locand began to talk again.

"So, what will the stakes be this time?” Stratton was quiet for a moment as he thought.

"The usual, we fight for bragging rights. Why, do you wish to raise the stakes?” Locand smiled as they came to the top of a small narrow staircase toward the back of the house that led to the kitchens. It was a back way that was often used when no one wanted to be seen instead of using the other stairs near the front of the house. Silence reigned for the remainder of the short walk, Locand already thinking about what he would bet when he had won.

Miranda rushed down the front stairs and walked quickly toward the sitting room where Madam Fairaday was supposed to be, but when she arrived at the doorway she wasn’t in there, nor were Rose, Lyle or Adam. Worry lined Miranda’s features as she glanced around the hallway. As she pondered where everyone could be, she heard laughter coming from the dining hall. She slowly walked toward the room and could briefly hear the conversations and laughter. Miranda felt guilty. She had been so selfish and stubborn, she was missing out on what sounded like a good time. As she came to the door she curiously peaked inside. To her amazement Lyle, Rose and Madam Fairaday were sitting at the large, eight person dining room table and were eating what looked like lamb. On the table were also potatoes, some fruits and other vegetables, breads, wine and several desserts. Miranda's stomach began to growl as she smelled the wonderful aroma of the food. She hadn't realized how hungry she was. As she looked around the room for Adam, she noticed he was lying in a chair next to Rose and had his head in her lap. He had fallen asleep. Rose's hand could be seen caressing his forehead and hair as she pleasantly talked with Madam Fairaday and Lyle.

Miranda admired the scene before her and was filled with envy. She quietly grabbed the door and was about to open it when she heard Madam Fairaday's loud laughter. Her eyes fell upon her and watched as she casually discussed the topic of court and how some of the ladies dressed and the men they had their eyes on. Miranda smiled to herself and glanced around the warm room. Madam Fairaday was a charmer with her warm and bubbly personality. Miranda was confident that no matter who the person was Madam Fairaday could befriend them in a matter of minutes, and they would be her most devoted friends for life. She thought about the words she had spoken to Rose about Madam Fairaday. She truly did think her to be the most wonderful woman she had ever met, and in truth she loved her, loved her like a mother.

Hearing Locand's story about his childhood and about what his mother had gone through gave Miranda a slightly different perspective of her. She was strong, resourceful and independent, but most of all Madam Fairaday was now her new mother. Miranda smiled with pride. She never knew her real mother, for she had died in childbirth, and Madam Fairaday was the closest she had to one. She had always guided her and helped her to fit in, protecting and teaching her the ways of the world from a woman's point of view. Besides Davy, she was her only true friend and companion. Miranda wouldn't have seen the several towns and sights around England if it hadn't been for her. She also wouldn't have been able to travel to Spain and Scotland if it wasn't for the friends that Madam Fairaday knew who cared for her enough to invite her to their homes and way of life. She learned a lot from her.

Miranda's eyes filled with tears and she was about to turn away when she heard a voice calling to her. "Miranda, is that you?" When Miranda turned around, it was to look into the eyes of Madam Fairaday. Miranda nodded her head quickly, her voice stuck in her throat. "Please, come in and join us." Miranda did as she was told and walked into the room. Her head was held high but she felt to be the lowest of all creatures. Rose, with a smile on her lips, glanced at Lyle.

"I think that it's time for us to go, don't you think?" Lyle glanced at Miranda and smiled but instead of saying anything to her he only glanced down at Adam.

"Yes, I think you're right. We should be going. Poor Adam has given up on us and needs to be put to bed." He stood up and walked over to Madam Fairaday.

"It has been a pleasure talking with you, dear woman. I'm glad we had the chance. It has been so long since I've spoken with you that I had forgotten how enjoyable it was." Madam Fairaday caressed Lyle's face and kissed him on the cheek. He then moved to Rose, bent down and lifted Adam into his arms. Rose stood from her chair and walked over to Madam Fairaday.

"Thank you for everything. It's a pleasure to finally meet you." Madam Fairaday wrapped her arm around Rose and embraced her.

"Now remember, Monday we are having tea with Lady Withering and her daughters. I will be picking you and Miranda up at noon." At the sound of her name Miranda raised her eyes toward Rose. Rose gave her a wink and nodded her head.

"We will not forget, Emily." Madam Fairaday smiled and watched as Lyle moved ahead of Rose to the door of the dining room. He stopped when he was right next to Miranda, Adam lying comfortably in his arms.

"Are you all right?" he whispered. His eyes held their concern and Miranda lifted her head confidently and smiled.

"Better now, thank you. I am so—" before she could finish he cut her off by clucking his tongue.

"Don't worry about it. We will see you later?" Miranda smiled and leaned forward as he leaned down to kiss her on the cheek. "Be good!" remarked Lyle jokingly as he gave her a dazzling smile and stepped out of the door into the hallway. Rose walked up to Miranda and wrapped her arms around her waist, her forehead touching hers in a sibling like manner.

"Everything is going to be just fine, I can tell. It took much courage for you to come back in here." She kissed her on the cheek and embraced her. "We will talk about all of this later. You are very fortunate to have such a wonderful woman like her to care for you so much– remember that." Miranda nodded her head as Rose separated from her and patted her on the arm. She glanced once more at Madam Fairaday and followed Lyle out the door.

When the room was emptied, Miranda and Madam Fairaday were left staring at each other. The silence was uncomfortable for a moment, but then Madam Fairaday held out her arms and Miranda ran hastily into them. Tears filled both women's eyes as they embraced each other. "I'm so sorry," Miranda began but was soon quieted by Madam Fairaday's words. "It's all my fault, I should have told you a long time ago. I love you, Miranda, and I don't want anything to come between us–ever." All that could be heard were the women's sobs. When they finally parted, Madam Fairaday grabbed a hold of Miranda's hand and walked her over to the table.

"Eat!" was all she said, and Miranda was more than happy to comply. A servant came–it seemed--from nowhere, and brought her a clean plate. Miranda eagerly filled it with the lamb and a few of the other foods. Madam Fairaday watched her all the while. As Miranda ate, she talked.

"Miranda, I know I should have told you sooner. When I was helping you prepare for Lord Hammil's gala I wanted to, I wanted to tell you all about us but I couldn't, you see–" Before she could continue Miranda held up her hand. After she swallowed her bite of food she said, "Locand already explained to me about your past." Madam Fairaday lowered her gaze to the table.

"He did?" her voice was timid and unsure.

"Yes," replied Miranda quickly, "and I don't care. What your husband did to you, what he did to Locand, was wrong and unfair. You shouldn't have had to live that way, to struggle for everything you have, but look at it this way. Out of everything that has happened to you, you have become one of the most popular women in this country. You are successful and kind. You have a wonderful husband, an adoring son– and me. Oh, Emily, you have our friendship." Madam Fairaday placed her hand on Miranda's arm and squeezed.

"So I am forgiven?"

"Yes, you are forgiven. Am I? I dearly hope so, for I have been acting so childish lately." Miranda smiled sweetly, placing her fork upon her plate.

"Yes, Miranda, you are forgiven, though to be honest, I was never really mad at you. I knew you would be angry at me for deceiving you, by keeping the truth from you. I deserved your malice, but I also knew that we could work through it. To be honest, I was more concerned about Locand's and Stratton's feelings for one another." Miranda raised an eyebrow in curiosity.

"Why?"

"Well, first I must say I was quite surprised to hear of your engagement." Madam Fairaday's tone had turned serious.

"He had told me he asked for my father's permission awhile ago, but he has only just made it official tonight before we came inside. I'm quite pleased by it. I love him, Emily." That was all Madam Fairaday needed to hear. A smile returned to her lips.

"Well, then it is a happy time indeed. I am glad for you. Stratton has often said how he wanted the two of you to marry one day, though now that he has his wish I am not sure how he's taking it. You are his only daughter you know, and my son is used to getting what he wants so sometimes they clash in opinion of how things should be done and when it concerns you, both think they know best." Miranda started to laugh and nodded her head profusely. "More often than not, of late, they have been butting heads so sooner or later they will come to a point where they will just fight it out."

"Do they do this often?" asked Miranda as her eyes filled with concern.

"Too often, I'm afraid, but no matter how many times I argue with them about it they don't seem to listen. Locand tells me it's the only way for them to see eye to eye." Madam Fairaday dramatically rolled her eyes and took a bite of some food left on her plate from before. After some time passed Miranda became full, then she and Madam Fairaday sat and talked for a long time, Miranda telling her about everything that had happened to her in the Caribbean. Madam Fairaday listened to every word intently, amazed at what had happened, though she already knew by several accounts from her son and husband. Even so, she could not get enough of the tale. After there was a pause in the conversation, Madam Fairaday felt it was time to ask the question she knew was burning inside of her.

"My dear, have you given any thought about the wedding and

where you would like to have it?" Miranda was taken aback by the question, yet her answer was immediate.

"A little, though to be honest I'm not sure of what Locand might think." Miranda glanced at her hands, then to the room around her. They had retired silently to a parlor where they took some tea. Miranda was stalling on the question and yet Madam Fairaday was not pushing it to be answered.

"I would love to be married back on Eleuthera Island. It is where I grew up as a child and I do have much history there. It is where my mother and father got married."

"I didn't realize that. Stratton never mentioned it to me. I wish I knew your mother, Miranda. I know from speaking with your father that he adored her. He told me how lost he was when she passed away." Miranda frowned slightly and then smiled in appreciation.

"I wish I had a chance to know her as well. I am named after her, did you know?" Madam Fairaday nodded her head remembering Stratton mentioning it.

"Well, what about a lovely wedding here in London? I know many people who can make sure the ceremony is done beautifully." Miranda thanked Madam Fairaday, but could not accept her offer.

"You're right. I do have a lot of history here, too. I grew up here as well but the one thing I am realizing is that our wedding does not have to be fancy or extravagant. All I want is Locand for my husband. We could be poor and it would not matter, for he would love me unconditionally. That is why I feel that a wedding here, on Locand's ship, would be the most appropriate place. It's simple and yet it will be memorable. We don't need to have hundreds of people we don't really know. All we need is you and my father, Davy of course, with Lyle, Rose and Adam by his side.

"A sailor is what Locand is. It is what my father is and though I know Locand is willing to change his ways for us, I also know he loves being the captain of his ship. He needs it as we need air to breathe. I think he would appreciate me giving that moment to him. What do you think?" Madam Fairaday raised a finger to her eye as she wiped a tear that had fallen away from her cheek.

"I think it is a wonderful gesture—an unselfish gesture. He will love it." Miranda smiled broadly and nodded her head in agreement. "Well, if that is what you wish, then let's start making the arrangements. You can never start too early planning these things, and I am sure that Locand will want to marry you right away. I will talk with some of my friends, and we will set your plans into motion. We must have parties and anything else that will celebrate this special occasion."

Miranda started to raise her hand, not wanting the affair to be too extravagant for it was not what she wanted. Miranda and Locand had simple pleasures, and too many things would be overwhelming to them. Madam Fairaday noticed Miranda's reluctance so calmly insisted, "Please, Miranda, if I cannot host the wedding at least allow me to help with everything else. Locand is my only son. Let me do this for the both of you." Miranda could tell how much the occasion meant to Madam Fairaday so she nodded her head and smiled. Madam Fairaday clasped her hands together and started giggling with delight, already having ideas popping into her head of what to do.

CHAPTER 24

In the weeks that followed, Madam Fairaday was true to her word. Miranda's and Rose's days were filled with elegance and excitement. They went to parties thrown by some of England's finest noble women and had tea with them often. They even went to a masked ball thrown by the queen herself. Miranda was used to doing these things with Madam Fairaday, though not as often and not to celebrate her wedding, but it was an all new experience for Rose. She was thankful to be a part of the experience and eagerly learned all she could from Madam Fairaday. Rose was starting to quickly learn who had the most pull in the queen's decision making. And Madam Fairaday, being an honest and forthright woman, always gave the queen her sincere opinion and only swayed her on her decisions when it was best for the people, not only for the crown, and she was richly rewarded for it. But she never betrayed her and always talked highly of the queen, which also showed her devotion and respect.

Madam Fairaday made sure that Rose had the most elegant dresses for everyday wear and colorful gowns for when they went to court. She liked the kind of woman she was becoming, but never forgot who she was, allowing the extravagances to go to her head like it has done to so many. Lyle noticed a change in Rose, too. Her language and features had become more refined, her demeanor impeccable, but even with all this she was still the same woman he met at Port Royal. Her sass always kept him on his guard, while her curvaceous body seduced him into doing what she wanted. He loved her. He truly did and though he liked her just the way she was, he knew she was happy and content with the life she was now living.

The men spent most of their days working with the LaRoices. There were ships to build, holds to clean and maintain, as well as to fix. They were very busy, and yet very content in their new lives. Often, Alex LaRoice would send them to do the testing of the ships to check and see if they were seaworthy. They had the best jobs in the world. They worked hard, got paid well and were making an honest living for themselves. A full month had passed when Locand and Miranda were wed. The ceremony was on Locand's ship, The *Soaring Eagle*. Stratton performed the ceremony with Madam Fairaday, Lyle, Davy, Rose and Adam by their sides as witnesses. They were truly happy. It didn't take long for Lyle and Rose to follow in their footsteps, and soon they became husband and wife. The family was finally together, and they were determined to let nothing come between them.

Time passed quickly and before they knew it a year had gone by. Locand had been summoned by the queen to sail for her. He had taken Lyle and Adam with him leaving Stratton and Davy to continue working. Though the men longed for the sea, they realized that at home was where they belonged. They were retired sailors, after all, whose lives were much simpler, and to be honest they liked it that way. They were now devoted to taking care of the women, who now needed them more than the sea. Miranda was now pregnant and close to term. Davy and Stratton swore to Locand that they would watch over her. Rose was faithfully by her side, as was Madam Fairaday when she wasn't by the queen's side.

Miranda's large belly made it hard for her to walk far distances, so her friends often came to her. Isabelle and Rochelle LaRoice had become her and Roses's most devoted friends and had dropped by to see them. For months now they had been spending time together, at social engagements or just for tea. They had helped Rose and Miranda fit more comfortably into society just by being loyal. They all remained faithful to themselves and did not let the politics of the town corrupt them, like they knew it had done to so many other women who cared only for social status. Maggie, Isabelle's daughter, joined them on occasion, for she was now in her early teens and needed to spend more time with other women.

Isabelle and Rochelle's younger children were being watched carefully by their mother who often traveled with them while their father left for weeks at a time to search for new herbs for his collection. He was a doctor and prided himself on the knowledge of healing the body naturally. The women were laughing together at Madam Fairaday's estate, for that was where all of them lived now, when Isabelle said, "You two must join us at Lord and Lady Chastwick's gala tomorrow. Antonio has returned home from his visit to Spain and Corinne wishes to celebrate it with some of their closest friends. Will you both come?" Rose glanced quickly at Miranda who smiled meekly while rubbing her belly.

"I'm in no condition to dance the night away, but Rose can go if she wishes. It sounds as if it would be a great affair," spoke Miranda.

"Don't be silly. I could not leave your side, Miranda," replied Rose as she turned to face Isabelle. "Thank you, but we must decline. We adore Corinne but—" Rochelle stopped Rose from continuing by touching her arm with her hand.

"There is no need to continue, Rose. We completely understand your situation, but we had to ask you none the less. Corinne wanted us to extend her invitation, though I am sure you will receive a proper invitation by messenger."

"We appreciate your thoughtfulness. We couldn't ask for better friends," replied Miranda as she extended her hands for all of them to take. An hour had passed when Rochelle stood to leave, not wanting to monopolize Miranda's time any further with endless chatter, seeing the tiredness in her features, knowing she needed rest. Maggie and Rose stood as well. Isabelle was about to join them when she could sense something wrong with Miranda and thought she might wish to discuss it.

"Why don't you go ahead ladies, I wish to speak with my dear friend alone for a moment." Everyone left the room and talked the entire time as if the request wasn't at all a peculiar one. "What is wrong, Miry? You seem—almost—depressed. And that is so unlike you." Miranda was not depressed, but worried. Not only about Locand, but the baby, and her lack of rest and everything else she could think of.

"Isabelle, I just have a lot on my mind. Forgive me for my distraction."

"Are you worried about Locand?"

"A little, in my heart I know he's well, so I try not to worry about him, but I am concerned about the birth of my child." Isabelle remembered well her experience with giving birth to her son. It was a pain she would never forget and yet it was a pain she would never have taken back. She adored her son.

"It is painful, but there are herbs and things that you can do to help you along. My father has often said…"

"No!" Miranda almost shouted shaking her head. "My mother died giving birth to me and that is what worries me. I don't wish to share her fate."

"Oh!" sighed Isabelle. "You mustn't worry. I'm sure you will brave through it. If you wish I can request my father to join us, if I can reach him in time that is. My mother knows just as much as he does for she has tended to many pregnant women, including myself, and almost delivered my child by the time my father arrived."

"That would be nice, Isabelle. I will contact you when the time comes." Isabelle gave her friend a reassuring smile, but secretly was starting to worry for Miranda. She could tell she would be due soon and knew that if she had complications with the delivery that she would need more than just a good doctor. She would need a miracle. A thought quickly came to her, and after kissing Miranda on the cheek, she excused herself to find Rochelle and Maggie.

The following day Locand returned at dawn. He was excited to be home and had missed Miranda deeply. He knew he couldn't have brought her with him because of her condition, but that didn't stop him from wanting her there. During his return home all he thought about was Miranda and was worried he would miss the birth of their child. If he did, he wouldn't forgive himself. With Lyle and Adam by his side, they stopped at The Oasis and talked with the LaRoice brothers for a little while to be kept up to date with what had gone on while they were away, then they went home. When they walked through the door it seemed like the activity inside came alive.

Miranda had been up all night for she was getting very little sleep these days. She was happy to see Locand and waddled her way over to greet him. Rose had kept Miranda company most nights and upon seeing Lyle ran to his outstretched arms. She then embraced her brother, kissing him on the cheek giving a silent prayer for their safe return. The men spent the day with their wives, and when Stratton and Davy returned from work, with Madam Fairaday not far behind them, had an extravagant meal to celebrate the occasion. The house was filled with happiness.

When night fell, Rose and Miranda encouraged Adam to attend Lord and Lady Chastwick's gala. Not being able to go themselves, and knowing that Maggie would be there, they convinced him to go in their stead. The women dressed him into clothes befitting a boy of his age going to a special occasion, and rushed him off. After he left, the men chastised them for interfering in Adam's life and making him go to an occasion like that by himself, but they soon quieted when their wives' lips touched theirs. The couples separated and both retired to their bedchambers.

When Adam arrived he felt intimidated by the massive house and estate that was the Chastwick's residence. The estate was in the country and at that moment the road was cluttered with carriages of various sizes and colors. He took a deep breath, puffed out his chest, and continued until he reached the door, handing the servant awaiting him the invitation that Miranda had given him to take, which had arrived only that morning. Adam was excited to see Maggie. They were often spending time together before he left with Locand on his ship and he hoped that wouldn't change after his return. He had a good friend in Maggie, and because they were close in age he felt a kinship with her. Isabelle had encouraged their friendship and though Alex never verbally said that he was against it, always kept a close eye on them when they were together.

As he walked in he was befuddled with all of the decorations. As he gazed around the room he took in the bright beautiful gowns of the women and the handsomely dressed men. Adam ran his hand down his stomach hoping he looked just as dashing, and yet knowing in his heart he didn't. He was still a boy in their eyes. Suddenly, Adam felt out of place and cursed himself for allowing Miranda and Rose to convince him to come. But then his eyes found Maggie and his once unsure steps had become more confident. She was beautiful with her pale pink gown and upswept hair. He wanted to see his friend. She was why he was there. Standing next to her was Andios and Rosemary. Lord and Lady Chastwick's twin son and daughter. They were dressed elegantly and were around the same age as he was. They all got along perfectly and were good friends. They were the kindest and friendliest group of people you would ever meet. He was thankful for them.

He then gazed away from his friends and took the time to notice the musicians standing off to the left side of the room while the guests danced artistically to the right. He wished he knew how to dance and made a mental note to ask Lyle if he could teach him. As he watched the dancers in front of him, almost in a trance, he heard his name being called. It was Andios trying to get his attention. When Adam looked in the direction of the voice, he smiled and waved. He then began to walk over to his friend when a man bumped into him. It was Alexavier LaRoice.

"Adam, I'm surprised to see you here. I thought you would be resting along with Locand and Lyle. I know you were all eager to be home." Alex's smile was kind and sincere, while his voice was filled with curiosity.

"Miranda and Rose begged me to come. They wanted to attend, but with their husbands being home, and Miranda's condition, they thought it better not to. So I was sent here on a mission to survey the surroundings and give them all of the juicy details."

"Brave man!" spoke Alex as he laughed and slapped Adam on the shoulder. They talked for some time about many things. Adam was thankful for Alex's friendship for he was now feeling comfortable and more relaxed. Samuel had walked up and the trio began another conversation but the moment was soon broken. Voices from somewhere behind them rose and caused, not only them to glance their way, but several others. They stopped and stared as the voices continued with their conversation.

Lady Chastwick was being held tightly in the arms of a man who was not her husband. This man had sent her several letters requesting her help, pleading for her to heal his wounds. Corinne had special healing powers. She could heal with her hands. It was a magical gift she possessed, and though she would use her powers to help many, it was sometimes a burden upon her. The man's request was not an uncommon one and yet the author of the note made her negligent of giving a response. She was appalled when he came to her husband's welcome home celebration and confronted her about it. When he had requested her to dance she would have insulted him by saying no, so she allowed him to guide her to the dance floor. Now, she regretted her decision, wishing she could have thrown him out instead.

"Milord, I don't appreciate you coming to my home and bombarding me with your demands. This is not how it's done. I have heard your reasons, and I will help you as soon as I can, but now is not the time and how dare you to think otherwise." Lady Chastwick was upset and gazed around the dance floor giving false smiles to her dancing neighbors. She glanced back at her dancing partner. He was a thin man and looked quite pale and weak, and yet by the grip of his hand upon her waist she could tell he was stronger than what he appeared to be.

"Lady Chastwick, I apologize for the inconvenience, but it was necessary. I am to see a dear friend of mine soon and do not wish for her to see me with this ghastly scar upon my cheek." The man turned his head to the left to show Corinne his scar. She had noticed it earlier but chose not to mention it. "I have a few others as well that also need your attention."

"And what makes you think I can heal your scars? When you wrote to me you had said that you heard that I was well versed in healing wounds and ailments with the use of herbs. Which is absolutely true, but what makes you think that I know how to heal scars?" asked Corinne as her gaze searched to find Antonio.

"I was assured by my good friend, Rolin McGrath, that you could help me." Corinne stopped dancing as her mouth fell open, her eyes wide with disbelief.

"Rolin died years ago," spouted Corinne in sudden anger.

"True," the man purred softly, "but I knew him well when he was alive, him and his son, Charles. In fact, I was the one who helped them find you and your mother." She had not once thought of Rolin since the day he had died. Her mother, Helena, was once married to Rolin, but he was abusive to her. Upon hearing of his death, Helena quickly married her lover. She had been happy for many years, until Rolin showed up trying to use Corinne to heal his wounds. He wanted to use her powers for evil, not for good. He even wanted her to marry his son, Charles.

Rolin had come up with a plan and kidnapped Helena and Corinne. He then forced them into marriage, Helena to Rolin and Corinne to Charles. With the help of Corinne's twin brother Patrick, and from Antonio, they were able to defeat Rolin. Both father and son perished in the battle. The monsters were finally out of their lives forever and yet here was a man in front of her who says he helped Rolin and Charles find them those many years ago and cause them so much devastation and pain? Corinne closed her eyes remembering being forced to marry Charles and then watching as Antonio had been beaten in front of her for mere pleasure. She tried to help him but she could not and instead had to stand out of the way as they fought. That day she had been forced to tell Antonio the truth about her magical powers in front of everyone, and she had remembered vividly the pain and betrayal in his eyes. The truth had almost ripped her and Antonio's love apart. She had hurt him much that day, and he her.

Tears sprang to her eyes as the memories came flooding back. They were painful memories and ones she wished could be wiped from her mind. The man reached to pull Corinne back into his arms when she shouted, "Don't touch me you vile creature. I will never help you!" The words caught Antonio's attention and he moved swiftly to his wife's side. When he touched her arm she wouldn't look at him. She couldn't. At that moment she felt like she was going to be sick. Antonio turned on the man who had caused his wife pain.

"How dare you, sir!" shouted Antonio, his voice filling with rage. His features suddenly expressed surprise, then anger again. "Lord Hammil, you have returned." Adam overheard the comment and gasped his surprise. Alex looked in his direction.

"What's wrong, boy?" Adam was instantly afraid he would be recognized by Lord Hammil but then relaxed slightly. He had grown much in a year. His features had changed and he was now taller. His body was filling out slightly. He was no longer the scrawny boy that he once was on Port Royal.

"Nothing!" responded Adam tersely. Alex glanced at Adam again, then focused his attention back onto Antonio.

"Yes, Lord Chastwick, I returned a few weeks ago. I have been in the Caribbean taking over as Governor of Port Royal. I had to do so when the other governor died from a knife wound given to him by some stranger. I couldn't leave until someone came to replace me." Adam's eyes went wild from the news and all he could think about were Miranda and Rose. He had to protect them somehow.

"This special occasion was reserved for my closest friends only," started Antonio. "You know you are not on my list so explain to me why you are here harassing my wife?"

"I was merely talking with her, milord."

"Yes, and something you said disturbed her." Antonio again looked at his wife but this time her eyes rose to meet his. She placed her hand on his arm while her eyes filled with her torment. He had seen that look before, a long time ago. He knew exactly what the conversation was about.

"William?" shouted Antonio. William, Antonio's most loyal friend, rushed to his side. Years ago they would make sport out of fighting, always competing against each other. William thought that was the reason why he was called to his best friend's side—to fight. He was disappointed when it was not.

"Please escort my wife away from here. Andios?" Andios, who had also been watching and listening to his mother's conversation with Lord Hammil, grabbed Rosemary by the arm and hastened quickly to his father's side.

"Yes, Father?" replied Andios, knowing by the sound of his father's voice he was troubled by something.

"Go with William and look after your mother and sister. You know what to do." Andios had been through many of these situations. His mothers healing powers were well sought after and there were times when her life, as well as their own, were endanger. He knew by his father's tone that he was right in his assumptions and he always did as he was told. His job was to arm himself and protect his mother and sister at all costs. He never failed, for his father taught him how to fight and disarm someone. At his age he was already quite good at it.

"Yes, Father. It will be done." He then steered Rosemary away from the group and waited for William to follow.

"Antonio!" Corinne pleaded, but Antonio only turned toward her.

"No! I will not let this happen again. I will handle this!" Antonio reached out his hand and caressed Corinne's cheek. He then leaned forward and kissed her, rubbing his cheek against hers affectionately. "Now, do as I say. Go with William and our children." Corinne took a deep breath and placed her hand on Williams' outstretched arm. He led her away to safety along with Andios and Rosemary. After watching Corinne and his children go, Antonio turned back to face Lord Hammil.

"I want you to leave, Lord Hammil, and do not bother my wife again with your problems. Next time you approach her, I will take you to a place that you cannot return from." The threat was loud and clear. Lord Hammil smiled and cocked his head to the side.

"You are very protective of your wife's talents, milord. I wonder why that is?" Antonio lunged forward to attack Lord Hammil but was swiftly stopped by Samuel. He had placed his arm around his waist and whispered something in his ear to calm him while he held him back. Lord Hammil ran his hand down his chest and coughed softly. He then turned to leave, his gaze quickly falling upon Alex.

"Why Mr. LaRoice, you are also someone that I wish to speak with."

"Whatever you have to say can wait, Lord Hammil. I believe you were asked to leave by our gracious host."

"Quite right, my good fellow." Lord Hammil took a few steps and stopped. "I am surprised to see you are here while your shop is left unattended. You have been busy as of late that I am sure you are looking for some extra help."

"We have no need of men who have worked under, or for you. We have plenty of trustworthy men working for us, and now partners." Lord Hammil gave Alex an evil smirk as he commented, "Yes, so I hear. Talented and experienced partners I wager. Still, a shop like yours that holds so much family value, and is so close to you and your brother's hearts, should be better looked after. I would hate to hear of anything happening to it." Lord Hammil went to walk away but Alex gripped his arm to stop him.

"Was that a threat?" asked Alex softly.

"No, Alex, merely an observation. Now, if you will excuse me." Lord Hammil yanked his arm away from Alex's grasp and continued on his way through the room to the doorway and then out the door. The comment left Alex feeling uneasy. He glanced around the room until his eyes focused on Isabelle, who was standing by Rochelle's side. Isabelle had overheard the conversation but shrugged her shoulders not sure of what it meant. After Lord Hammil left, Adam took his leave as well. He had to figure out what he was up to, so he followed quietly behind him not sure of what to expect.

Being concerned for their children, the LaRoice family left not long after Adam. The whole evening seemed quite bizarre to them all, and they discussed it during their carriage ride home. When they arrived all was well. Their children were safely sleeping in their beds. Isabelle and Rochelle's mother was also asleep. The servants that were awake assured them of no foul play. Isabelle felt more at ease, as did Rochelle. Maggie went off to bed while Alex and Samuel left to check on The Oasis. Lord Hammil's comment made them feel as if it were somehow in danger.

Rochelle retired shortly to her bedchamber, but Isabelle refused to sleep. All she could think about was what happened that evening, so she decided to wait up until Alex and Samuel came home. She knew that she should tell Miranda right away about Lord Hammil's return and what had transpired this evening, but decided to wait until tomorrow to bother her with such worries. Locand was home and she needed to be with him tonight. Isabelle knew that Miranda was once engaged to Lord Hammil and wondered how he would react when he found out that she was married to Locand and that they were expecting their first child. His reaction would be an interesting one to see. She could not stand Lord Hammil and his high and mighty ways. She would almost pay to see the surprised look upon his face.

As Isabelle's thoughts carried her away from reality, she heard a knock upon the front door. Isabelle waited to see if a servant had heard the noise but by the fifth knock figured they all went to bed and rose from the chair she was sitting in to answer it herself. She cautiously opened the door and inhaled a surprised breath as her gaze fell upon Lord Hammil.

"Lord Hammil?"

"Yes, my dear. I know that it's extremely late, but might I have a word with you?"

"Alex and Samuel are not here at the moment so I know that you will understand if I don't allow you entrance."

"Quite understandable, Isabelle. You are wise to be cautious." Lord Hammil pretended to turn and leave when he suddenly rotated and kicked the door in knocking Isabelle to the ground. Isabelle was shocked but rose quickly looking for a weapon. But before she could grasp a dagger that she knew was hidden underneath one of the tables Lord Hammil took the opportunity and rushed forward to stop her. He placed his hand around her throat and slammed her up against the wall. Isabelle's eyes expressed her fear as she fought for her freedom. Her fingers clutching at Lord Hammil's hand.

"Where is it hidden, my dear?"

"I don't know of what you speak of, Lord Hammil." Isabelle felt Lord Hammil's fingers tighten around her throat.

"The dagger, Isabelle! The ruby dagger you have hidden so well from prying eyes." Isabelle's forehead furrowed wondering how Lord Hammil could have known about her family heirloom, an heirloom that has constantly brought pain and sorrow to her family. The dagger was worth an insurmountable amount of money and there were only a few people who knew she had it in her possession, and other than her immediate family, those people were dead.

"I do not know of what you speak of, Lord—" But Isabelle wasn't able to finish.

"Don't play dumb with me!" shouted Lord Hammil. His features showed his anger as he pressed Isabelle farther into the wall. "I know you have it. James Kingston talked often about it." Isabelle started to shake her head at the mention of her uncle's name. He died a few years ago after trying to take the dagger from them by force and other means. He had kidnapped her sister Rochelle to get the dagger. He enlisted the help of Godfrey Langston to trick them all into revealing its location but for all of the deception and lies that had been told and revealed, Isabelle now had it in her possession. Through all of the pain she had endured since the ruby dagger had been entrusted to her and Alex, she was not about to give it up to Lord Hammil this easily.

"You will not get it, Lord Hammil. My Uncle never succeeded at getting the ruby dagger and when it did finally come into his hands, it was used against him. I outsmarted him, outsmarted his accomplices who hurt my family to try and get it. Don't think that I can't outsmart you, too, because I will stop you. I'm not a fool to trifle with." Lord Hammil laughed at Isabelle's arrogance.

"This I know, Isabelle, and it is a quality in you for which I admire. However, your arrogance makes you underestimate me and my abilities. I was not born a fool either."

"What do you want it for anyway? You can't possibly need it for some noble cause."

"Revenge is a cause that is noble to me and that, my dear woman, is all that really matters." Lord Hammil tightened his grip, then suddenly loosened it and let Isabelle go, but not before he raised his hand against her knocking her to the ground with the back of his hand. The blow caused Isabelle to black out. Seeing her go limp, Lord Hammil stepped forward to look at the bookcases in a room across from them when he heard a loud noise from outside. It was an approaching carriage. Cursing loudly, Lord Hammil ran through the lower level of the house and found a back door that led through the kitchens. He left without being detected. When Alex and Samuel approached the door, they could tell that it had been kicked in. Alex placed his hand at a dagger at his waist as he slowly opened the door. His heart raced painfully in his chest as his gaze fell upon Isabelle on the floor.

"Belle?" Alex whispered as he ran to her side, touching her. He exhaled sharply as he felt the warmth of her skin and saw her chest rise and fall. She was still alive. Samuel took off and checked on everyone else in the house while Alex lifted Isabelle in his arms and carried her to the closest sofa, which was in the room across the hall. After he laid her gently down, he fell to his knees and caressed her cheek. It already looked slightly swollen. Anger filled him for leaving her. He never should have left to check on the shop and yet he did so out of instinct. It never occurred to him until now that it was a setup. If it wasn't for Lord Hammil's remark, he never would have left. From the sound of Alex's voice, Isabelle's eyelids began to flutter.

"Isabelle? Isabelle, my love?" Isabelle's eyes focused on her husband's and she smiled.

"Alexavier?" Tears sprang to her eyes. "Lord Hammil was here!" was all that Isabelle could say. Her head pounded as she tried to focus her attention.

"I will kill him!" shouted Alex as he punched the cushion of the sofa.

"No!" began Isabelle, "you mustn't. He wants revenge against Miranda. Save her!" Isabelle spoke softly. "Save her!" Isabelle closed her eyes to rest, her cheek sore from talking. Alex kissed his wife's cheek as he ran his fingers through her hair. His concern right now was for his wife, not Miranda. Though he promised himself that he would go and see her first thing in the morning to warn her, he now needed to spend time with his wife. He promised her long ago that he would take care of her. Now he would stay up all night and watch over her like an angel to make sure that she was safe.

By early morning, Miranda's water broke and she started having contractions. Within a few hours they intensified and a doctor was called. Miranda was in too much pain to think straight though she did remember what Isabelle had told her. She had said that her mother would help with the delivery so she told Rose to let Isabelle know of what happened. As the day progressed, Miranda became frightened. So was Locand. He knew that Miranda's mother had died in childbirth and was worried that his wife would share that fate. He prayed frequently she would make it through this. She had to. He loved her too much to let her go.

The entire household had been woken up and they were all standing by her side wondering what they could do and how they could help. Labor had gone on for hours and, by midday, she had given birth to a son. Miranda was disappointed when Isabelle didn't arrive but was thankful none the less when the doctor had come. However, her body was weakening. She had no idea what the doctor had done, but she felt as if all of her strength was leaving her. She was losing a lot of blood, and the doctor said that he couldn't get it to stop. She was dying.

Once Locand heard the news he tried to remain strong. His eyes gazed upon his newborn son but he couldn't go to him. Instead, he moved hastily to his wife's side and clutched her hand in his. Stratton and Davy were there as well and both had placed a hand on his shoulder to comfort him. Stratton and Davy had both spoken to Miranda, both bearing a bit of their souls in the conversation but now they could barely hold on. Stratton had been through this once before and a part of him was dying each and every time he glanced at his daughter. Her pale complexion and weak smile caused him to leave the room, sobbing so loudly that Davy immediately followed doing the same. He could not watch as his sweet Miry passed away from him into another world.

"Miry?" spoke Locand softly while he caressed her cheek. Miranda turned her head, her eyes focusing on her husband.

"Locand?" Her voice was weak, and Locand couldn't help but to shed a few tears. "I'm sorry!" said Miranda as her head turned to the left. Locand cleared his throat so he could speak.

"Sorry for what?"

"Sorry that we can't spend the rest of our lives together. I love you so much and am so thankful for the time we have spent together, and—" Locand shook his head as he saw Miranda's face fill with pain.

"No, Miry! Don't leave me. I need you. Need you in my life! You are a blessing and have helped me become a better man. I love you so—" Locand started choking with his tears. "Please don't leave me!" Locand's voice failed as he leaned forward and held Miranda in his arms. Their cheeks touched as they whispered more words of love. However, their precious time together was short lived when the door quickly opened. When Locand looked at the intruder he saw Isabelle with Corinne hastily moving into the room.

"How is she?" asked Corinne sharply.

"She's dying!" yelled Locand as he raised his hands to his face. Isabelle and Corinne glanced at each other and then stepped farther into the room allowing their husbands access.

"Take him out of here, Alex. It will be easier if he leaves the room." Locand stood and stared at Alex. Isabelle had issued the order.

"I will not leave my wife's side. She needs me. I could not bear—"

"Antonio?" spoke Corinne sharply. "Please, get him out of here. I am losing time." Antonio and Alex both reached for Locand, but he fought them. It took the men several minutes to get him under control and they half-dragged him from the room.

"No!" Locand screamed. "Please, I may never hear Miranda's voice again. Don't do this." Antonio heard the door close behind them and lock from the inside.

"She will be fine, Locand. Look at me!" Locand focused his attention on Antonio. "Corinne and Isabelle can help her. She will live." Locand pushed away from Antonio and removed his arm from Alex's grasp. The hallway was empty. Locand tried to go back into the room, but Alex stepped in front of the door to block him.

"Get out of my way, Alex. You have no idea what I am going through."

"Actually," responded Antonio, "we do." Locand glared from one man to the other. "Each of us has a past, Locand, a past that we have learned from and hope to never repeat." There was a long pause before anyone could speak.

"I almost lost Isabelle," spoke Alex painfully. "It is a long story and one that I don't wish to fully share right now, but her uncle threw her over the side of a cliff five or six years ago because of a damn…" Alex had to take deep breaths, his words causing his voice to rise and anger to fill him as his memories ran wild. "Because of an heirloom. A dagger that is worth…" Alex had to calm himself, for the mention of its name would send him into a ranting session. He remembered the pain, the betrayals that James Kingston had caused and created. "Her uncle had—men hurt her—forced her to almost—me—my misguided—to the point, she almost died. It was the greatest pain I have ever felt and I promised myself that I would always cherish and love her after that. There are times when I worry that I might fail her." Antonio glanced at his friend.

"Are you all right?" Alex raised his hand and shook his head as he paced the hallway at a loss for words. Antonio shook his head and spoke.

"I had lost Corinne's love years ago when I wasn't strong enough to see through my own stubbornness. As with Alex's, my story is also a long one, so I will give you the shortened version to save me the same stress that Alex is now going through." Antonio glanced quickly at his friend who was still pacing the floors and ranting to himself. "These past years Corinne has been forced to endure so much pain because of her gifts of healing. There have been times when I could not save her from the pain she had to go through. Our love has been in the balance many times and we have hurt each other and done things that were almost unforgivable, and yet we overcame them. I promised myself that I would always protect her from harm. Save her like she has saved so many. I adore her and yet when I lost her love it killed me inside. We know the pain you are going through. If nothing else, we can say that we can empathize."

"Corinne's gifts? What do you speak of?" asked Locand in frustration, slightly confused and yet touched with his friend's words.

"Corinne is a magical healer, Locand. Her gift is being able to touch the injured and heal their wounds. Miranda will live, and it will be because Corinne will save her."

When the men left the room, Corinne rolled up her sleeves and stepped closer to Miranda. Isabelle walked to the doctor and took the sleeping babe from his arms and held him to her chest. She then escorted the doctor out another door that led into an adjoining room and locked it. As soon as the doctor left, Corinne went to work. She lifted Miranda's sheet that covered her lower body and saw the damage that had been done. Corinne shook her head and clucked her tongue.

"I have spent much time with your father when he has delivered babies and I will tell you this. Your father never cut or hurt the mother for the sake of the child unless absolutely necessary and, when he did so, he was meticulous about it. Look at her, the doctor was careless and incompetent. She is bleeding because of him and he would not stop it."

"Could he have?" asked Isabelle as her gaze fell upon the blood coming from between Miranda's thighs.

"Yes, Belle, he could have. Remind me when we are through to find the man and put him through the same torture. The incompetent ingrate," whispered Corinne, her features filling with the disgust she felt. "Better yet, tell our husbands what he has done. I believe the men will make sure the doctor gets what is coming to him. Besides, the task will keep them busy and their minds occupied." Isabelle quickly moved to the door and opened it, finding Antonio leaning against the wall beside it. Isabelle whispered to him and then closed the door. Corinne focused intently as she spent the next several hours healing every part of Miranda's body that had been cut, torn, bruised and injured from the childbirth, as well as from the doctor. She also healed the scar from the bullet she had taken in the arm for Locand. By the time she was done, not only was she utterly exhausted and ready to collapse, but completely satisfied. She had cleaned up the blood and disposed of any and all remnants of what had happened. Miranda's lower body was now in perfect condition. She was clean, washed and new sheets replaced the old. As Miranda's strength returned, Isabelle noticed the change and walked over to her, placing her son in her arms. He was eager to feed and had just started crying.

Miranda was eager to see her son and sat up hastily, feeling no pain at all for her efforts. She felt normal again. Isabelle showed Miranda how to nurse and after a few painful tries, the babe latched onto her breast and fed. Miranda had alternated him between breasts until he was full and content enough to fall back asleep. She then held him in her arms rocking him slightly.

"What have you done to me? I feel wonderful," said Miranda as she smiled. Corinne stepped forward slightly.

"I healed you, Miranda," answered Corinne. "I am a born healer, but you must keep it a secret. No one can know what I truly am or my life will be worth very little. As far as the population is concerned I am talented in the art of healing, using herbs and teas to heal the sick and injured. Though part of that is true, it is really my hands that heal the body." Miranda was amazed at what she had just heard and yet so thankful. She gazed down at the babe in her arms. He was so beautiful and serene that she started to cry.

"Thank you, Corinne, and you too, Isabelle. You have given me a chance to spend more time with the people I care for and love the most. Your secret is safe with me for I will never betray you. Your gift is a special one, and you have used it wisely, I'm sure. I will tell no one. I am indebted to you both. How can I ever repay—"

"No!" Isabelle insisted. "Friends do not owe each other, Miranda. You were in need of help and I promised that I would help you. I knew Corinne could save you and my good friend was more than eager to do it." Isabelle placed her arm around Corinne's shoulder and kissed her on the cheek. She then let her go. Isabelle wanted to say more, but knew that now was not the time. Miranda needed to spend time with her newborn son, as well as with Locand, who she had remembered was probably in the hallway waiting for them. Isabelle felt Corinne's hand on her arm.

"We will leave you now to rest, but we won't be far away if you need us. You need to spend time with your son, Miranda. Believe me when I say that they grow too quickly. We will talk of this more later. Your body is healed so you can do anything that you have done before, but I recommend resting a little. Our bodies are amazing things and sometimes rest is the best medicine to give."

"Thank you!" was all that Miranda could say as Isabelle and Corinne both leaned forward and kissed her on the cheek. They then kissed the babe softly on the head before leaving. As they opened the door, they saw Locand sitting on the floor leaning against the wall. His eyes were closed as his arms rested on his knees.

"Is he asleep?" Corinne asked as she closed the door behind her.

"He might be by now," replied Antonio who had been leaning against the other wall with Alex.

"Did you take care of the doctor?" asked Isabelle.

"The doctor will harm no more innocent women. This I assure you," replied Locand who had risen from the floor. "How is she?"

"She lives, Locand, and is currently spending time with your son. He is so beautiful."

"Is her body—" Corinne walked up to Locand and placed a hand on his back but upon doing so felt the hard lumps of his scars.

"Her body is the same as it was before she became pregnant. She will be able to bear more sons for you. Her condition had nothing to do with her mother. The doctor was careless and negligent. It was almost as if he were trying to kill her." Corinne saw the anger in Locand's eyes and decided to change to topic. "Locand, let me see your back." Locand instantly started to shake his head, thinking that Corinne might be appalled by the sight of his scars.

"Let her," spoke Antonio sharply. "She is only trying to help." Locand glanced at everyone in the hallway before taking off his shirt. He heard no gasps of surprise, but the clucking of Corinne's tongue.

"This will never do, Locand. I dare say that whoever did this to you had strong feelings of hate." Corinne ran her fingers along a few of the scars. "Do they cause you much pain?" Locand nodded his head and was about to put his shirt back on when Corinne stopped him. "Let me help you." Locand wasn't sure what she was going to do, but closed his eyes as he felt Corinne's hands move slowly across his back. At first he felt a soft pain, but then he felt as if his body was transforming. He stood up straighter as Corinne finished. She had removed the scars from his back. As Locand turned slightly, reaching his arm behind him to feel below his shoulders and back, he couldn't believe it. Tears sprang to his eyes. He was about to say something but stopped when Corinne held up her hand.

"Go and spend time with your wife and son, Locand. Let's not dwell on pleasantries. I know you are thankful for the gifts that you have been given." Locand leaned forward and kissed Corinne on the cheek. He then moved to Isabelle and did the same. "I cannot thank you enough."

"You don't have too. Your words are enough!" Locand took several deep breaths before he continued to the room and opened the door. When he saw Miranda sitting on the bed with their son in her arms, tears sprang to his eyes again, but this time they rolled down his cheeks. He ran to Miranda's side and kissed her. She began telling him about everything and placed their son in his arms so he could hold him. They cried together, relieved and thankful.

CHAPTER 25

When Alex and Isabelle, Corinne and Antonio, reached the stairs they heard a voice calling to them, a voice they dreaded to hear.

"Why if it isn't the LaRoices, and Lord and Lady Chastwick. Please, you must join us." Lord Hammil aimed a pistol in their direction which forced them to do as they were told. The room was filled with two other men who also held pistols, aiming them at the occupants of the room. Stratton and Davy were standing against the wall while Lyle and Rose were standing against the wall on the other side. Adam and Madam Fairaday were missing.

"Is Miranda dead?" The question was asked by Stratton whose eyes were red from the tears he had cried.

"No, she's not dead, Stratton," spoke Corinne. "She lives, as does her son." Stratton and Davy both exhaled a breath of relief. Lord Hammil grunted in frustration, his chance at extracting his revenge thwarted once again. Stratton heard the sound as well as saw the disappointment on his features.

"This is your doing?" Stratton became instantly angry and took several steps forward but wasn't able to continue for one of the men aimed a pistol to his chest. Lord Hammil laughed as he watched Stratton take several steps back. "Captain Ditarius the Deadly! You don't seem so deadly now, do you?" Lord Hammil's smirk caused Stratton's lips to press tightly together while his eyes narrowed. Lord Hammil then focused his attention on Corinne, knowing that it was she who saved Miranda's life. "Your gifts are a blessing, Corinne."

"Yes, they are, but a blessing for whom? You wanted us all here for a reason. You made it a point to get us here. Now, I want to know why?" Everyone's eyes focused on Lord Hammil.

"You will find out soon enough. At the moment I'm not in the mood to extinguish that curiosity for you." Lord Hammil's attention then turned to Lyle and Rose. "Now, I was surprised to see you here

Lieutenant Mansfield, and you Rose." Lord Hammil moved forward and lowered his pistol slightly. When he got to Rose's side he leaned forward and smelled her.

"Oh, my sweet, sweet, Rose. The moments you spent pleasuring me will not be forgotten."

"I have forgotten them, Lord Hammil. I'm not that woman anymore, nor will I ever become her again."

"I see you have changed, and honestly, I adore the new you. However, it has come to my attention that you were the one to help Captain Riveri escape from me on Port Royal— twice." Rose stood firmly and glared at Lord Hammil.

"Then do what you like with me, I don't care, but don't hurt anyone else here. If it is me that you want, then take your revenge."

"What a generous offer, but let's not forget your partner in crime, my ex-fiancée, Miranda. Oh, yes, let's not forget her betrayals. Now, even though Miranda used me as much as I used her, she has gained more than I have. I can't have that, so—come with me." When Rose didn't move forward another man with a pistol seized Rose by the arm and shoved her forward. Lyle advanced to stop him but Lord Hammil raised his arm and placed the barrel of the pistol against his forehead.

"Make your new wife a widow, I dare you." Lyle glared at Lord Hammil but took a step back when he saw Rose raise a hand to her lips, her eyes welling with tears.

"I will not give you the satisfaction." Lord Hammil laughed as he pushed Lyle back with the pistol.

"Bravery, another word for imbecile!" sneered Lord Hammil. He then turned and grabbed Rose by the arm taking her with him as they moved to the door.

"Let me be," shouted Rose.

"No!" replied Lord Hammil, "Nor will I until I get what I want. You will help me accomplish my goals." Rose shook her head but did not fight. "My dear Isabelle and Corinne, if you would be so kind as to join me as well?"

"We will not let you take our wives, Lord Hammil. You're crazy to think that we would give them up without a fight," spoke Alex.

"You are correct, however, a fight I'm ready for. If anyone resists I will shoot them without remorse. Could you live with the fact that you had killed one of these ladies because of your gallantry? I think not." Isabelle and Corinne both glanced at their husbands before slowly making their way to Lord Hammil's side. "Good, now all I need is Miranda."

"Here I am!" All eyes focused on the top of the stairs. There was Miranda, alone. She had dressed and her features looked serene despite the situation. She had left Locand asleep in the room with the baby.

"Ah, my sweet Miranda, you look wonderful. For a moment I wish that you were my wife in our home. It saddens me to think you are happy without me." Lord Hammil smiled only for a moment before a sneer replaced it. Miranda started to walk down the staircase enchantingly.

"Lord Hammil, our lives were meant to be apart. You used me to get to my father and almost destroyed my loved ones in the process, did you not think I would hold that against you?" Lord Hammil narrowed his eyes while producing a sly grin.

"It seemed fair given the fact that you used me in the same capacity." Miranda smiled as her eyes narrowed.

"Touché!" Lord Hammil's features became serious.

"I never lied about my love for you." Miranda stopped for a moment, taken aback by the comment.

"You have a strange way of showing love. Attempted murder, jealousy, rage, and betrayal? Yes, love is certainly in the air." Miranda continued down the stairs, with each step gaining confidence. When she reached the bottom, with catlike speed no one was expecting, Miranda pulled out a pistol and shot Lord Hammil in the thigh with wicked accuracy.

Lord Hammil, surprised by the attack, dropped his pistol. Rose took the opportunity to knock him to the ground while Isabelle withdrew a dagger that was kept in a sheath against her thigh and held it close to his throat daring him to move. The men took the opportunity to fight against their attackers. Stratton took out one of the men while Lyle took out the other. The men then surrounded the women, allowing them to finish what they had started.

Lord Hammil clutched at his thigh, his eyes filled with fear and surprise as he stared at the women surrounding him and watched intently as Miranda threw the pistol off to the side and walked over to him.

"If I die, Miranda, all of your secrets will be told to the queen. I've a man who is waiting for me to return, and if I don't his orders are to go straight to her, telling her everything about each one of you. All of your lives will be worth spit and everything that you have worked so hard to achieve will not be remembered." Rose, Isabelle and Corinne all glanced at Miranda to see what they should do.

"You're bluffing!" spoke Miranda.

"No! After the time we have spent together you must realize by now that I have a purpose for everything I do, and I always have a back up plan. Do you think that I would come here without having someone stay behind in the case you would kill me? Please, give me some credit."

Before any more words could be said the front door was thrown open and Adam entered with Madam Fairaday. Behind them were the queen's guards.

"I know what he was to use you for. Treason!" spoke Adam, answering an unspoken question.

"Arrest him!" ordered Madam Fairaday. The guards rushed forward. The women backed away as the guards surrounded Lord Hammil and lifted him from the ground. "Your man is dead, Lord Hammil, as are you. Do you think that the queen would allow you to start a war against her? All of these years you have been faithful and yet little by little you have plotted and planned to dethrone her. Well, as to repeat the words that you had said earlier, your life is now worth spit." Madam Fairaday motioned for the guards to take him away. When they passed her, she whispered, "Make sure that he's never found. That is our queen's orders and I am to see they are done." She then let them go to dispose of Lord Hammil in the way the queen had ordered.

When the guards left and the door was closed, Madam Fairaday ran to the arms of her husband, who kissed her passionately. The other men stepped forward and grabbed the arms of their wives, pulling them closer to them. Miranda was the only one left alone, along with Adam.

"Adam," spoke Miranda, "what was he going to do?" Adam stepped farther into the room.

"He was going to use all of the women to help him convince the King of Spain to fight against the queen, and in so doing remove her from her throne."

"How do you know this?" asked Rose.

"I have been following him since last night, since Lord Hammil disrupted Antonio's welcome home celebration. I followed him, he stopped at various places, including Alex's home," said Adam.

"Did you see—" started Alex, his features becoming hard.

"Yes! I saw him attack Isabelle." All eyes were focused on Isabelle now who felt slightly uncomfortable. "I also know what he wanted from her which she didn't give." Alex's eyes bore into his wife's. Isabelle looked away. She didn't tell Alex that Lord Hammil had attacked her because of the ruby dagger.

"I then saw him go to several other places and overheard his many conversations. He had something on almost every one of us, but mostly the women. It was them he wanted because it was only they who could help him with his cause. He knew nothing of me or of Madam Fairaday's and Locand's true identity. He did not know that Lyle and Locand were brothers, either. His attention was focused on the women only. Miranda and Rose he wanted for revenge, exclusively. He knew how much they had done to free Locand and the rest of us. From Isabelle he wanted the dagger, for he knew that she had it, and he was going to use it as collateral for his private war against the queen. It seems that he has been planning it for years, but as each plan failed he had to come up with new ideas, new ways to get money. For Corinne, her special powers of healing were going to be given to the King of Spain himself."

"Why?" burst Corinne. When she realized how menacing her voice must have sounded, Corinne quickly calmed herself before continuing, though her tone still held an edge. "He knew things about me, things he shouldn't have known. I want to know how he knew of my history— the men in my past—the betrayers."

"I want to know as well," added Isabelle. "How he knew of the ruby dagger. There are only a select few who know that we have it in our possession, and they are dead.

Miranda then spoke as well. "Now that you mention it, before we left to go to Port Royal, I found out that Lord Hammil was after my father and that he knew of the crystals we had that would be used to find the treasure. How he could have known about them still baffles me. The crystals were often hidden from view. We told no one about them. No one knew that my father was the notorious Captain Ditarius either." The words the women had told everyone sent the room into silence.

"I know how he knew," said Madam Fairaday as she stepped out from the comfort of Stratton's arms. Before she could speak, however, a voice from the top of the stairs did.

"It was Lord Havenor!" There were a few gasps from the women while the men quarreled to each other over it. When Locand awoke he had placed his son in the bassinet that was made for him and left to find Miranda. He had overheard the entire conversation and saw what the women had done to Lord Hammil.

"But why?" asked Miranda as she watched her husband descend the stairs. Once he did he moved straight to her side and grabbed her into her arms, kissing her softly on the lips. He then smiled briefly and pulled away.

"Because, he was the only one who had the power to know. The man was old enough to have known the men in all of your pasts and help them along with Lord Hammil. Those two men were very close and often did things together, though no one knew that about them. In fact, most people thought they hated each other, but that's not true—at least not entirely. Lord Havenor would find out the information, by any means necessary, while Lord Hammil did the dirty work for him, compensating him well for his efforts. They worked well together, but it was Lord Havenor who was going to tell the queen about all of you." He then raised his hand and swept it in front of the women in emphasis.

"How do you know that?" asked Stratton, surprised with the turn of events.

"Because—I was the one who killed him." All eyes were focused on Locand now. He then pulled out two pieces of parchment and waved it for everyone to see. "One of these is the information Lord Hammil had talked about concerning the women and their beloved secrets. Isabelle's family heirloom, the well sought after ruby dagger, Corinne and her wonderful powers of healing, and Miranda for being the daughter of the fearsome Captain Ditarius. It is all written here—condemning them all." All eyes focused on the parchment while Locand's eyes focused on Adam's. "You were mistaken about Lord Hammil, Adam, it was Lord Havenor who knew about our true identities--mine, Lyle's and my mother's. This other letter tells the truth about us, and our lives, too, were to be bargained for, but not to Spain, no, that would have been too kind a fate for us." Before Locand could continue another question was asked.

"How did you know about Lord Havenor?" The question came from Rose, but Locand glanced at Alex and Antonio when he answered it.

"Do you remember when we went to find the doctor?" Both men nodded their heads. After Isabelle told them what had happened, it put them all in a foul mood. So, they went to find the doctor, who had conveniently run back to his master. While Alex and Antonio went looking in other directions, Locand followed him. It was then that Adam had found Locand telling him that Lord Havenor had gone to see Madam Fairaday requesting to see the queen on some important matter and that she felt he should intercede. Madam Fairaday told Lord Havenor that the queen was busy and that she would send for him when she had an opening. Lord Havenor had then retired to his home to wait for the summons and it was there that Locand had found him with the doctor. Once he found out the truth and saw the letters, he killed them for it.

"When Adam had returned with the news from Locand, it was then that I got the queen's guards and brought them here," stated Madam Fairaday. "Lord Hammil's time was over, he just didn't know it yet and Lord Havenor got what he deserved."

"What do we do now?" asked Corinne.

"Well," answered Locand, "we burn these letters for starters so our secrets can never be uncovered." Everyone watched with anticipation as the letters were thrown into the fireplace. Locand then proceeded to light them with a candle and all watched as the parchment burned. When the letters were totally consumed, there seemed to be an easiness that emanated from them all.

"Now what?" asked Miranda.

"We move on," replied Davy. It was the first time he had spoken since Lord Hammil's arrival. "As far as I see it, we are all on even ground here and all of us have secrets that we wish to keep. Right?" Everyone in the room nodded their heads in unison. "Well, let's keep them. No one outside of this room knows about any of us and the knowledge about each other and what we do is something that will make us better friends. Our pasts brought us closer together, but it will not be the end of us. Now that we know each other's secrets we can accept them instead of hiding from them. For we all know how painful it is to hide them." There was a low murmuring in the room.

"Can we agree on the matter and live harmoniously again without fear?" asked Miranda.

"That would be nice," spoke Corinne.

"Yes, it would," added Isabelle.

"Do the men agree?" asked Davy. The men all nodded in unison. "Good! Now, I know Stratton feels the same way I do when I say that I would like to see my grandson now." After several more minutes of discussion, everyone dispersed. The women embraced saying their goodbyes, promising to stop by tomorrow, while the men shook hands and laughed. The atmosphere of the room finally lightened and warmed as laughter and acceptance filled it.

After her friends had gone, Miranda watched Locand as he sat in a chair and covered his face with his hands. Lyle had moved up next to him to talk. His eyes then focused on Rose and Adam, as they stood talking with Stratton, Madam Fairaday, and Davy. Miranda quickly walked up the stairs and slipped away to check on her son. When she stepped into the room he was sleeping peacefully in his bassinet like Locand had said. As she tiptoed until she stood next to the bassinet, she glanced down at the angelic form of her son. She then wondered what his future would hold. Would it hold happiness and peace, or would it hold pain and suffering? Miranda reached down carefully and picked him up. He was so fragile—so innocent. As she held him gently to her breast, Locand entered. As Miranda instinctively rocked her body back and forth, she stopped when she heard the floor squeak behind her. Her heart began to race until she saw her husband by her side. She relaxed as she saw the tiredness in Locand's eyes. She knew there was much to say about what had happened downstairs, but now was not the time. Locand moved in beside her and placed his hand on her arm. He wrapped his other arm around her waist, now having the responsibility of protecting two souls. But this was his family. That knowledge brought a smile to his face.

With Stratton, Davy, and his mother—yes they were a family, an odd family that also included Lyle, Adam, and Rose, but his son was something he helped create. Someone that he could help raise and be the father of. It was stability, a rock that he could always depend on, a love that would never fail. It was there that he promised to be a better father to his son, than his father was to him and Lyle. Locand raised his hand and gently stroked the soft and smooth cheek of his son. With all of the excitement going on he realized that they hadn't given him a name yet.

"We haven't given him a name," whispered Locand. Miranda exhaled, the realization hitting her.

"You give him it," she encouraged. Locand thought for several seconds.

"We will call him, Kanyn Locand Riveri. I never thought that I would want to name my son after me, but a middle name would suffice. It is a strong name." Miranda leaned over and pressed her lips against his. The kiss was soft and brief. As Miranda pulled away, her eyes fell upon her father's and Davy's as they entered. They were quiet as they moved forward.

Stratton reached out his arms for his grandson, but felt unsure. He always felt uncomfortable around babies. They were too delicate and soft. With his massively rough hands he felt like a brute in comparison. Miranda turned and placed her son in her father's arms. She didn't retract her arms away until she knew her father had a firm grasp. At first he just stared at the baby, he couldn't help but to have a few tears fall. Davy was standing next to him, tears falling down his cheeks as well. They looked quite the pair. Davy motioned to hold the baby, and Stratton placed him gently in his arms, exhaling his relief. He was so afraid that he would drop him. Too fragile.

"What's his name?" Davy whispered.

"Kanyn!" Davy smiled. Of all the parts of a ship, Locand picked the part that exploded. Well, it was also a part that protected and saved. Davy couldn't help but laugh as his gaze fell upon his grandson. After raising Miranda, he had no qualms about holding a baby. In fact, he relished it. Memories of Miranda's youth flooded him and the day Miranda was born filled his mind. He had held her the same way. But Kanyn's mother was here in front of him. That was the difference. It wasn't two men trying to raise a daughter. Kanyn will have his mother by his side, as well as a father, two grandfathers, and lots of relatives. The boy will be blessed. They will be blessed to have him in their lives.

Stratton pulled out something from his pocket, a uniquely shaped gold piece with markings on the side of it. All eyes fell upon it, and Miranda shook her head.

"No, we are not going." Miranda's tone was quiet, yet firm.

"You don't even know what it is yet," stated Stratton.

"I don't have to. I know you, Father. Where did you get it?"

"That doesn't matter; just think of it as a gift, a gift to be used for later, because now we need to spend our time raising this child." Locand accepted the gift, but refused to glance at it, not wanting it to drive him on another adventure with or away from his family, so he placed it into his pocket out of sight. Davy raised his head and gazed at Locand and Miranda.

"I have a feeling that you will keep him grounded, but it will be our job to teach him the ways of the sea. With having so many of us who have that love, we must pass it on. The gold piece is merely a gift for now, just keep in mind that when you need it, it will be there."

"What is it?" Locand's voice now sparked with interest.

"It's for Kanyn. Just promise us that one day you will search for it. It is our gift." Miranda did not protest, merely smiled. She loved Davy and her father so much. They were wild and free men, and though they pretended to be settled and changed men, she knew in her heart where they would rather be, and in truth, she wouldn't have had it any other way.